I0690700

In the Hearts

of Soldiers

———

A NOVEL

DOUGLOUS D. CLAMPIT

Cypress Gate Publishing

In the Hearts of Soldiers

Copyright © 2019 by Douglous D. Clampit

ISBN: 978-0-578-49368-8

First Edition: April 2019

10 9 8 7 6 5 4 3 2 1

In the Hearts of Soldiers

For Mom & Dad

"To err is human, to forgive, divine."
— Alexander Pope, An Essay on Criticism

ONE

I WAITED EIGHT YEARS to return what I had stolen. I stole from a dead man. An innocent man. A man who had a life outside that enduring war: a home, a wife, and a child. For the decision to return what I had stolen haunted me for too long. I'm frightened of a small lockbox hidden away in the back corner of the bedroom closet. I hid the box so I couldn't see it—and remember. But I would always remember, for the memories are always there—recollections of days no man should ever witness in his lifetime. The truth is: I needed to free myself of the secrets kept hidden away.

Every soldier of war has his secrets. Secrets ran thick. And I had mine. I thought I would take them to the grave, but secrets have a way of sneaking up on you when you least expect it. They keep me up at night. But it's more than secrets—perhaps it's a photograph hidden away in that lockbox. A photograph of a woman I once knew whom I befriended many years ago. But what part does a woman in an old photograph have anything to do with my story I am about to confess? For the moment, I will only say she is a woman I loved. Not a romantic love. Once I thought so, but I was too young to know what love was. It was an

innocent love—a fascination. But allow me to set all of my intimate feelings aside for the moment and let me say this specific woman is the
most crucial character in my story. But characters in stories are a fabri-
cation but let me say she is very real. As real as every character in this
story—myself included.

So this is my story. The story of a youthful army soldier haunted by a
woman in a photograph.

Yes, I was a soldier, technically I still am. I helped liberate cities,
towns, and villages along with my company of the 29th Infantry Division (the Virginia National Guard). The division along with others swept
through Europe, running the Axis Army out during the Great Second
War. "Twenty-nine, let's go!" was our motto. And I was damn proud to
serve under it. I brag it's the best division in the entire US Army. Others would oppose. There have been arguments of course. Sometimes,
fistfights break out among the younger folk, but I am too old for that
nonsense. As I learned, there will always be disagreements about what
division is the best. It all comes down to pride. And pride can force a
man to act foolishly. A hard lesson I learned one night outside a village
in Normandy, France. But that part will come later.

Now I would like to say that veterans of the Great Second War will
have their place in history. We are a specific breed of people. There's an
instinct implanted deep within our minds to always be alert. Always be
on guard. And after the war, that instinct stays within us—perhaps to
the day we die for there came many restless nights after returning home
to our beds. And over the years, those sleepless nights became a curse.
Each passing night only seems to stretch on longer and longer. I was
foolish to believe only I and perhaps a few other veterans suffered from
sleepless nights—the sudden dismay of past events: gunfire, explosions,
or watching a friend die before your eyes. It's not the instinct alone,
however. In part, it's the stress induced by the horrific memories of violence. Nightmares. It's clichéd I know but bear with me.

We all seen our fair share of violence; necessary violence though.
We've seen the worst in men, and we've also seen the best. Soldiers lived

among one another as a brotherhood. And a valuable lesson every soldier needed was to distinguish his friend from the enemy. But an enemy
can wear the same uniform. This is another lesson I learned firsthand.
Another lesson is that a friend can be found in the most unusual circumstances without knowing it. Now I never had much luck with
friends. Often I made enemies. But there are valuable lessons to be
learned from your enemies. The older I get, the more I understand that
now. I'm only thirty-three. The war has been over for over eight years,
and I had lived through times of unspeakable hardships and extraordinary events. Along the way, I learned valuable lessons. But I will reveal
these lessons in time.

So I am proud to have fought for my country of America and for other
countries all for the purpose to stop a mass murdering tyrant from his
reign of terror sweeping across Europe. And in doing so, saving countless innocent lives. Concentration camps were found scattered throughout Europe during the time the Germans lost ground in occupied territory. These camps were a sight to see—hundreds upon hundreds of
starved, defenseless Jewish civilians crammed together within a fenced
area. It was an unsettling sight. I saw it firsthand when my regiment
had liberated the Mittelbau-Dora camp near Nordhausen, Germany in
late April of '45. After our regiment had liberated the camp, Jewish civilians came up to the soldiers and hugged them and kissed them on
their cheeks, relieved to be rescued. Relief finally came for the poor
souls. I watched as the prisoners cry tears of joy and soldiers cry tears of
heartache for the prisoners. The prisoners were walking skeletons after
being starved to near death. But many others did not survive as many
bodies were discovered in small shacks and pits dug into the ground.
The Germans crammed these shacks and pits full of the dead. The discovered decomposing bodies left a foul and unforgettable stench in the
air that lingered on me for days. I couldn't get that stench off me no
matter how many times I bathed. But it could have been my imagination. During the war, a man's imagination can be dangerous. I walked
around the camp taking pictures of the dead and the living with my

35mm Rangefinder camera I purchased in Salisbury, England just months before. I didn't know why I took photos—perhaps it was to remind me I helped save many lives. But believe me when I say seeing something like a concentration camp would be difficult to forget.

All of my experiences I went through for the United States Army changed me. For it was the army that turned me into a man. Perhaps not the man I wanted to be or even the man I needed to be. It took eight years to see what sort of man I became and how I hated it.

Just two weeks after my return home, the 29th Division disbanded, and it disappointed me to see it go. Myself and along with many others transferred to other divisions, but the 29th reactivated a few years later. It didn't take long for me to put in my request to return. It was where I wanted to continue my military career. I can resign and leave the army, but life outside the military is too intimidating. It's scary to think about. There are only two professions I know how to do: soldiering and farming. But there is more to life than living on a farm by working endless hours of the day under a hot sun. That was not the life for me. It's not the life I wanted.

My profession is one I can appreciate. During my tenure in Europe, my superior officer promoted me to Sergeant First Class, and after the war, I became a drill instructor at Fort A.P. Hill in Virginia. Soon after, I put in my request to be transferred to recruitment. My superiors didn't object and approved my request within a few days. Not that I was a terrible drill instructor—working the recruitments hard was proven to not be difficult. You could say at times—I rather enjoyed it. I was a recruit myself before the war and savored in knowing how it felt to be the person ordering the recruits around. But the fact was—I was not much of a shouter. I didn't like stepping up to recruits faces and screaming at them until I was hoarse. That wasn't who I was. So I transferred to recruitment.

Now recruitment is not that difficult of a job, I must confess. I have to lie to possible recruits to get them to sign up. I'm not too happy about having to lie to them, but I must do everything I can to grab their attention. It's how I make my living. I wear my uniform with all my badges and ribbons with dignity and pride while recruiting to show my accomplishments during my tenure in the army for I believe it entices the recruits. I discovered that after working in recruitment, it's quite an experience to talk with young men interested in signing up. Being a young man in their shoes once and being like them, I didn't know what I was in for. Signing up for the army is the first step into manhood. You can say it's a warning to the recruitments. It's a warning I give on account that manhood won't be easy. Some challenges must be faced and often, faced alone. But win or lose any challenge that comes your way, is a step closer to nobility.

My good friend Andrew Decker once told me I had it way too easy. I suppose he envies me but who can blame him. Working as a recruiter is stable work. I could do it to the day of retirement if it so pleases me. Perhaps I will. I will work as a recruiter until a younger man replaces me and when that time comes, there will be no objections from me.

Working for recruitment grants a decent wage; there are no complaints there. My wife and I live comfortably in the town of Richmond, Virginia, just outside of Fort A.P. Hill. We settled in Richmond after the war due to life on the base was difficult on account of the many rules and regulations that needed to be followed. That was no way to live. I've had my fair share of rules and so I found a home off base.

The weather in Virginia is lovely: the summers are warm, and the winters are moderate. Pleasant.

Virginia has a different lifestyle than the south. Having been born and raised in Louisiana, a born southerner living in Virginia can make my life frustrating, however. I'm often taunted about my southern drawl; it's all in good fun, I know, but the jokes grow tiring. But my accent defines me. You can tell a lot about someone just by their accent: their backgrounds such as the history of their culture and intelligence. A person's accent is their character. And the south has a unique culture. A different reality. Every true southerner has a certain, profound trait of genuine self-respect that is carried around, even to death. That's just how we southerners are. Pride runs deep in the southern blood. Always have and always will. It's not that we believe we are better than other folk. I suppose our pride comes from a vivid fondness of the southern benevolence. It's a life that should never be taken advantage of. And I believe that's how all southerners live. The food, the language, and the mystery of its haunted, but yet beautiful land all captures the charm the south has to offer. It feels strange now to reside far away in Virginia. I feel like an outsider. But Richmond will have to do.

But even though the war is over and being back home, adjusting back to a normal and quiet life proved difficult, as with all veterans returning home from the war. A life a soldier once had may not be there when he returns. A once memorable home is perceived differently—foreign perhaps, after spending several years away in a different land. The man he once was has changed. He's distant, colder, and empty. It was as if something is lost; something that would be difficult to discover once again—or perhaps, not be found again at all.

It's the aftermath of war.

A soldier's profound change is most evident to the people closest to him. Sometimes, the transition isn't noticeable—not in oneself that is. It's a denial that lingers over in time until the truth will need to be admitted.

This had been my problem.

But I realized I wasn't alone. And due to the concern of my wife, I agreed to pursue help, but it had not been an easy decision. At first, there were efforts to cope with the troubles on my own, but the nightmares and restless nights were becoming worse. I was suffering, not only me but also my wife. She hated seeing me—her husband, in such a miserable state. I was eating less and less, and we were growing further apart from one another. There were large amounts of time I was alone, shutting myself away from the daily activities of life.

It wasn't until a long, difficult night I gave in to get help for her sake. Flashbacks of the war haunted me. Not only flashbacks but something else—something darker. A secret I presumed I would never share with anyone else. A secret I thought I would take to the grave. But I can no longer hold this secret in any longer. Something was calling out. Is it the lockbox buried in the closet? Delusions perhaps? Because of this, I questioned my sanity. I knew I had no choice now but to seek help.

This all leads me to this moment; I'm sitting in the empty waiting room of Dr. Winslow Gilliam's office with the small lockbox I had brought along. It was a modest room with only six chairs—three chairs in a row against the three connecting walls in the back of the room. The decoration consisted of a few plants in pots sitting on little tables, and a few paintings of landscapes hung on the walls. Near the entrance door, rested a small desk for Gilliam's secretary and next to the desk was a doorway that led into the doctor's examining area. It was early morning, and I was the only visitor at the moment. The receptionist was busy going through files and at times, glances up at me with her thick cat eye prescription glasses as I sat waiting to speak with the doctor.

The doctor ran his practice out of this little building with considerable dignity. I had never been a patient of his, but there are occasional news that spread around town about his practice. He never charged as much other doctors or hospitals would charge. I once heard he was popular among the children. He seemed to love them and never turned away any family who couldn't afford to have their child helped medically. It was a divine passion of his to help those who need it the most. I guess his motto was to never turn away the sick or the poor. If it was his motto, he without a doubt lived by it. Although he was a medical doctor by trade, he had agreed to speak with me about my problems after his visit to my home the previous night I had mentioned beforehand.

It was a night like any other; I suddenly woke in bed after having flashbacks of the war. My head felt hot, and I was drenched in sweat as my body trembled. The twin bell alarm clock on the nightstand read eleven o'clock from the moonlight that peeked through the window. In much need of some air, I slip out of bed as gently as possible as to not disturb my wife, who is sleeping next to me. Not thinking to put on my robe, I made it to the front door in just my paper thin pajamas and unlocked the bolts. I slowly opened the front door along with the creaky screen door, trying to make as little noise as possible. Once outside, I took a seat in a rocking chair on the front porch and listened to the illustrious sounds of the night and find comfort as I listen to the sedative cricket chirping and the occasional eerie hoot of an owl. I sit back and rock in the chair as I listen to everything around me.

It's early spring of '53 in Virginia, and it's a cool night—not as cool as usual, however. A gentle breeze drifting in the cool and crisp air made me shiver as the sweat that soaked my skin grew cold. I was tired, and my weariness tricked me into believing I could back to sleep but there would be no sleep. Even if I could, I would be too frightened.

So I sat on the front porch in my chair trying to calm my nerves. My mind is full of horrific flashbacks and guilt. The sudden feeling of sickness emerged as I trembled and sweat once more. Perhaps I could walk it off I thought—get my blood pumping. I paced around the front porch, but the pacing did not help. My heart pounded faster and more sweat dripped down my face. The pounding in my chest grew and grew as if my heart would explode from my chest at any moment. The pounding then evolved into a sharp and piercing pain; I dropped to my hands and knees as the urge to vomit arose from deep within my gut but the moment never came.

I didn't know how long I was on my hands and knees. My muscles felt weak and useless as I tried to pick myself up. There was no choice but to wait it out. My knees ached as they pressed hard on the durable and solid wood of the porch. To get comfortable, I stretched my limbs out and lay flat as my cheek pressed against the cold boarded floor, sending instant relief from the hot sweats.

I lied on the porch, motionless; too afraid to move. Dead perhaps. But I wasn't dead.

At last, my strength returned. My heart no longer pounded and the sweats and trembling ceased. After coming to my senses and lifting myself off the floor of the porch, I went inside and flipped through a little pocketbook full of phone numbers and after finding the number I was searching for; I made a phone call. It was a call to Dr. Winslow Gilliam. After a brief conversation and hanging up the phone, I turned on the dim outside porch light and returned to the rocking chair and waited for his arrival. I did all of this in silence and secret, not wanting to wake my wife. Let her sleep, I reflected. I'll explain everything to her in the morning.

After half an hour of waiting, an automobile arrived at the house. The headlights flashed as the car came near the house in the driveway. A short and portly man emerged from the car after the ignition turned off. He set his eyes on me the instant I stood from the rocking chair. As he approached, I recognized him for Dr. Gilliam. He had steel gray hair and wore thick round glasses in front of his wide eyes and wore brown slacks with black dress shoes and a white short-sleeve button-up shirt that looked as if it was just thrown on with no care. A medical bag hung from his hand at his side. He was the local town doctor, but I had only seen him very little. I wasn't a visitor to his office but my wife was a patient of his. And I only saw the doctor as we passed one another on the sidewalk. If I were to be seen by any medical doctor, it would be at the medical unit on base, but I had no desire to make a phone call to the base and disturb the medical staff there at midnight. Dr. Gilliam, however, was open to house calls no matter the hour.

"So what seems to be the problem, Mr. Conroy?" he asked in a loud and impatient tone as he stepped onto the porch.

"Not so loud," I said, sitting back down in the rocking chair. "Don't want to wake the missus." I gestured with my thumb at the house. Gilliam nodded his head in understanding. "And call me Vince. Anyway—I don't feel right. Something is wrong with me. I just don't know what." I then told Gilliam everything that had taken place in the last couple of hours, leaving out no detail.

Gilliam stood over me as I described to him my situation. He appeared to be deep in thought as I spoke. After I finished speaking, he said, "Well, let's have a look at you, Mr. Conroy." He then opened his medical bag and retrieved a stethoscope and listened to my heart and afterward placed the stethoscope on my back to listen to my lungs. Next, he took my blood pressure. When he completed the rest of his examinations, he placed everything back in the medical bag. "Your pulse is a little fast but how are you feeling right now?"

"Better I guess," I replied, although I felt a bit hot. "Still a little warm."

"Now tell me—has this ever happened before?"

"No."

"Tell me something else—have there been any big changes in your life recently? Perhaps you have witnessed or been through something traumatizing?"

"I fought over in Europe during the war. I try not to talk about it. I don't even like to think about it. Many bad memories."

"Europe, huh? What a damn tragedy all of that was. I knew people who want over there to fight. Some of those people were friends of mine. Some of them never came back. And the ones that came back—well they were never quite the same. But that's been over for about eight years now. What troubles are you specifically going through?"

"It's difficult for me to sleep."

"Trouble sleeping, I see."

"Yes."

Dr. Gilliam stepped back and put his hands into his pockets. "Have you been talking to anyone about your time in Europe?" he asked.

"No," I murmured. "As I said just a moment ago—I don't like to talk about it."

"Well, I've seen these kinds of things before. You went through something traumatic, and you don't know how to deal with it. Do you have nightmares? Is that why you are having difficulty sleeping?"

"Yes. I would say it's visions of what I went through. And to be honest, I'm just too scared to sleep."

"Well, I understand your frustrations. I'm only a medical doctor but what I believe is—that you have been suppressing a lot of bad memories from the war. You've been doing it for a long time. Your mind just needed to clear itself. That's why you had an episode. And it's not healthy to keep the past buried inside for so long. Eventually, the past wants you to remember." I listened to what Gilliam was trying to tell me. What he was saying was true, no doubt about it, but dealing with the horrors I experienced in the war was difficult to discuss with someone else. There was that undeniable feeling of not knowing how. "In cases like this," he continued, "it doesn't hurt to talk to someone about these kinds of things. You need to find a way of dealing with these problems." He gave me a look of concern.

But I acknowledged that he was right. If there is a chance to sleep at night, I needed to speak about my time in Europe. I believed Gilliam knew what he was talking about and if anyone could help me, it would be him.

"Perhaps you're right," I said. "Perhaps you could listen to what I need to say."

"Well now, I told you I'm only a medical doctor, son."

"Yes, I know. But the way I see it—any doctor would do right now."

The doctor placed his hand underneath his chin and held it with his fingers, occasionally rubbing it and again appearing to be deep in thought. "All right," he muttered. "Can you come by my office first thing in the morning? Let's say, eight o'clock? It's far too late at night to start this discussion now. A doctor needs his rest too you know."

"I can do that," I replied. "Eight o'clock it is."

"And try to get a little rest yourself, Mr. Conroy." Gilliam turned to step off the porch, and after taking a few steps, he halted and turned to face me once again. "I expect you, Mr. Conroy, to keep to your word. I know a person's past his own private business and often a man's past can be difficult to return to but in doing so is a good way to control or perhaps let go of some of those demons that have a hold of you. It doesn't do well to dwell on the past. Goodnight, Mr. Conroy." The doctor stepped off the porch and returned to his vehicle. The automobile purred to life, and in just a few short moments, he was gone, leaving me alone on the porch once again.

"MR. CONROY—THE DOCTOR WILL SEE YOU NOW," the receptionist said, snapping me out of my thoughts. I stood up with my lockbox as she opened the door next to her desk for me as I stepped through. Once inside the door closed behind me.

I was now standing in Dr. Gilliam's medical room. A fake skeleton hung from wires in the corner. An examination table was pressed against a wall, and large diagrams of the human body hung from the walls all over the room.

Dr. Gilliam was standing at the far back end of the room next to an open door. "Come join me in my study," he said.

I obliged and entered. He shut the door behind us and gestured for me to take a seat in one of the two chairs facing one another against the wall near the door. A dim light from a desk lamp filled the small office. There was a lingering musky odor coming from a large assortment of old medical books that filled large bookcases hiding an entire wall on the right side of the room. The air is sticky as I removed my suit jacket to get a little more comfortable. I sat down and placed the lockbox on the floor next to the chair as the doctor grabbed two small glasses and filled them up with what I believed to be bourbon from a small table near his desk which was settled in front the back wall. He gave me a glass and then he sat down in the chair facing mine. I took a swig of the liquor and discovered it was indeed bourbon.

"Now I have to remind you, Mr. Conroy," Gilliam spoke, "that I am only a medical doctor. I'll listen to what you have to say, and I'll see what I can do for you. And as I mentioned last night: sometimes it's best just to get these things out. Usually, that's all it takes to get better."

"I understand," I replied. "I wanted to thank you for taking your time to listen to what I need to say."

"Think nothing of it, son. I put all of my other appointments on hold for the time being—because I think I will be in for quite a story."

I smiled. "You can say that. A lot of this will be difficult for me to talk about. I try not to think about these things, but these memories have a way of seeping through from time to time. But I want you to promise one thing before I began, doctor."

"All right. And what would that be?"

"Please don't judge me on account of what I'm about to tell you. I was going through a difficult time in my life, and some events can change a good man into something else. There's a reason for the things I did; I'm not proud of it, but they happened."

"You have my word, Mr. Conroy. So I recommend that you tell me everything. Explain all to the best of your knowledge."

As I took a sip of bourbon from my glass, I leaned back in the chair and began to tell my story. . .

TWO

MY FAMILY'S TEN-ACRE FARM is just a few miles south from Natchitoches, Louisiana; a quaint and traditional old town nestled along the Cane River. I sat on a stool underneath Brownie—one of our two cows in the barn, milking, among the thick stench of manure and hay. My mother—Lucille, gave her that name because of her dark brown coat. It was late August, and the day was stifling hot. I daydreamed as I milked Brownie about being outside and running wild in the fresh air as children are expected to do but my father—William, had put me to work. My brother—Glenn, was spared from labor and disappeared into the woods at the first opportunity, presumably fishing. Glenn is one year younger than me and would only be in the way Father had told me. I was jealous of Glenn and furious at Father. But Father demanded that I should contribute around the farm more despite the protesting from Mother. At the age of just nine years, I thought being forced to endure labor should have been a crime.

School was dismissed for the summer, and I had been looking forward to the yearly break since January. Summer times in the south are long and hot. The perfect time to be outdoors. Glenn and I often filled our summer days with daily activities: fishing, blackberry picking, rope swinging in creeks, getting muddy, and playing in old abandoned barns acting out an adventure scene from a book we read in school. We ran barefooted in the woods, playing hide and seek, stepping on garter snakes—by accident of course.

Children such as us at a young age would have a fascination with snakes, frogs, and spiders. Searching and catching these creatures became a sport for us. Glenn and I would catch these critters and keep them in jars and scare girls our age with them at school. It was always fun for Glenn and me to do so. We'd chase them around with garter snakes wrapped around our hands and arms or taunt them with a spider in a jar. It was all fun and games until Glenn went a little too far and tossed a snake at little Janet Wells. A fight broke out, and Glenn came out of that fight with a bloody nose and a swollen lip. I think we were all surprised of what little Janet was capable of. After the fight, Glenn was suspended for his stunt. And there were no more taunting girls with snakes and spiders. Glenn was also at the end of much teasing for the rest of his childhood for losing a fight against a girl.

Taunting girls with critters were the only bit of entertainment I enjoyed at school. I didn't care much for learning and often saw it as a means of torture. On many occasions, I would try to fake sickness to Mother early in the mornings to stay home, but my foolish attempts would never work. Mother was too smart for that. She would whack my legs with a switch. "Don't play that with me!" she would shout. I would grumble and moan and force myself out of the comfort of my bed to endure the torturous day of education. Concentrating on my school lessons on account of daydreaming was difficult. I thought about being outside, running wild in the woods, building forts out of tree branches that fell to the ground, or lying down in soft grass, staring up at the infinite blue sky filled with clouds.

But Mother always pushed me to do well in my studies. I made a vow to work harder at my education. In a way, I idolized her; not only for her determination to make me more responsible but for her providing nature.

On the weekends, she would bring Glenn and me for walks with her outside the farm picking blackberries and honeysuckles. Mother would tell us stories about what it was like for her to grow up; stories often filled with moral lessons. This was her way of teaching Glenn and me. She always made it clear to us that we wouldn't be children forever. This was a message she was determined to sink into our stubborn little heads as much as possible. It's difficult to comprehend Mother's attempts at first, but she was persistent. And it was her persistence that turned her into a fine and unique woman. It was an endowment of hers that I never overlooked while growing up. Yet, her messages eventually settled into my brother's and mine skulls as we grew older throughout the years. I always looked upon her for guidance, and she never had the heart to ignore my pleas for help. Not only was she a mother but she was my closest friend.

However, there were different feelings I had for my father. Much like school, I wanted to escape any work on the farm on account I wished to not to be in his presence. He was a very irritable and demanding man with a tall and burly figure that intimidated me, perhaps even frightened me. Glenn and I would often be at the wrong end of his ugly temper when we misbehaved or disobeyed him. There were consequences to be paid, and those consequences resulted in a black and blue rear-end. Glenn and I had to learn to act appropriately around Father. One of the best lessons I learned was to avoid him as much as possible. The reason was obvious: fear.

There would be mornings when Father would stomp in our room in the morning and shake me awake yelling. "No school today! You are to stay home today to help me on the farm!" I would object, but Father would have none of it. I labored on the farm when he and Mother had fallen behind on their work, on account of rainy days. The usual farm work was done: feeding chickens, gathering eggs, milking the cows, painting the barn if needed, and repairing fences. Plowing was done with our two horses to grow vegetables. We ate and sold what we grew. This is how Mother and Father made their living. This is how we survived.

And in the summer of 1927, Natchitoches was lucky to not be affected by a great flood. The Mississippi River had flooded the northeastern area of Louisiana. It started with heavy rains, but the rain kept falling and soon, the overabundance of rain in the Mississippi caused massive flooding. By early '27, the Mississippi River had flooded over thousands areas of land. And so, land along the Mississippi Delta was under water, thus destroying crops and livestock and also, taking many human lives.

Many people were left homeless and were forced to relocate. With their homes and lands destroyed, many families came to Natchitoches looking for work and refuge. Mother being a gracious woman, wanted to help any way possible from the aftermath of the flood. So, she volunteered to help out at a relief camp set up in Natchitoches. The camp became overcrowded in a hurry, so Mother invited a young couple to stay on the farm with us for a few months. The couple claimed to have owned a small farm in Catahoula Parish, but the flood had wiped it out. At first, Father didn't approve when Mother first told him we would have company for a while. An argument broke out between the two of them. And after two hours, Father, at last, gave in; this was Mother's firm persistence at work. There came to be an eventual compromise: the couple would have to help on the farm if they wished to stay. "They will earn their place," I heard Father say.

Aren and Katrina came to live on the farm and had been doing so for half a year. Mother made room for them to sleep in the living area at night in our small home. They slept on a thin, stitched hay mattress with a few blankets and pillows given to them from the relief camp. There never came a complaint from their mouths about not having more for it was all we could give them. After all, we took them in when they had nowhere else to go.

Their abilities to work a farm were not impressive by any means. But it didn't take long for Father to whip them both into shape.

———

"YOU FINISHED MILKIN' THAT COW YET, BOY?" Father's voice rang out. I glanced up from my task and laid my eyes on him. He stood just out-side the large open doors of the barn in the sunlight with a hammer in his hand. Sweat gleamed off his leathery suntanned body from the many hours of labor working under a hot sun.

"Just 'bout, sir," I replied.

"When you're done, take that milk inside to your mother. Then come find me at the fence by the pecan tree. We got mendin' to do."

"Yes, sir."

Father let me be as I finished milking Brownie. Not wanting to rush to help Father with the fence, I took my time. Taking my time with tasks was something I became skilled at. I readjusted my position on the stool I sat on and collected milk from Brownie's udders. No need to start work under the sweltering sun right away, I thought. I should enjoy the shade while I can.

But it wasn't long before Brownie dried up.

I clutched the bucket, now full of milk, firmly by the handle and car-ried it carefully to the back door of the house so I wouldn't drop it and risk a whipping from Father. Our farmhouse is small, painted white that now shown signs of age. Bits of paint here and there were peeling off the weathered wood. It wouldn't be long before Father would have the entire house repainted. I went through the back screen door and found Mother and Katrina in the kitchen waiting for me to bring them the milk.

"Thank you, Vincent," Katrina said in a quiet voice as she took the bucket of milk from my hands. She had a petite figure with lengthy, honey blond hair and bright blue eyes. Beautiful in my eyes. She took the bucket over to Mother who was standing by the basin as if she had been waiting for my arrival. Katrina labored mostly with Mother since arriving at the farm: cooking, cleaning, feeding the animals, and gathering eggs.

I stood visibly in the kitchen gawking at Katrina like I had done countless times before. I was only a child but yet I thought she was the most beautiful woman I had ever laid eyes on. The way she went about was graceful—almost fascinating. The one thing I remember most about her was that she spoke very little. And when she chose to speak, it would only be a word or two—generally "yes" or "no." And she only spoke in a soft, innocent voice as if she was trying to hide a subtle accent.

It was only after two weeks that our guests had lived with us when Katrina unexpectedly spoke to me. That day, I sat at the kitchen table doing homework after coming home from school. Katrina was busy making bread. I became distracted by her fluid movements as she pressed the dough. Her hands and arms were covered with flour, working with devotion as if bread making was an art form.

Katrina must have felt me watching her. "You must pay attention to your schoolwork, Vince." She said with her delicate accent. She stopped kneading and turned to look at me and smiled: a sweet and virtuous smile that brought life to her face.

"Sorry," I said and returned to my homework.

"Perhaps you could take a break. I could use one myself." Katrina placed the dough she had been kneading into a pan and set the pan in the oven. She then sat down at the table across from me. "What are you working on?"

"Mathematics," I replied. "I hate it. It's my worst subject."

"I never liked mathematics either. I always preferred literature and poetry."

"Poetry? Yuck!" I said in disgust in a playful manner with my tongue sticking out.

Katrina let out a sweet laugh. "You're too young yet to understand poetry. Poetry is a way for a person to express their deepest thoughts into words. The words can be sad and tragic, or happy and joyful. Poetry can be beautiful if read and admired the way it's meant to be."

Katrina cleared her throat:

The wistful fall of snow covers the ground,
In this lonely and somber place.
Gently the snow falls without a sound,
A fall so graceful as it touches your face.
The grass and fallen leaves now covered with white,
Beautiful to behold.
Oh, what a sight.
But tonight is oh, so cold
As you lie in the earth underneath the twilight.
You will vanish to a place I don't know,
Sleeping away the years in peace buried in the snow.

Katrina gave me another gentle smile and stood from the table to begin work on another loaf of bread. The kitchen is now silent. The words of the poem echoed in my head.

"Who wrote that?" I asked to break the silence.

Katrina turned her head at me and smiled once more. "I did." She returned to preparing the dough. "I wrote that the day after my grandmother's burial. I was fifteen when my grandmother passed. We were very close. I wrote that poem and memorized every word. I recite it to myself every night before I go to sleep. It brings me peace. It's titled 'The Snow Requiem'."

"But doesn't it make you miss your grandmother more, though?"

"In a way it does. But every time I recite it to myself—I feel as though Grandmother is with me—watching over me. It's the only way for me to be with her, I guess."

Katrina fell silent and continued kneading the dough as I returned to my homework. After a few minutes, I lifted my head to look back at

Katrina. "What was your grandmother's name?"

"Katrina," she said as she turned to look at me. "I'm so named after her."

"Did you used to live in a place with lots of snow?"

"I did, yes. But that was a few years ago."

"I've never seen snow. I want to someday."

Katrina smiled at me. "Maybe you will. There is always something mystical about snow. I always loved to watch snowflakes fall to the ground when the air is free from harsh winds. I remember days I used to play in the snow on cold mornings with my parents and grandmother. Those are memories I will cherish for a lifetime."

The room grew silent once more. Katrina focused on the bread as I continued with my homework but had difficulty concentrating on account of thinking about her poem.

Katrina had let me in but only a little. Just enough. Things became different between the two of us after that day in the kitchen. From that moment on, I believed as if Katrina and I became friends. Perhaps we did. I had discovered that Katrina's words were just as beautiful as her looks and personality. She was a unique and stunning creature that possessed the gift of goodwill. I couldn't help but to admire her. To love her. Yes, Katrina was the first love of my life. A different manner of love; not a harmless schoolboy crush or deep affection love but a love that can't be described with words.

Katrina may not have known it or felt it. But I did.

Mother noticed my presence as she and Katrina began preparing the raw milk. "Go on outside now, Vince and mind your father. He needs your help with that fence." Mother was short and had shoulder-length brown hair she would hold in a small bun at the back of her head and had dark green eyes. "No need for you to be in the kitchen right now."

"Yes, ma'am," I said as I took my eyes off Katrina and rushed out the back kitchen door.

In no hurry, I walked as slow as I could to the large pecan tree that stood near to the house by the long barbed-wire fence stretching along the farm's property. Aren and Father were hard at work repairing the fence. Father saw the advantage he had at the farm with a helper and so worked Aren from sun up to sun down. Aren always did what Father ordered him to do with no question nor objection. No back talk. He worked till his hands and fingers bled and with a burned back caused by the sun, and with blisters on his feet caused by his boots for he had no socks. He worked on and on. At night Katrina would wash the blood off his hands and fingers and carefully wash his back and feet only to get up again early the next morning and go through the same torture once more. "Time for work!" Father would shout at Aren in the early morning when he would enter the living area. After I had seen this—I couldn't help but to feel sorry for Aren. I also felt sorry for Katrina. They had lost their home and traveled to get help over many miles away and were then forced to work like dogs; this forced me to resent Father a little.

Aren and Father were hard at work on the barbed-wire fence, replacing the old, rusted wire with new wire. Aren had a muscular body that overshadowed his average height. He had short sandy-blond hair and piercing blue eyes and spoke with a small accent much like Katrina. He worked devotedly at the fence as if taking pride in the labor; taking pride at the skill of wrapping the wire into sharp and dangerous knots. It was a delicate skill Father had shown him and me as well although I did not care one way or the other about how to wrap barb-wire. I didn't care for any of the skills taught by Father. He wanted me to be a farmer, much like himself. But I did not wish to grow up and do so. I was only a young a boy of nine years, almost ten, and had dreams of another life away from the farm once I became of age to make my own decisions. It was a secret I kept close to myself.

"There you are, boy," Father hissed once he saw me. He stopped his work on the fence and rubbed a palm across his forehead to wipe away the sweat the poured from his face, but it made no difference. "Start workin' on knottin' the wire at the gate and work your way down toward us. And take a couple of spare tools and gloves. You'll need em'."

"Shouldn't take long now," Aren said as he glanced at me. His eyes told me he felt sympathetic for my laboring. He knew I didn't want to work and just wanted to be somewhere else having fun. "We'll be finished before you know it."

"Go on now," Father said as he and Aren went back to work on the fence. Without hesitation, I grabbed the tools I needed: pliers and wire cutters, along with a pair of thick leather gloves and walked to the gate. No rush I thought. No point in trying to rush and do shady work and be forced to do it all over again. I hated Glenn for not helping. I wanted to lick him good when he returns from fishing, despite the consequences I would get from Mother and Father.

———

I WRAPPED THE LAST BIT OF STRETCHED WIRE and pulled the wire as tight as I could into a knot and clamped the knot with my pliers and at last, snipped off the remaining long strands of wire to sharp points. The fence was finished. It was also the end of a long and hard day of labor. The evening sun sunk low as the sunlight faded. Father examined my work. I knew what he was up to. He searched for anything to holler at me about as he's done so many time before. And he found it: on one particular knot, I failed to tighten it.

"This is the worst bit of tightenin' I had ever seen!" Father yelled. "You ever listen to anything I teach you, boy? You're damn lucky it's about nighttime or I would have you do the fence all over again!"

"Sorry, sir," I said with my head down. It was all I could say. No need to argue with Father for it would only make matters worse.

"Go on inside," he barked. "Your mother should have supper ready soon."

Without hesitation, I turned from Father and bolted for the house, wanting to be away from him. I was greeted at the front porch by Mother, who was holding a glass of fresh milk in her hand.

"Take this to Aren," she said as she handed me the glass of milk. I spotted Aren sitting underneath the pecan tree, relaxing. Father stomped passed me swearing under his breath and went inside the house. "Don't worry about your father. I heard him hollerin'. I'll talk with him tonight." I could feel tears in my eyes as Mother took my face with her hand. "Don't cry about it now, Vince. Be a big boy and let me deal with your father. Go on now and take that milk to Aren."

I stepped off the porch, fighting back the tears and walked toward the pecan tree where Aren sat. The birds were letting out their final sing-songs of the day, and the crickets and cicadas began their piercing night calls. A few fragile clouds creeping beneath the sky of an endless canvas of orange partially veiled the sun. There was always something so majestic about sunsets. The late evening was always my favorite time of the day. I had walked near the pecan tree where Aren was resting with his back against the large trunk as I stood mesmerized by the beauty of the sunset now suspended at the horizon of tree lines.

"Don't stare too long," Aren advised. "Even though it's setting, you can still burn your eyes." I took my eyes off the sunset and noticed Aren staring at me. He was right, however, about the sun burning the eyes. I could still see the image of the bright orange circle of the sun as I looked upon him; an image I was all too familiar with. "Is that for me?" he said pointing to the glass of milk in my hand.

Aren was soaked in sweat. His hands blackened, swollen, bleeding, and dirty from the day of work. His skin was dark and leathery, much like Fathers.

I gave him the glass of milk as he ran his fingers through his tousled hair. "Thank you, Vince," he said. He always called me Vince and not my full name. I sat down next to him and looked at the sunset once again. The crickets now chirped louder, and the sky was turning a dark orange as the sun was in its final moments in the sky before it would disappear behind the trees. "It's something to look at isn't it?"

"Yes, sir, it is," I replied.

"Come on now, Vince. I said you didn't have to call me that," he said with a grin on his face. He had told me many times not to call him 'sir' but being from the south—manners were taught at a young age. This was one of my mother's teachings.

"Sorry," I said. "It's a habit."

"Well, it's a good habit to have. And there's no need to apologize. Your parents are doing right by you. They're raising you right. You'll come to understand that one day when you're older."

I nodded my head in agreement. Aren took a drink of milk, and after a few minutes of silence, he turned to me. "You don't like your father, do you?" he asked.

"I don't know," I replied.

"I've seen the way you are around him. You act indifferently towards him."

"I just can't stand him sometimes. He's just too mean—especially to you and Katrina. I don't know why he is the way he is. He works you to death, and you say nothing to him about it. You just work and work."

Aren kept his eyes on me with a soft expression on his face for a moment before speaking again. "You know, Vince, your parents took us in to your home—and with two more people in the house is two more mouths to feed. So I have been working hard to keep up with the food needed to feed all of us and to keep up with the food and produce your family needs to earn money." He paused and took another gulp of milk. "So do you think it would be fair to your parents and to you and your brother if Katrina and I sat around all day doing nothing and eating your crops and taking away money that your parents need to earn to make a living?"

He was making sense and myself being my at young age didn't know any better. I gave a nod of understanding. "I guess I understand," I replied.

"Do you?" he asked once more.

"Yeah," I muttered.

"You see, Vince—I was new to farming before Katrina and I came to live here. We were struggling because we didn't know what we were doing. We thought it was easy, but we were wrong. So your father has been teaching all he knows about farming. I am now smarter and wiser for it. I've been learning many, many things and when we return to Catahoula, I will take what I learned here so I can run my farm and make a living. What your parents did for Katrina and I was a blessing, and I know there is no way we could ever repay your family for what you all have done for us."

The sun had now vanished below the horizon, and only a faint haze of orange was in the sky. A few stars were sparkling, and the mosquitoes flew about buzzing in my ears. I swatted a few away from my face before I said anything. "Ok, I guess it makes sense. I just hope he wasn't so mean about it."

Aren snickered. "It's just his manner. We all have our own personalities. Your father is just a little on the stern side is all, and there's nothing wrong with that. He puts you to work on the farm because he's just trying to teach you some responsibility before you're all grown up. He's making a man out of you. You need to understand that, Vince. He cares about you. He just has his own way of showing it. Your father is firm about mistakes because he wants you to do the right thing."

"Ok," I said.

More dim lit stars appeared and twinkled in the darkened sky above us. Mosquitoes now buzzed about and stung my arms, so Aren and I jumped up from under the pecan tree and dusted our bottoms off. Glenn then came jogging towards us from the trees across the farm, holding a few perch that hung from a threaded fishing line. As he got closer, I could just make out a smug grin on his face. He knew he had escaped the day from labor and was determined to mock me with his catch. "Look at what I caught today!" Glenn beamed at me, and if it hadn't of been for Aren standing next to me, I would have whopped him hard in the face. "Shame you had to work today, Vince. I had a good day fishin'." Glenn was rubbing it in harder. Now I really wanted to punch him to wipe that grin off his face.

Glenn held up the perch near to my eyes just to mock me, and then Mother's voice rang out from the front porch of the house. "You boys come on in! Supper is ready!"

Aren put his thick arm around me as we walked towards the house as Glenn walked along beside us.

"You're a good boy, Vince," Aren said. "And you too, Glenn." Glenn was busy swatting away at mosquitoes and perhaps did not hear what Aren had said. "You've got a good family. Katrina and I are hoping to start a family after we get back home and get our farm going again. I'll take everything your father taught me and I'll teach my boys the same. I'll make men out of them and when you have boys of your own some-day, you must make men out of them as well. Remember, we all have our own ways of doing things. We all love in our own way. Your father is a good man. You'll come to realize that someday."

I wanted to believe what Aren was telling me but I was too stubborn for that. It was then I realized I barely knew Father. He was only a presence in my eyes: a man who lived in my home, a man who gave or-ders, a man who showed no affection towards Glenn and I and never asked for it either. We were strangers living together.

The three of us escaped into the house away from the mosquitoes. The smell of hot and delicious food filled the air. My stomach grumbled for a hot meal after a long day of labor.

———

THE NEXT MORNING, I awoke to the alarming crowing of roosters. My hands and fingers were calloused and scabbed over—evidence of the work from the day before. I had a dream the previous night as if several people were watching me as I slept. There were words spoken, but they kept their voices low. But paying no mind to the dream, I gazed out through the window to see a bright day: few clouds in the sky and birds sang their morning songs. But something was missing: Aren wasn't any-where in sight. It was Tuesday and Father always had Aren working Tuesday. Perhaps Father gave him the day off, or he was letting Aren have a few more hours of sleep before putting him to work. But that wasn't like Father. There was a suspicion that something was not right.

I got out of bed and was careful not to wake Glenn up, resisting the urge to punch him in the face as he slept—wanting to get back at him for not having to work the day before. I stepped into the living area adjoining to the bedroom and found Aren's and Katrina's hay mattress gone, along with their belongings. There was talking coming from the kitchen, so I rushed in hoping to find them in there, but it was only Mother and Father. Mother was preparing to make breakfast while Father sat at the table drinking coffee.

"Where are Aren and Katrina?" I asked.

"They left for Catahoula earlier this mornin'," Father stated.

"They're gone?" I asked in shock.

"Yup."

"Why?"

"The flood water that covered their land is gone now. Your ma and I read about it in the paper yesterday. A lot of families are returning to their homes. Since their land is all dried up now, they can return and get back to their own lives."

I stood in silence, disappointed that Aren and Katrina didn't say goodbye. The urge to cry from disbelief came over me, but I fought back the tears, remembering Mother's words from the day before to be a big boy.

Mother spoke. "They made their minds up last night after you went to bed to leave straight away 'cause they needed to get back home. They wanted to say goodbye to you and Glenn but didn't want to wake the two of you. But they'll miss us and they thanked us for taking them in. And Aren told me to tell you, Vincent—to be a good boy and mind your father."

I stood in silence as Father glanced up at me. "Go on outside and enjoy your day, son," he said. "There'll be no work today. I'll get your brother up in a bit so he'll join you. We'll call the both of you in for breakfast when it's ready. Go on now."

"Yes, sir," I said.

And just like that—Aren and Katrina were out of our lives. Katrina—

the woman I secretly loved and Aren—the man who had words of wisdom for me when I needed them. I knew they couldn't live on our farm for the rest of their lives. I had counted on them staying with us and never leaving, but I didn't know it until now. But Aren and Katrina had their own lives to attend to. They were given another chance to start their own family on their own farm. I speculated if I would ever see them again. I hoped so. Perhaps one day when I'm older; the day I leave the farm or maybe they will visit in the years to come. I would look forward to the moment they return, perhaps with their children; I counted on it.

The sun was rising from the east over the tree lines as I stepped out into the bright day. The sky was blue, and a gentle breeze was at my back as I rushed toward the nearby creek with the entire day ahead of me. A good day to be a child once again. So it was time to catch snakes, frogs, and spiders.

Or perhaps go fishing.

THREE

IN THE EARLY HOURS OF THE MORNING, I slipped out of bed, put on my overalls and boots, and snatched a few dollars of my money before sneaking out the house in silence as everyone slept. The day was starting fresh; the air was cool, and the smell of autumn lingered. It's the year of 1938, and I was determined to make it into town to begin a new life I had been dreaming of for many years now; a life away from the farm and away from Father. Myself now being a grown man grew tiresome of the ordinary farm work. I longed for more. Now is my chance to have it. I'm now twenty-one, but still taking orders.

I wanted to escape the farm as soon as my schooling was over. But with no money and nowhere to go, my only option was to stay. Mother and Father could not afford to send me off to a college that would allow me to earn a degree. For America was deep into the Great Depression. And somehow, the farm held on by loose strings. Money was sparse, but we survived on what we grew. Glenn, now finished with his schooling, agreed to stay but I suspect Father had something to with that decision.

The farm had been lucky to survive. There were several attempts from bank workers to force Mother and Father to sell the farm. But Father stood firm on the matter and refused each time. But the bankers were persistent and patient. Each time they would return, the asking price would be raised, but Father still refused to sell. His intentions were simple: to wait it out; wait out the costs of crops to rise again, jobs to return, and wait out the bank associates patience.

And he did.

It was difficult considering we had one more mouth to feed. There came a new addition to the family: Little Julia. She was a fragile thing born with a full head of black hair and thick chubby cheeks. She arrived in '33. Mother instantly became attached to her and so did I. Whenever Julia would raise a fuss, Mother would sing lullabies to her, and she would just coo and fall asleep. She always kept Julia close and was firm on not allowing Glenn or myself anywhere near our sister for the early months. It was her motherly instinct to be protective. We learned to stay away until Mother felt we were mature enough to hold her with no accident. After the first time I did so, there was an unexplainable attachment. I was a big brother now to Julia and so, I needed to protect her.

But even with another mouth to feed, we survived. There were signs that the Depression was perhaps ending as the years rolled by. The price of crops rose—gradually. And jobs were on the rise. But faith in the stock market was at an all-time low, in fear the stock market could falter once more, as it had been throughout the times of the Depression.

But I remained optimistic, however, about the Depression ending. With the prices of crops picking up; I saw this by virtue to leave the farm.

In the previous months, I had been studying informative articles discovered in magazines in shops and diners around Natchitoches when I accompany Father when crops were to be sold and goods needed to be purchased. The stories were on the US Army, and after reading the first one, I grew curious and fascinated about joining up for the military. When I realized a recruitment office was in town, I decided to gather my courage and go speak with a recruiter about signing up. The army could be my way off the farm and I considered it to be best to keep my choice of enlisting a secret for the time being.

I arrived at the gate and halted. Paranoia forced me to turn around to look at the front door and windows to make sure I was not being watched. Father would be awake at any moment with daylight appearing in the morning sky. I could see no faces in the windows nor persons in the doorway. The coast was clear as I moved past the fence and onto the road, letting my legs and feet take me away into town for the day.

———

THE DIRT ROAD INTO NATCHITOCHES I walked on ran along several miles of vast pastures and farmlands with old abandoned barns possibly dating back to the 1800s. Magnolia trees can be spotted here and there along the way. I always loved the fresh scent of magnolia. The fragrance is unforgettable, and few trees are as beautiful in full blossom. Mother would ask Glenn and I to bring her a flower from a tree near our home and then place it in a jar full of water and set it on the kitchen table; the sweet bouquet of sweet magnolia would linger in our house for days.

The walk into town would be half an hour as the sun was now almost above the morning horizon and the heat had risen. It's late September but yet, the temperature is still warm.

After a quarter of a mile, I stopped at a shrub just a few yards from the road and treated myself to a few honeysuckles before I was to proceed into town. It has always been a tradition for Glenn and I to go honeysuckle harvesting. There is a skill in pulling the green bulb at the base of the flowers and drawing every bit of the nectar to suckle and to appreciate the delicious liquid. As a youth, I would spend large amounts of time by myself sitting by a thicket and enjoying honeysuckles while being lazy and relaxed. I felt like a kid again as I lied there covered with those little white flowers. But adulthood was far ahead of me as I wondered if I would have this freedom to act like a child again in the days to come.

My stomach growled. I was hungry and didn't think to take any food before I left, and I couldn't get my fill on just honeysuckles, so I returned to my walk towards town and got a breakfast of bacon, fried eggs, toast, and several glasses of cold milk at a diner once I arrived into town and to kill time before walking to the recruitment office.

Now is an opportunity to speak about Natchitoches. The town's charm is an alluring presentation of the south. Any traveler that comes into Natchitoches can fall in love with the town. Its beauty and the simplistic atmosphere was something I always admired. Hotels, general stores, and a lone diner ran down the main road of the town which ran along not twenty yards from the Cane River. The main street which is laid out in brick is not only used by automobiles but also horses and buggies. Oak trees filled the banks of the Cane River which provided cool shade on hot days. Old brick buildings and homes filled the streets behind the main road. But what made Natchitoches special was the community. It was the little businesses that allowed the small town to make a name for itself; this obliged everyone to know everyone. Everyone worked together to make the community strive. It was just the southern way of life.

I found the recruitment office to be empty, other than myself. A desk sat near the back wall with two chairs in front and behind the desk was a closed door. With no other person present, I strolled around the office looking at photographs hanging on the wall of soldiers and a few propaganda posters. My eye spotted a particular poster with a soldier pointing a finger at me with the words "There's A Man's Job To Be Done. Enlist Today." I stood staring the poster over when I heard a loud voice ring out. "Can I help you, son?"

Taking me by surprise, I spun around to meet a man in a brown military uniform glaring at me from behind the desk. He must have come through the door behind him and I had not heard him enter. He had short jet black hair with a stocky body. His coat was decorated with various ribbons, badges, and patches presenting his accomplishments. "Yes sir," I replied. "I would like to speak to you about enlisting."

"Is that right?" he said with a smile. "Well, why don't you take a seat at the desk and let's discuss it."

I took a seat in front of the desk as he took his from behind. After eye-ing me over for a moment, he spoke again. "So you'd like to join the ar-my you say?"

"Yes, sir," I said. "Maybe I could be useful."

"Good for you, son. We need all the recruitments we can get. I'm Staff Sergeant Charley Ward. And what's yours?"

"Vincent Conroy, sir. People call me Vince."

"Ok... Vince—so tell me... why you wish to enlist?" Ward said as he leaned back in his chair; his eyes focused on me as if studying me care-fully.

"Well, I'm a farm boy, you see. I've been working on a farm my whole life, but I figured that I don't wish to be a farmer for the rest of my life. But the thing is—my parents can't afford to send me off to college to get a fancy degree, and I have little money that I have been saving. So I guessed the army would be a good place for me to be. I've read that men who enlist get to travel and see the country and that sounds mighty fine with me. I have ambition; lots of it. The simple matter of the fact is sir: I'm tired of farm work. I hate it. So maybe the army can help me with my problem."

"So how old are you, son?" he said leaning forward and placing his arms on the desk and folding them.

"I'm twenty-one, sir," I replied.

He nodded his head and leaned back in his chair again. "I admire your determination, son. I also respect your honesty. You know, some kids often come in here and feed me a bunch of bologna on why they wish to sign up. They point out it's their patriotic duty and all of that other nonsense—but not you. Your honest and I can respect that. You say you hate the farm life and you believe the army is a way out from that. Well, it is." The recruiter snatched a pen off the desk and leaned forward once more to write something down on a form "Well, you look healthy. That farm life must have gotten you into shape."

"Yes, sir. It's all I know, but I wish to experience more."

"I know it's hard work. I did it myself before I joined up." Ward leaned back in his chair once again and scratched his chin. "Well, if you're serious about joining up—I have to say you should make a fine infantryman if that's what you choose to be. You got the look for it. The choice is yours though. Have you thought about what role you would be interested in taking?"

I had never considered about what job I would choose but when the recruiter said infantryman; I liked the sound of it. Excitement grew as I visualized myself as a soldier. "Infantry!" I spoke with excitement.

A smile came across Ward's face. "Well, you seem to know what you want. If you work hard enough, you can be promoted to a NCO."

"NCO?" I said with confusion.

"Non-commissioned officer. You'll start from the bottom as a Private and work your way up the ranks."

The thought of me becoming an officer was alluring. But there was one question that leaped into my head I needed an answer to. "I am curious where I will end up. I kind of wish to be placed somewhere other than here if that's not too much to ask."

"Well, I can understand that. After recruits finish their basic training, they're usually stationed somewhere near their homes so they can be closer to their loved ones. But in your case, I can recommend having you stationed somewhere else." This is what I wanted to hear, and I smiled. The recruiter picked up his pen again and began writing once more on his form. After a moment he looked up at me again. "Can you be here tomorrow at the same time?" he said after glancing at his wristwatch. "You will need to take the Army General Classification Test along with some other boys that are signing up. This is just to test your intelligence. After you take the AGCT, you will need to have a physical and go through any other tests if necessary. If everything goes smoothly, then you can sign the contract and take the oath."

"Yes, sir!" I said with excitement. "I'll be here first thing in the morning."

"Very good!" he said as we stood up. He gave me a vigorous handshake. "You're making a wise decision here, son. I know you'll make a damn good soldier. I have to warn you, though, being a soldier for the United States Army will not be easy. It will take a lot of hard work and dedication. Ever since the Great War, there have been many changes in how things are done. Training is vigorous. Some boys drop out, but I don't see you as a quitter." He gave me a hard stare. "Are you a quitter, Vince?"

"No sir," I replied. "I'll do my best." My attitude was cocky. I admit this because I was young and felt as if I was invincible.

"I'm certain you will," he said. "You know—I'll recommend you for the National Guard. That will be a good fit for you. It's a militia force that is responsible for protecting the U.S. from conflict and any natural disasters. The army currently has a Basic Training camp near Anniston, Alabama that is the best at training men for the National Guard."

"That sounds fine, sir," I said.

"Great! So I will see you bright and early tomorrow."

"Yes, sir. You will."

———

WITH MY SPIRITS UP, I was in no rush to return to the farm—not that I wanted to avoid Mother and Father about enlisting in the army; they'll be told of my decision once I arrive there in the evening. The full day was ahead of me, so after leaving the recruitment office, I walked a couple of blocks to a small bookstore and with the few dollars I had, I purchased a used copy of *Adventures of Huckleberry Finn* by Mark Twain.

Afterward, I took a walk down the main street with no particular destination in mind. With nothing to keep me in town, I returned to the dirt road leading back to the farm. After walking about halfway, I stepped off the road and wandered into a thicket of trees and shrubs for a quarter of a mile that leads into a small field settled at the edge of a bayou. The field was laid out with tall grass and partially surrounded by oak and hickory trees. At the southern tip of the field stood an ancient and massive live oak tree with Spanish moss that blew gently in the soft autumn wind.

I sat down underneath the canopy of the oak tree which provided me shade from the sun. From this spot, I can observe the field, listen to the wildlife, and relax. Glenn and I came here often for it was our favorite getaway from the farm. The bayou allowed the two of us to fish and the massive tree provided us shelter when we wished to just lay about and be lazy.

I had taken Aren and Katrina to this very spot several times to have picnics underneath the oak tree. We would all walk through the field chatting as we glided our hands at the top of the towering grass seeds. Aren and I did most of the talking as Katrina only listened.

The first night with them in the field, I taught the two of them how to catch fireflies. (I often called them lightning bugs.) The field would light up with hundreds of fireflies dancing in the night sky under a great and bright full moon. We'd catch as many as we could and put them in jars. The jar lit up, and Katrina's eyes glistened as she stared at the bursting luminous green light in her hands.

"It's beautiful," she said with a gracious smile.

For the finale, I would unscrew the lid of the jar and let all the fireflies out. We then became surrounded by the glow of the fireflies as they spread out into the night. All the lights around Katrina hypnotized her as she covered her smiling mouth as she giggled.

Aren only observed the happiness erupting from Katrina. He didn't seem all too impressed with the firefly jar trick, but he seemed content, at least for Katrina's well-being. On one or two occasions, I took a glimpse at Aren and perhaps witnessed a modest grin creep at the corners of his mouth as the fireflies danced all around the three of us.

I could sense the two of them were truly happy, even in that briefest amount of time. They lost so much but still had the gift to remain optimistic despite their troubles. There is something appealing about that. In troublesome times, it's best to observe the positives and feed off those emotions and ignore the negatives that only bring sadness and harm. It was an untouchable gift. A wonderful gift.

I made myself comfortable underneath the shade of the oak tree and dived into *Huckleberry Finn*. Reading had always been a favorite pastime of mine. I owned few books and was constantly hoping to broaden my meager collection and without a doubt—this book will be a great addition.

———

UNAWARE OF HOW LONG I had been resting under the tree reading, a voice rang out. "I thought I'd find you here." I jerked my head from the pages of the book and spotted Glenn limping towards the oak tree. The limp came from an incident a few years back when he fell from a ladder that leads to the loft in the barn. The ladder buckled under his weight as he climbed on account of it being old and rotted. Unfortunately, the fall broke Glenn's right knee, and the aftermath of that injury had caused permanent limp in his walk. But nowadays, Glenn along with everyone else has become accustomed to his limp and never acknowledge it.

Glenn halted just outside the canopy of the oak tree. He was drenched with sweat; no doubt from a busy and hard day at the farm. In some ways, Glenn and I looked very alike. He was a little taller than me, however, but only by a few inches. We both had the same dark brown shade of hair. His face was narrow much like Mothers as I had a stronger jawline like Fathers. But we both had the same ominous green eyes and a broad nose we both received with compliments from Father.

"You snuck up on me," I said while swinging my head away from Glenn to peer out upon the field. I picked up a fallen leaf from the ground and marked my place in the book and closed it. "Let me guess— Father sent you to find me."

"Yup," he replied. "He was really angry when he couldn't find you this mornin'. I helped him with some work, and then he sent me off to look for you. So... why did you run off?" Glenn sounded harsh. Annoyed perhaps on account of me skipping out on work.

"I'll tell you but say nothing to Ma and Pa because I will explain everything to them tonight."

"Tell me what?"

I took my eyes off the field and glared at Glenn. "I'm joining the army. This mornin', I snuck off and went into town to enlist."

"What?! Why?!" Glenn asked, staring at me with a look of confusion on his face.

"It's my way off the farm," I replied. "I'm off to do something more important. To live my own life. Farm life is not what I want. I can be a man in the army; a real man. 'Cause you know Mother and Father can't afford to send me off to college or anywhere else so I can learn a trade. Well, the army can teach me a trade and who else knows what. No more damn farm life for me."

Glenn only stared at me. He looked as if he wanted to speak but just couldn't get any words out.

"So just go on back home and tell Father that you couldn't find me. I'll be back home in the evening to tell them the news."

I diverted my eyes away from Glenn and opened my book to the page where the oak leaf was placed and began to read, but Glenn hadn't budged. He was still watching me.

"Are you sure you know what you are doing?" he asked. "If you spoke with a recruiter, he probably just fed you a bunch of horseshit on why you should join up. And besides, you're needed at the farm for at least a couple more years. Save your money and move on after things pick up. Things have to get better at some point. You're being stubborn, you know."

Annoyed, I placed the leaf back in the book and smacked it shut with my fingers and thumb and glared at Glenn once more. "It's not Ma's decision to make. It's not Pa's and it sure as hell isn't yours. The choice is mine, and I already made it. I'm going into the army, and there is nothing you can say or do to make me change my mind. The fact is, Glenn—I despise that damn farm. I hate working for Pa. You should understand that. You know what that man is like. I'm leaving, and that's all I'm gonna say about it."

Glenn didn't say another word. He just stared at the ground and nodded his head. He turned his back at me and disappeared into the thickets, leaving me alone at last; allowing me to continue reading and be left alone with my thoughts.

———

I LOST TRACK OF TIME as I read underneath the oak tree. The autumn sun was setting. The air became cooler. My stomach growled from hunger. I closed my book and left the shade of the oak tree to stretch and wandered around to get the feeling in my legs again. I felt well rested after a day away from the farm.

But it was now time to get home and eat a big meal and reveal to my folks about joining the army. I walked to the edge of the field, just outside the thickets and stared out over the ground once more. A loon call echoed out over the bayou as the crickets and cicadas began their songs of the night. The setting sun had enveloped the field with a faint light of orange. I glanced back at the old oak tree: the Spanish moss had now given the tree a haunting look in the dusk. The wind had picked up as the moss swayed back and forth strongly on the outstretched limbs of the oak tree. My body shivered from the cold breeze as I entered the thickets and headed home.

———

FATHER SAT IN HIS ROCKING CHAIR, fidgeting around with the radio as I entered through the front door. He was alone in the living area as I heard Mother's and Glenn's voices coming from the kitchen. The sound of static, jazz music, and news announcements from the radio changed from one second to the next. I closed the door behind me as Father looked up from the radio which he had now turned off. An expression of scorn came across his face. I stood at the door—frozen; aware of what was about to happen.

"So just where have you been all day?" His tone was harsh. From the looks of him, it looked as though he would explode at any moment. The talking in the kitchen ceased as Mother and Glenn stepped through the threshold into the living area.

"I went into town this morning—" I said. But before I could utter another word, Father interrupted me.

"Oh, really?" he said. "And for whatever reason for? Did you know I needed you to help me out with the work today? You left Glenn, your mother, and myself to take care of all the work today. We needed you, but you skipped out and disappeared into town. What is wrong with you, boy?!" His voice shot out throughout the house. I felt a shiver travel up and down my spine.

"I went into town this mornin' to enlist in the army," I stated before Father could speak again.

Father stood up; his face glowed red with anger. Mother gasped and covered her mouth in disbelief.

"You what?!" Father shouted. "Did I hear you right, boy?!"

"Vincent!" Mother said with distress.

"I spoke to a recruiter today, and I will be enlisting," I said. "I'm of age. Tomorrow morning, I need to go back into town to take a test and get a physical."

"Why are you joining the army, Vincent?" Mother asked.

"Yes! Tell us why!" Father shouted.

"It's what I wish to do. It's my choice. I don't wish to stay here on the farm. It's as simple as that."

Father scowled at me with anger. "You're a damn fool, boy," he said. "You have no business joining the army. Only fools join the army, and I won't allow you to become a fool. No, you are to stay here and help out on the farm. You're needed here. So tomorrow you will go into town and tell that recruiter that you've changed your mind and that will be the end of this nonsense."

"I can make my own decisions," I said, standing my ground. "When it's time for me to leave, I'm gone. I'm sure you and Glenn can run the farm yourselves. This is what I want."

Father inched closer to me which made me worried. Now my father had never struck me in the face, but there was a feeling he could do it right then and there. Instead, he only glared at me. "You don't know what you're doing, boy. I thought I raised you better than this. I raised you to mind your mother and me—to be respectful.

"Vincent, listen to your father," Mother pleaded.

This entire time, Glenn had kept quiet; he only stared down at the floor. I was glad he hadn't spoke for I was afraid he would only make matters worse.

I now realized that Julia was standing in the bedroom doorway on the other side of the living area. "Why is Daddy shouting?" Julia asked.

"Because your brother is being a fool," Father said. "He wants to leave us and not care about us any longer."

"That's not true," I stated. "I said nothing about not caring for all of you. You're putting words in my mouth."

Julia looked at me with sadness. Her large hazel-green eyes swelled with tears. "You want to leave us?" she asked. "Why are you leaving?"

Before I could answer, Mother stepped over to Julia and picked her up and took her back into the bedroom. She emerged a moment later in the living area and shut the door behind her.

"Please don't do this, Vincent," Mother pleaded once more. "Please listen to your father. The army isn't for you. You don't have a place there. I'm sorry that we can't provide to send you to college but why can't you stay here for a little while longer and wait for the economy to pick up. Then perhaps you can manage to learn a trade."

"I can't stick around a few more years. I want to leave. The sooner, the better."

Mother began to sob and rushed into the kitchen. Glenn shook his head at me. "You're a jack-ass," he scorned as he went after her.

Father hadn't budged from where he stood. He crossed his thick arms and glared. "You're a real piece of work; you know that, boy? I don't know what's gotten into you, but you are making a huge mistake." He turned away and stepped toward the kitchen before he stopped. He didn't look at me but lowered his head and rubbed his eyes. "After you leave for training—don't come back. You'll not be wanted here any longer. You can sleep outside in the barn tonight." He stepped into the kitchen with heavy footsteps that thumped hard on the floor, leaving me alone in the living area.

In need of something to eat, I peeked inside the kitchen; luckily it's empty. Shouting erupted from my parents' room; they all seemed to be engaged in a bitter conversation on my account. I scavenged the kitchen for a jar of milk, a couple of biscuits, along with an onion and apple and escaped outside. I went into the barn to put my food away before my wash up at the water pump. Afterward, I returned the barn and climbed the ladder to the loft and ate my meal before making myself comfortable as I drifted off to sleep.

FOUR

LARGE AND DARK STORM CLOUDS SHROUDED THE BLUE SKY like a blanket above the farm as I worked without end in the vegetable garden, picking lettuce when a heavy clasp of thunder exploded in the air, sending an icy shiver through my body. Rain was coming. I've always admired rainy days. There is something so alluring, so peaceful, about a rainy day. Perhaps it's that sweet, earthy scent of the land that rises and fills the air that I admire. It's a scent I came all too familiar with throughout the years. Even days after a rainfall, I can still smell it on my clothes and on my skin. The lands needed it. The winter weather had been dry and cool. Spring had not been different. There had been a few modest rainfalls in the past weeks; just enough to provide a few crops to flourish throughout spring but a solid rainfall would ensure a healthy harvest for the hardy vegetables.

It's mid-April of '39, and I have been waiting impatiently to leave for Basic Training. One factor I learned about myself over the years is that I am not a patient man. After taking the AGCT and passing my physical the year before, I expected to leave for Alabama right away, but instead, had to wait seven months on account that Fort McClellan was going through a massive expansion and until construction would be completed, I was to stick around the farm until called for duty.

Throughout the months, I grew restless as I lingered and worked on the farm. And it was during this time that Father and I could seldom look at one another. There was resentment between the two of us. His demeanor towards me was harsh as it had always been, but now it showed there was more feeling behind his mood; a hateful emotion he had for me and no one else. As the days passed, I became bitter with his behavior, and so I deemed it best to avoid him at all costs. It was intolerable to be around Father, so I accustomed myself to a daily working routine that would keep me far away from him as humanly possible. I often ate meals alone. But again and again, Glenn, Julia, and Mother would join me so I would at least have a little company. Once winter had passed, and the air turned warmer, I slept in the loft of the barn. I had no complaints there. I was free to come and go throughout the night without having to worry about disturbing anyone. The barn was also a place for me to have the company of a woman now and then.

"Vince!" Mother shouted out from the front porch as the distant rumbling of thunder echoed throughout the dark sky. "It's about to rain! Come inside before you get yourself drenched!"

I straightened myself up and waved at her to let her know I heard her, but I could at least pull a couple more heads of lettuce. My sack of lettuce was near full but I'm determined to carry all I can. Fewer trips that way.

Over in the distance across the fields, I spotted Father and Glenn by the barn moving the cows and horses in before the rainfall. Father was doing his usual cursing and griping, leading the horses and cows into the barn as Glenn limped behind them, keeping them from straying off. Another clap of thunder erupted as all the horses and cows became spook and shuffled away from Glenn. I almost dropped my sack of lettuce to run over to the barn to help, but Glenn hurried along in front of the animals and got them all under control before they ran off into the fields. The entire time, Father was swearing up a storm, being his usual ornery self. Once the animals were in the barn, the doors were closed securely as Glenn and Father began their walk back to the house.

I had just finished putting the last head of lettuce in the sack when the rain poured down. The rainfall was cold, but it felt refreshing as it washed away all the sweat and dirt off my skin. I swung the sack of produce over my shoulder and jogged back to the house. Underneath the shelter of the front porch, Mother was waiting for me with a glass of milk.

"How's the picking?" Mother asked. She now appeared as if she was another person: her once long wavy brown hair had straightened out and was now lightly stranded with gray. Her narrow face had become somewhat wrinkled, her eyes darkened, and her voice drier. It upset me to see Mother aging; it is not an enjoyable sight for me to witness. I wished that she could keep her youthful appearance forever but yet, she was still gorgeous in my eyes as she will always be. In her youth, she was spirited, but now it seemed her spirit was fading—perhaps on account of myself. I knew my enlistment in the army had worried her.

"Not too bad," I replied as I dropped the sack of lettuce on the porch floor and accepted the glass of milk from her. "Some were ruined." I took a generous drink of milk and leaned over the porch railing and watched the heavy rainfall that was at times interrupted with a clasp of thunder or a bolt of lightning streaking across the sky.

"That's to be expected." She smiled at me and gazed out into the falling rain. "I'm worried about you, you know. Your father and I have been hearing about some bad things going on over in Europe. We're afraid that if you get involved in the army—you'll get thrown into that mess. This country just got out of a war some years back, and from the sound of things, another one is brewing. I just want nothing to happen to you."

"I'll be fine, Ma. I can't stay on this farm for the rest of my life, or I'll go crazy. This is my chance to travel and visit other places. I crave more than just a simple farm life."

Mother sighed. "I know, dear." She kept her eyes on the rain. "Your father and I can't keep you here. I know your father can be really stubborn, but he doesn't look at you all grown up. In his eyes, he still sees a little child running 'round barefooted, jumping into creeks and stepping on snakes." She then looked at me with her delicate eyes, now swelling with tears. "That's how I see you too. You'll always be my little boy, and I just don't want to lose you."

I could hear the sadness in her voice; an accidental desperate attempt for me to view factors from her perception. I couldn't hold it against her. It was her maternal instinct kicking in, wanting to protect her son.

I took her into my arms and hugged her close, disregarding my wet clothes. "Pa doesn't want me to come back after I leave.

"Ignore your father. Just remember that you will always have a home here."

"I'll visit as often as I can. I don't know where I'll be, but I'll write to you and visit."

"That's good to know."

A swift flash of lightning and a booming echo of thunder broke my hold on Mother. My body tensed from the aftermath of the impressive sound.

"That was a big one," Mother said as I wiped her tears off her cheeks with my thumbs. She took another look out into the rain. "Now let's get inside because I know you must be hungry. You can sit at the table with us and don't worry about your father—just let him be. And if he starts up his nonsense, I'll set him straight." She gave me a consoling smile as she opened the screen door and stepped into the house with me trailing her and leaving the rainfall behind. I didn't think to snatch up the sack full of lettuce heads that sat on the porch.

Mother disappeared into the kitchen as I took a seat in a chair in the living area I placed by the window so I could watch the rainfall. The all too familiar scent of the rain filled the house as I opened the window to provide a cool breeze to flow through the house. Glenn and Father were nowhere to be seen. Plates and utensils clanged from the kitchen as Mother prepared a meal.

Julia emerged from the bedroom holding one of her dolls and hurried over to me and jumped onto my wet lap. "You'll get your behind wet," I laughed.

"I don't care," Julia giggled with her delicate voice. "I want to sit in your lap." She gazed up at me with her small hazel eyes as I gave her a small kiss on her head. I shook my leg up and down as she hopped up and down on my knee. Her thick black hair sprung from the top of hair into the air. She always loved when I bounced her. She shrieked with enjoyment.

When the bouncing was over due to my leg growing tired, Julia's little eyes gazed up at me once more. Her sweet and innocent smile had faded. She tugged on a loose string on my overalls. "Why are you leaving us, big brother?"

"It's something I have to do."

"But I don't want you to go," she sulked. "Why can't you stay here?"

There wasn't a simple way for me to explain to Julia why I was leaving everyone and the farm behind on account she is just a child. I shook my head at her. "It's just something I have to do," I explained to her once more. With nothing left to say, I became silent.

It was then; a figure appeared from the kitchen doorway. It was Father. His clothes were wet from the rainfall. A towel draped from his neck. He held a watchful eye on me as he sat in his rocking chair by the small table with the radio and a newspaper resting on top.

I gazed out the window once more to observe the rain as a sound of thunder erupted throughout the sky.

"You know, I understand that boys who go into the army are trying to prove themselves they are men but the army doesn't change them into men," Father said as kept his eyes on me. "No. The military doesn't turn boys into men. It turns them into damn fools. I knew a couple of fellas that signed up to fight in the Great War. And do you know what happened to 'em? ... They're dead. Those fools got there damn heads blown off."

"Julia, go into the kitchen with Ma," I said as I lifted her off my lap. Julia didn't hesitate as she rushed past Father into the kitchen.

"And the ones who didn't sign up got drafted," Father continued. "And do you know what happened to them too? They're dead. You don't understand... do ya, boy? The army is no place for you. And it never will be because it's suicide. You'll end up dead, just like all the other boys."

"So where were you?" I blurted out after surrendering my patience.

"What?" Father hissed as his short temper showed signs of flaring: his eyes flamed and his face turned a light shade of red.

"Where were you when they were signing up and being drafted? You must have been of age. So where were you?"

Father's face now beamed red as his eyes filled with anger. I knew I had made a mistake, but my temper was getting the best of me. "What are you tryin' to say, boy? You think your father is a damn coward? Is that what you're implying?"

"All I'm asking is why didn't you sign up when all the other men were going to fight?" I stated once more.

With that last comment of mine, Father stood up at once from his chair. His large and towering stature made me feel small and helpless. It's that imposing fear of him I would never outgrow. Father pointed a big finger at me. "Don't you forget your place, boy." His tone was sincere. "There is no place for you in the army. You belong here on the farm—where I need you. So you will stay here and work, and that will be the end of your nonsense."

I took my eyes off him and gazed out the window. It would be pointless to argue with him. It was a winless battle, and my best choice was to stay quiet.

"Are you listening, boy?!" Father snapped.

The house had fallen silent. I stood up wanting to walk out onto the porch, but before I made it to the front door, a hand clutched my overalls and spun me around. Father now stood within inches of my face. I could feel his warm breath on my cheeks. His eyes shimmered with fire.

"Please let go of me," I said with my eyes on the floor. My appearance was calm. But his grip only seemed to tighten.

"Your nothin' but a damn fool. I thought I raised you better. You disappoint me, boy."

I peered my eyes away from the floor and glanced over Father's shoulder; Mother and Julia were standing at the kitchen door with expressions of dismay on their faces.

"Let go of him, William," Mother trembled.

But Father refused to loosen his sturdy grip. "This *boy* of ours is nothing but a damn fool, Lucille!" His enraged eyes rested on me. His lips pursed and his face grew brick red. "Do you think you're gonna to be Mister Tough Guy? Well, let me *tell* you somethin', boy—if you want to leave so bad—then go. You're *no* longer welcome here in this house. I meant what I said when I told you not to come back the day you came home after signing up."

"It's pointless to argue with you," I said. "I'm a grown man and can make my own decisions, and I don't need you to do it for me. Why can't you understand that? You don't own me. I'm not doing anything you demand from me any longer. I'm not a little boy anymore. You're just too stubborn to see it." I grabbed hold of Father's hand to loosen his grasp, but it proved useless. My body tightened with resentment that fueled the desire to fight back at him. Father said nothing as he stared me down with anger. He paid no attention to Mother and Julia. His eyes focused only on me. "If you want me to go—I'll go," I said. "I'm done with you anyway." I had nothing left to say to him.

I didn't see it coming on account I wasn't expecting it, but the next thing I knew—I was on the floor. Father struck me hard in the face. I realized Father was a strong man, but I never expected him to be that strong. The impact from his big fist sent a sharp pain through my cheekbone that dulled my senses. There were moments after the incident that were hazy. I can remember shouting and crying. The left side of my face throbbed with pain. When my senses came to, all I could see was the wood floor beneath me. I tried to get back to my feet, but my knees buckled as I dropped back on the floor. I had to take it slow. Then Julia's tiny arms flung around my neck as she lied on top of me. She cried and screamed in my ear from the shock of seeing her big brother getting punched hard in the face by her father.

I looked up to see Glenn standing above me pulling Julia away, but she kicked and shouted trying to break free from the hold on her, but Glenn wouldn't let go. Mother took Julia in her arms and rushed her out of the living area and into the bedroom. She came back to the living area a moment later and closed the door behind her and stepped into the kitchen along with Father. An argument broke out between them as Julia's wails can still be heard coming from the bedroom.

"Can you sit up?" Glenn asked, kneeling down.

"I think so," I muttered.

Glenn helped me sit up against the wall just below the window. "Looks like he whopped you really good. I heard shouting when I was standing outside the back door. I came rushing in and found you on the floor. It's hard to believe Father would ever do something like that. That man is always full of surprises."

"To hell with him," I said as I held the left side of my face. The pain grew worse. "I can't wait to leave this place for good, Glenn. I don't think I'll ever come back." The words were bitter, and I believed them. I resented Father for what he did—maybe even hated him.

"You don't mean that."

"The hell I don't!"

Glenn sat down next to me underneath the window and sighed. "You're right—he can't keep you here. Believe it or not but I think I'm starting to understand where it is you're coming from. I've been thinking about ditching myself. I can't join the army because of my leg, but I'll find something. But I hope you know what you're doing by going into the military."

"I don't know *what* I'm doing, but anything is better than this."

"I have to admit though: You've got more guts than I do. Standing up to Pa the way you did. I would never have the balls to do that."

I gave Glenn a smile. When I will be gone, I would miss him. Mother and Julia too.

From the kitchen, I could hear Mother and Father still arguing.

There came the sound of a plate being smashed from time to time—from Father no less. His temper had no bounds. I had a fear of him lashing out violently on Mother, but the two of them only argued.

The sound of Julia's wailing had stopped. Glenn and I stood up from the floor, but I felt dizzy from the blow I received just minutes before. Glenn kept a firm hold on me to make sure I wouldn't fall as he helped me sit back down in the chair I had been sitting in moments before. "I think we should check on Julia," I uttered.

But before Glenn made a step toward the bedroom, there came a sudden knock on the door. He stepped over to the door and opened it. "We're looking for a Mr. Vincent Conroy," a male voice spoke from outside.

"He's inside," Glenn said as he gestured to whoever was at the door to enter the house.

Mother and Father stopped arguing and entered the living area as two men in military dress suits stepped inside. One was carrying an envelope, and the other man sat down a small black trunk. Glenn shot me a look of surprise. "Vince, these two gentlemen are here to see you."

I shot up from the chair as if a firecracker exploded from underneath me. "I'm Vincent Conroy," I stated.

"Mr. Conroy, I'm Sergeant First Class Ben Elliot and here with me is Sergeant Leroy Holbrook, and we're here from the United States Army." Elliot was tall—much taller than Father. He had a noticeable scar running down his right cheek that curved into a hook just as it reached his jaw. Holbrook was much shorter than Elliot and appeared younger, and he had a muscular frame that made his suit seem to be a size too small.

"How do you do?" I said as I shook the men's hands. "So what can I help you with?"

"We're here to inform you," Elliot said, "that tomorrow morning at precisely 1000 hours, you will need to be at the bus station in Natchitoches to travel to Fort McClellan in Alabama for Basic Training."

"Your time has come, son," Holbrook said, handing me the envelope in his hand.

I took the envelope and opened it up. Inside was a letter notifying me the army has called for my services, and I was to be at Fort McClellan by a specific date. With the letter was a bus ticket and currency—fifteen dollars. "1000 hours?" I said.

"That's ten o'clock in military hours," Holbrook stated. "Military hours will be something you understand in Basic Training."

"The currency is for your meals on the way to Fort McClellan and if you need to purchase any personal items," Elliot said. "We also brought a trunk for you to bring the necessary items. What you will be required to take is in that letter."

Everyone stood by in silence as the two men, and I spoke. "Is this your family?" Elliot asked.

"Yes, sir," I said.

"Well, you have a fine-looking family. And she's just darling," he said with a smile, peering at Julia who had just came from the bedroom. Julia looked up at the tall man, appearing bashful. Her eyes shown evidence of crying.

"Thank you," Mother said. "She's my little angel."

"Are you all right, son?" Holbrook asked, staring at my face. "Looks like you just got clobbered."

"It's nothing," I replied looking at Father. "Just a little accident I had." The pain was pulsing, and I was eager to see myself in the mirror to know how rough my face looked.

"You might want to put a slab of cold meat on that," Elliot said.

"Sure thing, sir."

"Would you gentleman like something to drink?" Mother asked. "Perhaps some coffee or tea?"

"Thank you kindly, ma'am," Elliot replied. "But we must get moving. We have other enlistees to see."

Elliot turned his direction towards me again. "Remember, 1000 hours tomorrow. Don't be late," he said with a stern voice.

"Yes, sir," I said. "I'll be there."

Elliot and Holbrook said their goodbyes as I followed them outside onto the porch. The rain eased as it now only drizzled. The men and I exchanged waves as they got into their automobile—a black Ford De Luxe and drove onto the now muddy road heading back into town.

———

I WOKE EARLY THE NEXT DAY to assure myself that I would not be late for the bus. I looked myself in a mirror to get a look at my face; it was blackened and swollen as if Father's blow implanted a wound deep in the skin. I went into the kitchen and held a bottle of cold milk to my face to help with the swelling. It took several tries to keep the glass on my face because of the pain. But at last, I could hold the bottle to my skin without cringing.

Afterwards, I studied the list of everything they allowed me to take with me to Basic Training: personal hygiene kit, briefs, socks, eyeglasses if required, and stationary material. Anything I did not have I would purchase at the general store once I arrive in town. I would also need ointment for the bruise on my face.

After a silent breakfast with the family, I stood outside the house with my small black trunk filled with what items I needed. Glenn sat in our brown rusted '33 pickup that didn't have much life left. Father had been too stubborn to purchase a new automobile throughout the years, but in his defense, the Depression was part of the blame.

"Ready when you are," Glenn said peering out the driver side window.

Mother and Julia had came outside to send me off. They were both in tears. "I guess this is it," I said to Mother. "You know... Pa said I was a disappointment."

Mother put her hands on my chest. "You listen to me... you are *not* a disappointment. Do you hear me? He is in the wrong for saying that. If anything, I am proud of you. Although I don't approve of you leavin' at the moment—I respect your decision because the decision is yours to make. It's not mine, and it's not your father's. It's *yours*. And you can come back whenever you wish. If things don't work out for you—please come home. You'll *always* have a home here."

I nodded my head.

Mother gave me a huge hug, and I thought she would never let go. When she released me from her long hold, I crouched down to pick Julia up as she folded her arms around me. I wiped her tears away and kissed her cheek. "I don't want you to leave," she whispered fighting back the tears.

"I know you don't. But I'll be back to see you. I'll bring back something for you from my travels, ok?"

She looked at me with her teary hazel eyes and innocent pouty face. "Promise you'll be back."

"I promise," I said as she hugged my neck.

"We best be off," Glenn stated. "Don't want to be late."

I set Julia down on her feet and threw the black trunk in the back of the pickup and hopped into the passenger side. I glanced back and spotted Father standing in the doorway of the house. He didn't come outside to send me off but just stood at the doorway watching my departure. I gave Mother and Julia a wave of goodbye as Glenn ignited the truck's engine and shifted the gears. He steered the vehicle past the gate and onto the dirt road leading into town. I swung my head around to peer out the rear window once more at Mother and Julia and waved goodbye once more as the farm became distant with each second. And at last, the farm was left behind in the dust.

And I was gone.

———

IT WAS NOW PAST NINE-THIRTY, and Gilliam had disappeared to the restroom to relieve himself. My throat was dry from speaking, so I took a drink of water from a water cooler in the examining room and returned to the study. Once I sat back down, I placed the small lockbox I had brought along on my lap and opened it. It had been many years since I had opened it; I filled its contents with memories I found difficult to turn back to, but now was a good time as any to at last open the box and go back to those difficult years and those painful memories that have plagued me; the contents: a German Luger, old letters I had received from Mother and Glenn when I was away from the farm, and many photographs of people I know or once knew, and places that are best left forgotten. After shuffling through the pictures, I came across one particular photo of me in my uniform with my 30 caliber M1 Grand rifle held to my chest with both hands, standing next to several men. My helmet unfastened and cocked a little to the side of my head, and my face wore an expression that no words could describe. Perhaps a look of astonishment and determination—perhaps bewilderment. I flipped the picture over to view the location and date: Normandy, France · June 6th, 1944. I flipped the picture over once more and stared at myself as a young man—the man I was—the man I wish never to be again.

I put the photograph back and shuffled more through the contents— and found what I was searching for—a locket. I held the locket in my hand as I observed it. It was small and square shaped, perhaps made from pewter and fastened with a thin chain and an intricate design of a tree is engraved on the front. A wave of emotion ran through me as I stared at this piece of jewelry. My hand trembled as the locket fell back into the lockbox. Not wanting to have another event like the one from the night before, I gathered all my concentration to keep my composure calm.

Gilliam stepped back into the study as I took out a few letters and shut the lockbox and placed it on the floor beside the chair where I had placed it before. Gilliam sat down and studied me as if he felt something was out of the ordinary. "Are you all right, Mr. Conroy?"

"I'm fine," I replied.

Gilliam took notice of the letters on my lap. "Well... what do you have there?"

"Just a few letters that were written to me is all. But we'll get to them later." I cleared my throat to signify a discussion of another matter. "So you see Doctor, my father was atrocious. He didn't care that I preferred to live my own life. He didn't care I wanted to leave the farm. All he wanted was to keep me there and work me to no end. His attitude toward me influenced me. The day he struck me in the face and expressed I was a disappointment was the day I had lost all respect for him. How could I respect him? Now maybe I didn't handle things as I should have, but there was still no excuse for what he did. I hope you can understand that. But I learned something throughout the years after I left the farm: the way my father treated me, believe it or not, would shape me into the man I would become—but not in a good way. There was hatred for him that evolved. A man shouldn't despise one's father, but there was hatred for him. So his attitude he reflected upon me would impact my life. A severe impact."

Gilliam seemed to be hidden in thought, and I doubted if he heard anything I said until he spoke up. "Was your father a drinker?"

"No," I replied. "In fact, I don't think I'd ever seen him drink at all."

He was silent once more for a few seconds as he adjusted the glasses on his face and then he spoke again. "It seems your father was arrogant—that's obvious, of course. I believe he wanted to control every aspect of your life because it made him feel compelling—even when you became a grown man and wanted to live your own life. When you were trying to leave the farm, he felt that you were challenging his authority. It would make him appear vulnerable. A man with his kind of persona wouldn't accept that by any means. He saw you as a threat."

"I wanted nothing more to do with him after I had left," I said. "I told myself that over and over how I never wanted to see him again. For the longest time, I actually believed it—but I'm not so certain now. The thing is: I have to make amends with him. Perhaps it's for the best to put all those awful things behind us."

"I see," Gilliam remarked. "But we can discuss more of that later. I'm keen to hear about what happened after you left the farm. Please, don't keep me in suspense now."

I leaned back in my chair again, took a small sip of bourbon, and took a heavy breath.

FIVE

"GOOD LUCK TO YA AND BE CAREFUL," Glenn said before I stepped onto the sweltering bus that would take me away from Natchitoches and onward to Alabama.

The army recruiters filled the bus with many young and eager boys prepared to take the journey to Basic Training to become men. They were eighteen or nineteen-year-olds, just out of high school and a few of them may have lied about their age because they looked no older than sixteen; they were kids who dropped out of school, and with nowhere to go and unable to find decent work, their only option was to join the military. I was perhaps the oldest recruit on the bus. It shouldn't have troubled me, but it did. I felt out-of-place being the oldest. I suppose this was the reason I kept to myself as the other recruits chatted along with one another. A few of them I recognized from high school; they were a few grades below me when I graduated. I hoped they hadn't recognize me for I was in no mood to socialize. Luckily, the other boys let me be so I could enjoy the bus ride out of Louisiana, through Mississippi and into Alabama.

The trip overwhelmed me with anticipation as the bus reached closer and closer to its destination. The ride was long—for there were several stops along the way at small diners to allow everyone on board to grab a bite to eat and to relieve themselves. The diners were rundown establishments that served mediocre meals and burnt coffee to the locals that had nowhere better to eat. Only the soda pop was fresh but never cold. I never tried the milk. These diners are not like those of Natchitoches. Far from it. The atmosphere of these places seemed foreign. My home was not far away, but yet a new environment is a big change no matter how close home is. And it was about halfway through the trip, several miles past Jackson, Mississippi that I had realized just how far the ride had taken us. Yes, I was excited to be on this journey, but I was also frightened.

"Be careful." Glenn's words stuck like glue.

Mother told me those exact words before I broke my arm. I don't think I ever cried so hard in my life. But it was just a simple fracture—nothing to get to riled up about. But believe me, it felt much worse. Breaking a bone is painful.

Father had taken Glenn and I fishing with him one evening when I was just eleven years old. He led us to a pond several miles from the farm. The pond itself could be difficult to find if you didn't know where to look. It's located a couple hundred yards off the dirt road leading away from Natchitoches and our farm, concealed behind thick shrubbery and oak and hickory trees. A person could well get lost if not careful. I never dared to venture into those parts of the woods if I did not know where I was going. Along the way towards the pond, the woods grow denser about one-hundred yards before reaching the pond. The pond itself is large, perhaps larger than most ponds, but not large enough to be a lake. Dragonflies hovered above the stagnant surface of the water covered with lily pads, and an infinite sound of croaking frogs traveled all around. The three of us would spend countless hours at that pond fishing the day away if Father saw fit to take a break from farm work. Mother would always wait for our return to see what we had caught so she may fillet and cook our catch of brim and catfish.

On one particular fishing trip, I hooked a large fish as I rested on the bank with my cane fishing pole and after several minutes of tug and war, I swung a massive catfish onto the bank. I had never caught a fish so large. Bigger than what I was used to catching. Its smooth large gray body flopped up and down on the ground as its mouth adorned with long black whiskers open and closed for air. I ballooned up with pride with my catch. The gratification of hooking such a large fish was nothing more but bragging rights. Glenn and I were always in competition with one another: who could run the fastest, eat the most, climb the furthest up a tree, and catch the most or biggest fish. Now I had hooked the biggest fish—and the bragging rights.

"How big do you think it is, Pa?" Glenn asked as Father worked on taking the hook out of the fish's mouth.

"I'd say it's at least six pounds," Father said. "Damn good fish you caught there, Vince."

After Father took out the hook, he asked me to rope the fish through the mouth so I could easily carry it back home. The smaller catfish and brim we hooked in the earlier hours were strung through gills and the bottom of their mouths as they lingered in the water off the bank to keep fresh. We now had plenty enough for a good meal.

The daylight was waning, and Father declared that it was now time to go back to the farm. I clutched the huge catfish by the mouth with my fingertips and as I reached to untie the rope strung with fish from a small tree stump, I stumbled over a thick root barely exposed from the ground and fell on my right arm on the bank. The sound of Glenn's laughing erupted after I had fallen. I felt a crack in my arm; a sharp pain caused an immediate anguish of tears. The large catfish broke free from my grip and flopped into the murky pond water, swimming away. I had lost my prized fish and along with it, the bragging rights. But losing my prized fish was not my biggest concern, however. This was the first time I had broken a bone; it's an experience that can't be forgotten.

Father flew to my side and rolled me over. He held my fragile arm in his hands and looked it over as I howled as an endless stream of tears poured down my face. "I think it's broken," Father said. Glenn's laughing stopped. Father then scooped me up into his powerful arms. I could feel his strength as he held me. It was as though I was light as a feather. "Glenn—grab the fishing poles and the rope. We need to get Vince to a doctor."

Father carried me all the way back to the farm. The pain in my arm surged, and it felt as if it would snap off at any moment. With each passing minute, the pain grew worse and worse. I did my best to keep myself from wailing in Father's ear and eventually I had composed my emotions about halfway back to the farm.

As Father lifted me back to the farm; no words of sympathy, remorse, or sorrow were uttered. There was only silence. Glenn appeared as though he would have a heart attack. He insisted on pestering Father with questions about my well-being, but Father ignored him. It was useless for Glenn to continue with his nagging questions. Father concentrated on getting me to a doctor as soon as possible as he hastened his walk—ignoring the lookout for snakes on our feeble manmade path through the woods.

It seemed like a lifetime before we returned home. Father carried me inside, and Mother jumped from her chair and bolted to Father's side to look me over. With her face brimmed with worry, she pleaded for someone to explain to her what had taken place. Father told her everything himself. I was too busy fighting back the tears to speak, and Glenn had disappeared as soon as we arrived at the house; perhaps he had enough of my wailing.

"I'll get the pickup ready," Father said. He laid me down on my bed and rushed into the living area as Mother drew up a chair by my bed and rested her soft hand on my forehead and viewed me with her warm eyes. Her touch soothed me. There is something compelling about a mother's touch. It permits the undefined power to create comfort on a whim.

"You'll be ok, Vince," Mother assured me. "We just need to get you to a doctor." I fixated on her sweet voice as she rubbed my forehead with her thumb. I had to be strong; strong for her. My tears and blubbering had at last ended although the pain in my arm was intense but I struggled through the pain. At this moment, I felt closer to her; closer than ever before. She was there for me. She was there to take care of her little boy.

Father had been the true hero of the day but I avoided that fact—or perhaps I didn't choose to accept it. The only person I needed by my side was Mother. She would take care of me.

I remained in the hospital that night to have my arm put in a cast. Mother never left my side. She fell asleep in an uncomfortable looking chair next to my hospital bed as Father and Glenn returned to the farm, but Mother never left me. And after that evening, she would present my affection in a more genuine and loving way than ever before. A heartfelt attachment developed between the two of us; an attachment that can never be broken.

"Be careful."

———

IT WAS LATE EVENING when the bus arrived at Fort McClellan. The sun hung low in the sky for its final hours of the day. The ride made me weary, and I wanted to be the first man off. And I was. I stretched my limbs as everyone aborted as the driver worked at getting the trunks off from underneath the bus. I nudged my way past the other recruits to find my luggage, and once I did, several men in military uniforms directed me to the National Guard Training Center building along with the other passengers.

Fort McClellan is located near Aniston, Alabama and is surrounded by the Choccolocco foothills of the Appalachian Mountains. The fort had been going through many developments. It amazed me to see a bakery, an auditorium, and a chapel. There was street lighting for paved roads, a firehouse, and to my most astonishment—an actual golf course. All of this I observed on my walk, dragging behind me my black trunk containing all of my belongings. It appeared as if the fort is now becoming a prominent army headquarters and training center as I observed, but much of the fort, however, was still under construction. Workers pounded nails with hammers, sawed lumber, dug into the ground with shovels, setting foundations for barracks for the many recruits that were arriving by the busloads.

It wasn't long before we all arrived at the enormous National Guard Training Center building. Standing outside the big front double door were two MP's. We all showed them our documents, and then we were all ordered to go inside. We stepped into a large area and then we were ordered to give our paperwork to a man in uniform sitting behind a table. He would look through it, checking for correctness, and if no problems were found, the paperwork was stamped and then placed in a tray on the table, and then we were directed to sit in chairs arrayed side by side in rows in the middle of the huge room. There were no orders for seating arrangements as I watched men taking seats where they so pleased, so I sat in an empty chair in the furthest back corner away from anybody else, not wanting to socialize.

The room gradually filled with recruits and after an hour, they had taken almost all the seats up. Voices rang out among everyone. With their patience running thin and empty stomachs grumbling with hunger, the angry talks echoed throughout the area and were close to deafening. I stood up to stretch, restless and wishing something would happen soon. I took my seat again and rubbed my eyes.

Boredom settled in. I nudged the person sitting on my left for some small talk. "About how much longer do you expect this is going to take?" I asked, unsure if he heard me speak over everyone else.

"Not a clue," he replied in a deep and grating voice. "I hope they get this show started or I'll start to rot."

"Yeah, you got that right," I said. I offered my hand and introduced myself. "I'm Vincent, but you can call me Vince."

"Roland Archer," he said as he shook mine with a massive palm and a sturdy handshake. He had piercing dark brown eyes with untamed, sandy brown hair and herculean body. He appeared as if he could wrestle a bear and win the fight.

"Where are you from?" I asked with curiosity. From the sound of his accent, he could not have been from the south—perhaps up north.

"Wisconsin," he replied. "I'm from this little town along Lake Michigan." (I can't recall the name of the town.) "It's just north of Milwaukee. It was time for me to get away from Wisconsin, so I joined the army."

"Wisconsin, huh? Never been there."

"Trust me, it's nothing too spectacular. I can tell you that much. The winters are long and cold, and there's just no damn sun. That's why I escaped from that hell hole. A man can spend his entire life living there and never get use to the winters. You see, I'm better off somewhere else—somewhere where I can stretch my legs. I've got ambition, but that ambition can't be used in Wisconsin. No, sir. I got out while the going was good."

There was boldness in the manner he spoke as I listened. He talked in a cocky tone of voice, but his face never changed expression once for he only had one: deadpan. I would go far as to say he was expressionless. His presence made me uneasy. Perhaps it was intimidation. Just the sheer size of him could intimidate any man. But Roland unawares took it a step further with his blank tone. There appeared to be no light behind those eyes—only desolation.

Before I could tell Roland my story, a voice roared and echoed throughout the room. "Everybody be quiet now!" A man in plain military uniform walked in front of all of us while we sat. His hair was jet black, and he possessed a vicious and sharp face that seemed to loom over his thin body frame. My eyes deadlocked with his as he shouted again. "On your feet!" Everyone stood in one swift action. "I am Drill Sergeant Paul Ramsey! You all have signed up to be part of the United States Army. The best army there is! For the next eight weeks, you all will learn how to be soldiers for the Army National Guard. You will learn how to stand in formation! You will learn how to salute an officer! You will march, jog, and run for many, many miles! You will learn how to load and unload and fire a rifle! You will learn the same with a pistol! You will learn hand-to-hand combat! You will learn fighting drills! You will learn all there is to know about being a soldier!" He was silent for a few seconds while pacing back and forth in front of us as if surveying everyone before speaking again. "Oh yes, you *will* be fine soldiers indeed. But as of now, I don't see fine soldiers. All I see is a crowd of fucking shit shoveling hicks and ratbag Yankees!"

He at last halted in the middle of everyone and faced us. "The first business I want you all to learn is this: whenever I speak—whenever I ask you a question—you will answer me with 'Yes, Drill Sergeant!' Is that understood?!"

"Yes, Drill Sergeant!" We all called out in unison.

Ramsey's face beamed red and he roared out. "What the *fuck* was that?! You all answer back at me like grown men and not some sissy school girls! So let's try it again shall we?! Whenever I speak—whenever I ask you a question—You will answer me with 'Yes, Drill Sergeant!' Now *is* that understood?!"

"Yes, Drill Sergeant!" we all shouted in unison and this time much louder.

"That's what I like to hear! Eight weeks, ladies! For eight long, grueling weeks—your asses belong to me or one of our other fine and handsome drill sergeants. We will push you. We will push you hard. And if I catch any of you slacking off—I will subject you to ridicule in front of the entire platoon, because I tolerate no slackers."

I hoped to not get stuck with Ramsey.

Ramsey then instructed everyone to follow him into a corridor in a single line while carrying our small trunks and we were lead to another big room for haircuts. All my thick curly hair was gone in less than a minute. Although not buzzed but thinned out to give the recruits a sophisticated look. Afterwards, we were all stripped naked of our civilian clothes and fitted into our uniforms which are beige long-sleeved shirts and trousers with leggings for covering our boots, along with new pairs of underwear and socks. Any personal items we had that were not permitted were to be packaged and sent back home; this included our wallets and civilian clothes.

After being fitted for our uniforms, Ramsey led the recruits outside and ordered us all to stand side by side in six rows, and each row comprised of twenty men. When everybody was in place, Ramsey stood in front of the rows and looked us all over for a minute while holding a pile of forms.

"Well, all of you shit-for-brains clean up fast! I like that!" He paced in front of the rows of men. "From this moment on—you are all Privates for the Army National Guard! I will now place you in your troop. Each troop will contain twenty men. Each man in your troop will be your brother for now on. After Basic Training, your troop will be placed in a regiment. It is your obligation for every one of you to watch after your brother in your troop. And your only daddy will be me or one of the other sergeants. Now when I call your name—you will come forward at once and stand behind me in a single file line. Is that understood?!"

"Yes, Drill Sergeant!" everyone shouted.

Ramsey began to call out names as I shook in fear of being placed under his training. Without a doubt, the other sergeants couldn't be as absurd as Ramsey. I mumbled to myself as he continued to go through the names. "Please, not me. Please, not me." It's foolish to behave in that sort of manner—I know, but fear can make a man act in strange ways.

After he had called out fifteen names, not one being mine, I felt content. "Maybe he won't call me," I thought. "I'll get another sergeant."

"Roland Archer!" Ramsey shouted. Roland's towering body slowly jogged to the rear of the line now standing behind Ramsey. "Pick up the pace!" Ramsey barked. A few more names were called out, and now there was only one last name left to announce. I was confident it wouldn't be my name. I felt the tension in my body ease but then. . . "Vincent Conroy!" The surprise made my heart sank. I had no choice but to get into line. In a lazy jog, I moved with my trunk towards Ramsey. "Move it, Private!" he commanded as I picked up the pace and vaulted to the back of the line.

Ramsey then marched to the back of me. "Everyone turn around and face me!" he shouted. We all turned at him in a hasty motion. We were already being trained, which we now act on instinct, much like trained dogs. It amazed me at how soon Ramsey had us taught in such a brief amount of time. "Now you all will follow me to your barrack in a single file line! Is that understood?!"

"Yes, Drill Sergeant!" we shouted.

"Good. Now keep up!" he barked.

We all moved in haste behind Ramsey as he lead the way to our barrack. I now got a further view of the fort and noticed that vast amounts of pine trees surrounded it. Several watchtowers stood alongside the edge of the trees, and each one contained a soldier or two who were observing the activities of the day or looking out among the woods as if to keep a cautious eye of any unusual activity outside the fort. I couldn't imagine why anyone would dare to attack this fort. Men marched and exercised as we passed. I watched as other sergeants shouted in recruit's faces. This forced me to realize that if I were to avoid any unnecessary confrontations with Ramsey—I would have to pay attention to fine detail to what he says, do what he says, and not stand out from the other men in any means. I made my first mistake by not moving quickly enough after Ramsey called my name to get in line. I couldn't allow myself to make another mistake. The way I saw it, one mistake is one too many.

We paced for over three hundred yards when we reached a broad green tent. The tent had a ridge height of about twelve feet and a wall height of about six feet. It stretched out for well over nine hundred square feet. A tall pole stood right in the front of the flap with an electrical wire that ran inside. Ramsey had ordered us to a halt right outside as he stood in the face of us by the tent's open flap. "Listen up!" he shouted. "This barrack, ladies—will be your home for the next eight weeks. I want the first man in line to take the last bed on his left, and the next man will take the last bed on his right. The next man will take the last bed on his left and so on and so on. Once you have found your bed, I then want you to place your trunk at the foot of your bed and stand upright by the right side of your trunk. Is that understood?!"

"Yes, Drill Sergeant!" we shouted.

"Good. Now get moving!"

Since I was the first man in line, at once, I moved inside the barrack and went to the last bed on the left. I placed my trunk at the end of the bed and stood beside it on the right just like Ramsey had ordered. I ob- served the other men do the same as I did. Ramsey watched during the entire time, shouting at the men to move faster when they were too slow. I took a moment to look around; long wooden boards covered the barracks floor along with the interior walls. Along the walls were twenty beds—ten beds on each side. At the back of the tent was another flap for entering and exiting. The ceiling contained a tall pole that stretched all the way through the tent and hanging from the pole were several large light bulbs. This was to be my home for eight weeks, and from one look of it, I hated it. The smell of fresh tarp and wood made me nauseous. The atmosphere was dull. But I guess army barracks doesn't need to be enticing. And I was to be here for eight weeks, so I had no choice but to suck it up. The entire barrack reminded me of small tents Glenn, and I used to sleep in when we camped out in the field back at the farm. Sleeping in a tent overnight was one thing but spending eight weeks in one is another. This had not been what I expected so far.

Once everyone stood in place on the right side of their bed, Ramsey paced through the barrack—inspecting. "Everyone is in place," he said. "Good. Maybe you all are not a bunch dumb shits after all. Now let's go to work!"

—

TRAINING BEGAN RIGHT AWAY. We first learned how to make our beds. It was the first day, and men were already getting screamed at. Ramsey had proven himself to be impatient and short-tempered. One slip up and he was in someone's face. He would inspect each bed, and if there were anything to be found not to his liking, there would be hell to pay. I know people can take their jobs seriously, but Ramsey was excessive. But I had been in luck. He examined my bed making and he then moved on. I didn't slip up. So far so good.

Once our bed making lesson was over, we all returned to the National Guard Training Center for an hour of lecture and training films to watch, and at last, to the mess hall for supper. Army food is nothing spectacular. My first supper (which Ramsey called chow) comprised of bully beef, canned peas, bland mashed potatoes, and a cup of water. Already I missed Mother's cooking. Right away, I knew army food was something to get used to. During lectures, we were all promised three meals a day. It implied the army had intentions of keeping its recruits healthy. And having three meals a day was the right way to go about it.

In the mess hall, I was eating supper across from Roland, who stuffed food in his mouth as if Ramsey would take it away from him at any moment. I wouldn't be shocked if that did happen. One thing I learned earlier is never let your guard down. The assumption that Ramsey would barge through the door and order everyone out during the middle of their meal harassed me. "So where did you say you from again, Vince?" Roland asked after taking a drink of water from his cup.

I never told him where I was from, but I humored him. "Louisiana," I replied after swallowing some mashed potatoes.

"Oh, that's right," he said. "You're an old southern boy!"

"That's right. Born and raised."

"Never been to Louisiana. Although, I hear the food is to die for."

"Depends on where you go I guess."

"Well, I can tell you one thing—it's got to be much better than this crud I'm eating now."

"It's not so awful." I didn't know why I said that. The food was bland.

"I'm from Wisconsin, see. My diet back home mostly composed of cheese, sausage, and beer. If they allowed us to have all of that in training, I'd be the happiest man in this camp. Hell, I'd take all three instead of a night with a lovely woman if given a chance."

Some men and myself included chuckled.

"You should never pass up a night with a beautiful woman," a man sitting next to me said. He had a medium build with wavy brown hair and bright hazel eyes.

"You got that right, Karl," a man with an athletic frame and dingy red hair and pale skin said sitting next to him. "I wish I had a proper woman right about now."

"Well you better get use to not having a woman for a while, Andrew," Karl said. "We're all stuck here for eight weeks."

Andrew shook his head. "Eight *fucking* long weeks. That's a *long* time without a woman and a beer."

"I've never actually had a beer," I said while stuffing my mouth with more mashed potatoes. My statement was true. I wasn't certain how my confession would make me look for I wished I had taken it back. Perhaps I made myself appear inadequate; not a positive first impression with someone I had just met.

"Never?" Roland asked.

I shook my head and continued to eat.

"Well that's a damn shame," he said. "Tell you what, Vince. First chance we get—you and I will have some fun. You will get your first beer and become a real man."

"Much obliged," I said as I smiled at Roland.

"I have to warn you though—" Roland said, "never try to out-drink me. That's a mistake you would regret—because you won't make it out alive." He let out an unpleasant laugh that made almost everyone sitting at the table stop eating and divert their awareness to his behavior. Roland appeared to be unaware of everyone looking. There was no mistake he needed to be the center of attention. I chewed my bottom lip as Roland continued to his obnoxious laughing.

"Jesus," I heard Andrew whisper. "Can't this guy shut up already?"

"He'll run out of steam soon enough," Karl said. "Or at least I hope."

Roland, at last, stopped laughing and allowed everyone to continue their meal. Small talk would break out between me and the other men, particularly Karl and Andrew during the remainder of their time. Roland would interrupt on occasions to get his few words in, but no one seemed to pay much attention to what he had to say. But it wasn't long before Ramsey pushed through the doors and declared that supper was now over.

———

AFTER SUPPER, WE WERE ALL SENT BACK TO THE BARRACK where we all gathered down in the middle of the boarded floor around Ramsey like school children sitting around the teacher as she read a story to us, however, Ramsey stood and explained military time. We had gone over it for about an hour and afterward, Ramsey called out a few names to translate regular time to military time. A test. I got the hang of it as Ramsey continued to explain the conversion from the civilian twelve-hour clock to the military twenty-four-hour clock. Everyone who had their name called out answered correctly. It was a relief on account I couldn't bear to listen to any more of Ramsey's shouting. He then went into an unnecessary lecture why this system is used, but I didn't pay too much attention to his ramblings.

When we had concluded, Ramsey then ordered us to hit the showers. The back flap of the tent leads us to outdoor showers. Each shower stall had a door that can be latched, and only cold water was available which was fine with me because the temperatures here in Alabama were hot— much like Louisiana. After we finished our showers and returned to the barrack, Ramsey informed us we had one hour of personal time before lights out.

As I sat on my bed, I ran my fingers through my short hair. It didn't take long for conversations among the recruits to fill the barrack, but I was too weary to join in. I was weary from the grueling bus ride, the orientation of Basic Training, a full stomach, and Ramsey's constant shouting.

I cringed for I knew the days to come would be difficult. Ramsey would not allow these eight weeks to be a cake walk. He had a job to execute, and the recruits under his belt would feel the wrath. He is to turn these inexperienced boys into men. There has to be a respect for Ramsey and his position, but I will come to despise him.

I knew what I was getting myself into when I signed the contract and yet somehow, I was unprepared. The illusion of glory of leaving behind the tedious farm life vanished before me. I realized there was no backing out now. This is what I wanted. I doubted myself. And my decision of coming here. Did I make the right choice? I can only hope so.

Eight weeks.

SIX

WAKE-UP TIME WAS STRICTLY 0500 EVERY MORNING. I concluded that wake-up time to be not all that challenging. I had grown acquainted to starting my day at dawn for I worked on a farm. Beds were to be made as neat as possible as Ramsey instructed us to do and after beds were made, we were provided time in the latrine before dressing into our physical training clothes: cotton t-shirt, shorts, and leather athletic shoes. The shoes I discovered to but uncomfortable. They hurt my feet.

For other recruits, however, had trouble adapting with the morning procedures. On the first morning after wake-up, I discovered the recruit next to me hiding under his bed sleeping. Not wanting the poor guy to get in trouble with Ramsey, I kicked at his feet to wake him, but he refused to wake up. Ramsey spotted this and trudged over to the recruit's bed with barred teeth, clutched the recruit's arm and with no difficulty, yanked him out from underneath the bed, holstered the young boy from his shoulders, and flung him against the wall. This was the first time witnessing Ramsey's strength, and there was no doubt he needed all the recruits to see what he was capable of.

"Remind me—what's your name again, Private?!" Ramsey barked

with his hands cuffed onto the recruits undershirt.

"Lester Spears, Drill Sergeant!" he replied with a look of fright on his face. Lester had blonde curly hair with squinty blue eyes. He stood thin among the other recruits and certainly among Ramsey.

"Private Lester Spears! Why are you sleeping during wake-up?!"

"No excuse, Drill Sergeant!"

Ramsey pulled Lester from the wall and slammed him again and again back into the wall for several seconds before stopping. Now all the recruits ceased what they were doing and viewed the scene taking place before them.

"Let me explain something to you, Private—you don't fucking sleep during wake-up. What's *wrong* you with you, Private?!"

"It was a mistake, Drill Sergeant."

"A mistake?! You should ask your mother and father about mistakes because from what I can see, they made a mistake by having you!"

"Yes, Drill Sergeant."

"Next time I catch you sleeping—I will personally drive my foot so far up your ass, you won't be able to breathe, and I'm gonna keep it there until you die! Is that understood, Private Spears?!"

"Yes, Drill Sergeant!"

Ramsey released his grip from Lester's undershirt, and his manner changed from diabolical to calm. "Good. Now do your morning routine, Private."

Without hesitation, Lester jumped to making his bed. Ramsey paced up and down the barrack—watching. At times, shouting at a few recruits to pick up the pace; Roland being one. Yet, he went about at his slow pace despite the warnings from Ramsey.

After everyone completed wake-up duties, Ramsey inspected each recruit's bed for neatness, and if a problem were to be found, he would toss the bed and force the recruit to make it again as he roared obscenities and insults. The men trembled to Ramsey as Lester did.

The first morning was the most difficult for the recruits. Young men needed to adapt to the routine. And our instructor's force of nature was challenging to withstand. For boys who join the army realize it's the first morning when reality hits. They are far away from home; away from their mothers, fathers, brothers, and sisters. All they have is the men in their troop. And Ramsey ensured playtime is over.

Once Ramsey was satisfied with inspections, he stood in front of the tent flap and shouted. "Outside! We are all about to have some fun!"

———

THE COLD MORNING AIR turned my breath into a faint mist as I stood shivering with the other men. Early dawns in April in the south has always been nippy. But the days grow hotter with the passing hours. Ramsey paced back and forth, observing every one of us. We had just been trained in how to stand in proper formation: five columns comprised of four men standing within four feet from one another side by side. Ramsey had pointed out to us that standing in formation will become a necessary formality during Basic Training. Once he was pleased, he halted in front while facing everyone and spoke. "From now on—you do what I say and when I say it without hesitation. It's my civic duty to change all of you dumb-shits into soldiers. I promise I will work you and work you hard. I will test you; test your physical and mental capabilities. Now you all may hate—perhaps despise me. But let me say this—I could not care less. Hate me all you want. You may hate me, but you *will* respect me. Because if you respect me, then I will respect you. I'm here to turn all of you into soldiers. And if any of you don't think it has what it takes to pass my training—then carry your sorry asses out of here. Because there is one thing I don't abide—and that is a worthless crybaby. You are here to develop into men. To become soldiers. And I will make soldiers out of all you who stick with me to the end... Now, let's go for a run."

———

MY KNEES ACHED and my legs felt like rubber. Cold sweat beaded down my forehead and the sweat from my body soaked my PT gear from underneath. The air turned warmer, but I wished it would remain cooler. I had been running for only five miles, and there was one more mile to go, but I worried I wouldn't make it. At any moment, I felt if I will drop to the dirt and pebbles beneath me. It wasn't long before I pulled behind the other men. I wasn't left out, however, for Roland was trailing behind the group as well. He appeared sick as if he would vomit at any moment. And as the run continued, more men were dropping behind. Before long, there was a group of eight of us pacing at a slower speed now—needing to preserve what little energy we all had left to make it to the end of the grueling run.

The trail we ran on is buried in the woods just outside Fort McClellan. There is nothing to look at but pine, hickory, and oak trees along with shrubs and fallen leaves and the faint sunlight that peeped through the branches from over our heads. From what I could understand, the trail was used often for exercises from other recruits throughout the years. At certain locations, other paths would branch off the main one, leading deeper into the woods.

The group of men running ahead of us must have been in better shape than the eight of us trailing behind. The distance between the two groups became further apart with each minute. Ramsey peered from behind him and noticed the stragglers. He said nothing, however, and carried his pace with the runners in front. After jogging for a few more miles around bends, the end of the trail was in view, and there stood Ramsey along with the other recruits that kept up with him. I continued my pace slow and steady when I, at last, reached the end of the run with everyone else. I stopped and crouched over to allow as many deep breaths as I could. At any moment, I thought I would vomit. Good thing I didn't have breakfast yet. Body aches soon made their presence known. My legs and arms were stiff as it became painful for me to move a muscle.

"So nice to have the rest of you men join us," Ramsey said. "Stand in formation!"

Without hesitation, everyman jumped or limped into position.

"Now you men may not know it," Ramsey said, "but the reason for these long runs is that I need to get each one of you into the condition I need you to be in for what is coming for the eight weeks of Basic Training. All of you need to be in top physical shape if you wish to be in the United States Army. There are no shortcuts. There is no leniency of any kind through physical training. So be prepared to run... a lot. Be ready for many hours of other calisthenics." Ramsey paused and paced along the front line of recruits. "Now I know that some of you didn't finish with everyone else. Don't worry about that right now. What's important is that you finished. But by the end of these eight weeks, I expect all of you to finish together." He took another pause and stopped in front of the center line. "Now let's get some morning chow."

———

WITH MY MEAL TRAY IN HAND, I drew a seat at the table occupied with the other recruits as they dug into their breakfast. My body ached, and I didn't expect I could make it the entire day without passing out from pain and exhaustion. I looked down at my breakfast, and it did not look appetizing, much like the meal the previous day. I had a cup of black coffee and two pieces of toast smothered with cream meat of some kind. Some other men at the table revealed the army calls the meal Shit on a Shingle. I can see the reason. With resentment, I poked my fork into the cream meat covered toast and took a bite. After the first swallow, I decided that I had worse meals but getting to eat this every morning would make me sick.

It wasn't long before Roland joined me at the table, banging his tray down and taking a heavy seat on the chair in front of me. "Goddamn run. It nearly killed me." Roland took off a huge chunk of toast from his fork and shoved in his mouth. "But at least we get some food. This stuff is not half bad."

"You like this stuff?" I asked.

"I'd eat just about anything," he replied. "Especially if it's free. And it's better than our meal we ate yesterday."

After taking a sip of coffee, I picked at my toast with my fork. I struggled to eat more as my weak stomach resisted.

"Are you hungry?" Roland asked.

I shrugged. "I don't know. Maybe not."

Without asking, Roland reached across the table and took my tray and dumped my food onto his. "I'm starving. Just two pieces of toasts aren't gonna do me any good."

Roland's greedy attitude unnerved me. I wished I told him I was hungry, but it was my mistake by making the claim I wasn't. I watched as he inhaled my food into his mouth. There was nothing more than I wanted than to reach across the table and take my food back but I didn't want to provoke a scene. At least I had my coffee. I cupped the tin mug and pulled it closer before Roland would try to steal it from me.

"Well, I don't know about you, Vinnie," Roland said, offending me by saying my name wrong, "but I guess this grub isn't too bad. At least the army has the sense to feed us."

I forced a small laugh to be decent, but it proved to be challenging. "I don't have an appetite this morning. It was that damn run."

"Running makes me hungry," Roland said with a mouth full of food.

"Lucky you," I muttered as I put my head down and sipped at my coffee, hoping Roland would just finish his breakfast and pay no regard to me. It was evident that I was exhausted from the morning's run and wanted nothing more now than to have a little time to relax. I kept my head down to avoid eye contact with Roland, not wanting to be bothered by any more of his rubbish.

I continued to sip my coffee as I listened in on a conversation Roland was having with the recruit sitting next to him. The two of them would talk and talk and at times, Roland would let out one of his obnoxious laughs that would send shivers down my spine. His laugh was like nails on a chalkboard. I mustered every bit of restraint I had from jumping up and shouting at Roland to stop laughing. I wanted to leave the mess hall, but I guessed that leaving until chow time was over was out of the question in fear of punishment from Ramsey.

At last, Ramsey stormed through the mess hall doors. "Time to move out! Time for some calisthenics!"

Every man groaned as they stuffed whatever food they could in their mouth before standing up and marching outside for the tasks to come.

My appetite had returned, and now I felt hungry as my stomach grumbled on my way out the mess hall doors. I could kick myself for allowing Roland to steal my breakfast. I would have to hold out for lunch, and it couldn't come fast enough. If I was to do well in these runs and exercises we would do throughout the day; I needed to keep my strength up so I needed to eat all I could.

No more mistakes.

———

AS THE FIRST WEEK WENT ON, it became problematic to get out of bed each morning due to aches and pains. Ramsey had kept his word—he worked us hard. Every day started the same: run in the morning after wake-up, breakfast, calisthenics before lunch, return to the barracks to change into uniforms, classroom instruction, and then drill and briefings before supper. At the end of the initial week, I don't believe I had done so many push-ups and ran so many miles in all my life. I knew boot camp would be challenging, but I was in for a surprise by how difficult it turned out to be.

I rested on my bed on Friday evening, drained from the day's workout and with a stomach full of food after I made it a priority to myself to eat even if I was not hungry. The evenings after meal time is the only time allowed for recreation. I use recreation time to shower, shave, clean the barrack, or just relax before lights out. We were not allowed to sleep and

Roland learned this the hard way.

Roland fell asleep in his bed, and Ramsey had entered our tent to check on everyone. He paced between our beds and came to Roland's as he was fast asleep. He put his finger to his lips to signal to everyone to be quiet as he put his face within inches of Roland's face. "Why are you sleeping, Private?!" he yelled at the top of his lungs. Roland shot up—his eyes bulging out of his head. I thought his eyes would have to be shoved back into their sockets.

"Sorry, Drill Sergeant!" he shouted.

"Twenty push-ups, Private Archer!" Ramsey barked. "Get on the floor now!"

Roland dropped to the floor and slowly did his twenty push-ups with everyone in the barrack watching on. He huffed as he called out the numbers each time he lifted his heavy body off the floor with his arms. Ramsey stood over him, tapping his foot, waiting for Roland to finish.

"On your feet, Private!" Ramsey barked once Roland had completed his push-ups. He hopped up as Ramsey stuck a finger in his face. "Now don't let me catch you sleeping again before lights-out. Is that understood?"

"Yes, Drill Sergeant!" Roland panted.

Ramsey then continued with his inspections after Roland finished with his push-ups. "Lights-out in fifteen!" he called out after the inspections and exiting the barrack.

Roland returned to his bed as I rubbed my legs. Bruises covered both of my limbs caused by Ramsey's steel rod he carries around with him during our runs and exercises. The morning runs had increased by length with each passing day. Now I know what the other paths on the running trail are. Each path branches off the main one to extend the run and then connect again to the main path once further on. And Ramsey rode us hard. Any recruit discovered to be slacking off during the run would get whacked with that steel rod.

On a positive note, however, my stamina improved with each run. With each passing day, I could run further than I had the day before without getting short of breath. But by the end of the race, I still fell behind with the other stragglers. Ramsey would whack our legs, determined to push us to keep us going. And if anyone was having a more difficult time than me, it was Roland because he got the worse of Ramsey's rod beatings out of all of us. His hulking body was quite a sight to see running along with men smaller than him. He looked out of place, or we looked out of place, however you want to look at it. Roland would always be the last man to finish to run. He also had difficulty keeping up with the other recruits in our exercises. Ramsey had made a habit of yelling in Roland's face, screaming insults at him, and whacking him in the legs with the steel rod. But Roland just kept up his sluggish pace and seemed to pay no mind to Ramsey. Motivating him proved to be challenging. For it didn't appear to work in the slightest. Perhaps he is just lazy and meal times was all he cared about.

It came as no surprise when Roland was once again screamed at by Ramsey for sleeping before lights-out. After he did his twenty push-ups, I sat up on my bed to write a letter to Mother with my stationary items. I pondered on what to say in my head before putting it down on paper. The best approach is to inform her I am alive and surviving boot camp and she shouldn't worry. I asked about Glenn and Julia, hoping that all was well on the farm. As I wrote the letter, I found it difficult to concentrate on account of exhaustion. The words on the page became blurry. I rubbed my eyes and concentrated on finishing what I began. I caught myself often from drifting off to sleep.

Once I finished, I sealed it in an envelope and addressed it. I lied down on my bed trying not to fall asleep when Roland stepped over by me and sat down on Lester's bed, who was away in the showers.

"Goddamn Ramsey," Roland said in a bitter tone. "One of these days I will grab that rod of his and hit him with it so he would know what it feels like."

"You don't seem to mind getting hit with that thing," I said. "Seems like you don't even notice it."

"I'm just waiting for the most convenient moment to snatch it from him and whack him in front of everyone. You'll see—the day will come."

I chuckled. "Well, give him a good whack for me, ok," I said, rubbing my legs. I joked with him, but I think he may have taken it seriously. "I've been hit it with that thing many times. Have you seen the bruises?"

"You're not a pansy, are ya?" he asked. "You'll live with a few bruises. But hey, I'll whack him for ya." He grinned, and it made me curious to know if he was serious or not. In fact, it made me feel uncomfortable. I feared that Roland's exterior masked over what lied inside. Could he be perverse and perhaps dangerous? I'm no psychic—far from it. But I have a talent for reading people. In Roland's case, I felt the tension he had been storing inside himself, waiting for the moment to lash out at anyone who wrongs him. "Let me ask you something," Roland said.

I rubbed my eyes and sat up in my bed. "Ok—shoot."

"I overheard Ramsey talking to the other sergeants about making someone from each troop a troop leader. They will have to make their choices sometime next week. I'm hoping I get chosen for this group. Do you think I could do it?"

There was an honest answer I preferred to give him, but this was not the best of times to be honest. "Of course," I said, shrugging my shoulders. A white lie. Growing up, Mother always lectured me that the best answer is an honest answer. But when I'm sitting across from a large man who can snap my neck like a twig, it's better to tell him what he wants to hear. "If you work hard enough at it—I believe you can do it." I was lying through my teeth for I knew he couldn't do it.

"Yeah, I thought so. I know I have what it takes." A smile stretched across his face—a cocky smile. "I've gotta say—you're all right, Vinnie."

Again, he called me Vinnie. "Thanks."

Before I knew it—Ramsey reappeared at the front of the barrack and shouted that it was time for lights-out. Roland returned to his bed as Lester came back to his and all the other recruits returned to theirs. Ramsey made one last inspection of everything before turning the lights out. No more shouting for the night. We were all left in peace.

Nights in the barrack is quiet until all the snoring begins. I always try to fall asleep before everyone else, but I don't. Lying in my bed, I felt alone. It's strange, however, I knew I wasn't alone but at nights—sleeping in that large tent with nineteen other men, I felt more alone than I had been in my entire life. It wasn't from being homesick; I was more than ecstatic to be away from the farm. But I missed Mother, Glenn, and Julia.

Something hit me with this feeling of clear loneliness and that coming here had been a mistake. The feeling burrowed deep into my mind. Perhaps I was homesick. Perhaps I was just too proud and stubborn to accept it. Stubbornness had always been one of my biggest flaws. As much as I hate to admit it—but I'm tenacious like Father. I suppose it runs in the family.

I was stuck here in boot camp and by some miracle, if I survive—if I could push through to the end, would there be some respect from Father? Would it prove to him I am more than capable of taking care of myself?

I was training to be a soldier. And if there is ever a time for me to serve my country by going to war, I wouldn't allow myself to wimp out. That would gain Father's dignity; even if I was to be killed in battle. It's a scary thought, however. After everything a recruit does—after all he goes through to learn how to fight—how to survive, that he can easily be killed by another man with the same training. No man is invincible. I know many of these young men sleeping in this cold tent believe they are untouchable. If war comes, they will want to be heroes. They will want to fight the war single-handedly and be the saviors of tomorrow. I thought I could, or at least I assumed I could.

But I was unprepared. And when I am prepared, will I have the bravery to fight among my fellow troops? The reality of the dilemma I got myself into came into plain sight. It scared me. But I had my pride and I had something to prove, and I will not back out now.

I nestled in my bed, trying my best to not stir up any pain in my limbs. I looked around the barrack in the dark—not knowing what I was searching for. Men coughed, snored, and slept in the blank darkness. They were here now with me and will be here the next morning: men with nowhere else to go, no other homes, no life out of the structures of this fort. I closed my heavy eyelids as I drifted off to sleep thinking about the farm. The last place I wanted to be.

SEVEN

IT DISAPPOINTED ME to learn that there are no weekends off at Basic Training. Saturdays are focused for exercising but the calisthenics are not as severe as they are during the week. However, Sunday allowed recruits to go to church—if that was their thing, and afterwards, it was time for strict barrack cleanings. No matter what hour of the day on any day, I belonged to the army. I had to cherish the small amount of free time provided before lights-out, even though the day's work exhausted me.

After the first week, eighteen of twenty recruits remained. Roland and I are two of those eighteen. Roland toughing it out impressed me, although I rather see him quit or get kicked out. But it was a great accomplishment in my eyes just to survive the first week of boot camp. The bruise on my face from Father's fist had healed, but a scar remained in its place—not a visible scar but an emotional one; a mark that reached deep into the skin, past the flesh, the muscles, and even the bone and at last stopped at my conscience. A mark like that can never heal.

There was pride—perhaps more than I care to admit but my survival of the first week of boot camp declared for a passion of triumph. It wasn't simple. I yet had forty-nine more days of training and counting the days down was not the way to go about it. I learned it's best to count down the weeks instead. Seven more weeks to go. How I wished these remaining weeks could fly by. But that is not possible, for I knew the prevailing seven weeks would be the longest of my life.

Can I tough it out? What if I concluded that the army is not what's best for me? Maybe I could leave voluntary; I volunteered after all, and if not, perhaps just run away. They would never find me. The first place they would search for me is back home. There was the mere possibility of never returning home for a time, but I could locate alternative places to hide before the hunt gets called off. They would no longer care for one deserter. It all seemed too simple for me to escape.

I knew this fantasy was naïve. They would find me. The possible scenario being they would charge me with desertion. There would be potential jail time. And jail I imagined, would be worse than boot camp.

Another thought that ran through my mind is if I quit—I would be too ashamed, especially after only one week. The United States government invested its precious time with me, and it would be best not to let my country down. Even worse, I'd feel embarrassed to return home with my tail stuck between my legs back to Father, and never be able to look him in the eye again. I put myself in this mess so there is no choice but to go through with it, no matter how strenuous it would be.

Many times during the initial week I wanted to quit. After every whack on my limbs from Ramsey's steel rod for not running hard enough, after every time Roland let out one of his obnoxious laughs during chow time, and after every early morning wake-up to begin the laborious day, I wanted to quit. But I couldn't for I wouldn't tolerate it from myself. More pain and torment lied ahead of me—this I knew; but if I was to finish boot camp, I would have to push myself mentally and as physically as I can. Don't quit; not after the first week. Quitting is not an option. There were doubts as there will always be. But doubts can drive a man away from his dreams—his ambitions. And I couldn't allow doubts to ruin my chance at something exceptional. Men must live the day and age with only confidence. I built that confidence within myself to continue. It wasn't easy of course. And Drill Sergeant Ramsey will test me with the impending days.

———

THE FIRST DAY at the start of the second week of Basic Training, after our morning run, we dressed into our beige long sleeve shirts, trousers, and boots and all sat in a classroom as Ramsey lectured on the use of a compass, reading maps, and navigating. Ramsey instructed the recruits the fundamentals of using grids on a topographic map and observing the terrain to figure out where you are, what destination you need to be, and how to get there. Grid lines on a military map measured one kilometer and by learning the different Norths: grid north, magnetic north, and true north; identify several known locations on the map and measuring the azimuth (a horizontal angle measured clockwise from an established baseline that shows direction) and convert the grid azimuth to a back azimuth (opposite direction) to determine the area on the map you are.

Classroom instruction on the basics of map navigating ended before lunch. With our bellies full from large roast beef sandwiches, the remaining hours of the day, were used for a hike east of the fort to the pine forest for camping and a test in navigating. Ramsey permitted each man to carry a few day rations: candy bars, biscuits, and canned corn beef, canteen filled with water, compass, small knife, flint and steel kit, blanket, and a small tent. All of this we carried in backpacks. Along the trail through the forest, as I swatted away mosquitoes, Ramsey continued his lecture on the importance of contour lines on a map and what each shape indicates to determine the surrounding terrain of an area. The men stayed quiet throughout the ten-mile hike. Listening to every word the drill sergeant said, afraid to interrupt him or talk out of line in fear of the consequences. Ramsey guided the troops up and over and around steep hills, explaining the importance of observing the terrain, looking for ridges, valleys, depressions, cliffs, rivers, creeks, and so on and so on. The hike was scenic—tall green pine trees towered from above, as thin strips of sunlight beamed through the branches. A powerful aroma of pine drifted in the air as I took deep breathes, savoring the fresh scent. Before long, Ramsey finished his lecture, and the rest of the ten-mile hike went on with nothing but silence except the chirping of birds and small insects buzzing about.

The hike lasted for almost half a day deep into the forest before Ramsey decided it was at last time to stop. The sun was dropping as we set camp in a small clearing. Each man set up his small private tent as Ramsey walked about, gathering fallen tree branches and sticks. This is a good time to point out what the men and myself truly thought about our drill sergeant. Underneath his flesh, there seemed to exist a depraved human being that had no regard for his trainee's safety. His brutal tactics for training caused little conversations to break out between the men about reporting him to superior officers as they set up camp. I for one would've been more than delighted to see him be discharged. But Ramsey had a talent in arousing fear in every man in the troop—especially myself. That was the presence he owned. In fear of what our drill instructor was capable of, the thought of raising concerns to superior officers was not urgent. No man dared to provoke him.

After every man finished setting up his tent, Ramsey shouted, "Every man around me!" Within seconds, he was surrounded by the troops. "Tonight all of you will camp here. I have one more lesson to teach for the evening. This is a lesson on surviving in the wilderness. And that is how to start a fire with no lighter." Ramsey had made a small fire pit in the ground. Inside was dried tinder from the fallen branches he gathered. We watched as he struck flint and steel together, creating sparks that created smoke on a piece of char cloth and the tinder. He blew into the burning tinder as a small fire ignited, and then a larger fire erupted. It took only moments. To start a fire that quickly must have taken years of practice.

After Ramsey finished the fire, he stood and shouted, "Stand in formation!" The troops took their places as he stood ten feet away facing the front row of men. "You men are to rest here tonight. All you have to eat for tonight is your rations. Tomorrow, all of you will study your maps for you will need to locate me in a given area. You will have until sundown to find me. I've taught you everything there is to know about navigating. Now it is time to put those skills to use. With the coordinates I will now give you—it is your duty to locate your current position on the map and to seek me out." He removed a slip of paper from his pocket and held it up in the air for everyone to see, unfolded it and read. "131181, 131182." He folded the paper, and stepped up to Robert Harris—a tall man with black hair, and handed him the coordinates. "Good luck." He stepped back once more. "As you were!" He then turned and began the walk to his destination, leaving the troops to do as they please for the remainder of the evening.

"The son of a bitch gave us two coordinates," Andrew Decker said as he snatched the coordinates from Robert's hand and looked them over. "We have to search two grids for him?!"

"I'm sure he has a reason for giving us two coordinates," Karl Lambert said.

Robert took the piece of paper back from Andrew. "No. You know what he's doing, right?" he said in a high pitched voice. "He's fucking with us. I bet you he doesn't even expect us to find him in just one day."

"Look!" Karl shouted. "We'll figure it out first thing tomorrow morning. It's getting too dark to look over the map. Let's just relax around the fire and then get some shut-eye."

All the men nodded their heads and muttered their agreements as we all sat down around the burning fire.

The entire week I spent with the men, I knew nothing to little about them. But this night, as we sat around the fire, I learned a lot. As it turned out, all of them except for Roland and myself come from or around the town of Harrisonburg, Virginia. They came from broken homes and with jobs scarce on account of the Great Depression and with no other way of making a living, the military was the only option available. They came from nothing. They are nobodies. These are the men the army relied on to protect this country from an attack from foreign nations—to protect its civilians from danger. It's ironic that these men are spit on by society and yet here they are with me, learning everything there is to know on how to protect the very same society that detests them—that demoralizes them. I often ask myself why the unwanted riffraff of civilization become the protectors of a nation. Is it really desperation to make a living? Is there a choice? There is always a choice. At this time, I could be home, safe and sound back at the farm, working and making a living but I decided to be here with these men sitting around the fire talking, eating bad food, joking, and laughing with them. I made my choice. Today, I have a theory for my question; perhaps it's a chance to prove to the society we are not the scum of the earth. We are better than that. We are human beings with something to prove—to either the country, our families, or even ourselves. The day will come when we will no longer be looked down on. The day will come when we will be remembered.

The late hours of the evening turned cold as men one by one stood and walked away from the warm fire to retreat to their tents. I was one of the last to do so. By that time, the fire had died down to a small flame. I ate the remainder of my chocolate bar and stood. Karl stomped out the blaze with his boot as we said our goodnights and went into our tents. I removed my boots and made a pillow for my head with my long-sleeved shirt as I bundled up beneath my blanket and fell asleep, listening to the crickets.

———

I WAS AWAKENED by Karl early the next morning. Today was the day of the test Ramsey presented the troops. Darkness began to fade with dim daylight, and the air was still chilly as I put my long-sleeved shirt and boots back on. Men were already emerging from their tents as I did so. I

blew hot breath into the palms of my hands and stepped over to a fresh-
ly started fire burning in the same small pit Ramsey made the day before. Several minutes passed as more men approached the fire, eating a
few rations. Some of them moaned 'good morning' to one another. But I
had a feeling this was not to be a good morning.

The last man to arrive was Roland. He rubbed his eyes, and his large
mouth opened wide for a yawn. "It's too damn early," he moaned. "Can't
we get another couple hours of sleep?"

Before I could interject, Karl spoke out. "We can't waste daylight.
Every second, minute and hour is crucial. We need to find the drill sergeant before dusk." Karl removed his map from his trouser pocket, unfolded it, held it close to the fire to study it. Using his compass, he directed the map north. The maps provided for the troops were 6 digit
grids that represented the pine forest east of Fort McClellan and the
fort itself along with displays of the terrain. "Now on our way here, we
walked along a creek for a good way. The creek runs straight, but there
is a large bend which would be about here." He placed a finger on the
map. "And it's the only bend shown on this map. So we hiked east along
the creek past the bend. Did anyone notice any large hills nearby?"

I studied the map and ran my finger down the displayed creek and
past the bend and to a large hill and stopped there. "Here," I announced.
"This has to be it. We passed around it and continued heading east. It's
not far from this campsite."

Karl studied the map once more. "Good. There's a smaller hill here,"
he pointed out, "that we went over to our current position which is about
here." His finger rested on a grid that represented a small hill and flat
land. "Now Ramsey wants us to find him at either coordinates 131181 or
131182. Which means we will need to travel north. And it's over... fifty-
six kilometers from our position."

Al the men cursed and disapproved the hike we would need to take.
"Fifty-six kilometers? Are you kidding me? I told you he was fucking
with us." Robert squeaked.

"That'll take all goddamn day," Andrew said.

"What choice do we have?" Karl said. "We have to do this."

"Yeah, but he could be in several places," Lester spoke up. "It'll take longer to find him. We can't do this before sundown. It's impossible."

"It may be impossible," I said, "but as Karl said, 'We have to do this.' We should pack up all of our gear and start the hike ASAP."

"I'd rather just hike back to the fort," Roland stated. "To hell with Ramsey. He can find me back at the barrack."

"We're all leaving here together and as a team," Karl stated. "If we show up without you—what is Ramsey going to think? He'll punish you, and he'll punish all of us because of your infraction."

"Think what you want," Roland snapped, "but I'm packing up my gear and heading back to the fort."

I expected Karl to lash out, but instead, it was Andrew. He beamed red in the face as he approached Roland and looked up at him. "You are coming with us, big boy. All of us will find Ramsey together. It's seventeen against one. You might take me down along with a few others, but you can't take us all on at once. When we're done with you, we will drag your ass through this forest if we have to. Got it." Andrew spoke with a stern and low voice. Not once did he shout. But there was passion in his voice; a scare tactic to intimidate. And it worked. Roland proved to be only a push-over.

Roland backed down. "Fine. Let's just get the hell out of here and find Ramsey."

After everyone broke down camp, put the fire out, and all belongings were packed away into our individual backpacks, we followed Karl through the pine forest in search of our drill sergeant. The simple idea of a thirty-five mile hike through a forest made me ill-tempered. We stopped to rest and eat rations for fifteen minutes once every three hours. Men bickered between one another about our task. They were as upset as I was. Roland stayed silent. He remained in the very back of the group, looking bitter and defeated—strange behavior from someone who wanted to be troop leader. He didn't appear to be capable of leading. Perhaps bullying his way to the top had been his course of action but it proved impractical.

Once we arrived at the first grid on our map, we halted to rest and to plan a course of action. Only an hour or two of daylight was available. If we were to find Ramsey, it needed to be done soon. We all kneeled together as Karl studied his map. "So each grid represents one kilometer. And we have two grids to search with little daylight left. What do any of you propose to do to find Ramsey?"

The men were silent, deep in thought. I pondered over the situation in my head when an idea came. "Well, I say we spread out side by side in a line. Let's say fifteen—twenty feet of each other. We walk at a steady pace and keep our eyes open. If anyone spots something, he'll let the man standing to his left and right about it, and the word spreads down the very last men in the line. And we do this through both the grids."

Karl and the other men nodded their heads in agreement. "That sounds like it might actually work," Karl said.

"Good thinking, Conroy," Andrew said as he rubbed the top of my head.

"All right! Everyone spread out," Karl said. "And walk side by side in a single line. Be no more than twenty feet from the man next to you, so you don't get separated. Keep both men in your sights at all times. Let's move out!"

My idea worked. With our maneuver, we swept up and down the first grid area of the map and didn't find Ramsey. By this point, daylight was near gone. And as we quickly swept through the second region, I was informed that one of the men spotted a fire and smoke rising from the trees. We all huddled together as we approached the fire. A camp had been set up and there by the fire, lying on a flat blanket was Ramsey with his hands tucked beneath his head and his legs crossed at the ankles.

As he spotted the troop, I figured congratulations would be in order, but he would not congratulate us, however. "Stand in formation!" He shouted. Everyone stood in formation as Ramsey paced up and down the front line. The fire glowed bright and red as he stared down the men he passed. "What took you so long, Privates!" he roared. No one dared to explain. "Well? Is anyone of you pathetic dumb shits going to answer me?! Or do I need to beat the answer out of someone?!" I sighted the steel rod in Ramsey's fist. He patted the palm of his hand with the rod, looking impatient and malicious.

"Drill Sergeant!" Lester shouted. I stood directly behind him the second row.

Ramsey strolled up to him and got inches from his face. "Do you have something to say, Private?" But before he could answer, Ramsey spoke again. "Who are you again?"

"Spears, Drill Sergeant!"

"Spears, huh? I don't like that name, Spears. Have I mentioned that before? Remind me again—what's your first name?"

"Lester, Drill Sergeant!"

"Well, we have Private Lester Spears speaking up for everyone. Isn't that sweet? So tell me, Private Spears—what took you so long?"

"We had trouble following your coordinates, Drill Sergeant! It's my duty to report to you that your instructions were poor, Drill Sergeant!"

Ramsey only smiled at what Lester said. I expected him to explode, but he only kept his calm. "Is that so? Well, let me apologize then, Private Spears. You are absolutely right. I did give you bad instructions, and it is all my fault." He took a step back. "And is that how everybody else feels?"

"I agree with Private Spears, Drill Sergeant," Karl shouted at the end the left end of the front row.

Ramsey stepped up to him. "What's that now? You agree with Private Spears? You agree that that my coordinates were bad?"

"Yes, Drill Sergeant!" Karl shouted. "It took longer to find you because you gave us two grids to search for you, Drill Sergeant!"

Ramsey stepped back and walked back and forth down the line again. "How about the rest of you men? Do you feel that my coordinates were bad?"

"No, Drill Sergeant!" the rest of us shouted in unison.

"Do you hear that, Private Spears?" Ramsey said as he stepped up Lester again. "The other men say you and Private Lambert are full of shit. What do you have to say now?"

Lester stuttered. "I-I... well we..." He strained to get any other words, not knowing quite what to say. Ramsey backhanded him.

"If you got something to say, then say it!" Ramsey barked. His face turned brick red. "Are you eye-balling me, Private Spears?!"

"No, Drill Sergeant!" Lester shouted.

Ramsey backhanded him once more and took a step back. "Step forward, Spears!"

Lester hesitated in stepping forward.

"Now!" Ramsey shouted. I guessed Lester would receive another backhand, but it didn't come.

Lester took a step out of line as Ramsey strolled up and down as he always did. "Now each and every one of you need to follow Spears' and Lambert's display of honesty. I intended to give you all bad instructions on how to get here because believe it or not—all your sorry asses will have to learn how to follow bad instructions as long as you are in the military. Because there will be times when detailed instructions won't be available when you are getting blasted with enemy fire. You all have to master the art of thinking faster and harder! This exercise is also about teamwork. All of you had to work as a team to find me, and so you did." Ramsey halted in front of Lester again. "Now... are we all on the same page?!"

"Yes, Drill Sergeant!" we all shouted.

In a split second, Ramsey punched Lester hard in the stomach. Lester gasped for air as he sank to his knees, clutching his belly. And in one violent swing of the steel rod, Ramsey struck Lester in the back of the head. He fell flat and motionless to the ground. He stood over Lester as he turned his limp body over with his foot. There appeared to be no consciousness in Lester's eyes. If he was conscious, he was good at playing dead.

"And never look me in the eye again you worthless maggot," Ramsey said, looking down at Lester. I wasn't sure if Lester could hear what was being said. Ramsey's eyes then shot back up at everyone else. "And that goes for all of you too! Is that understood?!"

"Yes, Drill Sergeant!" we shouted.

———

WITH THE EXERCISE OVER, Ramsey ordered two men—Roland and Robert to carry Lester on the way back to the fort by his arms and legs until he was capable of walking on his own. Our hike was not over. Hours passed in the night as the tall and endless pine trees reaching up into the darkness loomed over me. With no rations left to eat, my belly grumbled with hunger through the miles and miles of obscurity. No sleep for the night. A cold morning came as we reached just on the out-skirts of Fort McClellan.

Once back at the fort, Lester went to the infirmary and there, spent the rest of the day in bed.

Lucky bastard.

EIGHT

WITH THE NAVIGATING EXERCISE OVER, by mid-week, we began to learn hand-to-hand combat. The past several days exhausted me to my bones. Ramsey's map navigating exercise, endless miles of hiking, and lack of sleep turned me into a dead man. This was when I think I hated Ramsey the most. And there was no sign of him slowing down. After only a few hours sleep, Ramsey barged into the barrack and ordered everyone awake and to dress into their PT gear. After our morning run, the troop was directed to the sand pits to learn hand combat. If the time ever came to engage an enemy with nothing but your fists due to a rifle jam, or any other problem that may occur during combat, your next available weapon will be your fists, legs, and a bayonet or knife. Ramsey lectured on the importance of staying calm during a fight to allow yourself to think. Another important rule is always to be aware of your environment. Are other weapons available to grant you the favors in a match? Don't be alarmed if your opponent is larger. With speed and skill, aim for certain areas on the body to gain leverage. And the most important rule—never lose control of your wits during a fight.

Ramsey and the other sergeants demonstrated the stance, effective arm and leg strikes, choking, blocking, disarming, throw down techniques, breaking an arm, and even eye gouging. I have to admit, the thought of eye gouging made me squeamish.

Training was done outside under the hot sun in sandy and muddy areas. The routine and rules were simple enough; Ramsey would pair two men from the troop and at times, from different troops and those two men, would practice fighting techniques on one another. The drill sergeants made it clear the fights were not a competition and that no man was allowed to intentionally do any harm to his opponent. But rules were only words to naive short-tempered young men with something to prove to himself and his colleagues. The fights often got heated. Thankfully, the drill sergeants kept a watchful eye on the matches and intervened before any serious damage was done.

My first match, I competed with Arthur Bates, a man from my troop and lost. It was over before it even began. I made the mistake of charging, but his speed took me off guard as he dashed aside and took me into an unbreakable choke hold from behind. He locked his legs around my body as I fell backward to the sand and after several failed attempts to break free, Ramsey blew the whistle. My second match went better and longer, even though I still lost. This time I was paired with Robert Harris. Learning from the mistake of my first match, I kept a distance from him, planning my attacks and waited for him to make the first move. The first minutes we danced going around in circles with our fists raised, waiting for the first move but my patience wore thin. Suddenly I went for the left for a charge and then quickly went to the right for a fake and took him by surprise. I grabbed hold of his thighs and took his legs off the ground and flung him over my head. Thinking I now had the advantage, as I turned to jump on top of him, I see that Robert landed on his feet. He had an opening for a choke hold and took it for I was too slow to react. The whistle to signify the match is over blown. I lost the same way I had with Arthur.

After the match, we shook hands. "You'll have to teach me that move," I said.

Robert smiled. "After you teach me how to juke like that."

———

THE DAYS WERE DIVIDED from hand-to-hand combat, more calisthenics, and obstacle courses. I can't count how many walls, ropes, nets, I climbed up and down on. I can't count how many ditches I jumped across, how many beams and ladders I climbed across, and how many fences I vaulted over. These obstacles are to test our speed, strength, and physical capabilities as well as our mental abilities. The first runs I found to be enjoyable, but Ramsey's routine in training made it grueling. Now it became clear as to why Ramsey had us running so much during the first week. He made the statement himself in the first week that we needed to be in the condition he needed us to be in. I was glad though; I was now in proper shape, and this made obstacle courses easier to go through.

But Roland was being himself during the duration of obstacle course runs. He moved about at his leisure and cared not about Ramsey shouting obscenities at him. Roland would roll his eyes as an arrogant smile thinned out across his lips. But this made Ramsey try to drive him harder. And soon enough, Ramsey began to take his frustrations out on the rest of men as I became one of the targets for disciplining.

Before supper on a Friday, it rained. The obstacle course laid out with thick mud. I had just finished doing thirty push-ups after being punished for not completing an obstacle course fast enough. Mud makes this difficult. As I got to my feet, Ramsey still angry, growling with rage, whacked me hard with his steel rod on the back of my neck. It came as a surprise I had not been knocked unconscious. A wave of fury came over me as Ramsey shouted obscenities at me. He reminded me of an old rabid dog, foaming at the mouth, barking with fierce fanged teeth, always chomping down to bite. This time he bit. And will not stop until blood is drawn. "Get back on your feet, you worthless piece of shit! Because you will run that obstacle over again until you can finish it on time!"

Every man has a breaking point. The hate I had for Ramsey fueled the strength I needed to fight back. I grew irritated of his constant harassment. Without thinking, I jumped to my feet and seized the rod out of Ramsey's hands as I kicked his legs out from underneath him in one swift motion. The hand-to-hand combat training came in handy. Ramsey was flat on his back, lying on the ground spread eagle. And in my sudden burst of rage—I clobbered him with the rod many times on his chest and shoulders, making sure to give him a good wallop for what he did to Lester a few days before. Before I knew it, several men hauled me away—one of them being Roland. I flustered with anger as sweat dripped from my face. Wanting to keep the rod away from Ramsey, I flung it far away.

"Holy shit, Conroy," Roland whispered. "That was something else. You got to him before I could."

So much for me not standing out.

Other men from the troop helped Ramsey on his feet. At this point, I didn't know what he would do or what the military would do to me for that matter. Would I be kicked out of the army or arrested for assaulting a drill sergeant? After Ramsey had gotten to his feet, he only looked at me with contempt and thus to my surprise—he smiled. "Now that's what I like to see, Private!" he said aloud. "You've got a fire in you, son. I like that. And congratulations—you're now Troop Leader."

"Troop Leader, Drill Sergeant?" I said with confusion. It had come as a shock. This was not the reaction I expected. Not from this senile drill sergeant whose job it is to make my life a living hell. But here he stood, smiling at me. I questioned his sanity.

"That's right, Private! Troop Leader! From here on out, you will be in charge of these men. I know you will make a good leader. You will be an NCO someday. Now everyone to the mess hall. Chow time!"

———

I WAS STILL IN SHOCK during supper after Ramsey announced me as Troop Leader. I slowly ate my meal and tried to contemplate the situation at hand. I was now responsible for everyone. The last thing I wanted to do was mess it up. Ramsey must have been impressed with the way I handled the beating I received from that damn rod. Was there a possibility that maybe he did see something in me? And if that was the case, I didn't want to let him down. I sat there in front of my meal feeling an overwhelming responsibility on my shoulders which were heavy enough as it was and now, the weight became too much—far too much.

A feeling of sickness came over me. The food on my tray: corn beef, a roll, and greens looked unappetizing. But everyone else dug into their food as if it was the greatest meal they ever ate. I had a feeling. A feeling of uneasiness—dread; an unseen force that follows you in the darkest surroundings. It creeps into your very skin. Fear. Yes, it was the fear that I would let Ramsey down and not only him but the entire troop. "What have I gotten myself into?" I said to myself. I wanted to keep my head low and not stand out but failed. I was now Troop Leader, so I stuck out like a sore thumb among the other men. If I failed, Ramsey would replace me with someone else; someone who could get the job done. But Ramsey put his faith in me. After my little stunt at the obstacle course, I felt foolish. How could I do such a thing to my superior? And yet, I wasn't punished. Instead, I had been promoted. It's weird how things work out.

By the time I began to relax, I took notice of Roland eyeing me. I looked up from my meal and my eyes locked with his as he stared me down. His food had barely been touched. He wasn't devouring it down as he usually was. I felt uneasy from his long glare. He said nothing. Only sat across from me staring me down with a grim look on his face.

I forced down a couple bites of corn beef and tried to ignore the awkward stare, but I felt I had to say something. "How's your supper, Roland?" I asked with a slight smile, trying to be as friendly as possible. "Looks like you haven't eaten much."

After a long minute of silence, he at last spoke. "So you are Troop Leader now, huh?"

"I guess so," I replied.

"So do you think you're a big man now just because of what you did to Ramsey?"

"I don't think of myself as a big man, Roland. I got tired of being hit with that stupid rod. So I acted. You were saying yourself last week that you wanted to take a shot at him, but you never did. So I did it. I took matters into my own hands."

Roland's eyes squinted. By this time, I took notice of some of the men listening. "You're a real piece of work," he finally said. "So you think you are in charge of everyone now? . . . Are you in charge of *me*?"

He said those last words with audacity. I came to realize that maybe Roland grew jealous of me because of my appointed position.

At this point, I began to see what kind of person Roland really was. He was behaving as a spoiled brat. I visualized him growing up, that he had everything handed to him, and so coming to boot camp, he had the illusion he could work very little for a big payoff. It all made sense now. Since day one, Roland had been lazy. He slacked off in all our runs, our hike through the pine forest, and the obstacle courses. And now this one time, something doesn't work out according to plan, and that makes him feel like he had been cheated. I stole his shining moment away from him; unintentionally of course.

Still, as I sat there trying to eat, Roland stared at me with hateful eyes. I expressed a look of irritation, and at last, he took his eyes off of me and picked up his fork and dug into the food on his tray.

I felt relief, thinking his little episode was over until he put his fork down and spoke. "We'll see how long you'll last, Conroy. . . because as soon as you fail, I'll be taking over. And when that happens, you better watch yourself because I'm going to beat your ass black and blue with a metal rod much harder than Ramsey ever did."

That last remark sounded much like a threat. At this point, I had had enough of listening to Roland and only wanted to finish my meal. I wasn't, however, going to let him get the last words on me. My head felt hot. I could feel the heat burning in my face. "Well I'm sorry things didn't quite work out for you, Private Archer," I said to him with an impudent tone, "but as your Troop Leader, I suggest you finish your meal and speak no more about this tonight because I sure would hate to have to put you on potato duty." And with that, Roland's face became brick red. His eyes burned with fire as he glared at me. His staring had gone on long enough. "Oh, and quit staring at me because you're starting to freak me and some of the other guys out."

Men snickered as he went back to eating his meal. For the first time, I felt excited about my new position. I would need to fight to keep it, for I could not allow Roland to take my place. This is my moment, not his. And I'll be damned to see him ruin my chance to prove to Ramsey what I am capable of. I just need to believe it myself.

———

THAT NIGHT, BEFORE LIGHTS-OUT, I wrote a letter to mother informing her about what had been taking place at boot camp and that I had been made Troop Leader.

This was a position that I didn't ask for, but the conclusions I made after Ramsey handed it to me was to go with the flow. It's a sign of weakness if I back down now. I was responsible for all the men in the barrack, along with various other duties, such as barrack cleanliness, ensuring uniforms are neat and clean and informing everyone when it was time for lights-out. The responsibility can be overwhelming.

There is a positive, however, about my position; this was a grand opportunity to prove to Father that I'm making something of myself and I am capable of surviving on my own. I must be honest here—what I wanted is to make him angry. It thrilled me to feel this way. My confidence grew, and I was high on tenacity. I couldn't permit it of myself to remain as a soft, obedient little child, letting everyone walk all over me.

I finished writing the letter to Mother when Ramsey came into the tent and began tossing mail around. He had a distinct and difficult manner of doing things. A simple task, such as handing out mail had to be carried out in a deliberately unnecessary way. Mail flew through the air all around as Ramsey walked down the barrack. I had no hopes in expecting anything but to my astonishment; a letter came soaring towards my face. It dipped and hit my chest and dropped into my lap. A letter from Mother. I quickly ripped open the envelope and read:

Dear Vincent,

How are things at Basic Training? We all miss you, especially Julia. And even though your father has never said it, but I think he misses you too. You know how stubborn he can be. Don't be angry with him. I don't think he never meant to hurt you that day before you left. Things just got a bit out of hand is all. He loves you, you know. I just don't think he was ready for you to leave. I wasn't ready for you to go either. Things just feel different since you have been away, even if it has only been just a short time thus far.

On a lighter note, we are all ok. Glenn had been helping your father with all the farm work. But I feel that Glenn maybe up to something. I think he also is planning to leave the farm as well. I think you may have started something. He has been talking about wanting to get into a college somewhere. He wants to be a lawyer he said. But he knows that your father and I could never afford for him to go to college and yet he continues to talk about it. He seems to really have his heart set on it, but I have no clue as to how he will pay for it all.

Julia has been asking when you'll be back every day that you have been away. She also wants to know what gift you are going to bring her. You are coming back to visit, aren't you? Please do the first chance you get. Don't mind your father. I'll make sure that he behaves himself. I do hope that the two of you can work things out.

You remind me of him so much. There's a lot of you in him. Maybe you haven't seen it yet or felt it, but you two are so much alike. You are his son, and I hope that you love him. You are also my son, and I hope you know that I love you so very much. It's hard for me to understand that you are not a little boy anymore. I miss the days when I could hold you in my arms. I missed the days when you got hurt from playing outside, and I was always there to treat your wounds. How I wish to hug you again. How I wish to hug you so tight and never let you go. I want to keep you safe. But I know you are a man now. I told you before you left I am so proud of you and I meant it. You make me proud every day.

We'll always be here if you need anything. Be safe.

All my love,

Mother

I read the letter a couple of times before putting back into the envelope. I placed it into my trunk at the end of my bed and lied down. I lied there with my eyes open making sure I wouldn't fall asleep before lights-out. In that brief moment, I thought about trying to make amends with Father; deep down, I knew I wanted to. But even if I did, would he want to do the same? I didn't know the answer. The broad gap that had grown between the two of us had grown more extensive, deeper, and darker—far too dark. Standing at that fathomless edge, not knowing what move to make frightened me. The best advancement in this situation is no advancement at all. Be still. Stay where I am and let things play out to my advantage.

I looked at my wristwatch as it was now time for lights-out. And so I stood up and shouted.

NINE

"WATCH WHAT YOU'RE DOING, GODDAMNIT!" Father shouted at Katrina after she accidentally dropped a bucket of milk onto the kitchen floor.

"I'm so sorry, sir. It was an accident," Katrina quaked.

But Father had not seen it as an accident. He stood there red-faced and scowling as if his head would explode. "It's enough I let you people stay here, but I will not tolerate any foolish clumsiness! That was good milk you dropped on the floor!"

Katrina held her head low, not saying a word as if she was ashamed and that she deserved the torment coming from Father.

I had witnessed the whole thing. It *was* an accident. I held the back screen door open for Katrina to allow her to enter the kitchen when our mutt dog—Ziggy, without warning, scurried between Katrina's legs, making her lose her balance as the bucket of fresh milk slipped out of her hands and onto the floor.

Mother must have heard Father's outburst. She arrived at the back door. "What's all this shouting, William?"

"Look at what the girl did!" he said pointing at the milk covering the kitchen floor.

"Well, this is surely no reason to throw a tantrum, William! It's just spilt milk!"

Katrina sniffled, and Father glared at her. "You're not gonna cry, are you? It's only spilled milk, and there's no use in crying over spilled milk!" With those words, I couldn't help but let out a stifled laugh. Both Mother and Father's heads jerked in my direction. "What's so funny, Vince?" Father hissed. At once, I stopped laughing. I glanced at Katrina with her head still down, but I could see her face turning red and her mouth trembling with a smile, trying not to snicker at Father's comment.

"I-I don't know," I murmured. "Nothing."

Mother grabbed towels and began cleaning the floor. Katrina knelt down to help, but Mother stopped her. "It's ok, darling," she whispered. "Go into the living room to sit down and rest."

Katrina did as Mother told her without hesitation and I followed her to the living area and heard no objections.

I heard Father cursing to himself as he always does when something happens. That man knew how to curse. Words that should never be said in front of children would pour out of him like liquid. The vilest and cruelest things I had learned was from him. Father seemed to not care about what he expressed in front of his children. I came to live with his daily profanities. Sometimes, the obscenities would amuse me. Other times, I had no clue what he was saying, less talking about. But there were words and phrases Father used, that even in my age, I will refuse to say. I guess I have standards. I wouldn't want any person hearing me say those sorts of things. It would be unethical of me.

Katrina sat down on the couch, and I did so also right next to her.

"It wasn't your fault," I whispered. There came a need for me to make the poor girl feel better, even at my youthful age. Aren worked in the fields outside, oblivious to the milk incident. So I felt I should try to comfort her. But being a boy, I didn't know how and yet I needed to in some way.

Katrina smiled. "Thank you," she said in a gentle voice that was like honey—bright and sweet.

We both nestled up together on the couch, saying nothing, enjoying one another's silent company. We didn't need to speak. I can smell her hair and the fragrant scent of her perfume. It smelled of wildflowers. To this day, I can still smell her perfume as if she was sitting right next to me.

I took to her as a friend. And desired she felt the same way about me. Years later, I came to understand what a close friend she had been. Not once did she raise her voice at me, scold me, or ridicule me like Father. She reminded me of Mother. I can visualize Aren and Katrina as the parents I never had, or perhaps the bigger brother and sister I never had. Thinking back on all of this now, I wanted the two of them to live with us forever on the farm, and take weekly picnics to the field on sunny days and wait until sundown to watch the glowing fireflies move about at night.

How I wish.

But friends are challenging for me to come by these days. Instead of friends, I made enemies. I guess it came with the territory when Ramsey appointed me as Troop Leader. Being in a position of a greater power is frowned upon among the men.

And yet, Roland wanted to be Troop Leader himself. But failed. Ramsey yanked the opportunity from him. When the position had been assigned to me—Roland grew cold. I can't say I'm disappointed for I never considered him to be nothing more than a team member. But the change in his manner was clear. The simple fact is—he now despised me. Hate peeked from underneath his boisterous persona. His colorful character altered into something vicious. And since my appointment of Troop Leader, I became a burden needing to be put in place. He ignored my daily 'Good Mornings' and only scoffed. During chow time, he sat far away from me at the table. His changed demeanor toward me should have been enough to warn me to be wary. I should have been. But I wasn't.

———

THE ARMY ISSUED the troops an M1 Garand rifle, Colt M1911 pistol, and dog tags during the third week at Fort McClellan and for the first time, I felt like an actual soldier. The remaining six weeks were to be challenging but exciting—not to mention dangerous. One example of dangerous is the barbed-wired infiltration course. The simulation is intended to give the experience of what it's like to be under enemy fire. I have heard stories of men being killed in these simulations due to carelessness. Men get overwhelmed by the burden of the gunfire and stand up suddenly, wanting to get away but only to be shot. I had never witnessed this myself, and I am thankful I hadn't. Every man is to crawl three-hundred meters on the ground in thick mud that smelled of feces under barbwire as live M-60 ammunition rounds fired above our heads. My ears rang from the deafening barrage of gunfire. The shouts from Ramsey were faint, making it impossible to know what I should have been doing. Was I moving too slow or too fast? So I only did what the other men did: don't fret about the drill sergeants shouting; just complete the course. And as if the live gunfire was enough to worry about, Ramsey also instructed us to keep our rifles clean as we crawled on our stomachs through the mud. A rifle fouled with mud meant a redo of the course.

The troops and myself had difficulty of keeping oneself from getting caught in the barbwire. Cuts and scratches across the face and hands and ripped uniforms were a common problem, but the injuries are looked upon with pride. The scars to be left behind from the cuts are to be signs of courage and toughness.

After the first time running the course, I made it to the end with a clean rifle but several men failed to keep their rifles clean and were sent back to the beginning for a redo. And Roland was one of these men. Every man who failed, only made Ramsey direct his attention toward me with anger. This was my cue to ride the troops harder, and Roland is to be no exception. "I don't want to see any of your rifles with mud on them!" I called out. "Put your asses into gear and finish this course with a clean rifle!" I yelled myself hoarse during the exercise. But I had to convince Ramsey that I can do my duty. My primary target, however, was Roland. Now's the time to get back at him for the threat he imposed on me in the mess hall.

Those who failed the first time ran the course a second time and kept their rifles clean, except for Roland. I ordered Roland to repeat the exercise yet again. "Do it again, Private Archer and keep your rifle clean!"

He stared at me with a smug face.

"You know what? I'm feeling a bit tired," Roland said. "I think I'll sit this one out."

Roland turned to walk away from me until I rushed in front of him. This is the time to intimidate him as Andrew Decker did during our map navigating exercise. "Do the exercise over again, Private Archer!" I yelled. "That's an order!" I could feel my face burning red with anger. "I am Troop Leader, and you will do the exercise over again until you can keep your rifle clean from mud!"

Roland stood there with an ignorant look on his face, not moving. But I was standing my ground with him and had no intentions of backing off. At last, Ramsey stepped between us and stuck his finger in Roland's face. "Do the exercise over again, Private! Or I will knock the dog shit out of you!"

He scoffed and with hesitation, returned to the beginning of the course as I kept a careful eye on him. His heavy body crawled through the mud with difficulty, struggling to keep his rifle clean and struggling to keep himself from getting caught in the barbwire which he did so frequently. He slowly but surely made his way to the end of the course and by some miracle, kept his rifle clean from mud. I wanted to be finished with this damned exercise, so Roland's completion sent a flood of relief. The excessive M-60 gunfire had created an unpleasant ringing in my ears. I imagined myself being deaf by the end of my military career.

I expected that that would be the end of the simulation. My ears rang, mud painted my entire uniform, and the stench was unpleasant. But Ramsey will order every man to work the course again in the coming days. And with that, the troop lost two more men, bringing the total to sixteen. But Roland remained. Too stubborn to quit.

The tension between us grew raw and perhaps dangerous. Roland testing my patience had been intentional. His mission is to ruin me. But his plan failed. It's my role to be verbal but lashing out physically would be unacceptable on my part. I was only Troop Leader and not a drill instructor. Roland played a game, but I refused to participate. Another time will come when he will make a move once more. I had to prepare myself for the unexpected.

I had to learn to look over my shoulder at all times.

———

SINCE I NOW HAD MY RIFLE AND PISTOL—target practice began. The first time at the shooting range wasn't disastrous, fortunately, I proved to be more than capable of aiming and firing a rifle and a pistol. Growing up, I went hunting many times, but there is always more to learn. And I needed to comprehend the art of shooting and since I would be an infantryman—I had to learn all there is to know.

The M1 rifle, I discovered to be a bit heavy. It took time to get use to. But I also learned the M1 to be accurate. I guess you can say, 'take the bad with the good.' There was no surprise why it is "standard issue" in the army. The Garand—is a .30 caliber, gas-operated, rotating bolt semi-automatic rifle with a single clip containing eight rounds and once I got the practice of loading and reloading, I could shoot about forty rounds per minute. I came to love the distinct 'ping' sound of an empty clip discharging from the rifle.

I also grew to love the Colt M1911 pistol. The weight, like the Garand, is heavy, but after a time, it became comfortable in my hand and the trigger, light and satisfactory. The Colt is also accurate. With my admiration for the pistol, when the time came to clean it, along with my M1 Garand—I cleaned them right. I took pride in cleaning my rifle and pistol. Every time Ramsey would inspect them for cleanliness—he always made a positive comment about my cleanliness. Perhaps the brute was respecting me. Earning his respect is difficult but possible I suspected. And if I could earn Ramsey's esteem, I would be untouchable. Ramsey wasn't aware, but he became my protector. Only a fool would dare challenge me now, and even Roland is not stupid enough to do so, not whilst Ramsey is at my side.

The shooting range, I grew fond of. This was the time that Ramsey was the most pleasant. The targets were large plywood with painted circular targets and in the center is the bulls-eye. Firing my rifle and pistol came to be my favorite activity at boot camp. Who wouldn't enjoy the opportunity to take concealed frustrations out on a target by firing bullets? The experience is thrilling. Ramsey and other sergeants would coach the recruits along, teaching different procedures to improve one's aim. But guidance can go so far. Another valuable asset is talent.

And I am always eager to learn more and turned to a few other recruits for guidance—Andrew Decker and Karl Lambert. The two men stuck close to one another throughout boot camp as if they were longtime friends, seldom leaving one another's company. They sat together during meals, kept each other company in the barrack, and worked closely at the shooting range. The companionship between them appeared strong and reliable. An impacting bond is impossible to break. It's the friendship I longed for with my brother Glenn. Our childhood together had been barren. Ridiculous conflicts that often rises between siblings divided us. But now a moment lays out before me. If not to be a better brother, then a better ally.

When the time was right, I approached Karl and Andrew to ask for pointers after watching the two of them shoot their rifles for half an hour. Shot after shot hit the bulls-eye or close to it. Needless to say, I was impressed. They were damn good. Even though I am not a bad shot myself—a few tips wouldn't hurt. After speaking with them for a few minutes, I learned that both were from Huntington, West Virginia and signed up for the National Guard soon after I enlisted. They have been close friends for much of their lives and from my knowledge, became inseparable.

"Shooting is all mental," Karl stated. "Always keep a clear and focused mind. No distractions. Because distractions are your worst enemy."

"Never focus on using one position for the whole day," Andrew said. "Practice all positions. Practice one for half an hour and then move on to the next one."

"Make sure you're doing your daily exercises," Karl said. "Believe it or not, but those exercises help. They help you get and stay into your positions much easier."

"And learn how to read the wind," Andrew said. "Pay attention to the flags. The flags are there for a reason."

"And if all else fails," Karl said, shooting his rifle in a prone position, "you better be damn good with your bayonet." Both Andrew and Karl laughed. It was a joke; I thought it wasn't amusing. I'd rather much shoot a man from a distance than stab the poor soul with a bayonet. Perhaps I am squeamish. I didn't laugh at the quip. Didn't grin either. Karl continued firing his rifle as Andrew observed. "All right, Vince— let's see what you got," Karl hopped to his feet, satisfied with his rounds.

I hit the ground in the prone position and fired away. I did well the first couple of rounds, but afterwards, my shots were drifting away from the bulls-eye. After more lousy shooting, Karl stopped me.

"Not bad, Vince, but you're losing focus. Remember to focus on every shot. Imagine that that target you're shooting at is the enemy rushing towards you and you have only one shot left, so you need to make it count. And look at the bulls-eye as the enemy's heart. So focus and make the kill-shot."

With those words, I took a deep breath and aimed. Andrew and Karl watched me with firm eyes. After everything they told me, I didn't wish to disappoint. My ability to focus, however, is not hopeful for I could feel their watchful eyes on me. But I had to stay sharp. The tricky part is focusing; it's not the aiming or the setting of your position—it's the concentration. Any man can aim a gun and pull the trigger, but to make a precise shot, concentration is key. I focused on Karl's words again. I envisioned an enemy rushing towards me. No ammo left. His only weapon: a bayonet. But I have one shot to take—one bullet. If I miss, the two of us will engage in hand-to-hand combat. But the situation can be avoided with my rifle. One shot. Make it count. I take a steady aim at the bulls-eye. The heart. The kill-shot. And fired. Direct hit. The enemy is dead.

It was the next late afternoon at target practice when Ramsey approached me as I practiced my shooting at the target, remembering everything taught by Karl and Andrew. Ramsey stood next to me, observing. "Ignore him," I said to myself. "Pay no regard to him and only focus on shooting." Round after round, I fired. Each shot just as direct as the next; in or close to the bulls-eye, until at last, my shots strayed further and further away like the day before. I couldn't concentrate. Ramsey's presence got the best of me. I was losing focus. Then Ramsey lied on his stomach next to me, peering through a pair of binoculars at the target I had been shooting at.

"Hold your fire," Ramsey said as he peered through his binoculars. His face transfixed with a close inspection of my target. "Very good, Conroy."

"Thank you, Drill Sergeant," I said with confidence. I relaxed after Ramsey had made a decisive comment on my shooting capabilities.

"Watch your breathing," Ramsey continued. "Try taking a few deep breaths and then fire when your lungs are exhausted."

I did as Ramsey instructed and my shot hit the bulls-eye. Nearly dead center. I was in awe for a few moments. My mouth dropped as I starred at the target in disbelief. One of the first lessons I learned since arriving at boot camp is always do what the sergeant tells you to do.

"Atta boy, Conroy. Just keep doing that. Continue," he said as he stood up to watch over the other men. Instant relief came as he left my side; it's problematic to focus on shooting with him breathing down my neck. But now with Ramsey gone, I loosened up.

I continued for another hour shooting my rifle, practicing my breathing as Ramsey taught me along with Karl and Andrew's teachings.

There came a considerable difference in my shots. My rifle remained steady, and the shots fired more precise. The real talent of a marksman.

———

WE ALSO RECEIVED BAYONETS to attach to our M1 rifles. Ramsey set up exercises for us to use our bayonets to jab at dummies. He exhorted us to use much aggression when using a bayonet during the training. "If you are to kill a man with your bayonet—you need to be fierce!" He paced through the rows of men plunging their bayonets into dummies, observing. "You must not hesitate when it comes time to gut your enemy! Because if you hesitate—your enemy will get the upper hand! You must never allow the enemy to get the upper hand! Is that clear!"

"Yes, Drill Sergeant!" we all shouted.

Ramsey intended to make it clear to us that war is not pretty. And if the time ever comes for to us to step into battle, then we must be ready for it. A soldier's job is to protect his country and in doing so, perhaps die for it. Death in battle is part of the job. It's a risk that every soldier must accept when he signs those papers as I did. My body, mind, and spirit now belonged to the army. It was the army's sole purpose to turn men into skilled killing machines.

I, at last, comprehended all of this during our bayonet exercises. But I considered the reality of stabbing an enemy soldier. I can stab a fake, emotionless dummy, stuffed with cotton, but could I stab or shoot another living human being who bleeds the same blood as I do? Would I be capable of looking another man in the eye as I jab a bayonet into his gut?

It's much to comprehend—killing another man for the purpose of battle—for war. In war, there is a need for killing for an undefined purpose. A sole purpose only based on another man's ideas. Ideas are dangerous. Ideas placed into the wrong hands can cause damage never thought possible. War begins with an idea—even a simple one. But ideas expand with time. Ideas grow and grow until that one, small idea has evolved into many. And yet, it nevertheless grows and will continue to grow, until at last a decision to act out based on that one idea from where it all started. The course of time can change based on one idea. A solitary truth is buried in the idea that is often overlooked. And if one truth can be discovered, the underlying potential of war can be diverted. But there are those among us who refuse to acknowledge that truth, on account of purely being blind.

TEN

THE WEEKS WENT BY AT BASIC TRAINING. Daily routines were set. And I remained as the Troop Leader. But now is the time to mention that Alabama weather is hot—much like Louisiana. As the weeks passed through May, the air grew warmer and thicker with humidity. And in this weather, we marched, speed marched, and jogged long miles in full gear, carrying heavy packs on our backs along with carrying our rifles in our hands. These marches and jogs were brutal under the sweltering sun. It amazed me I hadn't suffered heat stroke from the harsh hot weather or any of the other recruits. We all had water in our canteens but were never allowed take a sip unless at certain times that Ramsey specified. And if he caught anyone drinking water—he would apply severe punishment. "If you want to be tough—you don't need water!" Ramsey barked as we marched under the hot sun. Many times, the heat tempted me to sneak a drink from my canteen, but each time, I resisted the urge. It has been some time since Ramsey whacked me with his rod and I want to keep it that way.

From what I can recall, we had short time for calisthenics, classroom instruction, and target practice. Now, most of our time was focused on marching. We also marched throughout the night—which was a relief from the blistering heat of the daytime. And this was the first time in my life I felt perfectly fit. My body displayed muscles on my chest, stomach, arms, and legs—muscles I didn't know I had. My physical body changed. I no longer appeared to be that pudgy and out of shape man I used to be. In his place now stood a soon to be U.S. soldier with a well-defined physique. How I wish Mother could see me now. She would not recognize me. I wanted her to see me—not to impress, but to reveal to her how much I have changed in these past weeks.

With the great satisfaction for my physique and a feeling of triumph for completing these long marches, my feelings and attitude towards the men became brash. Resentment grew among them. I learned from Ramsey to never be weak but to be tough. The men will respect and fear you. Being soft, you will be disrespected and deceived. I thought I'd earn their admiration for making it this far. Further than the quitters. That at least stood for something. Not once did I try to resign or run away, yet I imagined doing so. But it was foolish thinking. If I made it this far already, why not continue? Why not finish what I had started? There remained only a week left of Basic Training. There was an obligation to fulfill, and I had every intention to see it through. But the glares and the talks were a distraction. The men didn't respect me; they hated me. I admit I perhaps took my role too passionately. Barrack clean up time was inspected with no room for error. Lights-out was always nine o'clock sharp. No exceptions. I yelled at men who I perceived as slackers during exercises and was quick to punish. I often sent Roland to latrine duty. The power assigned to me by Ramsey went to my head. But I did not realize it.

But I must have left a good impression on Ramsey. He kept a watchful eye and was swift to correct any mistake I made regarding my duty as Troop Leader. I believe the purpose of assigning someone this onerous task is to test the man, whom the sergeant considers could make a capable leader. This opportunity allows a chance for building skills in toughness, leadership, and authority. These skills would be an absolute necessity if a soldier wished to move up in rank. Even though I didn't want the job at first, but now I was proud to be in my current position despite the extra work and stares of resentment from the other recruits. This would be a great convenience to show the army I have what it takes to be an NCO.

But it was a long and challenging road ahead of me if I wished to go down that route. The idea of me becoming an NCO was first ignited on that day I met with the recruiter—Staff Sergeant Charley Ward. He had an exceptional way of reaching out with people. He used his skills of conversation and charm to persuade me to work hard to become an officer—and the funny thing is—I didn't realize it until now. Isn't that something? Perhaps it was one of those subliminal messages. An idea can be placed into a person's head unaware, and after a time, that idea blooms, until at last, the idea consumes you. It drives you. So that one, simple idea planted into my mind from Ward about becoming an officer was driving me. It drove me to be the best damn Troop Leader I could be.

I was, however, finding it difficult to balance my personal time and my duties as Troop Leader. The position entrusts me to take on more responsibility, so I became busy every night with my nightly duties, overseeing that everything is in working order promptly to please Ramsey as I mentioned before. There wasn't much time for me every night before lights-out. It had taken me three nights to write my final letter to Mother. It was one week before graduation. I chose to tell Mother I would be home soon to visit for I had put in my request for a week-long furlough after my completion of Basic Training.

I lied in my bed, exhausted one evening after a long day of marching; after sealing the letter to Mother and placing it under my pillow, Roland approached me. He sat down on Lester's bed and gave me a casual expression. This look differed from the looks I always got. His manner was calm: his eyes were soft and courteous, and the expression he wore was peaceful. I didn't know whether I should be worried about this behavior or thankful. But I became perturbed when he did not speak. He only stared at me, and before long, my patience had worn thin. "What is it?" I asked.

"You know, with the way you have been acting," he replied, "I'd say you have your head so far up Ramsey's ass, that you have turned into his little brown-noser."

I decided that it would be best to ignore his comment. He was playing a game with me, and his intention is to get me upset. But I couldn't allow myself to become rattled. "I do what I have to get through training, Roland. Nothing more."

"You're so full of shit, Conroy. I wanted to warn you that you need to watch yourself. Ramsey will not be by your side all the time, holding your hand. Something bad may happen when he is no longer around." A menacing smirk came across Roland's face. The old familiar look slipped through the cracks and exposed itself. His comment made me sit up in my bed.

"Are you threatening me, Roland?" I fumed.

He stood up and peered down at me. His colossal body shadowed over me—his face stern with bitterness; and eyes filled with resentment. I felt small and helpless. "Just watch yourself," he said, pointing a fat finger at me.

Roland returned to his bed, leaving me to contemplate over what he had just said. I looked around the barrack and spotted several other men eavesdropping on our little conversation. Karl and Andrew being two. Some of them went back to what they were doing, and others only presented looks of concern.

But Roland was right. Ramsey wouldn't always be there for me. A fear came over as I tensed up. I thought about Roland's words over and over—and speculated he was threatening me. What was he plotting? When the most opportune moment arrived, he would make his move on me. But what could I do to prepare myself? Another idea occurred: is

Roland only trying to scare me? I didn't know. I wanted to believe his intentions were to frighten me but I knew it not to be true. But I couldn't allow him get to me. Roland acted like a juvenile; an enormous and foolish child wanting to play a game.

———

RAMSEY WAS DECENT ENOUGH to reward every man a weekend pass before our last week of boot camp. All inspections passed on Friday afternoon and we were all rewarded the evening off. I never foresaw this from Ramsey; perhaps the cruel bastard had modesty. But I couldn't help but recognize how unbalanced Ramsey was. His persona made me believe he had a split personality. It was unsafe to assume what would come next: would he lash out for honesty or applause it? Would he be sympathetic for the inability to keep up with the other recruits on runs or condemn it? Ramsey played it both ways. Whether it is intentional or not—it's genius. And I caught on to his plot: always keep the recruits guessing; never allow them to get comfortable. That's how to break them. It all comes down to mind games, and Ramsey was good at it. It all came naturally for him to twist a man's mind around. Twist long enough, and the mind will snap. This made me question his sanity.

The excitement came from all around from all the recruits—the barrack filled with laughter, conversations, and clothes packing as the men prepared to leave for the weekend. I looked forward to getting away from Fort McClellan, even for just a few days. A change of scenery would be good for me. The everyday landscape of the fort grew tiring. I longed for more contact from the outside world. Meet new people and perhaps enjoy the company of a woman.

I chose to go to the nearby town of Anniston and find a room in a hotel for the weekend. I overhead some men were headed there and I wanted to join in. There was still currency left given to me before I left Natchitoches. I stood at my bed, stuffing my duffel bag with clothes and toiletries for my leave when the mail arrived. Ramsey paced down the barrack, flinging mail once again when a white envelope flew on my bed addressed from Mother. I sat down and ripped the envelope open:

Dear Vincent,

I am so proud to learn they have made you Troop Leader. You are growing into a man now. I am happy for you.

But I am sad to say while things are going great with you— things are not going so great here back at the farm. Your father had an outburst when Glenn told us he was leaving the farm to find work elsewhere. He is desperate to learn a trade and work his way into paying for college. As with you, Glenn is a grown man, and we can't keep him here, but your father thinks differently. The two of them had a huge argument, and after it was over, your father and I had a disagreement. Julia cried the whole time. I wasn't sure if I wanted to mention this in the letter because I don't want to upset you, but you have a right to know.

I know your father loves you all but his ego is getting a bit out of hand, and this concerns me. Many times I tried to talk sense into him, but he refuses to listen. He's grown way to stubborn for his good. Not once has he spoke of you since you left until our argument. He says he blames you for Glenn's decision in leaving. I told him he was wrong, and that Glenn is a grown man just like you and that he can make his own decisions. And I even explained to him the Julia will be a woman one day, and she will have to leave us as well, but he doesn't want to understand.

I also spoke to your father about hiring help for the farm because I expect that will be the only thing we can do. Your father and I are getting older, and this makes it difficult to do specific work. I believe a hired worker would solve that. He has said no, but I have been pestering him, and I believe he will let up soon. Eventually, he'll see that that will be our one and only option. I am sorry for expressing all of this, and I wanted to write you a letter that was more cheerful. I am sorry this couldn't be that letter.

Julia still keeps asking about you because she misses her older brother. I am looking forward to seeing you again. I will wait for your return.

All my love,
Mother

Like the first letter I received, I read it a second time and then placed it in my trunk. The contents of the letter did not stray far from my mind as I finished packing for the weekend. Best not to pine over it at the moment. A weekend of rest and relaxation lay ahead of me; an escape from the boring barrack, a modest bed, and an insane drill sergeant. But I couldn't get the letter out of my head. I lacked the capability. The more I said the words to myself, the angrier I got. I noticed I was forcing my clothes into the duffel bag. My head felt hot with anger. I took a few heavy breaths to control my composure in the presence of the men. My hands trembled as I put my last t-shirt in the duffel bag, but I did so calmly.

After zipping the bag up, I slung it over my shoulder and made my way to the front of the barrack, but Ramsey blocked the way out. "Be back here 2000 hours Sunday night," he stated.

"Yes, Drill Sergeant," I replied. "I'll be back here on time."

"Good," he said. "And one more thing before you leave..." Ramsey leaned forward and whispered in my ear. "Go to the pool hall on Fifth Avenue in Anniston and be sure to tell the bartender I sent you. You'll thank me later, but just don't overdo it. You need to be sober and ready for work next week. Got it?"

"You have my word, Drill Sergeant."

"Very good, Private. Dismissed."

I JUMPED ON A SWELTERING HOT BUS and left camp filled with enthusiasm with many other recruits relieved to have a short break away from training. Men laughed aloud, hooped, and hollered for their brief vacation. After spending weeks in a barrack with fifteen other men, I wanted my privacy. A room to myself. So a weekend elsewhere was just what I needed.

My body is sore and stiff from all the long, laborious marches and calisthenics. Ramsey had once made a comment that a soldier fights through the pain no matter what. Aches and pains are never to stop you when the time comes for saving a fellow soldier's life. There is no rest in the army. But rest I desired more than ever. I forgot what rest felt like.

Luckily, the trip to Anniston had not been long. A mere fifteen-minute drive from the fort. Once off the bus, I went in pursuit for the closest hotel. I strolled down the streets with my duffel bag tossed over my shoulder in search of a decent hotel, desperate to beat all the other men from snagging the rooms first.

There's not much to say about Anniston. It's a small humble town with a southern charm that reminded me of Natchitoches: streets lined with tenement houses, modest diners, and pawnshops. The townspeople sat out in chairs on the sidewalks and in front of their homes smoking cigarettes, drinking liquor, and mingling amongst other folks.

I stopped and asked few elderly gentlemen whom I saw standing outside a barbershop for the closest lodging. They directed me to the Wallace Hotel on Fifth Avenue. Ramsey had told me of the pool hall on Fifth, and the Wallace Hotel would be most convenient.

I found Fifth Avenue and entered the Wallace Hotel to check to see if a room was vacant for the weekend. I was in luck—there was, and it was a room for myself. Other recruits were filling into the lobby as the desk clerk handed me the room key. The clerk waved his arms in the air to gain everyone's attention and announced that only a few rooms were available. The men swarmed to the front counter eager to get a room. They shouted and elbowed each other demanding they were the first in line as the clerk struggled to obtain control and organize the situation. I couldn't help but to smile as I shoved my room key into my trouser pocket and made my way up the stairs to the second floor.

The hotel would be the perfect remedy for my well-deserved leisure. The little currency I had would be used to purchase meals, since I could drink all I wanted from the pool hall—thanks to Ramsey.

I set my duffel bag inside my room and locked the door securely. Men still shouted in the lobby downstairs as I exited the hotel. I stopped at a small dinner for food close to the hotel and ordered a chicken-fried steak with gravy, mashed potatoes, and a glass of sweet tea. The food was delicious. For a few days, I am free from the bland army meals I received from the mess hall. I told the waitress that served me I would come again. She beamed at me with large brown eyes. Her long blonde hair hung over a cheerful and neat face. She looked older than myself, but I couldn't help myself but to flirt. I had not been with a woman in over seven weeks, so urges are hard to resist. But my teasing proved to be useless once I saw the wedding ring on her left hand. I tipped her a quarter anyway leaving the diner and made my way to the pool hall.

The air inside was thick with cigarette and cigar smoke. Local gentleman and recruits filled the rooms, drinking with no regrets and speaking out loud to one another with vague obscenities. The sound of pool balls clacked as a game of billiards was underway in the back of the room.

I took an empty stool at the bar as the bartender hobbled over. "What'll it be?" he asked. He was tall and stout, similar to Roland's build but seemed far less dangerous. He was also much older than Roland which I believed shifted the pleasantness in how I regarded him. A gentle giant sort of speak.

"A beer," I replied. He poured a mug of beer as if it was an art form and set it down in front of me. "Paul Ramsey sent me."

The bartender looked me over a little. "You come from Fort McClellan?" he asked.

"That's right," I said. "I'm Ramsey's Troop Leader."

"I had you figured for an army man."

"My uniform must have given it away," I said as I chuckled.

"You could say that. Well, drink up then. There's plenty more where that came from," he said while pointing at the mug of beer in front of me.

"Thanks."

"You bet," he said as he shuffled away to serve other men sitting at the bar.

It was so I took my first sip of beer. The flavor I discovered to be crisp and invigorating. Taking the initial sip of beer is never forgotten. This is what I needed because the beer was keeping my thoughts away from my mother's letter. I closed my eyes and only tried to imagine life after Basic Training was over. Where would I be sent to next? Sinister things were escalating over in Europe. Germany's leader—Adolf Hitler had been opposing the treaties after the Great War and invaded Czechoslo-vakia. And because of this, tensions were rising between other European countries and Germany—particularly Great Britain. Newspapers and radio shows filled the headlines with this information every day.

I continued to drink my beer in vital silence as I glanced around the room. The observation led me to believe drunkards and smokers filled this place come here to escape the realities of their lives. This place was their haven, perhaps their only haven. It's their place to escape their wives and children, if only for a short period. It's their place to drink their troubles away and feel untouchable from life—even for a moment. I felt it too. Everyone deserves that peace—peace from worries and the mundane repetition of their daily lives. How extraordinary that can happen in a place like this; a smoky run down old building where all cares can be set aside.

I had finished my first mug of beer, and the bartender (whose name I found out was Bert) poured me another. The fuzziness of the alcohol crept through my body as I sipped my second round and got lost in thought once again; this time about the field back home. How I yearned to back under the huge oak tree and how I wished to see the field light up again with fireflies. Thoughts of Aren and Katrina flashed in front of me. I imagined us having a picnic under the oak tree like we once did before years ago. My eyes closed and saw it and for a brief, content moment of time, it all seemed so real.

Then came an abrupt shout that broke my thoughts as my eyes popped open to see Roland along with Lester and Arthur Bates, standing not far away from me. Roland appeared to be drunk. His large head nodded as he struggled to keep his eyes open. He stood out from everyone else because of his huge frame. How long had they been standing there? They must not have taken notice of me. I kept my head low and went back to drinking my beer, trying to avoid any confrontation with him.

I tuned out the squabbling of the room as I did before until a couple of fingers jabbed me in my back. "Didn't you hear me?" a voice said. "What brings your sorry ass here, Conroy?" It was then I realized that Roland must have been speaking to me, but I did not hear him.

"Mind your own business, Roland," I replied as I glanced at him. "I'm just here to have a few drinks and relax. I'm not looking for any trouble."

Roland let out his boisterous laugh. "You're not looking for any trouble?! Well, you've caused me nothing *but* trouble!"

His speech was slurred, and at this point, I could see just how inebriated he is. "Please let me be, Roland," I demanded. "I recommend you find a place to sleep. You're obviously drunk."

Lester and Arthur took hold of Roland's shoulders and tried to pull him away, but Roland shoved them both off with his strong arms. "Are you trying to tell me what to do? We're not at the fort right now, so you have no authority over me. I can do whatever the hell I want, and you cannot say otherwise!"

"I only recommended it, Roland. And you're kind of making a scene here." Indeed he was. The patrons stared at us because of Roland's obnoxious shouting. I couldn't help but to feel embarrassed as I could feel my cheeks burn red.

Lester took hold of Roland's arm and tried to pull him away from me. "Come on, Roland. Let's get out of here."

Roland used both of his hands and shoved Lester away from him, forcing him to trip over a bystander's feet while stumbling backwards and then he hit the floor hard on his rear. Arthur rushed over to help Lester up. I stood up to face Roland, who was being nothing more than a bully. Roland jabbed me in the chest with his finger. "Didn't I say to you the first chance we get I would take you out for your first beer?" He reached behind me and grabbed my mug. "Well, have a beer on me!" Roland splashed the beer in my face and whooped. He handed me the empty mug. "There! It's on me!" The pool hall had grown silent and now the patrons watched the unpleasant scene taking place before them. I only stood there, wiping the beer off my face with my hand. Roland laughed right in my face and then took his eyes off of me to look around at everyone to encourage them to laugh with him, but there was not even a chuckle. "Come on! That's funny, right?" With Roland occupied with the other patrons, he left himself wide open for an attack.

This was all I needed.

With one swift motion, I punched Roland right in his thick stomach when he didn't expect it and then smashed the beer mug on his nose. Shards of glass flew all around. He gasped for air as he covered his face with his huge hands as blood seeped through his fingers. I then pushed him with all of my strength away from me, forcing him to stumble backward and fall onto a table. The top of the table broke from its legs and shot up, hitting Roland in the back of his head. He fell hard onto the floor and remained still as blood gushed from his nose. Lester and Arthur rushed over to check on him. Sweat poured down my face as my anger reached an unusual level. A frightening level.

"Get him out of here and let him sleep it off!" I scowled at Lester and Arthur. The two didn't object as they both tried to pull Roland by his heavy shoulders but failed, so instead they each grabbed him by a leg and pulled him as his head thumped on the floor of the uneven floorboards out the door.

Afterwards, everyone returned to their drinking, talking, and billiard games. The feeling of embarrassment still lingered. Bert looked at me with bewilderment on his face. "What do they teach you in the army these days?" he asked.

I didn't answer as I guessed it was just a rhetorical question. "I'm sorry about all of this. What's the damage to the table?" I asked while holding up currency. I glanced all around at the broken bits of glass on the floor. "And for the mug?" I wanted to pay for the damages and be as friendly as possible on account I didn't want the police getting involved or even the army. If word would get out about this incident—I could be court-martialed.

"Don't you worry about it," he said. "I saw the whole thing, and it wasn't your fault. The bastard had it coming."

"Are you sure? It's no problem if I pay for it."

"Your money is no good here. But I have to confess though—this has been the most exciting night here in a long time."

I gave him a chuckle and apologized once again before leaving. I thought it was best for me to call it a night and return to the Wallace Hotel for the evening. The sun had now set and the evening air felt cool on my skin. I was victorious for the moment, but there will come another time I would have to fight Roland again. He won't let this one skirmish slip past him. I may have won this round, but next time, Roland will know better than to be inebriated to fight me again. But Bert was right. The bastard had it coming.

The haziness of the alcohol hit me as I entered the Wallace Hotel. Drowsiness had draped over me as I took it step by step up the stairs to my room. Upon entering, I locked the door firmly behind me, due to a ridiculous fear of Roland bursting through the door, wanting to go round two in a fight. I opened the one window in the room to allow a breeze to come through. By the window was the bed. A large bed. I stripped off all my clothes and climbed in on top of the sheets and blankets naked. It was too hot. But how great that large bed felt as I slipped away for the night.

ELEVEN

I DIDN'T SEE ROLAND until I returned to Fort McClellan on Sunday evening after catching a bus with the other recruits leaving Anniston. Our weekend of freedom was over. A feeling of dread came when it was time to return to camp, but my undesirable return was inevitable. I wished the short bus ride had taken longer. Why couldn't have there been a breakdown or a flat tire? Any delay would have been a blessing. But no setback came, and the bus arrived at camp on time, and with an agonizing hesitation, I stepped off the bus with the other recruits who walked in my same shoes. The men grumbled and cursed amongst themselves as we all arrived at camp and reported to our barrack. But the bright side for our return: there remained only one week of Basic Training to go. And what a long seven weeks it has been.

Roland sat on his bed as I went inside the barrack; his nose was bandaged, and both eyes were surrounded with a subtle shade of black. His face displayed an expression of anger. I stifled a laugh as I tried my best to hold it in. He glared at me with fury as I walked past him. I tossed my duffel bag on my bed and unpacked.

Ramsey came in the barrack and immediately called everyone to attention. In an instant, all the recruits did as they were instructed. Ramsey strolled past the beds and halted when he spotted Roland's bandaged nose. "What happened, Private?" he asked, "Wouldn't pay the hooker?" Every recruit snickered, including me.

I expected to get a scorning glare from Roland but instead, his blackened eyes remained attached to Ramsey. There was no amusement in his face. His expression told me he felt humiliated and irate. There was to be no more buffoonery—only sheer determination. Determination to make me pay for what I had done to him in the pool hall. I turned into a target. That's what I came to understand. He needn't look at me to tell me this. It was all in his face, his eyes, and his manner.

A smirk appeared across Ramsey's face as he continued his stroll through the barrack. "Everyone is here!" Ramsey shouted. "Excellent! As you know, ladies—this is your final week of Basic Training. And for this week, I will push you harder than you have ever been pushed. It is my duty to turn you into soldiers, and by god, I am going to that. You all graduate on Friday, so on Thursday at 1900 hours—I will speak with each one of you about your impending profession for the National Guard. After you leave here, you will go into your next stage of training. You will learn how to do the specific job you signed up for when you enlisted. Work hard, and you may move up in rank as NCO's. I ask one thing from all of you and one thing only: don't let me down. Now is that understood?" Ramsey's words were genuine and his tone honest. These words came from a man who was ruthless but dedicated to doing his job correctly. Maybe there was human in him.

"Yes, Drill Sergeant!" everyone shouted.

"Wonderful! You all have one hour before lights-out. As you were!"

——

BEFORE LIGHTS-OUT, I showered and shaved and afterwards, propped my head on my pillow, missing the hotel bed I slept in the preceding two nights. I felt well rested but there were a few aches and pains that lingered, so I did not look forward to the eventual remaining five days of boot camp. Ramsey clarified we all were to be pushed harder than we had ever been. But how hard? The unwanted feeling of dismay came. Will I be prepared for the final week of training? The more I stressed over the forthcoming week, the more I wanted it to be over. Perhaps one more good night's rest should do the trick. That's all I needed. By early tomorrow morning, I will wake up refreshed and determined.

I relaxed, for I knew, I stressed over nothing. I wasn't expecting Ramsey to murder all the recruits. He is perhaps insane, but he isn't that insane. Then came a hasty speculation that Ramsey was trying to play us with one of his cruel mind games. A trick. The week to come will be challenging but to what extreme? I couldn't allow him to get in my head and stress over nothing. I'm prepared. In fact, I'm more than ready. I chased away the butterflies in my stomach.

I checked my wristwatch—only twenty minutes before lights out. With tired and heavy feet, I paced throughout the barrack for a brief inspection. All the recruits had finished their showers and now lingered about or lied in their beds. I found everything in order except Roland was nowhere to be found. I checked the showers and latrine but no trace of him. He seemed to have vanished. The men had seen not him, including Lester. But Arthur, the other recruit drinking with Roland at the pool hall had information for me.

"I watched him leave out the front not over five minutes ago when you were busy with your inspection," Arthur spoke with arrogance. He lied down on his bed with his fingers clasped together under his head. He peered at me with his thin brown eyes set tight in his bony face. Perhaps he's angry with me for smashing Roland's nose.

"He did not comment on where he was going?" I inquired.

Arthur squinted at me. "No. He just left. I guess you have to find him yourself."

I didn't have much of a decision in this issue I had with Roland but to leave the barrack in search of him. He needed to be found and brought back before lights-out. The option of reporting to Ramsey on this matter was out of the question in fear of the resentment I would receive for the lack of supervision I had. He would be furious with me for not handling this situation myself.

There is one thing I want to point out: I am not stupid. I imagined Roland hiding somewhere outside, waiting to ambush me once I exit the barrack. Perhaps this is all a ploy he devised to do me some payback. But what choice did I really have? Disturbing Ramsey is unthinkable, so I had no choice but to go it alone. Or did I? I needed back up. Arthur and Lester wouldn't do it. The two of them became Roland's lackeys in a way. And I didn't know the other men all that well. But Karl and Andrew would help. I hoped they would provide me another hand as they did at the shooting range. I'm not ashamed to say I was scared of leaving the barrack alone. Yes, I was scared. Scared of Roland.

But for some odd and unexplainable reason, I left behind the barrack in search of Roland without Karl and Andrew's help. Doing so could be a mistake. A careless mistake, but seeking help would make me appear weak. No, this was my mess I got myself into, and this is my mess I must deal with on my own. I only hope to have a reasonable argument with Roland before he did anything irrational. It was worth a shot.

I proceeded outside and stepped around the other barracks in the area with no luck in finding Roland. No other soul moved about in the night time. I could hear conversing and laughing from the neighboring barracks—the men inside them are going about their nightly duties before lights-out. I could also hear the faint sound of cards being shuffled—a game of poker was being played. After several minutes of exploring, I spotted a huge figure standing below a bright barn light hanging from the top of a shed. After the figure saw me, he made a dash behind the shed and out of sight. I knew it had to be Roland. But why did he let me see him? I now regretted my decision in not asking for any help. But I couldn't turn back now. Time was running out. I needed to get Roland back to the barrack before anyone would notice we were missing and we would both encounter the wrath of Ramsey.

I had to be cautious.

I took light steps past the shed light towards the rear of the shed. Moths fluttered about in the bright light from above. No need to rush, there is still a little time. I leaned my back against the boarded wall of the shed and peeked my head around the corner. Roland disappeared. Disappointment came over me. But before I could turn around, an arm reached around me and put me in a bear hug while another hand cov- ered my mouth. "You try to yell, and I'll snap your neck," a menacing voice said. It was Roland. I know that voice from anywhere. I tried to break free, but his hold on me was tight. He carried me behind the shed and then bashed me in the chest again and again with his thick arm while keeping his other hand over my mouth. I tried to claw at his face and grab hold of his injured nose, but it was to no avail. I struggled to break free from Roland's hold but failed. Before I knew it, I'm thrown to the ground with a great force, and then I was kicked violently in the chest many times. There was no chance for me to defend myself as I had been so trained. My defenses were weak and pointless as I tried to pro- tect my body with my arms. A strong kick to the stomach knocked the wind out of me, so the only sound I made were gasps for air. It proved useless for me to put up any sort of fight. All I could do was take the punishment. Roland was too much for me to handle. I didn't have a chance. Then with one swift, sharp kick to the side of my head, I fell on my back—beaten.

My head spun from the kick as I went in and out of consciousness. Nausea came. The pain in my body grew intense. It felt as though I had a possible fractured rib or two. I somewhat returned to my senses as air filled my lungs once again. "Now we're even you cheeky son of a bitch," Roland said as he crouched over me. "I warned you I would beat your ass black and blue. And if you mention any of this to anyone, especially Ramsey—I *will* kill you." I didn't look at him. I couldn't look him in the eye not after what he had done. He grabbed my chin and jerked my head towards him. "Understand?" His eyes pierced deep into mine. I stared into the eyes of a raving sociopath. I wanted to break away from his grasp, but his grip on me was secure.

I feared he really would kill me if I spoke to anyone about what just happened. Roland showed his brute force, and I knew I had gotten lucky a few days ago in the bar. I caught him off guard. He was inebriated. I was a little drunk myself, but at least I kept my wits. But now, he had the upper hand. The chances of winning in an equal fight against this huge man were inexistent. Maybe, just maybe I hoped this would be the end of our feud and let bygones be bygones. He said we were even, and I wanted nothing more to do with him.

"So this is what will happen—" he continued to speak with his hand clasped on my chin, "we are going back to our barrack together and walk in together. I left no bruising on your face so suspicion won't arise amongst the other men. If anyone asks, we are to say we only had a minor discussion in private. I can see you are in pain, but you better try to hide it. I believe we only have a few more minutes to get back to the tent before lights-out so remember what I said." Roland's voice was sincere and threatening. It came to me he had all of this planned out. He intended to keep his beatings away from face and only focus on my body for the punishment. I realized perhaps he was intelligent—something I did not expect.

Roland seized me from underneath my arms and pulled me up. I grimaced as pain shot through me. My ability to walk straight due to being kicked in the head proved problematic. Roland took hold of me. "Get it together, Conroy. Walk straight and upright."

The dizziness wore off as soon as we got to the barrack. "Remember what I said," he whispered as he opened the flap and gestured for me to walk in first.

I stood up straight as I went inside, trying my best to hide the pain I was in. I recall little about making it to my bed. I could, however, feel eyes on me. Many eyes, as if the men's suspicions were getting the better of them. Arthur knew and perhaps Lester. But what of the other men? There were whispers. But I didn't care. I knew Roland's beating couldn't remain a secret. Secrets can't be kept among all the recruits in the barrack. If they didn't know now of the incident that occurred out-side just moments before, they would know soon enough. Word will spread—from either Lester or Arthur. Perhaps from the both of them. Or Roland will laugh about it one day in the mess hall to mock me. Yes, word will get out. It's only a matter of time.

This is not how I wanted to begin the final week of boot camp.

TWELVE

FRIDAY, LATE AFTERNOON—the day had been bright and hot—so hot, it became difficult to breathe. It's a dreadful feeling of trying to inhale fresh air, but all you get is warm, sticky air instead. I cringed at every deep breath I took. The bruising on my body began to vanish slowly throughout the passing days, but the pain was still there.

It's the final hours of training. The final test. All recruits held in formation just outside the camp as Ramsey stood firm and faced everyone. We were all dressed in our beige uniforms in full gear, carrying a forty-five-pound pack on our backs. "You've all made it this far, and I'm damn proud of it. All of you only have one last task to complete—and that is a twenty-five mile forced march. We will start here, and we will end here. Now during this march—no one, and I mean absolutely no one, is to take a drink from their canteen. Doing so will cause harsh punishments. If you accomplish this task—you will be a full-fledged United States Army soldier for the National Guard. Questions?" No one said a word, and after a moment, Ramsey spoke again. "Good. Now let's get to it." There came no shouts from Ramsey. Instead, he talked in a benevolent tone.

The march began, and since I was the Troop Leader, I marched at the front of the line as Ramsey did so in the back to keep his eyes on any water drinkers. Keeping the recruits from drinking water during a very lengthy forced march on a hot day is torture. Ramsey perhaps had intentions to kill us. If so, I believed it. But it wouldn't be long before the daylight departs and the air would become cooler.

We started on the usual trails that circled the camp but eventually, we marched off into unfamiliar territory. Ramsey would bark an order at me on where to turn off the trail onto another trail that leads to another. It would be too easy for a man to become lost in this endless maze of trails if he didn't know where he was going. But he had fascinated me yet again; his knowledge of these trails was remarkable. I couldn't help but wonder if he made a habit of running these trails throughout the years. Perhaps he knew the trails like the back of his hand. The layout is all embedded in his mind like an unseen visual map that knew every fork, turn off, and mileage.

I was in rough shape just a couple miles in. The illusion of being unfit to complete the final test stimulated my morale. But I knew I had to keep going. I couldn't stop.

Roland had been responsible for causing the final week of Basic Training a painful and problematic challenge. The damage inflicted on me from Roland's beating put me in doubts on whether I was capable of finishing the week. Sure, I could run to Ramsey and inform him what took place and have Roland kicked out of the army, but I assumed that all of this was my fault. In truth, I delivered the first punch at the pool hall, but Roland provoked me with his taunting and then splashed beer in my face. Smashing the mug in his face had not been my wisest decision, and I could have dealt with the situation better but for the sake of my argument, I was inebriated and being inebriated can drive a man to take regrettable actions. I learned this the hard way.

I took a beating from Roland and had injuries to show for it. It proved difficult to hide my bruising from the other men in the showers. I learned this the day after Roland had attacked me. The only solution I came up with is wait until everyone else was done with their showers and then I would go in last to take mine. I hoped the cold water would help with the healing. After I finished my wash on Monday morning before our daily run, Karl and Andrew came searching for me after I disappeared from the barrack. I wrapped myself with a towel around the waist as Karl and Andrew examined my injuries; shades of blue and purple, near black painted my chest and ribs. My ribs were most sensitive. No matter how much I didn't want to believe it, but I feared a few may have been broken.

And with no excuses, I revealed what had happened. "Tell Ramsey," Karl said as he eyed my body over.

"... No," I said with hesitation. "Not even a doctor. I'll get put behind if I say anything—and who knows where I'll end up if that happens. And besides—I'm not a snitch. What will the men think of me if I go babblin' to Ramsey about what happened?"

"Well then just give me the word, Vince. And I'll put a stomping up Roland's ass for you," Andrew said. "I'm sure I can take him. He may be a big guy, sure—but he's just a pushover. And a pussy at that. What kind of man ambushes someone from behind?"

"Take it easy, Andrew," Karl advised. "No one here is gonna start a fight with Roland."

"Well, he sure as hell can't get away with this!" Andrew snapped. "That bastard needs a good ass-kicking!"

"And I suppose you'll be the one to do it?" Karl inquired.

"You're damn right!" Andrew grunted with barred teeth. "I just said I would!"

"Just calm down!" I demanded. "Look—I appreciate that you guys want to help but I'm afraid if you confront Roland or Ramsey about this, it's only gonna make things worse. This is my problem and not yours."

Karl sighed and placed his hand on my shoulder and gave it a slight squeeze. "I hope you know what you're doing. If he threatens you again or lay another finger on you—say something to Ramsey." I gave him a nod of understanding. It bewildered me that Karl took to me the way he did. There are few living bodies on this earth that possessed the same vigilant personality he had. He offered me a tender and comforting smile that lifted my spirits. "Let's get out of here before Ramsey begins the morning run," He slapped Andrew on the shoulder and walked out the showers.

Andrew said nothing more. He shrugged his shoulders and shook his head at me before following Karl out. They left me alone in the showers. I carefully slipped my undershirt and underwear on and before I left, I considered my options. Perhaps I should see a doctor. But what lie could I give him about how I had sustained my injuries? And Roland made his threat quite clear: I was not to inform anyone what had happened or he would kill me. But is he really capable of killing? Or perhaps he only made the threat just to frighten me? I lacked the courage, however, to challenge that threat. Roland had made an example out of me. Whether there was truth behind the threat, Roland proved he was not to be intimidated and brushed aside. At the moment, he was in control. I knew it. He knew it. But I wouldn't allow Roland to win. I was down but not out. With one week to go, determination awakened me to finish no matter what condition I was in, no matter how painful it would be. Yes, it will be tough but I must carry on.

I must finish.

That morning, Ramsey strolled up and down the front row of men as he regularly did as we all stood outside the barrack in formation. His presence seemed different from usual: tenacious and more focused. I knew then all of us weren't dealing with the same Ramsey we came to known. He had now shifted to a darker being that was hell-bent on crushing everyone's spirit. His body language and irate facial expression said it all. At any moment, I expected him to start foaming at the mouth like a rabid dog I always visualized him as.

"Listen up, ladies!" Ramsey shouted. "As you all know—this is your final week of Basic Training. Just because this is the final week, doesn't mean I will take it easy on you; quite the opposite, actually. The final stage is to test how much you have learned during your entire tenure here at the fort. I guess you can say—it's just one large, grueling test." Ramsey stopped pacing and stood in the center of the front line facing the men. "Now, I have worked too damn long and too damn hard with every one of you just to have one—two—maybe three of you to disappoint me by failing this final week. Because *if* you fail—you do not only make yourself appear incompetent, but you will also make me look bad. And I cannot allow that! So failure is not an option!" His voice roared with devotion and sincerity. "Because no one ever makes me look bad! So I want all of you to remember this: if you fail—it will be the biggest mistake of your pathetic life. Because you will have *me* to answer to. Now, do I make myself clear?!"

"Yes, Drill Sergeant!" we all shouted.

"Good. . . now let's get to it."

And as it turned out, Ramsey was a man of his word. He drove everyone harder than we had ever been before. Each day just as intense as the next. Every activity we performed at camp was put to the test: calisthenics, map reading, hand-to-hand combat, bayonet exercises, target practice, obstacle courses, and so on and so on. And no mistakes were allowed or Ramsey's wrath would be unleashed.

My daily exercises jogs, and runs were painful due to my injuries. Doubts about not having the strength to finish the week plagued me, but I was determined to finish or die trying. Hand-to-hand combat drills were excruciatingly painful; the sharp pain restrained me from fighting to my full potential. Karl volunteered to skirmish with me on account of wanting to protect me, but even as he held back, the drill proved difficult. But I continued. I did my best to not show any signs of weakness to Roland for I wanted to prove I am strong enough to overcome the grueling training, just to detest him. I wanted to demonstrate that his ambush on me would not force me to fail, no matter how much damage he inflicted on me.

But for the entire week, I cursed Roland under my breath for what he had done. His observant eyes watched me at all times, laughing at me behind my back. I caught him making casual glances at me with a smug look upon his face, knowing the pain I endured, enjoying as I suffered. For he wanted me to. He wanted the last laugh, but my determination drove me further each day.

I will get the last laugh.

And as the last march continued, Ramsey returned to his old cruel ways and taunted everyone with obscenities—one of the mind games he liked to perform throughout my entire time in Basic Training. But I tried not to focus on Ramsey's insults. My focus was on finishing the march. It became worse when he taunted us by drinking out of his canteen. He even dared us to take a drink from our own, but no one was foolish enough to do so.

Sweat streamed down my face as the sunlight, and hot air burned my skin. Several times, the heat tempted me to sneak a quick sip from my canteen, but my conscience would get the better of me. Ramsey would notice, and I would pay the price. But every man has his limits and mine were being tested.

The march continued and the heat began to drop as the sun made its descent. The desired relief came over me. The miles racked up until there were only several more left to go. I knew this on account of Ramsey shouting out the countdown. If only I could rest. If only I could take a drink out of my canteen—I would feel better. Drenched with sweat, my body stiff and in pain—all I could think of was jumping in a deep cold lake. I kept that image of a crisp blue lake in my head for the duration of the march. I imagined there being a lake and a drink of cold water waiting for me at the end. The lake and a glass of water was the reward. I must claim the prize so I pushed on. I pushed on harder and harder. The more my body ached with pain—the harder I marched. I pushed to the very end.

———

THE MARCH WAS AT LAST FINISHED. We were all back where we started—outside the front of the fort. It was dark and the fresh night air stimulated my skin. My eyes are heavy from exhaustion. I died of thirst, along with the other recruits. My backpack seemed ten pounds heavier than it did before. The entire troop along with myself could barely stand up straight in formation. The march had done its number on my injuries, and all I wanted now was to drain the water from my canteen down my throat and get some much needed rest.

Ramsey began pacing left and right in front of the men and halted dead in the center before he spoke. "Congratulations, troops. You all have just completed your twenty-five miles forced march. Now I'm sure everyone one of you is tired and thirsty, so I now authorize you to drink."

Without hesitation, I twisted off my canteen lid as fast as possible and began pouring water down my dry throat. The water wasn't cold, but refreshing. The clear liquid had never tasted so good. After a minute of drinking, Ramsey spoke again. "Every one of you is to return to the barrack and shower. You all have exactly one hour to shower before lights-out. Is that clear?!"

"Yes, Drill Sergeant!" Everyone shouted in unison.

"Good! Now hit the showers!"

———

ALL THE MEN HOOTED AND HOLLERED in the showers, excited to be finished with boot camp. Standing just outside, I would hear the occasional snap of a towel on someone's rear end, followed by a playful scuffle. They were having fun, and they deserved to have it. It's curious how grown men can act like children. But we were to all be soldiers now. That's worth celebrating.

I was the last man to enter the showers after everyone left. The cold shower was stimulating. It now felt like I bathed in that frozen lake I envisioned during the march. This is to be the longest shower I have ever taken. The cold water had a positive effect. I rested under the gentle stream and let it soothe my aches and pains. I needed this moment alone.

Eight weeks of hell was at last over and I could not have been prouder. An instant feeling of gratification came over me. I allowed all of it to sink in. There was an eagerness to leave this camp once and for all; an escape that couldn't come soon enough. After my shower, I put on clean clothes and headed for the barrack to stretch out on my bed. The bed felt soft—softer than I can remember.

The men still had their fun, but eventually, the fun wore down, and the barrack grew quiet before lights-out. Everyone was exhausted after the long day. Yawn after yawn from the recruits was let out one by one as they nestled into their beds. These men I had lived with for eight weeks are now my brothers. Ramsey stated that on the first day. There were, however, mixed feelings on that subject with Roland. I didn't see Roland as a companion, nor will he ever become that. There are no ill regards towards Lester and Arthur; they cowered with fear when it came to performing their roles as Roland's lackeys. It's simple: they feared Roland as I feared him. But in their case, they are too frightened to stand up to him. I expect that my defiance over Roland will someday be a wake-up call for the two. No man can make a name for himself hiding behind another man—a valuable lesson I taught myself.

After inspection, I ordered for lights-out and slipped into bed. I realized this would the last time I would sleep in this little bed. It was a great feeling that this barrack and this bed will be a memory after tonight.

As soon as my head hit the pillow, I closed my eyes and fell fast asleep.

———

EARLY THE NEXT MORNING, Ramsey sent the recruits to the mess hall for our last breakfast at Fort McClellan. Afterwards, we were sent to the National Guard Training Center. There, the superior officers briefed us on what to expect in our advanced training. We all sat in a classroom sitting in chairs listening to them speak for what felt like hours. They explained it to us that Advanced Training will be similar to Basic but we would have considerably more freedom, but are required to keep our-selves in shape, however, and that it was our obligation to do so. I found it difficult to focus on what was being said due to the high anticipations of leaving.

We were at last sent back to our barrack to retrieve our belongings after the lecture was over. Ramsey was there waiting for us. He handed out envelopes to everyone. My envelope contained bus tickets. One tick-et was back home for a week furlough, and the other ticket was to Fort A.P. Hill in Virginia. It relieved me to know they approved my furlough and that I would see my family before leaving for Advanced Training. But Ramsey warned all of us to be at Fort A.P. Hill by a specific date, or there would be consequences.

Afterwards, Ramsey called everyone to attention. "I want to let every one of you know it has been an honor to train you gentleman. You're no longer recruits but United States soldiers." He paused from speaking as he shot a look towards Lester. "I'm very impressed with you, Private Spears; you took a beating from me and yet you did not quit like the other recruits who couldn't tough it out. You should be proud, son." Ramsey took his gaze off Lester and looked right at me. "And you, Pri-vate Conroy—you made one hell of a Troop Leader. You should be proud as well." I gave Ramsey a little smile and nodded my head to return his gesture. "This may be the last time I see you gentleman again. I must remain here to train more recruits in the coming months. You will all meet your captain upon arriving at Fort A.P. Hill. So allow me to say one more thing before I dismiss you: you're doing your country a service. Now there are rumors about war possibly breaking out over in Europe. Some man named Adolf Hitler is causing a lot of commotion, and by the looks of it, he doesn't wish to settle down—not anytime soon that is.

"And if that time comes and you all get called for your duty to go to war, you shouldn't be scared. You should be fierce. You should be strong. You should be willing to die for your country if that time came. No man should join the army if he is afraid of death. Dying in battle is an honor. It's a privilege. If you die in action—you will die a hero, and that is what you will be remembered as—a hero. Die a hero. If you can do that—you will never be forgotten."

Ramsey's words struck me as poetic and passionate. This had been a side of him I never witnessed. And then, at last, he said the one word I was desperate to hear. "Dismissed!" he shouted with a salute. We all returned his salute as I could see the pride in Ramsey's eyes. He looked proud. He reminded me of a proud father watching his sons leave to face new challenges. But he would get a new recruits to train soon enough, and we would just be a distant memory.

———

I STOOD OUTSIDE FORT MCCLELLAN as the bus arrived. There was no bitter sadness about leaving; I never want to see this place again. Fort McClellan will be a memory and nothing more for I was eager to return to Louisiana. A long bus ride lay ahead of me. I said my temporary goodbye's to Karl and Andrew and a few of the other men. They had other buses to catch; different destinations ahead of them. Before I stepped onto the bus that would take me home, I took sight of Roland glaring at me from a distance. I smiled at him. A sarcastic and cocky smile that would perturb him. A smile that told him I couldn't be beaten, and he had lost.

Roland looked away from me as I stepped onto the bus. I took an empty seat near the rear and rested my head on the window as the bus drove off. The men I had ridden with after leaving Natchitoches now joined me on the trip home. I daydreamed of returning to the farm, seeing myself hugging Mother and shaking Glenn's hand. I could see Julia running into my arms as I pick her up to give a huge hug.

Boot camp was over, and now there's time for my wounds to heal.

THIRTEEN

AFTER HOURS OF TRAVELING, the bus arrived at the station in Natchitoches after 8 pm. I stepped off the bus and stretched my legs, thankful the long ride was over. The depot was quiet and near empty from travelers save the recruits and myself. I said my temporary good-byes to them before renting a storage locker from the clerk. I placed the items I wouldn't need for the week inside and the remaining items: clothes, toiletries, and Julia's teddy bear I purchased at a small toy store in Jackson, Mississippi on the way to Natchitoches, into my duffel bag.

It was too late in the evening to take a walk to the farm; exhausted and wanting a comfy bed to lie in, I decided I would take the walk the next day, bright and early, to make my surprise return home. With the hours free to myself, I walked through the busy late afternoon streets of Natchitoches. Crowds of men and women dressed in their finest clothes prowled the lighted streets with energy in the waning hours of the day's heat. A long and entertaining night was laid out ahead of them. The traces of the depression seemed to have not mattered as patrons filled the few bars I passed, drinking the night away.

I made a stop at the Nakatosh Hotel on Front Street, which fortunately was just a short stroll from the bus station. Once inside, I reserved a room with the pay I received from completing Basic Training, and the clerk had a bellman carry my duffel bag to my room. I then located a bar inside the hotel and thought I could help myself to a couple of drinks before calling it a night.

The air was thick and smoky with potent cigar and cigarette smoke. It made my eyes water. Jazz music played from a radio placed next to a shelf filled with beer mugs. I sat down at the empty counter and the barkeep—a thin elderly man with dark brown skin and thick, springy silver hair, who was wiping down the counter took, notice of me and limped over.

"So what'll be, sir?" he asked with a warm smile and raspy voice. He had a welcoming personality—the sort I would not expect from a barman serving drunks on a nightly basis.

"Just a beer," I replied.

"Coming right up." He poured me a mug of beer and set in front of me. I handed him a dime for the drink and took a few sips of the cold alcoholic liquid. The barkeep limped away and proceeded to wipe down the counter. After a few minutes, he came back. "You an army man?" he asked.

"Yup," I replied. My uniform must have given it away. "Just finished Basic Training. I'm on leave before I leave for Virginia. That's where I've been assigned."

"Well, congratulations. You from around here originally?"

"I lived on a small farm just outside town. I'm heading there tomorrow to visit family. They will be excited to see me because they don't even know I'm here."

"Is that so? Well, you showing up should make for one hell of a surprise for 'em. Especially looking all nice and handsome in that uniform you wearin'." I smiled. "Well, if there's anything else you need—don't hesitate to ask. The name's Frederick."

"Thanks, Frederick," I said as I shook his heavily callused hand, which told me he must have lived a long life filled with hard work—

which could have explained his limp. Frederick returned a friendly smile and started serving patrons sitting down at the counter. I went back to drinking my beer.

A few mugs of beers later, the bar became crowded with more patrons as the minutes passed. Loud chatting and laughter and jazz music bursting from the radio made my ears ring. The smoky air became thicker and warmer. I loosened up my tie and unfastened the top buttons of my shirt so I wouldn't overheat.

I continued to drink my beer in peace, keeping my head low, choosing to stay away from socializing until I heard a woman's voice pass through the calamities of the other patrons' conversations. "Would you mind buying a lady a drink?"

My head shot up, and I turned to my right to meet eyes with a beautiful woman sitting next to me. She had straight and long red hair that commended her charming face. Her lips were concealed with crimson lipstick, and her green eyes were complimented with long eyelashes. Her petite frame balanced out the fancy dark red gown she wore. I wasn't sure of her age, but I would have guessed around my age or just a little younger than myself. She didn't appear too young but had traits of a more mature personality. "I'm sorry, I didn't mean to interrupt. You looked like as if you were deep in thought," she said with an inviting grin.

"Um, no actually, just the opposite. I wasn't thinking at all."

She smiled and rested her face on her hand with her elbow resting on the counter as she gazed at me with notable curiosity. "So are you going to buy me a drink or not?" she asked after a moment of staring.

"Oh, sure," I said without hesitation. I called over to Frederick who limped over after finishing serving a couple of men sitting at the counter.

"So what'll it be?" Frederick asked.

I noticed my mug was almost empty. "Another beer for me and whatever the lady is having."

"Scotch on the rocks," she said in a sly way. Frederick left us and returned with our drinks a minute later. After I paid, he left us again to continue his busy work for the evening.

"From the looks of you, I'd say you are in the military," she said. "Dangerous lifestyle isn't it?" She raised an eyebrow and took a sip of the scotch out of her glass. The ice cubes rattled as she set the glass down on the counter.

"I guess you can say that," I said after taking a sip of beer. "It isn't so dangerous as long as there are no wars to be fought. And I'd say by the looks of you; you must love the color red?"

She leaned her head back, letting her long hair fall from her shoulders as she laughed. "Oh! You are a sly one aren't you?"

She stared at me, not answering my question. We sat in silence as the scene grew awkward. "So what is it you do?" I asked, desperate to start a conversation with this beautiful woman sitting next to me.

"Me? Oh, let's just say I have had quite a few occupations throughout the years. I've done this and that. But never found my true calling." The more she talked, the more I realized how alluring her voice was. Her words were soft and dreamy, as if her mood could put someone's anger and troubles at ease. She had a natural behavior that some men would find seductive. "How come I've never seen you around before?"

"My folks run a small farm just outside town. That's where I grew up. Never really had any reasons to visit except to help my father with selling produce."

"Well, that's too bad," she pouted. "But you're here now." She perked up and took a sip of her drink. "And you're here with me having a nice chat over some drinks." It impressed me she could drink such a strong alcoholic beverage such as scotch. I always thought of it as a manly drink.

This evening I thought I wanted to be alone, but I guess a few words with a charming woman wouldn't hurt. And it felt nice to have a little company.

The woman opened her purse and took out a small, slender metal case. She opened it and took out a cigarette. "Cigarette?" she offered while holding it up.

"No thanks," I replied. "I don't smoke."

She shrugged her shoulders and lit the cigarette in her mouth and took a deep drag and blew the smoke out across the counter. "I guess that would be a good thing since you are in the army and all. So tell me... what's the army like?"

"It's nothing spectacular. Shoot guns, run, march, and get yelled at a lot."

The woman let out a soft laugh. "You're funny." I wasn't sure why she thought I was funny because what I said was the absolute truth. She kept her eyes glued to mine with a quirky smile spread across her polished red lips.

I tried to keep our little talk going. I felt it was getting too awkward with neither of us saying anything as it was moments ago. "So do you live close by?" That was all I could muster to say. I feared now she would only think of me as a fool who didn't know how to speak to women. Her presence influenced me like nothing I had ever felt before. I became flustered. Here was a beautiful woman sitting next to me in a bar and we're having drinks together, and I couldn't think of anything to say to her.

"I have an apartment just a few blocks away from here," she said taking a sip of her drink. "I like to come in here once a night and mingle with people." She winked at me.

My anxiety lifted. She didn't seem to resent my boring question. She seemed to enjoy our small talk. I loosened up a little more, feeling comfortable with her. "Are you here by yourself tonight or are you waiting for someone?" I inquired.

"I'm alone tonight—well until I sat down next to you," she said with pleasure as she gently touched my thigh. "Did I mention how handsome you look in that uniform?" Her seductive tone had cast its spell, and I became seduced. I'm embarrassed to admit how simple it is for the opposite sex to seduce me. She leaned a little closer. I got a good whiff of her perfume; something I hadn't detected before, perhaps from the overwhelming smell of cigarette and cigar smoke that filled the room. Her perfume scented her with a light fragrance of jasmine. "I don't see a lot of men around here in uniforms, except for men over at the army recruiting office." It was then I noticed she had set her hand on my thigh. She leaned closer with a flirtatious smile on her face. "You look tense. Anything the matter?"

I felt tense from just being in the company of perhaps one of the prettiest women I had ever met. And here she was sitting next to me; speaking with me with her hand on my thigh. I became aroused. "No, I'm ok," I said in a shaky voice. I tried to speak again, but I could do was stammer a little. I felt foolish, as if I was a pathetic virgin who didn't know how to act around a woman. But the thing is: I'm not a virgin but this woman sitting next to me, this woman I'm having drinks with, and speaking with had me behaving like a skittish school boy terrified of the opposite sex.

She giggled playfully and kindly. "What are you so afraid of?" she said as she tickled my thigh. "I won't bite."

"I'm sorry," I said. "It's just that I haven't been around a woman in a long time. You know, because of boot camp."

"Well, you have nothing to be afraid of. Let's chat for a while until you loosen up some more, ok?"

"Ok. . . but I have to be honest—I wasn't sure if I wanted company tonight, but I think you changed all of that."

"You're sweet. Well, why don't we order a few more drinks before we engage in more friendly conversation." She winked again.

"Ok," I said. It surprised me that she was interested in me. But I had an undeniable feeling about who she was. She kept a secret she did not wish to tell me, but I suspected the truth. There isn't a need to admit it to myself, but it was just a feeling. I didn't care, however. I pictured the two of us becoming lovers. Even for just one night. But I wanted more than one night. I wanted a lifetime. The time I spent with her, I felt a connection. It made me happy just being in her company. For the night, this woman belonged to me. I had her all to myself.

—

"I'M SORRY, BUT I NEVER GOT YOUR NAME," I slurred. We had been speaking for an hour now over several drinks. The alcohol did its job for making the evening hazy. And it never occurred to me to ask for her name until now. The company of a beautiful woman and a night of drinking can make you forget simple details or questions to ask. However, asking the right questions will allow her to invite you in to her secret world. But there was no need to get into her affairs. And there is no need for her to get into mine.

"It's Catherine," she said with a smile. A smile I became acquainted with. I can't picture her beautiful face without it. "Catherine Barlow. May I ask you yours?"

"Vincent," I replied. "But everyone calls me Vince. But I guess it's Private Vince now." I spun my pointer finger in the air as I spoke those last words. The alcohol was in effect, and I couldn't take another drink in fear of somehow making an ass of myself at some point in the evening, although I wasn't wholly inebriated, but I would be if I continued to do so.

Catherine laughed at my foolish manner. "Well, *Private* Vince—do you have a room here for the night?"

"I sure do," I responded. I kind of knew where the evening was going. And I would not allow this opportunity to pass me up; drunk or sober, especially with a beautiful woman like Catherine. I had been away for over eight weeks and hadn't been with a woman the whole time. Sure, I could have had a woman during that weekend leave in Anniston but my attention at the time was elsewhere.

"Aren't you going back to your family's farm tonight?"

"Not tonight. I am first thing tomorrow mornin'. And besides, I wouldn't want to return home after I had a few to drink."

"Well, why don't we just get out of here and then go to your room," she said in a seductive tone.

"You got it," I responded without hesitation. Catherine's alluring manner forced me to say yes. She was charming all right. I spotted a subtle glimmer in her eye as she stared at me. She was hooked, and so was I.

Catherine finished the last of her drink. I paid Frederick what I owed him along with a small tip. Fredrick kept watchful eyes on me as he stood behind the counter with a bottle of scotch in his hands; his face beamed at me as if he knew what was going on between Catherine and I. Once we were out of the bar, we ascended upstairs to my room side by side and arms linked.

———

CATHERINE LIED ON HER STOMACH, facing me on the bed in my room with her arm draped across my chest. It's early dawn. About six o'clock and I could hear birds chirping their morning songs through the open window. Sunlight peeked through the white drapes. I gently caressed her upper arm as she let out a soft moan. Her skin felt smooth. I never touched a more delicate body than hers. We had lain together the night before (on several occasions), but I thought there would be no lasting romance between the two of us. Suspicions rose about what she did for a living, but I wasn't positive. I had my doubts as we talked over drinks at the bar the night before. But she's too gorgeous and far too classy for that kind of profession, but looks can be deceiving. But I have to admit—she gave me the best night of my life. I feared I wouldn't have been able to perform correctly because of my injuries but somehow, I fought through the pain. I heard no complaints, so I guess I did just fine. A little fun being back in Natchitoches is what I needed. Precaution was used, of course. The last thing I wanted right now is to become a father. I had no children—at least none I was aware of.

Catherine adjusted her position as she woke and ran a finger up and down on my chest and stomach tenderly. "What happened?" she asked, taking notice of my injuries. Over the passing day, the bruising diminished some, and the pain became mild, but I still had trouble moving about on account of stiffness.

"It happened at Basic Training. A little accident is all," I answered. I didn't want to tell her the actual story. Why should I? Some things just shouldn't be discussed. I also didn't want her to think of me as some kind of wimp even though I was assaulted from behind from Roland and had no chance of fighting back.

"It makes you look more rugged," she said. "I like rugged." She propped herself up on her elbow and kissed me on my lips. Her makeup worn off throughout the night but even in the early hours of the morning, she remained beautiful. She then lied down on her side and snuggled up close next to me.

I hoped, for her sake, that she someday finds a legitimate occupation and settle down with a husband in a lovely home. Maybe even have a few children. I wanted this for her. She deserved it. Any man in Natchitoches would be lucky to have her. There was no opportunity for me to give her that kind of life. I am to be stationed in Virginia and knew she would never want to leave Louisiana. She had a life here, and I didn't.

But I couldn't explain it; it was during this moment with her in my hotel room—I felt a connection to Catherine. In just this brief amount of time, my heart had a soft spot for her. It was possible I felt awful for her. I didn't want to see her live this kind of lifestyle. There came a great desire to help her, but how?

We lied on the bed for a few more minutes in silence, deep in one another's arms, listening to the morning songs from the birds when she spoke again. "I'm not a prostitute, you know." I was taken aback! "Last night, I saw you sitting in the bar all alone, and it made feel sorry for you," she said as she caressed my chest and stomach once more. "So I thought I would just sit down with you and give you some company. And then one thing lead to the next."

"I'm not gonna to lie to you—" I said, "but I thought that's what you were." I wasn't sure how she would take my honesty. I only hoped for the best.

"No," she muttered. "But don't worry, I'm not upset with you thinking I was. Any man can make that suspicion." I kissed her on the top of her head and held on to her firmly. "Did you mention last night you were to be sent to Virginia?"

"Yes," I said. "I'm only here for a week before I have to travel there to be ready for Advanced Training."

Catherine sighed. "I wish you could stay longer and spend more time with me."

"So do I. I have to go to the farm today to visit my family. I'll most likely be there for the rest of the week. But can I come to see you before I leave for Virginia?"

"I'd like that."

At first, I believed there would be no deep romance between the two of us, but I couldn't have been any more wrong. How was this even possible? In just this short amount of time we spent together, I had fallen for her. But had she fallen for me? We were both young, and a full life lied ahead of us. We both had all the time in the world to find love, and yet we discovered love in our youth—here and now. I loathed the thought of me taking off for Virginia and leaving her behind. How I wish I could stay or take her with me. But here, she had a life and it would be selfish of me to take it away. I wanted to be part of it. I wanted to be there for her when she would need someone; hold her during the hard times and celebrate with her during the good times. Catherine was a sweet, innocent young woman who fell in love with the wrong man. There was plenty of fish in the sea, but she hooked me.

The wrong fish.

———

WE MADE LOVE once more that morning and afterwards we stayed in bed, cuddled up together. By late morning I was getting hungry for some food. We eventually escaped the comfort of the bed and did our daily morning routines before leaving the room. I closed the door behind me with my duffel bag in hand. We ate breakfast at the hotel and afterwards I suggested to Catherine I walk her home after I checked out of the hotel. She obliged. She led me to a small tenement building near to the hotel as she had stated the previous night.

"Come see me before you leave, ok?" Catherine said as she hugged me. Her tone was soft and melancholy as she spoke and was careful not to hug me so tight.

"I will," I said in good spirits.

She kissed me on the lips and stepped into the building. She kept a watchful gaze on me as she teased me with that smile of hers. The door closed and she left me all alone.

I debated whether I should see her again. I couldn't shake the belief that perhaps the two of us could be lovers. It's what I wanted or at least thought I did. I didn't know what I wanted. But Catherine realized something last night I also noticed: there was fear; not fearful of her but fearful of getting too close. She had the uncanny ability to look past that. I admired her—perhaps even loved her. Truly love her.

I turned away from the closed door that shielded Catherine from myself, and began my long walk towards home.

FOURTEEN

THE DAY GREW HOT, but the heat was tolerable. I could feel sweat beading on my forehead and dripping down my back and legs as I wandered down the old familiar road towards the farm. Sweat will tarnish my uniform in a matter of hours. There is a slight breeze in the air, but the breeze did little to cool me off. I chose to look presentable to Mother when I arrive. I adorned my uniform with my ribbons and badges to present the accomplishments I made thus far. It will surprise her when she sees me on the front porch, knocking on the door. Her little boy that left eight weeks ago has come back a matured man.

I envisioned the times I walked this lonely dirt road with Glenn or in my subtle loneliness. But there are memories of sitting with Father in the pickup truck heading towards town to sell produce to earn money. Father always has been traditional. That is something I respected about him. He told me stories of what his life was like back before automobiles. Before automobiles, there were wagons. They were more straightforward and cheaper to maintain. He believed it was a simple waste of money to invest in an automobile, but Mother had said otherwise. He felt inclined to use a wagon with a horse, but Mother said the times are changing. Wagons are a part of the past. Father remained stubborn, however. Horses are cheaper if one was in need to be put down. That's Father's way; save money with the most affordable solutions. It worked too. But Mother wouldn't give in too quickly. She pressed Father to purchase a pickup truck, and each time he refused, she would lose her temple and scold him to no ends. Eventually, Father gave in. He was a beaten man by a woman smaller and weaker than him. But not because Mother had demanded it. The primary reason: he loved her. He wanted her to be happy, no matter how much he hated purchasing a pickup.

Father always said the world moves too fast; it's all becoming too sophisticated. The world didn't need to be that way. Everything only needs to stay pure. Life would be easier. Perhaps he was right. Or perhaps he was wrong. However, the world can never remain the same. Throughout humanity, life has evolved. Mankind has progressed to the next stage of unavoidable change. There will always be change; there's no way to stop it, control it, or even slow it down. Father wanted not to progress forward and had succeeded in some ways. Perhaps the change would not come easily for him in his lifetime. But he cannot, however, control change for his children; it's not in his power to do so. Children will have to continue with humanity's progression forward. It's inevitable. And for my sake, I embraced mankind's progress. Everything changes. Time changes. It catches up whether or not you want it to. So why not give in?

I gave in when I joined the army. I gave in at the moment I stepped onto that bus headed towards Alabama. And because of it, I'm living life on my terms. It's because of the army I became strong-willed, which drove me to have a conversation with a beautiful woman I met the previous night; alcohol doesn't hurt either. Tasteful images of Catherine kept peering into my mind. I struggled to shake the thoughts of her out, but it was of no use. Many times, I told myself that Catherine was only a fling and nothing else, but I wished not to accept it. After the memorable night and morning we spent together, I couldn't help but feel a sudden attachment to her, and I expected she felt the same way. But curiosity made me wonder why she had sat down next to me and started a conversation in the first place. She expressed that she wasn't a prostitute. But what if she was? But she wanted no money from me. She didn't ask for anything. Had that been a sign?

The more I reflected of her—the more I wanted to see her again. I only had a few days to spend at the farm before I have to travel to Virginia, so I looked forward to returning to town just to gaze upon Catherine's beautiful face once again. This mysterious woman somehow touched me inside and forced me to long for her more than she could ever imagine. I saved a mental picture of her lying next to me in the bed in my hotel room. She was beautiful—even in the morning, and I know people look their worst in the morning, but she looked magnificent.

I never had a girlfriend, and I thought of us being together, but I knew it couldn't be possible. The distance that lied before us would be too great. I concluded she was just a good time and nothing more. But I knew I would never feel the same way about another human being the same way I felt about her.

Or so I thought.

———

I CONTINUED MY WALK and along the old road, I stopped to pick a few blackberries from a thicket for a quick little snack. How I missed the sweet juices of a blackberry running down my throat. I remember from my childhood, Glenn and I picking as many blackberries as we could and giving them all to Mother. She would then take all the blackberries and make a delicious cobbler. How I miss blackberry cobbler.

After my snack, I soon approached the barbed-wire fence in the front yard. The same barbed-wire fence I had helped wire all those years ago with Aren. Before walking onto the property, I looked the farm over. How can something look so different even though nothing had changed? The farm looked the way I remembered it when I left but yet, somehow—it's not the same. It was like a distant memory buried deep inside that slowly comes into focus. It seemed strange but even though I had been gone for only eight weeks, it didn't feel the same. Even though I wanted to escape this place—I somehow missed it. I still remember the day I left—riding in the pickup truck with Glenn off the farm, leaving everything behind. Mother and Julia watched me leave. I left them both in tears. It saddened her to see her baby boy go. But I was home now, even if it was only for a few days, and being here was all that mattered.

I took a deep breath and crossed through the open gate of the fence, glancing around the farm, seeing no one in sight. In the horizon, I spot- ted dark clouds forming and heading in my path; then arose subtle dis- tant claps of thunder in the distance. A storm was fast approaching. The brightness of the day is vanishing as it grew dark and dreary. Not the welcoming I was expecting.

After crossing the yard, carrying my duffel bag, I walked quietly onto the porch and up to the front door, wanting to surprise everyone. There is only silence coming from inside. I gave the door a couple of knocks before I heard footsteps marching from inside. I adjusted my necktie to appear proper. The door opened as I now stood face to face with Mother. An expression of awe swept across her face as I smiled at her.

"Hello, Ma," I said.

Mother stood for a moment with shock before rushing into my arms. I tossed my duffel bag on the porch and held her in my arms for what felt like an hour. She hugged me with all of her energy which sent a jolt of pain through me, but I didn't have the heart to tell her she was hurting me. "You're home!" she said as she kissed my cheek over and over again. "My baby's home!" Tears swelled in her eyes—tears of happiness.

"I'm home. But just for a bit." It was the only thing I could get out. She kept kissing my cheek with her hand latched on to my chin.

After a few minutes, she at last released my chin with her grip and composed herself. She took hold of my arm and led me inside as I scooped up my duffel bag and shut the door behind me. There were no signs of Glenn, Julia, and Father. Much like outside, nothing had changed inside. Still, all the same old furniture were in the same places when I left. Father's chair sat by the table with the radio by the entranceway to the kitchen. Many late evenings, I remembered listening to that radio with the family: music, newscasts, and half-hour radio programs. How I missed those nights. This was the house I grew up in. Memories overwhelmed me as Mother lead me into the kitchen. Those eight weeks of being away now seemed like a lifetime ago.

"Come sit in the kitchen while I prepare us something to eat," she said as she adjusted my necktie. "Oh, you look so handsome!"

"I'm not hungry," I replied, still full from a large number of blackberries I ate moments ago.

"How about some coffee then?"

I sat down at the table and didn't have to answer as Mother was already pouring me a cup of coffee. At the center of the table was a glass vase with a beautiful bloomed white magnolia suspended from the top. The fresh scent of magnolia lingered in the air. Mother set the cup of coffee down in front of me and gently ran her hand across my shoulders and sat down next to me on my left. Her appearance was different. Bags formed under her eyes making her appear exhausted and the gray in her hair had now spread but only a little.

"So where is everyone?" I blurted out.

"Julia is outside playing somewhere," Mother said. "She'll be along shortly. She'll be so happy to see her big brother, you know. So how long you will you be able to stay with us, Vince?" She spoke fast, just capable of containing her excitement for she neglected to mention Glenn and Father.

"Only a couple of days," I replied.

"Really? Just a couple days," she said with sorrow.

I took a sip of the hot coffee. "I wish I could stay longer, but the army has stationed me in Virginia. I'm only on a week furlough."

"Virginia!" she gasped. "Virginia is so far away. How often will we get to see you?"

"I'm certain I can make a couple of trips a year to the farm."

Mother's face fell. I could see the disappointment. "A couple of times a year?"

"It'll be all right," I said. Her hand rested on the table as I set mine on top of hers.

"I know it will," she whispered. "If only you could stay longer and be stationed somewhere closer. I also wish Glenn was home now too."

This came as a surprise. "Glenn? Where is he?"

Mother sighed. "He left us. He said he no longer wanted to stay here. So he traveled to New Orleans to learn a trade."

Mother had mentioned about Glenn wanting to leave the farm in a letter, but I didn't know why I was so surprised. I should have been expecting it. "So he really left? How long has he been gone?"

"It's been a week now. I miss him." Mother let out a slow sigh. "Your father hasn't been like himself anymore. Ever since you left, he's been distant from me—and Julia. It got worse when Glenn left. I know your father has always been bullheaded, but now I feel as if something has truly changed in him. We don't talk much. He barely acknowledges Julia. He just works and works all day. It worries me how often he works: he fixes things that don't even need to be tended to, paints walls that don't need repainting, and tends to the crops more than he should. He seems lost. It's as though something is missing from him—maybe a part of him is missing. He's just not the same. He worries and he upsets me too much. Sometimes, I feel as if I don't know who he is anymore. It's like he's someone else."

Mother grew silent and stared at the magnolia in the vase at the center of the table. I could hear the bitterness in her words. I felt as if all of this trouble had been my fault. Perhaps it was my fault for Father behaving the way is. It's my fault that Glenn left for New Orleans. That's how Mother made me feel. It was all my fault. And I couldn't stand to listen to any more of it. Anger boiled from inside.

I wanted to get out of the house. This had not been the welcoming I hoped for. Mother made me feel guilty as I sat at the table speaking with her. "Where is he?"

"He's outside somewhere working on who knows what?" she replied, not taking her eyes off the magnolia.

I stood up and looked down at Mother. "I know I'm the last person he wants to see right now, but I want to see him before I leave."

"Before you leave?!" Mother's voice rang out as I walked through the back kitchen door.

———

I FOUND FATHER TAKING A REST on the side of the barn. He leaned against the boarded wall with one shoulder and arms crossed over his white shirt that was covered with dirt and soaked with sweat. His skin is wrinkled and tanned. As I neared, it appeared he hadn't noticed me. He stared out into the grassy lawn, appearing as if not a simple thought occupied his brain. It was as if he wasn't there at all. Just a barren shell of a human being a presence had once filled.

I approached him but there no words interchanged between the two of us. There was considerable tension. After a few moments, it turned unpleasant. Neither of us had anything to say it seemed. I found this my cue to leave but as I was doing so, Father at last spoke. "Do you know why I didn't go into the army when the Great War came along?" His question I left unanswered, for I took it as a rhetorical question. "It was because I was too damn scared," he continued in a low and steady tone, diverting his narrow eyes at me. "I was a goddamn coward. I dodged the draft and went into hiding deep into the swamps below New Orleans. I knew they wouldn't find me. How much fuss were they gonna raise for one draft dodger? My place wasn't in the war. That mess was none of my business. My place was at home. But all my friends and some of our relatives got drafted and were shipped off to fight in Europe. Many of them never came back alive. So while my friends were getting killed in a war, I was safe and sound at home with a clean conscience. Not a dirty conscience, remind you; a clean one. But all of that changed when I heard your Uncle Eugene was shot through his head. You never met your Uncle Eugene because he was dead before you came into this world. And so here I am, alive and well while my brother decays in some worm infested grave who knows where. But now my conscience is dirty, you see. Your grandparents didn't want much to do with me anymore after they got word that Eugene had been killed. Why? Simply because I'm a coward." He became silent and glanced out into the lawn once more before diverting his eyes back at me. "So do you think coming back here, dressed all nice in your military uniform is supposed to impress me? Shit boy—if anything I'm ashamed of you. You being dressed like that only tells me that you think you're better than me—that you're a somebody and your old man is a no good fucking coward." Father had not raised his voice, but there was bitterness in his tone. Once again he shifted his eyes onto the lawn. "Now I meant what I said that I didn't want you to come back here. So the only thing I recommend for you to do is just move along. You're not wanted here."

But I didn't wish to leave just yet. "I suppose you blame me for Glenn leaving? You blame me for many things. No. . . I'm not the one to blame. Everything that has happened is your own doing. You're just too stubborn to see it. That day you struck me in the face is the day I lost respect for you. I just wanted to let you know that. I don't respect you anymore. You say you're ashamed of me well I'm ashamed to have you as a father." With that, I turned to walk away but felt as though I should have one last word with him. I turned to look back at Father who had not moved from his position against the barn wall. "I may not be a better man than you," I said, "but your brother Eugene. . . he was a bigger man than you will ever be." Thunder rumbled close by as the wind picked up and drops of rain began to fall from the dark clouds above as I made the short walk back to the house.

———

I STORMED THROUGH THE BACK DOOR and lumbered through the kitchen to snatch my duffel bag, not acknowledging Mother as she still sat at the table. She stood up and walked over to me. I opened my duffel bag and drew out the teddy bear I got for Julia and thrust it into her hands. "Give this to Julia for me."

I turned to leave, but Mother tried to pull me back. "What happened, Vince? What did he say? Please tell me!"

"I'm leaving. To hell with him."

Mother, yet still tried to pull me back with her but I resisted. She couldn't keep me in the house. I stomped through the living area and out the front door as it now poured heavy rain outside. "No, don't leave, Vincent!" she cried. "Don't listen to your father!"

I stepped off the porch and swung back to look at Mother; her eyes were swollen with tears. "Please don't leave, Vincent," she wept as she clutched the teddy bear to her chest. "You can work this out with your father. I know you two can work it out."

I shook my head. "No. We can't work it out," I snapped. "He doesn't want to. He's just a miserable old bastard, and we can't see eye to eye. There's no chance to for the two us to work it out. . . I'm sorry. Goodbye, Ma."

And with that, I walked away. I made it to the fence before turning my head around to see Mother collapsed on the porch only holding herself up with one arm and still clinging to the teddy bear to her chest with the other. She was weeping uncontrollably. "Please come back!" she cried.

I should have gone back to her and carried her back inside to her bed, but I didn't. And if I knew of the events that were to come at the time, I would have gone back. I would have picked her helpless body up and brought her back inside and stayed with her. But I didn't. There are certain events in my life I wished I could have changed. This was one.

Instead, I returned to my walk away from the farm in the heavy rain, not looking back ever again. When I crossed the fence, I heard Julia's voice ring out not far from behind me. "Why are you crying, Momma?! Who's that man leaving!?"

———

I SAT UNDERNEATH THE EDGE OF THE CANOPY of the great oak tree, watching the rainfall. I had removed my dress shirt and necktie and stuffed it in the duffel bag and only wore my undershirt, along with my slacks and shoes. The smell of rain hung in the air as the sound of thunder and flashes of lightning erupted through the dark and clouded sky. I closed my eyes and listened—cherishing the gentle noise of raindrops as it pelted the ground and leaves of the surrounding trees.

But I felt sick to my stomach. Perhaps I overreacted back at the farm. Mother didn't deserve it. I became too much like Father: stubborn and cold-hearted. I left her on the porch, crying tears of heartache, and yet I did nothing. I didn't want to imagine what that grief felt like. A moving image played in my head over and over. It's a vivid picture that will haunt me for the years to come. An image I can't erase no matter how hard I try.

I could make matters right. I knew I could return to the house with my tail tucked between my legs and apologize for my rash behavior, but in my heart, I knew I wouldn't. To face my parents now would be a challenge. "I'm ashamed to have you as a father. . ." The words I said to Father echoed in my head. Now there is a valid idea in those words. I understood now I was no better than he was.

After some time, the rain lightened up, but I became too lazy to move. The day grew late, but I had to get back into town for I was in need of a good meal and a place to sleep. By the time I decided to leave, the moderate rain turned into a light drizzle. This was the best chance I had to hike to town, just in case the rain would start up again. I gazed out on the open field. An eerie mist had now coated the ground. It all seemed strange. For what I thought had been my sanctuary, now felt much different. As odd as it is, there arose a sign that the field wanted to tell me something. A sudden chill ran through my body even though the air was muggy.

After leaving the shelter of the canopy, I turned around to observe the oak tree. The tree itself also seemed unusual. Everything appeared different. The tree, the land, the atmosphere—all different from I remembered. Time slipped away from me as I stood there regarding the tree; had it been a few minutes? An hour? At that moment, I closed my eyes, and a flood of memories swept through me. Memories of me as a young boy, spending time in this field and sitting underneath the tree. I remembered the days I spent with Aren and Katrina here. What I wouldn't give to have another day like that with them here. I longed for it. I thought of the times I spent here with Glenn, Julia, and Mother. But those days were long gone, and I knew there was nothing that could be done do to get those days back. I hadn't realized I was crying—not an intense emotional cry but a soft weeping.

Then came a swift gust of wind that snapped me out of my trance; a sign for me to leave. The field had made its point, and it was telling me it's now time to go. I dried my eyes with my hands in the misty air and left. It was to be the last visual remembrance of that place. Maybe this would be the last time I would ever see the field and the great oak tree again.

———

I MADE THE WALK BACK TO NATCHITOCHES and stopped at Victor's Diner for a bite to eat. During my meal, I had decided to take the bus to Virginia the following day. I didn't want to stay in Natchitoches any longer and concluded that I should get to Virginia to start my new life. A mystery lay ahead of me. It intrigued me to know how my new life will begin.

After I finished my meal, I visited Catherine hoping she would be home. In this hour of need, I missed her and felt I needed her now more than ever. Dark clouds still covered the sky, but the rain had ceased. The town was quiet as if the storm had forced everyone into hiding.

I stood outside the door of the tenement building where I had left Catherine just earlier this morning. Nervousness rattled my bones before I knocked. I was eager to see her again but frightened. After a moment, the door opened and there stood Catherine, smiling at me as she stared. "What are you doing here?" she asked. "I thought you said you wouldn't be back in town for a few more days."

"My trip back home didn't go so well," I uttered.

"What happened?" she asked with concern. Her smile vanished.

"I don't want to talk about it. I just wanted to see you." There was hope Catherine would listen and not push the matter. I didn't wish to talk about what had happened. This was the time I wanted to be alone with her once again. I wanted her maternal instincts to kick in, for my emptiness and loneliness led me to her. I needed her to make everything ok.

I stood outside her door like a scared child before she invited me in. "Well, come in and sit with me," she said.

We sat down together on her sofa close to one another—fingers almost touching. Her apartment was small. Nothing of great value seemed to lie about. The meager decor and furniture expressed an absence of passion. The odor inside the room was musky with age.

"Are you sure you don't want to talk about it?" she asked. I should have known she would try to get what was troubling me out. I mustn't blame her though; it was her maternal instincts I relied on. But I was determined not to let up, no matter how hard she tried.

"Yeah, I'm sure."

Catherine took hold of my hand. Her touch felt the same as it did before. "I missed you today. I couldn't stop thinking about last night and this morning. All day, I had been thinking of you, and now you're here."

"I thought about you today, myself." I paused for a moment to consider my next words. "Listen... I came here to tell you that I had chosen to leave for Virginia tomorrow. I wish I could take you with me but you have a life here, and I can't take that away from you. And I don't know if this morning or last night meant anything to the both of us. I mean—we just met. Maybe its lust—and not love."

She said nothing at first, instead only stared at me with a frown. Her hand still gripped mine as if she did not want to let go.

"No, I don't have a life here," she mumbled. "I'm not even from around here." Her tone of voice and facial expression told me she was speaking the truth. She appeared serious and somewhat dismal. "This isn't even my apartment," she confessed. "It's my friend's apartment. I'm from Mississippi, and I ran away from home when I was seventeen. You see—I even lied to you when I said I wasn't a prostitute. I did things like that to earn some money while travelin'. I often stole clothes, food, and money from unsuspecting people. Nearly all the clothes I own are stolen. When I arrived here, I fell in love with this little town, so I stayed. I haven't been here very long. My eighteenth birthday was just a few months ago. Sometimes I lie about my age in bars to get drinks, and if that doesn't work, I flirt a little with the bartenders. I met my friend at the same place I met you. I told her my sob story, so she helped me out by letting me stay here with her. I work odd jobs to help pay the bills. Any bit of money helps. And I haven't sold myself to any man ever since I've been here. And that's the truth." She rested her head on my shoulder and sighed before speaking again. "I hope you don't think different of me."

At first, I didn't know what to think. She told me who she was. I didn't know if I should be angry, disappointed, or both. In a way, I felt relieved. Catherine displayed an enormous amount of respect to tell me the truth, and I needed to respect her for it. It was odd, but I didn't feel angry. I felt content.

"Are you mad?" she asked after a moment of my silence.

"No, I'm not mad. I think I'm rather pleased you told me."

"This morning, I didn't lie when I said I wanted you to stay longer with me. I wish you did. There's something about you, Vince that I like. I'm not sure what it is, but I feel myself drawn to you. So I'm glad I met you. I'm glad I sat down next to you at the bar and had a conversation with you. And I'm glad we spent the night and this morning together."

"Me too."

"Did you mean what you said a few minutes ago? Do you want to take me with you to Virginia?"

"I meant it—at least, I think I do. . . I don't know. My head is messed

up right now. Everything is confusing. I'm not sure what I want anymore."

"I want to go." She lifted her head off my shoulders and gazed into my
eyes. Her eyes told me the truth. She wanted to escape with me to Virginia. She wanted a new life, and she wanted to start it with me.

"Ok," I said. "But I'm not certain about all the rules of living on an
army base. Once I get settled there, I'll send word to you. We can start a
life together, Catherine—if that's what you really want. I guess I want it
too. So if you're prepared to wait—we can be together. Will you wait for
me?" I felt as though I had meant every word said. I wanted to be with
her, but would she be willing to wait for me? It was much to ask for but
perhaps, she would.

I held my breath with anticipation, waiting for her response.

A little smile appeared on her face. "Of course I'll wait for you. No
matter how long it takes."

We kissed deeply, and we then proceeded to the bedroom. She explained that her friend wouldn't be home for another couple hours. We
made love. And it was how I remembered it from the night before and
this morning. Our craving for one another was being filled. Our love-
making was passionate and at times, intense. I knew there was no denying it—we were much in love. I can't explain this phenomenon of the two
of us being in love when we had only known one another for only a couple of days. There was lust, but this was more than just lust. I just
knew. At least, I hope I knew.

———

CATHERINE RESTED ON HER STOMACH, spread out on the bed, nude,
without a sheet or blanket to cover her. Her red hair draped across
much of her face. The room was sweltering hot. I eased myself out of bed
to not disturb her and I put on my clothes that stuck to my damp skin.
After searching around for some paper and a pencil in the sitting area, I
discovered an envelope with the apartment's address written on it. I

scribbled the address on a slip of paper and shoved it into my pocket; then I wrote Catherine a note on another sheet of paper, explaining to her I would write her once I get to Virginia, so we could keep in touch and I expressed how much I long for the day we would be together.

After it satisfied me with what I had written, I carefully slid the note under her hand and removed some of her hair covering her face and kissed her cheek. She did not stir from her deep sleep. I took one last moment to study her face, wanting to remember her just as she is. I had seen no one as beautiful as she was. After one final kiss on her cheek, I then quietly slipped out of the apartment into the late evening light.

Street lights guided my way back to the Nakatosh Hotel where I checked into a room and slept away the remainder of the long and provocative day.

———

WITHOUT DELAY, I HEADED to the bus station. The fresh morning air was damp, and I can still smell the rain from the day before. Very little sunlight shone through the many clouds that still hovered in the sky. As I sat waiting outside for the bus to arrive, I could only think of Catherine. We were to be together, at least I hoped. I now had something substantial to look forward. A dream to hold on to.

It was nine o'clock when the bus arrived. Anticipation made me ready to get on the road and be away from the place, perhaps once and for all. This is a town I will always love, but part of me wanted to let it go. I found two vacant seats side by side near the back of the bus and claimed them. A very long trip is ahead of me, and so I made myself comfortable.

As many times I had been on buses, they felt like a home. I had become too familiar with them: the smell, the noise, the people. After every stop in some modest and stranded town, someone gets off, and someone gets on. Every person who rides along all have one thing in common: they have a destination. It's everyday people in search of a journey; a new beginning or a return to an old life. Sometimes, that destination may be unknown. They go only as far as the trip will take them and nothing more. I didn't know of my destination just yet or if I would ever find it. I didn't know what I was searching for. Something perhaps I couldn't reach yet. But there was a long and obscure road ahead of me. Calling me. Where am I going? What would I find?

———

DR. GILLIAM'S OFFICE had been silent, other than my voice. It's now a little after eleven o'clock. Gilliam uttered not a single word as I dragged on my tiring story. There were moments I thought I had lost him; he would close his eyes with his cheek resting in his palm, his head tilted down with a blank expression on his face as if he was sleeping. I would pause to check on him, and his eyes would flash open. "Go on," he said. "I'm listening." I realized that he wasn't sleeping, but deep in concentration. This proved that Gilliam was dedicated to listening and helping.

"These are matters I have never spoken to anyone about," I mumbled. "It's kinda a relief to finally say it all out loud."

"This is all very interesting," he said. "Tell me one thing, though, if you will?"

"Yes, of course," I replied.

"Didn't you feel as though you wanted to rush things with Catherine?" I said nothing. "You had just met this girl," he continued, "and yet, you wanted to be with her. She confessed that she was a runaway and a prostitute. She used men to get what she wanted, and yet, you willingly fell into her arms. Was that wise on your part?"

I couldn't help but feel a little perturbed by Gilliam's remarks. Maybe even angry. There was a sense that he was judging me. "I was young," I snapped back. The words slipped out unexpectedly in that manner. But I had kept my composure as I continued. "When you are young, you make choices, sometimes without thinking. Trust me, Doctor—I've made many choices I regret when I was younger, but I thought perhaps, I could help Catherine. Because I saw the real her. Perhaps the person no one else could see. I didn't see her as a manipulative prostitute. She was a sweet girl who just fell on difficult times. Everyone must find a way to survive even if it means going to extreme measures to do it. She reminded me a lot of myself, actually. She ran away from home to escape a miserable life, just like I did. I felt connected to her. I'm *not* a stupid man; perhaps naïve, but not stupid."

"I'm not calling you stupid, Vince. Of course not. I'm only seeking to understand your decisions, is all. I need to know this information in order for me to help you."

I focused in on Gilliam's words like a hawk. "Of course, Doctor. But I need to reveal everything to you before you can truly help me—so that you can understand."

"Yes. . . you are right. My apologies. But I must say, Vince, that I am finding your story quite fascinating. Depressing but fascinating. Something I want to know is: did you try to contact your mother after leaving the farm?"

"I mailed her a letter some days after arriving in Virginia, explaining to her why I did what I did. I feared that she wouldn't forgive me. I even thought she hated me. The fear of your mother hating you is difficult to live with. As I mentioned before—I wish I never left her weeping on the porch. I'm ashamed of myself for what I did to her. She didn't deserve it. But the sad truth is: I never received a letter in return from her. I believed that perhaps she really did hate me."

I stared at my shoes resting on the floor, stricken with grief. I tried to speak, but no words came out my mouth. The agony from my guilt cut deep. Deeper than I never thought possible.

The silence in the room grew longer. Gilliam studied me with a sympathetic expression. He cleared his throat. "We can stop for the day—if you want, Mr. Conroy. You need some time to compose yourself and gather your thoughts."

Gilliam began to arise from his chair. I did need to stop for the day, but I knew I couldn't. If I need to tell my story, I needed to do it now. "No," I blurted. "I'd like to continue—if that's ok?"

Gilliam froze in his somewhat standing position for a moment and then sat back down. "All right then." He cleared his throat. "The way I understand it: you blame yourself more than you realize, Vince. You shouldn't criticize yourself for misgivings beyond your control. I believe your dear mother understood the situation you were in and so she couldn't find it in her heart to write to you because it may have been too difficult for her to do so. There are some feelings that can't be expressed in written words. So I don't believe your mother hated you. I find it impossible for a mother to hate her child. The bond between mother and child is always strong; no matter the circumstances."

I nodded my head.

Gilliam leaned back in his chair and again rested his face into his hand. "So please go on, Vince. I'm eager to hear the rest of your story."

FIFTEEN

I STEPPED OFF THE BUS and realized I was further away from home than I have ever been, which was fine with me. I wanted to be as far away as possible.

Fort A.P. Hill, I soon discovered, differed from Fort McClellan. One aspect I first noticed is that it's smaller. But many army units have now been assigned here for training. The fort lacked the features that McClellan processed, such as constructs for entertainment: golf course, auditorium, and so on. And the roads weren't roads—they were long strips of mud. That is what I remember the most: the mud. It was difficult to wander around in a mess. The smell of muck putrefied the air with its foulness. You would assume I would be used to this, seeing I came from a farm, but the mud in Virginia is much different. Not what I was used to. I'm now in a strange piece of land, far from home, no relatives, no friends, and no direction to go in.

I made my way to the central office building just a few blocks from the bus stop after presenting my papers to an MP standing outside the main gate of the fort. The temperature is mild and sky was overcast with heavy clouds. A recent rainfall had tarnished the ground with thick and foul mud. I trudged in the wet dirt with my duffel bag slung over my shoulder towards the office building, nodding at other soldiers passing by. Only a few returned a gesture, such as a head nod or a quick wave of a hand. Others did not. And I could feel eyes following me, curious as to who I am. I felt out of place and alone, being here by myself with no friends.

I struggled to pick up my pace to the office building, for it turned difficult due to the thick sludge. Eventually, I hopped around to find drier, firmer spots to walk on but this proved to be not much help. It wasn't long I soon realized that I was making a fool of myself. I gave up on trying and with no other option, walked through the mud to the front entrance, trailing the mud in from the bottom of my boots.

Once inside, I found a young woman sitting behind a big desk, looking over some papers. She adorned herself in a woman's military-style uniform: beige skirt, button-up jacket, and black shoes. At first, I assumed she was in the army, but no rank insignia nor badge decorated her sleeves. Her long brown hair was styled neatly on her head to not allow any strands to drop past her shoulders. Her face wasn't particularly pretty but she adorned herself by shadowing her long eyelashes with black mascara and masked her lips cherry red with lipstick.

The interior of the building was dull. The entrance was a big open room with chairs lined along the walls, and large prints of landscapes and the fort itself decorated the white walls. Many closed doors were scattered throughout the room, creating a mystery of what could be behind them.

"Hello," I said as I approached the front desk.

"Can I help you?" she said, looking up at me with a smile.

"Yes, I'm Private Vincent Conroy, and I have orders," I said as I gave her my papers, "to report here for my advanced training. I just finished boot camp."

"Ah, I see," she said looking over my papers. "You must be one of the FNG's."

"FNG?" I said with confusion.

"Oh, nothing," she said. She removed a folder from a drawer in the desk and flipped through it and pulled out a page with a list of names on it and looked it over. "You're right here. But you weren't expected for a few more days."

"There was a change of plans. So I arrived early."

She shrugged. "No matter. Everything is already arranged for you." She handed me a folder. "This is all the information you need. You won't need to report to your training until Monday, so you got a little free time to look around the fort and get acquainted with everything. Where you will need to go for your training is in that folder, so don't lose it. Some-one will drive you to the barrack where you will be staying. You have the entire barrack for yourself for a few days so enjoy the privacy while you can. You'll be sharing it with all the other men from your Basic Training unit. And if you need anything else, my name is Lucy Good-win." This was just my luck. Once again I will share a barrack with Ro-land. She could see the disappointment in my face. "It won't be too bad," she assured. "The pay gets better when you move up in rank. By then, you'll be able to afford your own home. But you're still training—and trainees, I'm afraid, just don't earn the accommodations the official ranked troops receive."

"It is what it is," I uttered. "Well, thank you, ma'am." I stepped away from the desk and sat in one the vacant chairs against the wall.

She gave me a thin smile and picked up her telephone and made a call. After a few minutes, a soldier came from a door on the far end of the building.

"Hello, Sergeant Aschner," Lucy said as he approached the desk.

"Ms. Goodwin," replied the soldier. Aschner was tall with a sturdy build. He had dull brown eyes and black, short trimmed hair. "Is this the FNG?"

There was that acronym again—FNG.

"Yes," Lucy replied. "This is Private Vincent Conroy. Private Conroy, this is Staff Sergeant Daniel Aschner. His barrack is Number 15 on Timber Street."

"Very well," Aschner said. I stood from my chair, and we shook hands, and afterwards he lead me back outside the way he came in. We hopped into an open top green Willys MB jeep after I tossed my duffel bag into the back. Aschner turned on the ignition and pulled the vehicle onto a marshy road. The ride was slow and the wind hitting my face made me cold. I flipped the collar of my dress shirt up to protect my neck from the sharp wind. I imagined how bitter the winters would be. It's late May but the air is crisp.

We kept silent during the early minutes, as we passed other jeeps on the road. In the distance, I spotted men doing various exercises in an open field. The recollections of Basic Training came rushing back. But as I watched, they all worked at their own pace, and no drill instructor was yelling at them. Perhaps this will be the sort of recreation I earned for finishing boot camp.

After a few minutes had passed, Aschner broke the silence. "So where are you from, Private?"

I diverted my eyes away from the group of men exercising "Louisiana," I replied.

"Never been there. Where did you do your Basic?"

"Fort McClellan, Alabama."

"Never been there, either. I trained here. I was born not too far from here—a little town called Rockville. It's a cesspool of a town. Nothing to do and nowhere to go. I got out when the getting was good, so I joined the army; best decision of my life."

"Rockville. Never heard of it."

"Doesn't surprise me. It's the sort of town that many recruits are coming from. Towns no one has ever heard of. Men from these little towns join up for the military because they have nowhere else to go. It's those little towns that form the backbone of America. And no one knows it. Most of these men come from the filthiest, most remote corners of the US. All their lives, they've been spit on, ridiculed, and detested. They grew up with barely enough to eat and barely any education. So what do they do when they become of age? They join the military because the military is all they have. What about you, Private? Where did you come from?"

"You could say I came from one of those places. My folks ran a farm. We didn't have much, but we survived. I graduated high school, so I have an education, but my folks could never afford to send me off to college. So I joined up for the army."

Aschner nodded his head. "Any siblings?"

"My brother—Glenn, who is a year younger than me. A much younger sister—Julia."

"Is your brother educated?"

"He graduated high school, like me. The last I heard, he's in New Orleans somewhere, trying to gain an internship at a law firm or something."

"So your brother is trying to make better use of his life in an office, away from the dangerous life of the military. Why didn't you try to follow the same route your brother took? If he can get into an internship at a law firm with only a high school diploma—why can't you?"

"Law doesn't interest me. I know nothing of it, nor do I want to know anything of it. I mean I think I would make a crummy lawyer or an assistant. My point is: I have little talent. I can shoot a gun, but what kind of job could I get that would allow me to shoot a gun any time I wanted beside the army?"

"But you didn't join the army so that you could shoot a gun."

"Well, of course not."

"So what's the real reason why you joined the army?" I was silent. "From what I understand: you came from a family that made ends meet, you are educated with a high school diploma—so is your brother, and you had the opportunity to find a better life than the one you're in now. Your brother sounds smart. He took an opportunity and seized it. So my question to you is: why did you sign up for such a risky lifestyle when you could have taken a safer route? You can't tell me the army was your only option. Most of the recruits here who came from those unknown little towns would have shot themselves in the foot for the chance to walk the path your brother had taken and a path you could have taken. But you didn't take that path. Instead, you chose the dangerous path— the path of a soldier for the United States Army."

"It was this or farming, and I didn't want to be a farmer. I didn't want to be a farmer like my father and his father and so on and so on. That's where I come from—farming. And there's nothing I want to do with it."

Aschner shook his head. He pulled the jeep onto the side of the road. I had caught a sign on the turn he made that read Timber Street. "No. It wasn't about farming. It wasn't about your family. You joined up because you have a backbone. You could have chosen a different life, but you didn't. Your brother doesn't have a backbone, but you do."

I shook my head. "Glenn can't enlist because he broke his knee. He walks with a limp now."

"But would he have joined up if he hadn't broken his knee?"

I thought the question over before answering. "Probably not."

Aschner nodded. "So do you understand? Don't be embarrassed by where you come from. Because a lot of these recruits are ashamed of where they come from. They sign up because they had nowhere else to go but no backbone. You could have given yourself a much better life, but you chose a dangerous life. And that says a lot. Believe it or not, you're bigger than any of the recruits here." Aschner pointed past me. "This is you."

One side of Timber Street was aligned with barracks that all looked the same much like the one that stood next to it: large tents constructed for sleeping many troops. The other side of the street—the same. Lawns were just mud much like the roads. I also noticed a great absence of trees. The only trees I saw were far off in the distance of the fort. I realized this fort had been constructed not to impress anyone. The very bland structure was far inferior to that of Fort McClellan. The ones responsible who built this wasteland did not seem to put too much of an effort in it. I now hoped I would get transferred somewhere else; from the looks of it, any place would be better than this mud pit.

From the outside, the barracks looked very much like the ones at Fort

McClellan. There was no denying it—but it appeared I would have to get accustomed to barracks for a long time. No matter how much I hated them—they were to be my home.

I carefully stepped out of the jeep, so I wouldn't slip and fall in the mud. I grabbed my duffel bag from the rear of the jeep and looked over the barrack.

"It's not much," Aschner said with my back turned to him, "but you might find it to be quite cozy. You got the whole thing to yourself for a few days. Enjoy the free time while it lasts."

I turned back to Aschner. "Nothing cozy about them. I should know. I lived in one for eight weeks."

Aschner smiled. "You'll get used to them... eventually. So let me be the first to welcome you to the Virginia National Guard. And hey, listen—it's not so bad here. It'll grow on you. And If you're ever hungry—the mess hall is just a few blocks from the office building on Hill Drive."

"Got it," I replied. A question popped into my head. "So what about you? Do you have a backbone? Or are you here because you had nowhere else to go?"

Aschner smiled. "I'll leave that discussion for another day."

Before he drove away, I asked him another question that had been nagging me. So now was the time to get to the bottom of it. "By the way—what is FNG?"

Aschner smiled again. "Fucking new guy," he said before driving off.

SIXTEEN

THE ONLY TIME I spent in the barrack was for sleeping. The few days I had to myself came and went. You would guess after living eight weeks with many other recruits in a tent wouldn't be a hassle—but you'd be mistaken. On Sunday evening and Monday morning, the barrack filled with the same men I trained with at Basic Training along with a few new faces. They arrived, much like myself, to continue with their training to become full-pledged soldiers. Their lives had returned to the grounds of rules and obedience—an unwelcoming restraint on freewill and carelessness. The civilian lives we once possessed is now the property of the United States Army. We were civilians no longer. We were now citizens—but the price is a heavy one. Citizens are governed by a different set of laws and regulations that civilians are not constricted by. This is the life we chose; some of us were not sure why, some men had their reasons, and other men needed an escape. I concluded that escape was my reason. It always has been. But which of the others became citizens for escape. This I can't tell you. These other nineteen men I share a barrack with are a mystery. I don't know all their histories, past jobs, education, and families. I could have imagined it. At times I did, unaware of the reason. I have an untamed imagination. But the men are as unfamiliar to me as the first day of Basic Training. It's how I wanted it, for there is no place for me in their lives. They had no place in mine. But sometimes we never get what we want.

The first day of Advanced Training surprised me. We still had to stand in formation next to our beds when a superior office called for attention, but to my relief, no one yelled in my face, demoralized me, or whack me with a metal rod. Captain Albert Hull paced down the barrack for the first-day inspection. He was about thirty years old, perhaps older—with short light brown hair and wore a neatly trimmed thin mustache on his upper lip. His ears were a bit large for his head, making him appear almost comical. "Listen up, Gents," I am Captain Albert Hull. And I would like to welcome you to Fort A.P. Hill and to my Company. You are all here because you have completed Basic Training. Congratulations. But now is the next phase of your training. We start every morning at 0500 hours. All of you have exactly half an hour before we begin PT. After PT, there will be breakfast, and afterwards, each of you will report to your destined practice area for the position you are assigned to."

Walking next to Hull was another officer—Lieutenant Emmet Hastings. He kept quiet and seemed uninterested in what Hull had to say as he carried around a clipboard, making small notes on paper with a pencil. He appeared to be in the late twenties—with neat cropped chestnut hair with hazel eyes and average height.

Hull rambled on about what our daily activities will be like. A speech I am all too familiar with. Advanced Training wouldn't differ so much from Basic, but one exception: weekend passes. At the end of each week, if we would satisfy him with our conduct, each man will be allowed a weekend pass. As you can guess, this inspired every man to exceed beyond expectations to be rewarded a couple days' worth of freedom at the end of each week.

Hull was fair with our daily activities. He was no brute like Ramsey but yet, he was stern. He was a demanding figure who never failed to make his presence known. I learned the hard way about failing to keep cleanliness appropriate after being placed in his company. He ordered everyman to be well groomed at all times for he wanted the best-looking group of soldiers the army has to offer. At first, I thought the man jested but learned quickly that he was serious when I neglected to shave one morning. He ordered me to do various workouts all day, and it did not stop until late in the evening. Exhausted and with little to eat or drink the whole day, I dry heaved the small contents in my stomach in front of him. The man reminded me much of Father. I had to learn my lesson fast while being in Hull's company. It felt as if he took his job a little too seriously—much like Ramsey had done back in boot camp. Even though I didn't like him much, I respected the man. He contained much knowledge and took it upon himself to act as an important authority figure.

So I spent the majority of my time outside exercising or attending classroom instruction. I used half of the time indoors and the other half outside with hands-on experience: combat drills, fighting positions, weapons and vehicles maintenance, and target practice. The infantry-man was my career choice. I worked together with the other infantry recruits as the superiors sent off the others to separate areas to train for their chosen career.

One aspect I enjoyed about Advanced Training is no sergeant yelling in my face or forcing me to do push-ups if I made a mistake. Instead, if a mistake had been made, the instructors would point it out calmly and coach me on how to correct or improve on what I had done wrong.

I found this technique of instruction satisfying. It made training more comfortable and likable. The men finished with boot camp didn't need to be shouted at and insulted every minute of every day. We earned that privilege, a passing as you will say, to be treated with dignity and re-spect. And for the first time since I joined the army, I was enjoying my-self. There came a change in my attitude—a new me. Desire filled me, and I became devoted to learning all there is to know about being an infantryman. What I lacked in talent, I made up for with continuous hard work.

———

AS I MENTIONED, I didn't like staying in the barrack. Captain Hull granted passes at the end of each week, but I always stayed on base. But if I wasn't training, or doing exercises, or at the target range, I was often at the main office building. Believe it or not, but most of the time, it was near empty. It had its peak hours only during certain hours of the day. But once those hours have passed, the main office became a ghost town. And if I was ever in need of some peace and quiet, that's where I could be found. The men and women who worked there had grown accustomed to my presence. Eventually, we all became acquainted. They allowed me to walk about the area to my heart's desire. They even let me access to the break room, where I could take naps on the sofa, listen to the radio, or write letters in peace away from the men. It became my private escape when I needed it.

Lucy worked at the front desk full time, shuffling through documents and files and making phone calls; work I never imagined myself doing. But if I ever desired company, she was always willing to strike up a friendly conversation if time allowed her too. Her warm and upbeat manner was most welcoming. During her downtimes, she sat at her desk trimming her nails or read magazine articles.

Early Friday evening, I wandered in through the front entrance as men in uniforms stepped past me, eager to escape the long work week. I finished my days' worth of training and now had time for recreation. I met Lucy at her desk. Her eyes glued to a magazine. I leaned down and crossed my arms across the desk. "Hello, Lucy. Did you miss me?"

"Hardly," she joked. "You should try getting out more. You're not restricted to just the base you know. That's *why* there are weekend passes.

You should at least get off the base occasionally." She flipped a page over in her magazine.

"I know," I said. "But I like pestering you."

"Why not try going to a bar or something," she muttered, flipping another page over. She hadn't taken her eyes off the magazine since I met her at the desk. "Soldiers are always going to bars outside the base. It'll be good for you to get out of here and join them for some drinks. I mean, it's Friday night for crying out loud."

I let out a small laugh. "If I knew any better, Lucy—I'd say you are trying to get rid of me."

She, at last, drew her eyes off the magazine and studied me. "Of course not, Vince. I just think it's doing you no good to be sitting in here all day."

"Well, I like being in here. There's no trouble, and I'm free to annoy you as much as I want."

She laughed and tossed the magazine on the desk and stared at me hard. "Well, tonight's not your night, mister. I'm taking off early because I have a date."

"A date!" I said surprised.

"That's right—a date. So, I'm afraid you will need to find someone else to pester." She stood up and seized her purse and walked to the front entrance. Before opening the door and stepping out, she swung around and looked at me with an apologetic expression. "I'm sorry, Vince. But I have to go. Take my advice and get off the base for the night or even the weekend. Find a bar and try having some fun for a change, ok?

"Ok," I said.

"Good," she said with a smile. "I'll see you Monday." She left, leaving me to myself.

I agreed it was in my best interest to take her advice to escape the base for a little bit. I didn't know for sure what had been holding me back. And it couldn't hurt to have a little fun. I had been cooped up on the base so perhaps a few drinks with the men would be entertaining. And I had no desire to return to the barrack, so the temptation to leave became overwhelming.

———

I SNAGGED A JEEP after I left the office building. The vehicles were free for borrowing, sort of speak. No one seemed to care if you borrowed one, as long as it was driven back and parked where you found it, clean, and in one piece. They spread out everywhere among the base. Parking lots would be full. Keys were always found in the ignition or under the driver's seat.

So I drove off base, with no set direction in mind in search of a bar. In the passing weeks, the temperature grew warmer. But there is always a chill in the wind when driving in an open top Willys MB Jeep. The first time driving off base alone is unforgettable. I forgot what true freedom felt like. Rules and regulations I followed through my training ceased for the moment. I thought back to my weekend alone in Anniston, Alabama, recalling the immunity of strict guidelines that every soldier must follow. Now a suspicion struck my brain as I drove in the cold winds of Virginia: rules had been holding me back. It's because of rules I had been afraid to leave the base. The army turned me into an obedient individual. But this once, I broke free from my cautious routine in pursuit of something new. And I found it a few miles away from the base in the nearby town of Bowling Green.

THE BLUESTONE PUB.

I sat in the jeep for a few minutes, to gather enough courage to go inside. Maybe it was that the only bars I have visited, an unexpected event occurred—my dispute with Roland in Anniston and the woman I fell in love with in Natchitoches. Trouble as it seems, seeks me out. "But not this time," I said myself before entering through the front.

Walking in, the scene was busy: tables were filled with chattering and chuckling soldiers and civilians. Soldiers sat in groups of their kind, and the civilians did the same. The scenario reminded me of two separate factions keeping to their own, and that intermingling is frowned upon.

I spotted an empty stool at the bar, but it took much effort to reach it as drunks bumped into me. A few drinks spilled over, but no commotion came up. The bartender who appeared as if he had seen better days poured me a mug of beer and let me be, wanting to have no conversation for the likes of a sudden newcomer.

I drank my beer in silence, savoring the crisp taste of alcohol until the occupied stool next to me became vacant and then promptly taken up by a new owner. It was Staff Sergeant Daniel Aschner. He had given me a ride to the barrack after my arrival to Fort A.P. Hill. He called for a beer and then took instant regard of me. "Well, hello there, Private Conroy. Never seen you in here before." I had never come across Aschner much at the base. He was a fleeting shadow on the road or in the mess hall.

"It's my first time," I replied. "Guess I should escape the base for the night and have a little fun. Lucy's suggestion."

"Lucy, huh? I love that girl. She just doesn't know it."

"Well, I hate to burst your bubble, but she has a date tonight."

Aschner laughed. "Don't let her fool you. She always has a date. She says that to me every time I ask her out. Cunning, she is. But I think I'm wearing her down. I have a feeling she'll say 'yes' here pretty soon."

I only nodded and took a sip of beer. Perhaps Lucy was trying to be rid of me for the evening. I had been spending an enormous amount of time at the office building, and sometimes, I can overstay my welcome without regard. Tonight she needed a break.

"So what about you, Conroy?" Aschner said.

His question confused me. "What about me what?"

"Do you have a girl—someone waiting for you back home?"

I thought of Catherine. Boundless memories of my brief time spent with her hit me like a ton of bricks. I could see her beautiful face crystal

clear in my mind and I could smell her lucrative scent as if she was sitting right next to me. "Yes—well, it's sort of complicated," I said staring
into my beer mug.

Aschner gave me a look of doubt. "Let me guess: you don't know what
to do about her. You're all the way up here, and she's all the way back
home. You're worried that she'd soon move on with someone else and
forget you."

I sighed. "Something like that." I realized Aschner could see right
through me.

Aschner smiled. "I wouldn't worry too much about it. If she truly
loves you—she'll wait for you."

"I hope so," I said.

Someone broke our discussion up with some obnoxious laughter carrying throughout the bar—a laugh I was all too familiar. I glanced
around the room and spotted Roland near the back at a table filled with
other soldiers.

Roland had not been a problem with me since I arrived at the fort. He
lived in the same barrack with me, and his presence was one of the reasons I avoided it. The best way to keep the peace is to stay away. It had
worked to my advantage, but I wondered how far the peace would go
before there would be an intrusion.

The night shifted from pleasure to worry. But I didn't want to display
to Aschner that something troubled me, so I stiffened up and continued
to drink.

———

TIME HAS A WAY to jump ahead when alcohol is consumed. Sometimes
it's erratic; it makes you wonder where the lost time had gone to. Several hours slipped by me unnoticed. I glanced at the clock above the mirror behind the bar. The hour and minute hands told me it was past elev-
en o'clock.

Aschner had been on some rant about how easy officers have it made.

I lost track of the conversation two or three beers ago. The effects of the alcohol now took a firm hold of me and were not letting go. I looked at my beer mug which was still half full. But I couldn't take another drink. I wasn't entirely drunk, however; I felt tired, but not drunk. Or so I thought. I needed to drive back to the base, but I didn't know if it was possible.

". . . officers sit in the back during battles," Aschner said, "or they sit comfortably in their offices while enlisted men such as ourselves are thrown right up front in the excitement of battle. You're more likely to get yourself killed. I'm not complaining about officers—don't get me wrong. Officers have a very important job, but they have it a little too easy." Aschner stopped talking and finished his beer.

I buried my face in my hands. The evening had gone on long enough. The endless loud murmur of the patrons and my need to sleep made me want to leave and return to the base. "What do you say we head back?" I asked. "I think I've had enough drink and conversation for one night."

Aschner seemed to agree. "Yeah, I guess you're right. It is getting late." He stood up from the stool with no trouble—but me, it took several struggles to get my footing. I followed behind Aschner as we walked out the door as I shuffled my feet.

Once outside, I found Roland by the door, leaning against the wall, smoking a cigarette. He looked at me and scoffed. "Can't hold your liquor, Conroy. You pussy."

Now I could stop and confront him, but I thought it would be wise to pretend to ignore that remark and keep walking towards the jeep. Another scuffle with Roland will prove nothing. And all I wanted was a bed to sleep in.

"Don't turn your back on me!" Roland barked. Again, I pretended to ignore him and kept walking. But before I could enter the jeep, Roland grabbed my shoulder and spun me around. "I said don't turn your back on me! Didn't you hear me?!" He was now in my face, jabbing me in the chest with a fat finger. I could smell the liquor and alcohol on his breath. It was strong and vile.

"Let me be, Roland," I demanded. "I don't want to fight you. We settled that back in Alabama." I was doing my damnedest not to start a fight.

"Oh no, shithead!" Roland barked. "We settled nothing."

But before Roland could get another word out, Aschner stepped in between us. "What's going on here, Private?!" he said in Roland's face. Aschner's tall body was almost even with Roland's but he wasn't as big as him.

"Who are you?!" Roland argued.

"I'm Staff Sergeant Daniel Aschner, and I'm demanding to know what's going on here?!"

"This is none of your damn business—*Sergeant*!" Roland mocked.

Aschner got into Roland's face. They nearly touched noses. "Stand down, Private! That's an order!"

Roland's face turned blood red.

"I said stand down!" Aschner roared.

Roland took a few steps back and then pointed a finger at me. "Just keep that pathetic piece-of-shit away from me." He then barged his way back inside the bar.

I felt relieved. "Thanks, Sergeant," I said.

"What was that about, anyway?" Aschner asked.

"It's a long story," I said. "And I'm much too sleepy to tell it."

"I understand that. Get back to base and get some shut-eye, Private. It looks like you need it. I'll report him first thing in the morning for you."

"Thanks," I muttered.

"Don't mention it," he said. "And hey, if he gives you any more problems, don't be afraid to come to me."

I nodded and sat down in the jeep, turned on the ignition, and shifted out into the road. My condition insisted I find another way back to base. I had an opportunity to ride back with Aschner but doing so would involve abandoning the jeep. And that would not be an option. I could make it. I knew I could. Concentration is the key. Ignore the alcohol and weariness. Watch your speed. Focus on the driving, and I'll make it back safe and sound.

———

THE NEXT DAY, I awoke to the sight of vomit on the floor next to my bed. Lying stomach down, my head hung off the edge of the bed. The stench of the vomit had smothered the entire tent. My head pounded. Getting out of bed was challenging. It took several tries as my head spun each time I stood up.

At last I kept my balance and staggered to the restroom at the back of the barrack and buried my face under the faucet to allow the cool water to work its magic. So this is what a hangover feels like. "Never again," I told myself. I felt lucky, due to it being only Sunday, and there is no work on Sundays.

I took a cold shower to allow the icy water to work more of its magic on me. During the shower, it became difficult to stand, so instead, I sat down in the stall to absorb the water to sober up.

I made it back to my bed after the shower and threw a towel on the pile of vomit and put on some clean clothes. The barrack is near empty of other men except for a few still sleeping in their beds. I imagine the smell of the vomit had run everyone else out. The keys for the jeep I borrowed the previous day were on my trunk at the end of the bed. I thought back to the night before but couldn't remember where I left the jeep.

After walking outside, I spotted the jeep. It nestled unharmed in the yard surrounded with circles implanted into the ground, obviously made from the tires. Had I done this? I couldn't remember. I couldn't remember much about getting back to base. The drive back was in blurry, flashy images: bits here and there and nothing else. I didn't even remember falling into bed.

My first instinct was to return the jeep to the main office building. There was no use in attempting to repair the lawn. I thought of how many people had already seen it. Afterward, I would go to the mess hall and try to eat breakfast, but what I needed the most was coffee.

———

THE DRIVE TO THE OFFICE BUILDING made me feel better. The morning air was cool, and it helped with the headache. I parked the jeep, leaving the keys in the ignition, and trotted to the mess hall. It's not a long walk but it felt as if it was. My head continued to pound, and I could feel the nausea in my stomach churning. Before I knew it, I was on my knees dry heaving. Whatever had been in my stomach the day before, had been expelled sometime last night after I had fallen asleep. It was still early in the morning, so not much people were out and about to watch me suffer. After several minutes of continuous dry heaving, I lifted myself back up to my unsteady legs and continued my slow walk to the mess hall with muddy hands and trousers.

Hoping that that was the end of the dry heaving, I grabbed a cup of coffee once I arrived at the mess hall. I sat down by myself at an unoccupied table and buried my face in my hands in desperate need for the hangover to end. Eating any food was out of the question, in fear of vomiting it up. Just thinking about food made me uneasy. Instead, I took slow and little slips of coffee as to try not to disturb my weakened stomach.

After several minutes, Andrew and Karl joined me at the table with their trays filled with breakfast food. The feeling of nausea returned. To not got sick again, I kept my eyes glued to my cup coffee.

"Rough night?" Andrew said with a mouth full of scrambled eggs.

"You can say that," I murmured.

Andrew and Karl laughed. "Yeah, we've all been there," Karl said. "I can't count how many times it's happened to me. But you'll survive."

"The one good thing, though," said Andrew, "the more you drink, the more you can tolerate."

I rubbed my temples with my fingers. "Can we not talk about drinking?" I requested.

They both laughed again. "Sure," Karl said. "It's not the end of the world. Your hangover will pass. Drink as much of that coffee up as you can. It'll help. You should try to eat something too, perhaps some eggs. Eggs are good for a hangover."

We sat during the rest of breakfast, mostly in silence. I tried to take Karl's advice about eating a few scrambled eggs, but my stomach wouldn't allow it. Karl and Andrew had a small conversation about the revival of the 29th Infantry Division. The possibility of its restructure could take place within the next couple of years for preparations for the possible war now looming in Europe. The US military was in works of reorganizing on account if the US was ever to join in the war against Germany.

———

AFTER I FINISHED my second cup of coffee, I thought it would be best for me to escape to the break room at the office building to sleep off my hangover. I left Karl and Andrew and retreated outside. There, I was confronted by Lieutenant Hastings. "Private Conroy. A word please," he demanded.

"Yes, Lieutenant," I replied, unsure as to why he wanted a word with me. But I remembered the tire tracks outside the barracks made with the jeep. Perhaps I had been caught. Maybe someone discovered I had been responsible and reported to Hastings for my drunken foolishness.

Hastings cleared his throat. "Staff Sergeant Aschner from B Company came to me this morning and explained to me that Private Archer drunkenly confronted you last night and tried to start a fight with you. Is that correct?"

I tried to recall the events the previous night at the BLUESTONE

PUB. The events of the night were still hazy, but I did recollect an argument with Roland. I thought of this as my chance to have Roland removed from the army and out of my life for good. "Yes, Lieutenant. That is correct."

"I see. Well, it is from my understanding that Captain Hull will want to take immediate action at this sort of misconduct. You can expect to see Private Archer doing latrine duty for a week or two."

"Latrine duty, Lieutenant?" I became disappointed. "I thought perhaps he would be kicked out of the army."

"Captain Hull needs all the men he can pull together, Private. And so does the US Army. Just in case you haven't realized—this country is in a state of mania. We can be heading to war in the near future, so the US Army needs every available man to fight."

I nodded my head. "Of course, Lieutenant."

"Good. I'm glad we understand one another. Or at least you understand what this country needs right now?" I nodded my head again. "And Private Archer will be dealt with. You needn't worry."

I did understand the country needs men to fight for its side, but there are men more capable than Roland. But I knew latrine duty is the only punishment Roland will endure. "Lieutenant," I said as I saluted Hastings.

But before I could make my way to the office building, Hastings took hold of my arm with a tight grip. "Oh, and another matter of business, Private," he said. He let go of my arm and removed an envelope from his coat pocket. "This came for you yesterday. I meant to give it to you, but you had left the base. There had been some sort of mix up with the delivery, so it's a few days late." He handed me the envelope. The return address was from Catherine. Before I could give Hastings my thanks, he spoke. "As you were, Private."

Hastings entered the mess hall for his morning breakfast as I made my way to the office building. The front entrance was unlocked as it always is. Even on weekends, the building remained open, but there's always a lack of activity. Lucy was not present for she did not work on the weekends. I caught a glimpse of a few superior officers passing through doors, and I spotted a janitor wiping down desks as I made my way to the break room for some privacy to read Catherine's letter.

I sat down on a sofa, satisfied to be off my feet again and opened the letter. But I was afraid of what the contents of the letter would be. I wrote a letter to Catherine every week since arriving to base. It has been nearly four weeks now. And this is the first letter I received. I shook as I unfolded the paper due to nerves and the hangover I suffered:

Dear Vince,

This letter is being written to you as I am sitting at the bank of the Cane River of a beautiful morning. I wish you were here now, right next to me. Listening to the flow of the gentle river and the sweet songs of birds. If only you were with me, this morning would be heaven.

I have received all of your letters. Thank you for writing to me. I'm sorry I haven't written sooner. Several times I tried, but I just couldn't find the right words. I'm glad you haven't forgotten me. Every day, I think about you since you left. You are never far from my mind. I'm still waiting for the day when we can be together again. The sooner, the better. How I long to be held in your arms again.

I am happy to know that you are safe and sound in Virginia. Please get a home of your own as soon as possible if you can. I look forward to the day of leaving Natchitoches to be with you. And please visit me when you can. Have you asked about getting some time off?

Also, I wanted to let you know I am being faithful to you only. And I hope that that hasn't been a worry for you. You are my one and only. I know it may seem hard to believe but I fell in love with you after that short time we spent with one another, and I wasn't lying when I told you that there is a connection between the two of us. The connection can only be described in ways I can't explain. I truly hope you have felt it as well. You are the only man for me—my one and only.

Love,
Catherine

P.S.
Please write again.

Relieved, you could say—so much relief. Catherine's letter convinced me of our alluring relationship. Her writing seemed too authentic to be a lie. This is what I needed—a simple reassurance of an infinite feeling of belief to pick up my spirits. Catherine is waiting for me.

I slipped of my boots and swung my feet onto the couch to stretch out, and I closed my eyes, having a moment of reassurance and gratitude. Yes, I was grateful that Catherine is waiting for me. But when would I see her again? How long would she remain waiting? These were questions I required answers to. I felt I had to see her again. But when? When will I get the chance?

The time would come soon enough.

SEVENTEEN

ON DECEMBER 7, 1941—the Japanese Army bombarded the United States Naval Base at Pearl Harbor on the island of Oahu, Hawaii. It had been a surprise attack. Nearly three hundred and fifty-three Imperial Japanese fighter planes, bombers, and torpedo planes attacked eight U.S. Navy battleships, and four of those ships were sunk. Twenty-four hundred Americans lost their lives and over a thousand were wounded.

The attack on Pearl Harbor forced America to declare war on Japan the following day. President Roosevelt delivered his Infamy Speech in front of the U.S. Congress to enter the war, and it only took Congress less than an hour to decide. With the US now involved with the war, Germany and Italy then declared war on the United States on December 11. There came a great panic that fell upon the people of America. Fear had swept the nation.

US Congress issued a draft in October 1940, and soon after the Pearl Harbor attack, the draft continued further. Many young men were plucked from the comfort of their homes and placed into military ser-vice. And now under the urgent circumstances of war, the military at last organized divisions into fighting units. The army reactivated several of Fort A.P. Hill's regiments into the 29th Infantry Division. The men I trained with were now officially part of C Company of the 1st Battalion in the 116th Infantry Regiment. And now, I suspected it would only be a matter of time before I am called upon to fulfill my civic duties as US soldier. This is what I had signed up for. I knew the risks and the dangers. It wouldn't be easy when the time would come. But this is my career and there would be no choice but to continue on. I couldn't back down. The military would brand me as a coward and a deserter if I tried to find a way out or run from my responsibilities.

The time will come but almost every soldier, myself included, had been left in the dark about what appropriate steps were being taken about America's involvement in the war. The truth: no one knew much of anything. Word only spread throughout the base based on rumors and hearsay. Each passing false news was about as ridiculous as the next. Everyone wanted to know the truth. There were many questions we all wanted to be answered; questions that would drive any man with insanity to discover the harrowing truth. But there remained a lesson to be learned—there was a need to be patient and eventually, the answers will come. This can be difficult, however, because many people lack the required know-how for being patient. I'm guilty of it myself. But no matter how much the impending war had troubled me, I thought it would be best to let the war find me. I'll understand all there is to learn in due time. I'll know when I'm ready. There would be no reason to chase after answers like a madman.

Wait for them, and they'll come.

———

I WAS OFFICIALLY RANKED PRIVATE after graduation, even though Private is only the starting rank, I realized all my hard work was paying off. And with the help of a former drill instructor of mine, I was being promoted quickly. The night we all graduated, we took it upon ourselves to have a night of celebration at the BLUESTONE PUB. We all put on our finest military suits decorated with our badges, ribbons, and insignias and drank the night away with the endless clanking of beer mugs, conversations, jokes, and laughs. Some men flirted and conversed with the women, but I wanted no part, even after the endless nagging of Andrew to join him in a little fun at a flirtatious blonde's home near the bar with her friend. I declined to Andrew and urged him to find another partner in crime. I vowed to Catherine and myself that I would not touch, kiss, or lay with another woman.

Catherine and I exchanged letters throughout the months, confessing our need to be with another when given the initial opportunity. But for this dream of ours to become a reality, I need to move up in rank, so I could afford a home and at last, escape the dreadful barracks. It came as a disappointment that a Private's pay was anything but grand. I'm a trained US soldier and was paid with peanuts. A measly salary is a slap to the face—an insult for deciding to become a citizen. A private's starting pay is not sufficient to move off base to purchase a home; that's why we were all forced to be crammed in barracks like sardines. Barracks are an establishment to throw the lower ranks of soldiers into to house them for they had nowhere else to go. Privates are the lowest of the low; the rougher class of the military society. But every enlisted soldier has to start somewhere. For me to move up in rank, I needed to prove myself, yet again to my superior officers. Eventually, with enough hard work and time, I will afford to escape the barracks and secure a home for Catherine and myself. And in due time, perhaps marriage, and who knows, perhaps even children. A life for the two of us remained far from reach—but in sight. At the present moment, it's all fantasy—a fantasy I wanted. It's a vision that would take time and patience, but I didn't know how much patience Catherine had. I explained all of this to her in letters, but Catherine has hopes one day it all will happen. She swore she would wait, no longer how long it took. It had been too long since we last seen one another. But she possessed one thing I remember the most about her—it is her finest feature: her beautiful face. This fascinating woman waits for me, and I was determined to deliver to her the best life she could ever dream of. But all I needed was time. And lots of it; as much as she would give me.

I sat at a table with Karl and Andrew, enjoying cold beers. The flirtatious blonde sat in Andrew's lap, giggling at Andrew's obscene jokes; jokes I did not find amusing. They were sexual. Not the jokes to be told around young children and not around a lady but the blonde didn't seem to notice, perhaps it was because she was just as drunk as most of the soldiers.

But I had learned my lesson about drinking so for our night of celebration, I swore only to drink a little, hoping to avoid another evening of amnesia and a horrible morning suffering a hangover. I peered behind me and at the other end of the bar at a table in the corner, sat Roland, Lester, and Arthur. I could hear Roland's loud, obnoxious laughter over everyone's conversations. No matter how many times I had listened to his laugh, it still makes me shutter. Nails on a chalkboard. That was always a teacher's way of getting her students' attention when there was too much rowdiness.

"Well, it looks like we're going to war after all, boys," Andrew said after taking a drink of beer. "I don't know about you guys, but I'm aching to get over to Europe and teach those sons-of-bitches a lesson or two."

"There are many army divisions as of right now," I said. "You don't think they'll send us over there, do you?"

"The military wouldn't reactivate the 29th Division if there weren't any plans to send us over there," Andrew stated. "The government wants to be prepared. So I wouldn't be surprised if they sent our sorry asses over there tomorrow."

"Too soon," Karl interrupted. "Just today, I saw recruits arriving at the fort for Basic Training. Those poor boys are about to be trained to join us in the 29th. Their draftees. And draftees don't make the best recruits."

"They just need a foot in the ass," Andrew said. "And we may have to be the guys to do it." He let out a laugh.

The blonde sitting on his lap laughed as well. "My hero Private Deck-

er here will make men out of those boys," she said as she pinched Andrew's nose.

"That's right, Evie," Andrew said as he winked at her. "They'll learn
from the best."

"Those kids are frightened," I said. "How would you feel if you were
taken from your homes to fight in a war you have nothing to do with?"

"Those bastards are getting drafted because we need them," Andrew
snapped. "Hell, we need all the men we can get. So don't tell me you are
soft on those guys?" He paused for a moment as he gazed at me. "Does
Private Vincent Conroy have sympathy for poor little draftees that have
to train to fight?" Andrew continued to stare at me with a stern and
drunken face. The blonde on his lap again laughed at his talk—a laugh
that seemed to mock me.

"I think that's enough, Andrew," Karl insisted.

Andrew kept his gaze as I stared at him unamused until he cracked a
smile and erupted with laughter. "I'm just fucking with you, Vince. You
should know that. You need to loosen up a little. Don't be such a stiff all
the time."

I played it cool and laughed along with him although I knew he
hadn't been joking. Luckily, Karl was there to keep the peace.

At that moment, the front door of the bar swung open, and Captain
Hull stormed inside. "Listen up, Gents!" he shouted. Every soldier stood
up at once. The blonde sitting on Andrew's lap almost hit the floor. "Finish your drinks and head back to base. That's enough fun for all of you
this evening. Your soldiers now. Not a bunch of drunken buffoons."

All the men grumbled as they downed the last of their beers and prepared to pile out the front door. As I forced my way to the door, Captain
Hull grabbed my arm and drew me away from everyone else as if wanting to speak in private. "How sober are you, Private?"

"Fairly sober, sir," I replied.

"Will you remember this conversation in the morning?"

"I believe I will, sir."

Hull nodded his head. "Good. Because there's something, I want to discuss with you if you're interested."

"All right, sir. What do you wish to discuss?"

"Well as you know, some draftees have arrived at camp for some training to become US soldiers. I've given Lieutenant Hastings the responsibility to train a platoon that will join C Company. He will need a devoted assistant to get these recruits into shape. Lieutenant Hastings has asked for your help personally. So what do you say?"

At first, I didn't quite know what to say. Hull's proposition had taken me off guard. I never thought of myself becoming an assistant to an instructor. My first instinct would be to ask for reassurance. Perhaps Hastings confused me with someone else. A mix up of names perchance. But I could feel Hull's observant eyes on me, waiting for an answer. "I would have to accept, sir," I blurted out.

"Good. That's damn good, Private. I'll inform Lieutenant Hastings first thing tomorrow morning. And consider this a quick promotion for yourself. Officially tomorrow, you'll be promoted to Corporal."

"Yes, sir. Thank you, sir," I said as I saluted him.

Hull returned my salute. "Now report back to camp and get some shut-eye. You'll need your rest."

———

HULL WAS GOOD ON HIS WORD and promoted me to corporal. Granted the pay is better but not enough to move off base. And being promoted to corporal has its perks: I am no longer the lowest of the low. I now had authority over fellow troops and new recruits, and there also came the respect. Moving up in rank was proving yourself—demonstrating that you are sufficient to handle the strenuous life as an army soldier.

Hastings had command over twenty men, and it became his duty to shape up these draftees in eight weeks. I can still remember the eight weeks of hell I endured during boot camp. So I won't lie—I enjoyed watching Hastings put these kids through the tough training I went through. And now I stood on the other side of that training. My duties included: barrack inspections with Hastings, supervising, and recording the daily counts of performed calisthenics during PT time. The work was uncomplicated and yet satisfying. The recruits, most of the time, never seemed to pay me much attention, as if I didn't exist. I was just an assistant, but there came times when they needed to be put in their place for disrespecting a superior rank: extra push-ups, running extras miles, or potato duty were a few of the punishments I would implement among the recruits. I pleased Hull and Hastings with my performances with the draftees, and it wasn't long before Captain Hull promoted me to sergeant.

I was moving up in rank—thank goodness for it. Along the way, I made a name for myself at Fort A.P. Hill, although it had not been a good name among fellow troops; Roland, being one them. My quick promotion in ranks through the year provoked jealousy. But Roland is intelligent; not dumb. He's smart enough to never criticize or demoralize me in front anyone. The reason: I'm under the protection of Captain Hull and Lieutenant Hastings. I became untouchable.

By July, I wish I could say that all was now going my way, but I can't. On a Monday evening, I returned to the barrack after spending time at the shooting range to find an envelope waiting for me on my bed. Written on the envelope was a message: *We Deeply Regret to Inform You.* I sat down on the bed with the telegram in my hand, tapping it on my knee, fearful about what I am about to read. And after several hesitant tries to open it, I ripped the envelope open and read:

Vince,
  Mother has passed. Funeral will be next Monday at Evergreen
  Hill Church. Nine o'clock a.m. Come home. Glenn

I grew numb. I read the tiny sheet of paper over and over to know if it was real because I didn't want it to be. The words then became jumbled after reading through it again and again that I could no longer look at it. I tossed the telegram with anger away from me, believing none of it was true. All just lies, I told myself, over and over—all lies. Glenn is toying with me. Having a little fun. Only a cruel and sick joke. But eventually, it all sank in. I had to accept the truth.

Mother was gone.

Over the next couple days, I reported to Hull that I was ill and put in a request for an emergency furlough. Hull granted me a few days of leisure but only a few days and no more. He seemed sympathetic. I explained to him Mother's passing and I expressed my desperation in returning home for the funeral and also my need to see Glenn, Julia, and Catherine. But there came no definitive answer from the captain.

By Saturday, my request for a furlough had not yet been approved until Hull called for a briefing with his entire company: the 29th Infantry are to undergo rigorous training in preparations for the upcoming invasion in Europe to push Germany back from occupied territory. This is all the information that Hull disclosed. It made me question if he knew more than what he was telling us. Or it was the only information he is allowed to reveal. Keeping classified information disclosed is a talent. Captain Hull declared he knew no more, but underneath his calm exterior, I read his face, tense with uncertainty, as if debating he should reveal what he truly knows. Yes, he knew more than what he explained.

But endless questions spilled from the lips of the troops. They wanted answers, and a small non-detailed discussion is unacceptable. They grew angry with their questions as Hull did his best to answer all of them, but he had no answers that would violate classified intelligence. Shouting and profanity from the men filled the barrack. I wouldn't be surprised if a fight were to break out at any moment. But to calm matters down, Hull stated that each men are to be given a two-week furlough before our training begun. This settled everyone down. A two-week furlough had been unheard of. Now I would have guessed this announcement from Hull would have pleased everyone but instead, the men shook their heads and cursed as they walked out the barrack in resentment or returned to their beds to sulk in their self-misery.

"Sergeant Conroy," Hull said as I walked past him. "A word please."

Hull and Hastings led me outside and into a small building next to the barrack. It was Hull's private office. Once inside, Hull sighed as he sat down behind a desk, leaving Hastings standing beside him with arms crossed, appearing strict and onerous.

"Have a seat, Sergeant," Hull said as pulled out three small glasses and a bottle of whiskey.

I sat down in the chair in front of the desk as Hull filled the glasses and set one glass down before me and handed another to Hastings and the last one he picked up for himself.

"Sergeant, I wanted to speak to you," Hull began, "about the news that all of you were just given."

"Well, I have to admit, sir, that all of this had been expected but very little has been disclosed among the men. They want to know more." I said.

Hull grinned faintly. "Believe me, Sergeant, I know this news isn't easy for you and rest of the men, but I wanted to tell you I am not holding anything back. I disclosed with the men everything I learned. I wish I knew more, but the simple fact is: I don't." I wanted to believe him, but I didn't. Hull took a drink of whiskey from his glass and twirled the glass around in his hand before taking another sip.

"Well, is there anything I can do for you, sir?" I asked.

"I think I'll let Lieutenant Hastings answer that for you, Sergeant."

Hastings took a swig of whiskey from his glass and cleared his throat as if he was now the person with authority in the room. "Captain Hull and I both agree that you are a capable man worthy enough to take charge of a platoon in C Company. We spoke with your old Drill Sergeant—Paul Ramsey; and he spoke highly of you. And so, Captain Hull and I have decided to give you 2nd Platoon, with me in charge of 1st. We discussed this matter last night, and we believe you are more than capable of taking the job. What do you say?"

This news had came unexpectedly. Now I took a swig whiskey. I almost coughed from the strong burn of hard liquor. Hull offered me the opportunity to take command of 2nd Platoon. A great responsibility is taking charge of a group of men. This was a job I didn't know much about, granted I had been the troop leader in Basic Training, but that was just training. I was being offered to command a group of soldiers going into war. I can make mistakes while training, but in war, mistakes can't be made. Errors can lead to someone getting killed and the possibility of myself getting killed. I wasn't sure if I should take their offer in fear I would let them down and that I would embarrass myself, forcing Hull to never trust me again with such an enormous responsibility.

I wanted to say 'no.' But I couldn't. I nodded my head as I sputtered my answer. "Y-yes."

Hastings smiled. "You have my full confidence, Sergeant. And you may find yourself promoted to Staff Sergeant soon enough."

"You're a good man, Sergeant," Hull stated. "I know you'll do the two of us proud."

"Thank you, sir," I said. "I will truly do my best."

"I'm sure you will. Now there's another matter I wish to discuss with you."

"Sir?"

"I understand that there has been some issue regarding something back home. You requested a furlough to head back to... Louisiana— was it?"

"Yes, sir. There has been a passing in the family—my mother. This news has came as a shock, sir."

"Ah, that's right—my condolences. You already know I have granted every man in my unit a two-week furlough, so you are no exception. So you have my permission to leave first thing tomorrow to Louisiana and take care of whatever it is you need to do. You have two weeks, Sergeant. Be back here in two weeks. We have preparations for war to attend to. Your training at commanding begins then. Dismissed."

I finished my glass of whiskey and stood up as Hull and Hastings did the same. We all saluted one another before I left the office.

EIGHTEEN

IT'S THE DAY OF THE FUNERAL. I woke around seven in the morning with Catherine lying beside me—asleep. Bright morning light glared through the hotel room's only window. The window's curtains were drawn back, allowing the sun and heat to invade the room. I lifted myself out of bed, careful not to disturb Catherine as I peered out the window. The townsfolk were already bustling in the streets, on their way to start the day as horse-drawn carriages rattled on the brick road of Main Street.

After my morning routine, I kissed Catherine on her cheek and put on my slacks, brown leather shoes and a white t-shirt before my walk to Evergreen Hill Church. It was eight o'clock—one hour before Mother's funeral. I packed my military dress suit in a duffel bag; no need to wear it yet. Save the best for the burial. I quietly slipped out the door to allow Catherine to sleep in peace.

———

I ARRIVED AT NATCHITOCHES the previous day, in time for the funeral.

My head swam with proper measures on when to tell Glenn and Julia about my upcoming departure to Europe. The news will no doubt come as a shock, but it's not best to keep secrets from those close to me. I should tell them before they discover the secret some other way: radio newscast or newspaper. Soon, the entire United States will know of their army's departure to England to fight in the war. War has been declared so it would only be a matter of time before action took place.

On Main Street, I picked up a newspaper and read an article regarding Japan. America's war with Japan has not been easy. For the moment, it seems, Japan has the upper hand. Since the attacking of Pearl Harbor, the bitter relationship between the US and Japan had been ugly. And it implies the tensions between the two countries will only rise. Japan had been invading islands, and other countries and the Allied armies had accomplished little to oppose them. The battles had been bloody and torturous. There had been reports of massive surrenders from the Allies for the Allies were unprepared to engage the Japanese. A hard lesson learned as now constant preparations for the invasion of Europe were underway. This is a war we couldn't lose. Every precaution must be taken to assure a solid victory for the Allies. Failure for the US was not an option. Only victory.

INSIDE, THE CHURCH WAS HOT. Several ceiling fans spun around on its highest setting, not circulating cool air, but instead, circulated warm air. I patted my forehead with a handkerchief to wipe away the beading sweat dripping down my face. The large room was empty, save for myself, until the two front doors swung open as Glenn stepped through, with Julia close behind him. He was dressed in a three-piece gray business suit, presenting himself as professional and driven. Julia appeared older—but she had held on to her sweet, childlike nature as I remembered before leaving the farm.

Once Glenn spotted me, he pointed me out to Julia, who came sprinting into my open arms. She latched onto me as tight as she could as I picked her up and hugged her. "I missed you, big brother!" she shouted with excitement.

"Well, I'll be damned," Glenn said with a smile as he approached. "Looks like the army really made a man out of you."

"You don't look so bad yourself," I said after setting Julia back on her feet. "You look like a hotshot lawyer or something."

"Not quite a lawyer just yet. It's been hard work. It's mostly classroom instruction. But I've been interning and earning my stripes."

"I've been earning my stripes as well. Your brother is a sergeant now. I'm responsible for a platoon of men. It's hard work, but I'm learning."

Glenn only nodded as he stared at the floor. He had a look as if something complicated and troubling was on his mind. "Listen... Vince—" he said, "about Ma—"

"How did she go?"

Glenn looked down at Julia. "Go sit at the front pew while I talk to Vince, ok?" In a heartbeat, Julia ran to the front pew on the left of the room and took a seat, leaving the two of us with some privacy. "I hated to be the one to send you that telegram. There was so much I wished to tell you, but I decided just to wait and tell you face to face. She had been ill for quite some time. She wanted to write to you about her condition but just didn't know how. It had been devastating for me as well with Pa and Julia. Julia cried non-stop. Pa rarely speaks nowadays. He only works and works. I think he's only tryin' to keep his mind occupied.

"I left New Orleans to come back to the farm for the time bein'. Pa had written me and told me about her condition. The last few days before her death, I was at her side, holdin' her hand. I talked to her to let her know I was there. I talked and talked so much. And she mostly listened because she had a hard time speaking. She only lied in bed with a teddy bear she clutched to her body. She wouldn't eat and wouldn't drink much water. A doctor had prescribed her medicine, but she refused to take it. She only lied there in bed with no hope—no desire to fight her illness. I think she accepted her fate.

"Julia would come into the room to see her but wouldn't stay long. She would eventually run out of the room crying because she couldn't bear to see Ma like that: frail and dyin'. On her last day, Pa never came into the room. It was only me who stayed with her in her final hours of the morning. I held her hand until she was gone and continued to hold her hand. I don't know why but I just did as I sat by her side looking at her and talking. Talkin' to her for what felt like hours. Maybe I couldn't accept her passing. I guess that's why I continued to speak to her because I couldn't let her go. Her hand turned to ice as I held it. I remember several times telling her to wake up. But she never did. She only lied there... cold and still.

"And so, it wasn't until the doctor arrived that I finally left the room. I broke the news to Pa and Julia. Pa only sank into his chair, motionless and not speaking. I picked Julia up and held her while she cried and wailed, 'I want Mommy! I want Mommy!' I did the best I could to calm her down and let her know everything would be ok. After a while, she finally calmed down long enough for me to put her to bed for the evening. Ma's body was removed the next day and taken here into town.

"Julia hasn't gotten over it yet. I haven't either. It's gonna take time for the two of us. I don't know how long but soon, I hope."

I stared at my feet on the floor as I listened to the words of grieving spilling from Glenn's mouth. In part, I felt guilty for Mother's death. She suffered on account of me, and I felt the guilt pounding down on me without remorse. But mentioning to Glenn that Mother's death was part of my doing seemed uncertain. I guess you could say I'm a coward. I was a coward to confess to my brother the guilt that weighed me down. Glenn would despise me. I hated myself. Is it reasonable to say I had killed her? In my mind—yes. Mother couldn't let go of me. It had been her maternal instincts; that's what killed her. Her love was as great as I had ever witnessed. And I betrayed her love with my arrogance.

Glenn doesn't know, nor Julia. They need not know, or so I thought. This is a secret I will keep to myself, only for the time being. For how long, I don't know. Perhaps when I'm ready to confess; if I'm ever ready to do so. But the secret would emerge soon enough. Sooner than I expected.

———

BEFORE THE FUNERAL BEGAN, I was clothing myself with my military suit in a private room when Glenn entered, still dressed in his business suit but he removed his coat. "Looks like it's only gonna get warmer," he said peering out the window.

"Looks like it," I said as I buttoned up my shirt. "Has Pa arrived yet?"

"Yup."

"I have nothin' to say to him," I stated. "I don't even want to be in the same room as him."

"Well, I got something to help you out with that," Glenn said as he reached into his vest pocket and removed a small flask.

I laughed. "You know, I don't think I should be drinking before a funeral."

"Just take a small swig," he said passing the flask to me. "It'll calm your nerves some."

"Why not?" I muttered to myself, giving in and taking a small sip. The aroma was powerful as it burned my nostrils and the taste of the strong bitter liquor burned my throat, causing a coughing fit. This was much different and much stronger than the whiskey I had drank with Captain Hull and Lieutenant Hastings.

Glenn laughed as I handed the flask back to him, coughing. "It'll take a few swigs to get used to it," he stated.

"It isn't too bad," I said as I continued to dress as Glenn stood there by the window, staring at the floor. His manner was distant. It appeared as though something was on his mind but had a difficult time letting it out. After a few minutes, I became anxious and decided just to ask him up front. "So what's on your mind, Glenn? It looks like you got somethin' to tell me."

Glenn took his eyes off the floor and glared at me. "I know how things are with you and Pa. . . "

". . . Yeah?" I said with reluctance as I worked on my necktie, peering at my reflection in the mirror in front of me. I wanted to imply to Glenn that my relationship with Father is one I did not want to discuss.

"But perhaps the two of you can—I don't know. . . work things out."

"I don't think that's a good idea," I said as I continued to work on my necktie in the mirror with patience and technique while making casual glances at Glenn's reflection in the mirror.

"You see—Ma threatened to leave him if he didn't make things right with you before she passed."

"I'm not surprised. Perhaps she should have."

"Yeah. She mentioned we have family in Vicksburg, Mississippi. And that she would take Julia with her to stay with them. Ma cared too much about you, Vince. She threatened to leave Pa for you. My opinion—I believe he feels responsible for what happened to her."

I nodded my head as I folded the collar of my shirt down over the necktie and swung around to face Glenn. I couldn't keep my guilt away from Glenn. But this wasn't about keeping secrets; it was about respect I had for my only brother. He had a right to know. "No. I'm responsible for what happened to her. And I really wouldn't care if Pa blamed himself or not. Perhaps he should blame himself, the more I think about it."

"Why are you blaming yourself? It wasn't your fault. And it wasn't Pa's fault. It was her fault, Vince. She didn't know how to deal with the family being broken up. She wouldn't eat, and she wouldn't drink. She let herself die. It's all it was. It's all it ever will be." I said nothing but only stared at the floor, as Glenn had done minutes before. "So please," Glenn pleaded. "Work things out with him."

"I tried that once. It didn't work out. Did you hear about that?"

"Yeah, I heard about what took place. But please at least try to talk to him once more. If not for you, but for Ma. . . and for me. Please."

I put on my coat. "I just don't think he'll listen, Glenn. That man is a stubborn mule, and I feel I'll only be wasting my time. Besides, Ma isn't here anymore. And it was my fault. I left her when she needed me the most. I walked away from her because I only thought of myself. She could still be here if it weren't for my ignorance. If you should blame anyone—perhaps it should be me."

Glenn shook his head at me to admit defeat. He then looked at me. His face was bitter "You can be really stubborn, you know. You're just like Pa! More than you will ever know!"

I gave Glenn a sarcastic smile. "The thing is, Glenn—I don't want to work things out with him. I don't care for that sorry SOB. I will not waste my time on a lost cause. You see—I'm leaving for Europe in a matter of months." I didn't realize it, but I let it slip I would leave to fight in the war. "And all I want is to get through this funeral with no confrontation from Pa. If I try to talk to him, things will only get worse. It's just not worth the trouble.

"Ma died from a broken heart, Glenn. I broke her heart. She fell on the front porch after I stormed out of the house after my talk with Pa. She cried out to me to come back to her, but I didn't. I just left her there on that porch sobbing, and I did nothing but walk away!"

Glenn put his hands into his pockets and stared down to the floor once more, looking disappointed. "Ok then. I think I know when there is no point in trying anymore."

"I'm sorry, Glenn. I am. I'm done with that man. It's my final word on the matter."

"If you feel so guilty about what happened to Ma than perhaps you did drive her to the grave. That's a heavy burden to live with, Vince. And now you're telling me you're leaving for Europe soon. Perhaps you should take that burden with you over there and then you will understand."

"Understand what?"

Glenn sighed. "That you're too damn stubborn to realize everyone makes mistakes. And that one mistake you feel so guilty about makes you weak. You admit it because it's what you believe, but it's not what I believe. You can't survive drownin' in your mistakes. Mistakes make you stronger—wiser; because you learn from them. But you are becoming weaker. Perhaps one day, you'll see that. No one's perfect, Vince. We all make mistakes. All I'm asking is—don't brood on yours. They'll get you killed."

Glenn stormed out of the room, not saying another word as he slammed the door behind him. I dropped down into a chair and scratched my head. My days of worrying over Father were over. The truth was—I wanted him out of my life for good. But Glenn didn't understand. He couldn't understand. However, I couldn't help but admire him. He was sensitive on the issues within the family and had made a faithful mission to keep it together, but he was failing or perhaps failed already.

———

TOMBSTONES BLACKENED WITH AGE occupied the small and old cemetery where Mother had been laid to rest along with a fresh stone with a new engraving that had been recently planted into the ground. I had only visited the graveyard on one or two occasions in the past. Father once told me that several of our distant relatives were buried there, but I knew nothing of them; Father nor Mother ever spoke of them. I wondered if the dead relatives were much of a mystery to my parents as they were to me. Were they Cousins? Aunts? Uncles? I didn't know. During the funeral in the church, I sat far away from Father as possible. Not once, had there been any acknowledgment of one another's presence; not even eye contact. The same behavior lingered in the cemetery as Mother's coffin was being laid into the deep ground. I stood far from him, but at times, I laid sight on him to observe his sunken eyes, and a face weathered down from exhaustion, age, and sadness over the tragic loss of his wife. Before the casket lowered, I took one last look at Mother's face before Glenn clamped the lid shut. Her face was as I remembered it: softly aged with an expression of grief. And yet beautiful. She suffered for too long because of me, but now she sleeps in peace.

After the burial, many of Mother's friends insisted on speaking to me with no end, wishing to express their deepest sympathies for our loss but the same words were echoed by each person. Words I had heard countless times in just one afternoon. One by one, aged men and women shook my hand, kissed my cheek, or embraced me because of my loss. It became maddening, and I needed to get away. It was all condoling, I agree, but my patience wore thin. I grabbed Glenn by his forearm and begged him to grab Julia so we could leave cemetery and to do so in a hurry.

I came back to the hotel room along with Glenn and Julia after Mother's funeral. I opened the only window in the hotel room to let a breeze flow into the stuffy room. A note left behind from Catherine had been placed under a pen on the small desk under the window informing me she had errands to run and would return later in the evening.

I sat on one of the two chairs with Julia resting in my lap with her head on my chest as Glenn sat in the other across from me. With two small glasses of whiskey in our hands, we saluted to the ceiling, saying our final goodbye's to Mother.

"Pa has to be told, you know," Glenn said after taking a swig of whiskey, "about you leaving for Europe."

"You're leavin' again, big brother!" Julia yelped, taken by surprise.

I let out a heavy sigh. "I'm afraid so, sweetheart. I have an essential job to do very far away from here across the ocean." Julia pouted. Her lips quivered and her big eyes filled with tears as she rested her head on my chest. "Do what you must," I said to Glenn. "He wouldn't care anyhow."

"You don't know that."

I shot a sharp gaze at Glenn, letting him know I was finished on the subject with Father, hoping he will get the hint.

"How long you will be away?" he asked, now avoiding the subject with Father.

"I don't have the faintest idea. I know as much as you do. All I know is that I'm leaving. I don't know exactly where, or how long I will be there, or if I am even coming back at all. A lot of us won't be coming back. This is war. But this is what the army trained me to do. They have called my number, so I have to pay the piper my due."

"Are you scared?"

I gave Glenn another sharp gaze. "What do *you* think?" I took a drink of whiskey from my glass and with a firm grip, rested it on the thick cushioned arm of the chair.

He scoffed. "There's no need to get worked up, Vince. You know you put all of this on yourself? That day when I found you in the field after skippin' work at the farm; I told you not to let that recruiter fill your head with a bunch of nonsense. But you went with it anyway—because you are one the most stubborn people I know. What did you think would happen? You knew what was going on over in Europe before you signed up. We all knew. Hell, we all tried to talk you out of it, but you wouldn't listen. Or perhaps you listened and just didn't care."

"It's a decision I made. There's no takin' it back. Had I known what I knew now—would I still sign that contract. . . who knows? Maybe."

"You might not realize it, Vince, but believe it or not, we only tried to protect you. Pa too. Do you think he would want to see you go away and be killed? No father would wish that for his son."

"I've heard the story, Glenn—about what happened to Father during the Great War—about how he was a damned coward. And I thought I had made it clear that I don't wish to speak about him anymore, especially in front of Julia."

Julia lifted her head from my chest and glanced around as though she had not been paying too much regard in the conversation. She was perhaps asleep. "It's ok, sweetheart. Your brother and I are just talking."

Julia let out a sleepy yawn and rested her head on my chest again.

"You really are stubborn, you know." Glenn muttered.

"As you said before," I responded. "It runs in the family I suppose."

"No point in arguing with you there."

After a moment, the both of us laughed but the laughter died down in an instant. Glenn took a drink of whiskey and me the same.

"What if you don't come back?" Glenn asked. "What kind of state is that gonna put me in? And Julia? We just lost our mother. We can't lose you too."

"I don't have an answer for you, Glenn. I wish I did, but I don't. As I said before—I don't know if I'm coming back. If it's my sole purpose in life to die in hostility, then that's the way it's gonna be. I can't change that. Who knows? Maybe I'll come home wounded or maybe come home without a scratch on me. I don't know. I wish I did, but I don't. And to answer the question you asked me earlier—yes, I am scared. I'm scared to death. And you're right—I am responsible for putting myself in this position. But it's a choice I made, and it 's a choice I must live with. But perhaps by some chance, I come back home alive; I may say I had done something remarkable. I had done something that no one could ever take away from me. No one could deny or ridicule me for. Do you know what that will be?"

Glenn shook his head. "No. What is it?"

"I lived, Glenn. I lived my life. Lived it to the fullest. And no man on this earth will ever take that honor away from me—no one. Perhaps that's what I'm doing this for. Perhaps I will have a story to tell my children and my grandchildren about what their Father and Grandfather had done with his life. Maybe you'll tell your children and grandchildren what I had done so they will grow up to respect their uncle and maybe Julia's family as well. One day perhaps, they'll know I was no coward. I fought in a war that needed me." I gave Glenn a sharp look. "Pa can't say that about himself to us. But I will."

Glenn took a sip of whiskey and stared down at my feet on the floor. "Goddamn right," he whispered. His response somewhat surprised me. It was as if now he had last understood.

Julia let out a loud yawn, showing that she was sleepy and was in a desperate need for a nap.

"I think I need to get her back to the farm," Glenn said as he downed the rest of his whiskey. He set the glass on the small table by the chair and stood. I stood up and passed Julia's tired and limp body over to Glenn. She wrapped her little arms tightly around Glenn's neck and collapsed her head on onto his shoulder.

I escorted Glenn and Julia downstairs and outside to Glenn's automobile—a dark green '38 Plymouth Sedan.

Julia woke as Glenn gently lowered her into the front passenger seat. She rubbed her sleepy eyes and looked at me. "I don't want you to leave again, big brother," Julia said in a sleepy voice. "Why can't you stay?"

"You need to take a nap," I replied, wanting to avoid the subject. "You're too young to understand why I have to go."

"But I don't want you to go," she said again as her eyes filled with tears.

"I have to leave to make the world a safer place, sweetheart," I said as I knelt down by the passenger seat. "I have to help people who are going through a tough time right now."

"But why?" she asked with a delicate voice.

I knew I couldn't explain to her that my job entitled me to leave the US to fight in a war. For her age, she could not understand.

"Because sweetheart. . . I want to be a great big brother to you. I want you to be proud of me for the sacrifice I have to make to ensure your life and other people's lives are safe: such as Glenn's, and even. . . Pa's. I'm also doing this for Ma, even though she's not with us anymore." I could feel my eyes beginning to tear up. "One day, you'll look back on this terrible war that's happening, and you'll tell people your big brother was there—fighting for peace. Fighting for other people's freedom. I don't know when I'll be back, sweetheart. It could be a long time. But I want you to know I'll be back, ok. I'll be back to see you again."

Julia lifted herself up and hug me around the neck, crying. Her grip was tight as if she never wanted to let me go. I held her for a minute and set her back down on the seat and kissed her forehead. "Goodbye, sweetheart," I said, fighting back the tears.

"Goodbye, big brother," she whispered as I shut the automobile door leaving her as she wiped away endless tears streaming down her eyes.

Glenn stepped up to me and held out his hand. I gave him a firm handshake and grinned at him. "You know, if you hadn't busted up your leg, you would probably be going over there with me?"

"Yeah," Glenn said. "Nothing can be done about it now."

"No. I guess not."

"Well, good luck, Vince. Please be safe so you can come back to us."

"Thanks, Glenn. I'll come back. I'll see to it."

And with that, Glenn stepped around his automobile and entered the driver side, igniting the transmission and driving off with Julia, leaving me behind in the smoke and nauseous exhaust fumes. My reunion with Glenn and Julia had been brief. They came back into my life, but were departing once more, wanting no place in the obscure and distant portions in my part of the world.

———

"IT FEELS LIKE MY HEAD IS ABOUT TO EXPLODE," I said staring at the dark ceiling. The room was pitch black but my eyes adjusted to the darkness. I thought of turning on the lamp by the bed, but the light would only burn my eyes.

Catherine snuggled closer to me. Her warm breath blew on my cheek. "I wasn't that rough with you, was I?"

I chuckled. "No, it's not that."

"Then what is it?"

"I have to tell you something. I don't want to, but I have to. It's just difficult to get it out."

Catherine propped herself up on her elbow beside me; only a thin sheet covered her naked body. I could still feel her warm breath on my cheek. "What is it? Is it bad? Did you find someone other woman to be with up in Virginia?" She sounded bitter as if preparing herself for a late evening of yelling, disappointment, and foolishness: foolish for believing she had found someone to be with, foolish for wasting time on someone who would leave her. Yes, I was leaving her but not with another woman. I was leaving her for my duty—for my country.

"No," I replied. "I'm not leaving you for someone else. But I am leaving the country in perhaps a matter of months. I've received my orders to start training for the war. I have no say in the matter. The only choice I have is to go."

It was now quiet as if Catherine had stopped breathing. "I had a feeling that something like this would happen. You know... I don't want you to go." Her tone now became different. I could hear the sadness in her words.

"Part of me doesn't want to go because I would miss you too much, but another part of me wants to go. I'd rather not go into this conversation again. I already had it out with Glenn just hours earlier." Now I propped myself up on my elbow and gazed at Catherine in the faint darkness. "But I have to know something, even as selfish as it may sound. But I have to know."

"Have to know what?"

"Will you wait for me? Will you wait for me 'til I come back? And if I don't come back, will you wait until you get word I didn't make it?"

"What do you mean if you don't come back?"

"Who knows what'll happen to me over there. I could be killed or taken a prisoner to never see the light of day again. Anything can happen."

"You mustn't speak like that, Vince. You're coming back. And when you do, I'll be here waiting for you."

"Can you promise me?"

"Yes, I promise." Catherine rested the palm of her hand on my cheek. I took hold of her hand with mine and kissed it. "It comforts me to know that I am just more to you than just sex. Because that's how I feel about you, you know. I don't see it as sex. I hope you know that. I see it as something different, something more intimate. Do you know how excited I was to see you yesterday? I opened my door, and there you stood all handsome in your uniform. Everything stopped right then. I waited so long for you to return and then there you were. So yes... I will wait for you. No matter how long it takes—I will wait until you are here with me once again. I promise."

Catherine fell silent, only because she began to cry. And I believed what she told me. I believed every word she spoke. I took her face in my hands to feel her soft skin—as soft as I will always remember. I kissed her forehead and then she rested her herself on my chest once again. "That's all I needed to know," I said before falling asleep with her in my arms.

NINETEEN

I TRAVELED WITH THE REST OF THE 29TH INFANTRY on the *Queen Mary* for Europe on the 27th of September in '42 along with other army divisions. We departed from New York City for Gourock, Scotland. By estimation, the trip would take five long days and four long nights. Before I stepped onto the ship, a superior officer gave me a blue-colored button that affiliated with one of the three color-coded sections of the ship. My unit had been placed in the stern of the ship. I remember watching the harbor disappear as we left. I was now leaving America for the first time in my life, going to a distant continent—a strange place, not knowing what to expect and it scared me to death.

The morning I departed from Natchitoches to return to Virginia, Catherine cried. I wanted nothing more than to stay with her, but I had my orders. The evening before, I convinced her to take a walk with me around the town; we walked together mostly in silence, holding hands. There was much I wanted to say to her—far too much: my entire life story, my dream of starting a life with her when I return, children, and growing old. But there was a complication I couldn't hide. Catherine and I both knew—I would be away but for how long? Perhaps several months, a year, or longer. And there's a chance I may not come back at all. The thought of me dying in battle had kept me awake for many nights before the time came to step aboard the ship and sail across the vast Atlantic Ocean.

So on my last day with Catherine, I thought it would be best to not mention my upcoming departure and instead, only speak of more pleas-ant things. We came to a secluded area overlooking the Cane River and sat on an empty bench. The sun began to set as we watched the evening light fade. No stars were visible yet. It was too early. The river's water rippled gently and glowed with orange. We were together and yet, I felt alone. The entire day, Catherine distanced herself. She stayed silent and never looked at me. I didn't believe she did this intentionally. My departure was to blame. She turned bitter because I had to leave her yet again; not by choice, but by my duty as a soldier—a life I had chosen.

I needed to console her. I needed to say everything and do everything I could to assure her I would be ok. "Catherine—I know you're worried about me. Tomorrow, I depart for Virginia, and in due time, I'll be leav-ing for Europe. Other men are leaving as well. They're leaving behind their wives, girlfriends, siblings, and parents just like I am. And I know a lot of them won't be coming back. But I will come back. I'm a trained soldier, and I'm gonna use everything I've learned to make it back to you. You have my word on that."

"But what if you don't come back?" she asked. "What will I do with myself?"

"I know there is nothing I can say to convince you that everything will be ok," I said. "And there's nothing I can do to get out of this mess besides shooting myself in the foot or something." I chuckled to lighten the mood, but Catherine didn't laugh. Not even crack a smile. "But then I would be court-martialed or something." Catherine still was silent. "Please, listen for a moment..." I took her face in my hand and gazed into her green eyes, as they swelled with tears. "I'm coming back. And when I do, we will start a family. We'll have and raise kids and watch them grow up, and we'll grow old together."

"I want that more than anything," Catherine said. "So I want you to promise me you will do everything in your power to return home. Don't be careless or stupid over there. Just be smart and careful. Will you do that for me?"

"Of course," I replied.

"Write to me."

"I will."

We then walked back to my hotel room for our last night together—a memorable one.

The next morning, I traveled on a bus to Virginia to begin preparations for the upcoming mission that no one and myself knew nothing about. After intense training, the 29th shipped to Fort Blanding in Florida for a month of rest. Before leaving, Lucy embraced me and cried, sad to see me and the other men whom she got to know leave her behind. She told me to come back safe. I said I would. We stayed at Fort Blanding until the 19th of September. Afterwards, we all traveled to Camp Kilmer in New Jersey. It was a staging area for our deployment to England. Shortly after, we were all on the *Queen Mary*, leaving New York City.

Being on a large ship with thousands of other men is quite the experience—a very unpleasant experience. We were all given two square meals a day, on account, there were so many men on board. Meals had to be in six settings. And my setting was last. I ate breakfast (bacon, eggs, and coffee) around eleven a.m. and dinner (beef stew, couple slices of bread, and juice) around seven-thirty p.m. The food was bland, but with nothing else to eat, there is no choice but to eat it. But we were provided small stale pork meat sandwiches to snack on throughout the day to keep our calories up.

As if problems with bad food weren't enough—there was fear among myself and all the troops that enemy submarines could wreck the ship. The thought of this kept me awake at nights and kept me always on guard. I wanted to be ready. Along with difficulty sleeping, because fearing the ship being sunk and disappearing into the depths of the Atlantic, the ship was crowded with men. The *Queen Mary* carried over fifteen-thousand troops, making sleeping arrangements difficult. The sleeping quarters were too hot due to overcrowding. We all slept in bunks stacked up to six-feet high with an eighteen-inch clearance between each bunk. These bunks became drenched with sweat from the occupants because of the intense heat. It was hot for me, even though I am from the south, and that's saying something. It relieved me to find out the sleeping arrangements rotated. Every soldier aboard would sleep two nights inside and two nights outside. I preferred to be outside. It's much more relaxed and I had a better chance of survival if enemy submarines sunk the ship. I also liked to be outside because I was away from the putrid smell of vomit from seasickness, sweat, and cigarette smoke. But there is a rule for anyone outside the ship: helmets and life-jackets are to be worn at all times, even for sleeping. No exceptions.

During the last day of the voyage, I thought it would be best to occupy my time with some gambling, which is forbidden on board but many of the men ignored this rule. Swearing and boozing were also banned. All the men would swear, myself included, but we did not do this front of superior officers. "What they don't know, won't hurt them," I said to myself as I got into a card game of gambling with a Karl and Andrew. I never gambled with money in all my life, but I decided to learn. The game I stuck to the most was poker. I caught on to it after a few rounds, and I became a few bucks richer. Perhaps I found my calling.

But our poker game was interrupted when a powerful noise thrashed throughout the ship. The fear of being attacked seemed to have become a reality. Everyone downside jumped to their feet and grabbed their gear and ran topside. Not thinking, I failed to put on my helmet and life-vest as I ran out from below. Once I reached the outside the ship, I looked around for planes flying above or ships and submarines in the water. But I discovered no planes flying overhead and saw no submarines. I questioned about what the thundering noise was until someone towards the front of the ship yelled that the *Queen Mary* had struck the *Curacao*—one of our British escort ships. I fought my way towards the front to examine the scene. That's when I heard the screaming and noticed smoke rising into the air. I moved my way to the side railing and to my horror, saw a smaller vessel divided into two. Fire blazed throughout the sky as I saw men yelling for their lives. Large amounts of oil covered the ocean water as men fought to survive, swimming and trying to grab hold of anything that would float. Many of them drifted motionless in the water—dead. To my astonishment, the *Queen Mary* only sailed on, as if nothing happened. I remember shouting out if those poor souls in the water were to be helped, but no one heard me. All I could do was watch on as the massive ship continued its course and the wreck of the *Curacao* vanished into the vast horizon.

I encountered my first taste of war. And that first taste wasn't against our enemy—but our allies. And I could do nothing to help them. This is no dream I lived in. This is reality, and then I realized there would be many more deaths for me to witness in the upcoming months, maybe years to come. But there is no turning back. I was stuck here on this ship and held in the war until I am killed or wounded.

As the ship moved on, I couldn't get the image of all those poor souls in the water fighting to stay alive and the dead sailors drifting in the water. Many of the troops had already cleared off the top deck and retreated below as I trotted around outside to locate an area of privacy. I discovered a secluded area on the starboard and just in time too as I leaned my head over the railing and vomited. I wanted to do it away from the other men, for they may think of me as being weak. For several minutes I heaved before getting control of myself. I turned around as my back moved down the railing so I would be off my feet. Sweat streamed down my face as I wiped my forehead with my sleeve. The air outside wasn't warm, but I felt hot. After several minutes, I felt better and expected I could make my back down below the ship until a voice rang out. "Where's your helmet and life vest, soldier?!"

I jumped to my feet as it surprised me to see standing just a few feet away from me was Aschner. "You scared the hell out of me, Aschner."

"You didn't answer me, Sergeant! Where's your helmet and life-vest?!"

"I-I'm sorry, sir—I didn't think to grab my helmet and life-vest before running to the top deck."

"You didn't think?!" he growled. "Tell me something, Sergeant: what if we were under attack and you came running out here without your helmet and life-vest? What kind of situation would you find yourself in?"

"I-I don't—," I stammered.

"What kind of situation would you be in?!" he barked.

"I would be in a fucked-up situation, sir," I blurted. It was the only answer I could come up with. I felt foolish.

Aschner then smiled at me and laughed. "Good answer, Conroy."

I became relieved and chuckled with him. But I felt ridiculous I didn't see through the ruse. "What was all of that about?" I asked.

"Sorry, I couldn't resist, but I'm only teasing you."

"You did give me a scare though."

Aschner laughed again. "I apologize. I have to work on my skills at being a leader."

"Well, please don't practice your skills on me too much, will ya?"

"Sure thing."

Without warning, the uneasiness I felt moments before came back. Perhaps seasickness, as I gripped the railing of the ship.

"Are you all right, Conroy?" Aschner asked. "You're looking a little pale."

"Yeah, I think I'll be fine," I responded. "Just a little seasick is all."

"This wouldn't have anything to do with what just happened, would it?"

"I don't think so," I replied. "Just seasickness." I didn't want to tell him the truth. I felt hot again as beads of sweat on my forehead dripped down my face. My legs became unstable, making it challenging to stand. I needed to sit again.

"Easy, Conroy," Aschner said. "Sit down and relax a little." Aschner took hold of my shoulders with his hands and helped me off my legs.

"Thanks," I said. Sitting down did indeed help. Now that Aschner mentioned the incident with our escort ship—I grew curious if he had seen anything other than what I saw. "Did you see it happen?" I asked.

"Yeah, I saw it," he replied as he sat down right next to me. "I was standing at the bow with some other men, discussing a few things. We chatted and watched that escort vessel coming up to the ship too damn close. This ship had been zigzagging. This is a measure to throw off enemy subs. But that vessel just kept getting closer and closer. Then it got too close. And collided with this ship. So that's what happened. I witnessed it with my own two eyes."

"I feel sorry for all those men aboard the vessel," I said. "Will those men in the water be helped? Why didn't we stop?" My head filled with questions.

"It's just policy, I reckon," he replied. "It would be too dangerous for us to stop and help them because this ship would be too vulnerable for an attack. And yes, those men that did survive will be picked up. You don't need to worry." I nodded my head, unconvinced, however. "We'll be in Scotland very soon," Aschner said as he turned his head, looking out over the blue ocean. "That's the coast of Ireland there." I turned my head around and watched my first glimpse of foreign land pass by. We were quite away from the coast, but the land was visible. "Yep, it won't be too long now," Aschner continued.

"Good," I said. "The sooner I get off this damn ship, the better."

Aschner laughed. "I don't blame you. I wouldn't mind stepping off this ship myself and stepping onto solid dry land."

My thoughts wondered. The understanding of being back on land would only bring battle, and I would be in the middle of it all. "Can I ask you something?"

"Well sure."

"Are you scared?"

Aschner fell silent at first. He didn't look at me, only at the ship's wall about ten feet away. "Yeah. I guess I am. How about yourself?"

I took a moment to answer. ". . . Yeah."

"It's nothing to be ashamed of, Conroy. Because I can guaranty you, there isn't a soul on this ship that isn't afraid."

I nodded my head.

"Just remember your training, and you'll be fine. You'll go home when all of this blows over. We'll all go home and carry on with our lives as if nothing ever happened. We'll be back to getting drunk in bars, sleeping with our women, and having kids and raising them."

"Yeah," I said. "All of that sounds nice right about now." I paused, unsure if my next words should be expressed to Aschner. "I don't know what I'm doing here. You know—I put myself into a huge goddamn mess. And when the time comes to pull the trigger—I don't know if I'm strong enough to do it."

The feeling to vomit soon emerged again. I jumped to my feet and leaned over the railing as I did before. I regurgitated while Aschner patted my back. "Get it all out, buddy. You'll feel better. Trust me."

"Thanks," I said after it was over. "I'm feeling better now." I sat back down again and glared at Aschner. "You know... you never answered my question."

"What question?" he asked with confusion.

I smiled. "The question I asked you back at Fort A.P. Hill. Don't you remember? Did you enlist because have a backbone? Or are you here because you had nowhere else to go? I think now is a good time for an answer."

Aschner shook his head. "The funny thing is: I don't rightfully know. We all have our choices. You have yours and I have mine. And how we stand by those choices define who we really are. You should remember that." I nodded my head and said nothing. "Try to find a place to lie down for a while. Somewhere cool if possible. I need to report to my superiors. And I'll see you on land. Once you get back on land, you'll be feeling much better."

"Yeah."

Aschner walked away, leaving me alone.

I thought of the choice I made when I enlisted. But I wasn't ready to fight; I came to understand that. It wasn't seasickness or the horrific

image of the escort ship sinking forcing me to vomit anymore. I was terrified of this war. Now more than ever, I wanted to run home back to
Catherine like a damn coward. Like a dog with my tail tucked between
the legs. But I remembered Aschner's words. I made my choice, and I
need to stand by it. And years later I understood that he was right. The
choices we make and how we stand by those choices define who we really are. I only wish I realized it then.

———

I MADE MY WAY BACK DOWN to the sleeping quarters and squeezed my
way through the men in search of Karl and Andrew. Roland passed me
on the way, looking angry as he slammed his huge shoulder into mine.
"Watch it, you fucking prick!" he shouted as he stomped past me. Arthur
followed, keeping his head low and avoiding eye contact.

After shrugging off Roland's immature manner, I soon found Karl and
Andrew playing a game of poker with Lester. They were crammed between a couple of cots near the floor, struggling to enjoy a comfortable
game. I knelt down to make my presence known. "I don't know if I'll
ever forget what I had just seen."

"That makes two of us," Lester said. "We just left them in the water
to die. How fucked up is that?"

"What could any of us do?" Andrew asked.

"Someone could have done something," I replied.

Andrew gave me a cold stare. "Yeah? Like what, Conroy?" I didn't
have an answer, but Andrew had put me on the spot. Karl and Lester
gazed at me, waiting for an answer. But I remained silent. "What could
any of us have done to help those people? Were you thinking of saving
them yourself? Did you wanted to jump in there with them? If you had
done that—what could you have done to help?"

Again, I had no answer. I felt embarrassed by my statement earlier
and wished I had never said it. The three men sealed their stares at me.
Then I mumbled. "Nothing. There was nothing I could do." They

switched their curious eyes from me and back to their cards in their hands.

"You may be a sergeant, Conroy," Andrew said, "but don't try to be a fucking hero—especially if it's gonna get you killed. No one could have done anything to help them. *No* one."

Karl came to my rescue. "Back off, Andrew. I'm sure there were plenty men on this ship that wanted to help those people out."

Andrew scoffed as he threw his cards down. "I'm out."

"Me too," Lester said as he threw down his cards also, leaving Karl the winner of the hand.

"Deal me in," I said as I threw a dollar down into a meager pile of money, trying to move away from the conversation.

Lester looked at me. "Well, I'll be damned, Conroy. Never took you as a gambling man. You're just full of little surprises."

"I'm learning the game," I replied.

"Well, you still have a lot to learn," Karl said.

"As I recalled," I said, "I took money from you guys earlier this evening."

Andrew scoffed. "Don't get too cocky, Conroy. Roland was arrogant, and he lost some dough to us just a few minutes ago."

"Is that why he was so upset?" I asked as I rubbed my shoulder.

"Could have been," Andrew replied.

"I don't know why you like to hang around that guy, Lester," Karl said. "He's a sleazeball."

Lester dealt out five cards to each man for the round to start. I had a pair of fours. "He's good at winning fights. As long as I stick close to him, no one will mess with me. I mean, he's like a bear. And no one tangles with a bear. Because let me tell ya—he's pulled me out of some tricky situations. And the poor guy doesn't have many friends, so I guess I owe it to him."

"I'll take two," Andrew said as he threw two cards down. Lester passed Andrew two cards. "Don't be a goof, Lester. That son of a bitch could barely get through boot camp, and he didn't fare much better during our advanced training. Because let me tell me—where ever we end up over in Europe, Roland will get himself killed, and he's gonna get you killed too if you hang around him. He's clumsy, smug, and fucking slow. He'll be the death of ya."

"Nope," Lester replied. "I don't believe that one bit. We'll watch each other's backs over there."

"Yeah fucking right," Andrew griped. "Just you wait and see."

Lester exchanged himself three cards as a few more dollars went into the money pile. "Shit. I'm out." Lester threw down his cards and stood up. His eyes went sharp. "We all need someone to watch our backs over there. That's one of the first things we learned in boot camp: we all watch each other's back. I'll take my chances with Roland. And I know we're a long way from home. And who the hell knows what we're heading into. All this training we've been going through is all because of this dictator who wants to control everything. Because of him—we're all sailing onboard a crowded ship to stop him and his army. We could be home right now—safe and comfortable. Instead, we're traveling across a fucking ocean to take part in Hitler's war." He then stormed away from the card game—angry and hard-nosed.

"Little shit," Andrew remarked.

I came to recognize this wasn't the same Lester I remembered from Basic Training. He was no longer the frail man who took a beating from Ramsey. No, this was someone else. He may look the same and even talk the same, but he was someone different. A fire had been lit underneath him. And in some ways, I felt that same fire being lit underneath me. It's a small fire, steadily rising to no end—a fire that would refuse to burn out as long as I still breathed. I reflected that most of the men on this ship had that same fire underneath them. Their eyes told me. I thought of the conversation with Aschner once again when I first arrived at Fort A.P. Hill. Nearly all of these men came from towns no one has ever heard of. Volunteers and draftees who are uneducated, and with nowhere else to go are now disciplined soldiers for the United States Army. They are here now on this overcrowded ship sailing away to a distant land to engage in a war for the sake for the greater good. But Aschner was wrong about one thing: these men didn't sign up because they had nowhere to go; it's the willingness to serve and perhaps die for a country that calls for them for the sake of patriotism. It's every man's duty to protect his country in the hour of need. The soldiers for the US Army had a good fight in them. They'll defend it until their dying breath. All for the sake of freedom.

TWENTY

THE JOURNEY ACROSS THE ATLANTIC had been eventful. One's first voyage across a vast ocean is not easily forgotten. In my case, it was the wreckage of the *Curacao* that made an impression—a grim impression.

But at last, The *Queen Mary* arrived in Gourock, Scotland on the fifth of October. For the first time in my life, I now stood on foreign land. Gourock, a small fishing village, was used as a port for incoming military ships. Troops stayed for the evening for sleep and traveled the next morning to Tidworth in the south of England for more training for preparations for the Allied assault. In Tidworth, we slept in uncomfortable barracks: the bunks had straw mattresses, there were no pillows so spare clothing had to be used to rest my head on. And what I remember the most is the cold. The barracks were not heated, and this made sleeping a nightmare. I huddled under the one blanket I owned in my bunk, trying my best to keep warm. Believe it or not, but I looked forward to the training, on account I was outside and moving around, allowing heat to build up.

The American and British troops are to be supported by the Soviet Union and China armies. Germany, along with Italy had invaded much of the European territories. The primary purpose during this time was to cease the Axis armies advancement throughout Africa and westward through Europe. And now the training began. The training became laborious. The entire 29th Infantry marched throughout southwestern England for endless miles in full gear. Our uniform comprised of our helmet, boots, leggings, undershirt, jacket, and trousers. Along with that, we carried our rifle, handgun, bayonet, spade, canteen, ammunition, grenades, and a combat pack which had personal items. During these marches, we dug and slept in foxholes for many days. My blanket came in handy for keeping bugs away during the night. I could never become accustomed to bugs and worms. The mornings after waking up, everyone needed to brush and flap their blanket like a madman to remove every bug crawling about. Insects and worms were a nuisance, but it would be best to tolerate them, for I knew I had to live out my days in this war sleeping in foxholes.

We performed daily exercises to remain in shape and did target practice to occupy the days with activities necessary for our discipline. We were instructed how to use explosives and probe for mines. The daily routines reminded me of Basic Training. And that's where I thought I was. Ever since I finished boot camp, the training continued and on and on. There was no end in sight.

We remained in Tidworth for over seven months, then proceeded to Dartmoor for yet more training. But this was something new. Something different. Now our focus was different. The first day learning amphibious assaults confused me for I did not understand what I was doing. We started by jumping in and out of boats on land to get us comfortable before superiors instructed us to train in the water. This may seem simple enough, but there were procedures that all troops had to tolerate. We used these procedures to learn the vital goal of teamwork.

Dartmoor, however, felt like a marsh. It's difficult to locate any piece of solid dry land. The weather is miserable, due to continuous rain. When our amphibious training, at last, moved to waters, we stayed wet from head to toe throughout the day. And cold. Any soldier could practice all they with the formations of vaulting in and out boats on dry land, but there will be slip-ups along the way in the water. I can't recall how many times I had failed to drop into the boat either by my foot slipping off a net or the boat suddenly rocking because of waves.

We not only practiced jumping in and out of boats but also how to attack pillboxes (large concrete structures with loopholes used for shooting a weapon). This involved six separate teams on the same boat. The first team is the riflemen; they are the first off the boat after the ramp drops and are responsible for covering fire. The second team off the boat are accountable for carrying Bangalore torpedoes (long pipes stuffed with dynamite) to blow trenches in a sand wall. Next, the third team is off the boat and they must cut wires to create a breach for a narrow passage under barbed wire. The fourth team are machine gunners, responsible for covering ammo carriers and mortar gunners. Finally, the last group off the boat are the flamethrowers and dynamite team. This team's task is to blow up the pillbox.

Our superiors watched as we performed these exercises and were quick to correct any mistakes and make suggestions. As time passed, our amphibious training became more monotonous and the more we trained, the more I grew to despise it.

As if training wasn't bad enough, the food was terrible as well. Nothing was fresh. We ate stale sandwiches with jelly or a thin slice of meat and had very little fruit to eat. All there was to drink was stale burnt coffee.

Our barracks in Dartmoor were no better than the barracks in Tidworth. The Dartmoor barracks were more like huts. The British built them for the American troops arriving for training. And much like the Tidworth barracks, they were cold and uncomfortable.

This became my life now. The entire 29th Infantry and I trained almost every day for two years. And I waited. I grew anxious as to when the skills I learned would be put to the real test. The time would come soon enough. Learning everything there is to know about being a soldier requires patience. But my patience was being tested. I had an itch. I couldn't scratch it or relieve it myself. The only way to do so is to wait for the orders to come. But when will the orders come? After several years of training, I felt like a weapon of the US Military. Now here in England, amongst many other American soldiers, I grew eager to fight.

And now the time to fight drew closer. I felt it in my bones.

By late May of '44, after several years of training was over, Captain Hull granted me a pass to nearby Salisbury along with Karl, Andrew, and Aschner. Passes were scarce, and I was shocked to receive one. I needed a temporary leave from Dartmoor. The gloomy and stagnant surroundings of Dartmoor would not be missed once I would leave it for good. And I hoped it would be soon. I was glad to be going to Salisbury for a change of scenery, even if it was just for a few days.

My visit to Salisbury had left me stunned. The town is surrounded by dense grassy meadows. And the old timbered buildings gave it a gothic atmosphere. A cathedral, erupting so notably in the sky, dominated the small town with influence and importance that no one could look upon its magnificent architecture without admiration. Never had I been in a place so rustic and charming.

Military officials had evacuated most residents of the town in fear of German bombings. Even though evacuation was voluntary, they per-suaded parents to send their children away to live with strangers in safer areas. The town is now being used by the Allied armies as a re-treat for troops and refuge for the injured. They erected hospitals throughout Salisbury and doctors and nurses from all over were arriv-ing in preparations for the war.

The four of us strolled the streets of Salisbury in search of nothing in specific. The pubs weren't open, being only ten in the morning; Aschner made the recommendation we get soup to eat before the pubs open. So we went in search for a nearby cafe.

The day was wet. It had rained in the early hours, and now an over-cast remained. The clouds still dropped a few drips of rain here and there. We were all dressed in our finest military clothing. Our attire caught the eyes of the local women, something the local men shunned.

We did our best to keep to ourselves, but soon the women would rush up to us and shake our hands and try to start small-talk. I was hesitant at first to speak to them, but it didn't take long before I gave in. These women were glad to speak to us and we thought it be best to oblige them—not wanting to be rude.

So the four of us talked and flirted with women as we made our progress down the streets. We passed a little shop when I spotted a black and grey camera with several knobs on top and a round lens in the center of the front displayed in the window. Wanting a closer look, I broke from the group and slipped inside the little shop. It was a quaint little place with a musky aroma in the air. A large-set clerk that wore small glasses on his round face stood behind the counter as I wondered about, looking at various little trinkets and small furniture. I paced around for a few minutes observing the contents of the shop before making my approach to the camera in the window. I didn't know why but I wanted it. I picked it up to observe it closer.

"It's a 35mm Rangefinder," a voice with a thick British accent said from behind me. I spun around, almost dropping the camera, to find the clerk smiling at me.

"35mm Rangefinder?" I said.

"That's right," he said. "Are you interested in that camera? You've been staring at for quite some time."

"I suppose you could say I'm interested," I replied.

"Well, it was produced in 1940, and the lens is 51mm. It has various functions and whatnot. It's a great camera, but unfortunately, these sorts of cameras are quite expensive."

"That's too bad. I would have liked to own this."

"Well, that camera has been used before. A gentleman sold it no more than a few months ago. So secondhand brings the value down."

"Hm. So what price are you asking?"

"You're an American soldier, yes?"

"That I am. 116th Regiment with the 29th Infantry," I stated. Saying it made me feel important but I may have been filled with too much pride.

"Well, we're all glad you boys are over here helping us out and all. So what I will do for you is sell that camera to you for twenty-three pounds. How does that sound?"

In my pocket, I carried about eleven pounds. My other funds were being held for back-pay which I'll collect when I arrive back to the States. "I would love to have this, but I'm afraid twenty-three pounds is out of my budget. I'm sure it's worth that, but I'm not carrying that kind of currency."

"Yes, like I said—these cameras are not cheap. It's a fine camera, that is." Before I could set the camera back down in its place in the window display, the shopkeeper took hold of my arm. "If you don't mind me asking—but how much currency do you have on you?"

"Only eleven pounds."

"Eleven pounds, you say."

"That's right."

"Well, I'll tell you what I can do for you; you seem like a nice young man. You're an American soldier over here helping us fight this war... so how about seven pounds, and the camera is yours."

I almost dropped the camera a second time. "Seven pounds?! Are you sure?"

The shopkeeper nodded his head at me and smiled. "I'm sure. Seven pounds."

I fumbled around in the pockets of my trousers before I found the small wad of British cash and coins. I flipped through the currency and counted out what I owed and handed it to him. "Seven pounds it is. Thank you for this."

"You're very welcome, young man. And I hope you put it to good use."

"I will."

"Oh, one other thing," he said, walking behind the front counter. He pulled out a couple of film rolls from underneath the counter and handed them to me. "You might need these. Free of charge."

"Now I'm asking too much. I can at least give you another pound for the film."

"As I said—free of charge. And it's my pleasure. I have an impression with the America's involvement in this war—we will surely win. This is the least I can do." The shopkeeper's words were sincere and filled with hope. I didn't want to let him down.

I was now grateful for visiting Salisbury. The last I expected to find was the generous warmth of a shopkeeper optimistic about the war. His good will toward me gave me a new perspective. There's faith among the people that the Allies can win. And with enough faith, the tide can change. America's involvement lighted the spark needed to give the civilians hope of driving the German army back. And along the way, if I survive, I want to record the events with my new camera. I had a suspicion this will be a time I will not wish to forget.

———

AFTER I LEFT THE SHOP, I caught up with everyone else as they were entering a small diner. The smell of food and coffee was strong and it made me hungry. Small tables furnished the floor. The decoration was old-fashioned, much like the medieval image of Salisbury. Pictures of the Cathedral hung on the wall along with maps of England. Bookshelves filled with various books and knickknacks were lined up near the top of the wall.

"Where did you disappear off to?" Karl asked as we sat down at a corner table in front of a large window. He stuck up four fingers in the air and called out for four bowls of cheese soup.

"I went into that little antiques shop we passed and purchased this," I replied, holding up the camera.

Andrew whistled. "I've seen one of those," he said. "They're nice. How much did you pay for it?"

"I'd say I got a reasonable deal on it," I replied. I didn't want to reveal how much I paid. The last thing I wanted was for word to get out and that poor shopkeeper would need to put up with many other American soldiers harassing him for discounts on his items.

"I'd take real good care of that," Aschner said. "You're lucky you got one."

A young woman soon came by and gave us coffee and bread to eat as our soups were being prepared. Andrew kept his eyes on her as she poured hot coffee into mugs from a pot. She smiled at him with big brown eyes as she turned to retreat into the kitchen. Andrew watched every movement she took with fascination.

"So what's happening now?" I asked Aschner. "There isn't more train-ing, so something has to happen soon."

"I'm not sure myself," Aschner replied as he stuffed bread in his mouth. "I only go by hearsay. But... I heard a rumor we will ship out to France."

"France!" Andrew shouted. "Well, it's about fucking time! If you ask me—we've been wasting too much time on training. Haven't we trained enough? We need to get over there ASAP and go to war!"

"Easy with the language, Sergeant Decker," Aschner scolded. "And keep your voice down. It's only a rumor. But if it is true, it should be only a matter of time before we invade."

"I hope so," Karl said. "Believe me when I say I don't know how much longer of Dartmoor I can take."

I sat and drank my coffee and ate warm bread as the three men chat-ted. After my fill, I fumbled around with my new camera. I discovered how to put the film roll in and I played around with the knobs and switches. Once satisfied I had everything figured out, I took a photo of the men as they chatted. This would be the only photo I would take with all three of them together.

"So what do you think, Conroy?" Aschner asked. "You've been awfully quiet."

I had no clue what their discussion had turned into. "I wasn't paying attention," I replied.

Karl laughed. "He's too busy experimenting with that camera." Bits of bread crumbled out if his mouth as he spoke.

"I was wondering if you think we're welcomed here in England?" Aschner said.

"Why wouldn't we be?" I replied. I thought of the shopkeeper. "We're over here lending a helping hand to our allies. They'd do the same for us. They need all the help they can get."

"See," Karl said. "He gets it. But Andrew here doesn't."

"I only know what I know," Andrew said. "It's a surprise the men around here don't spit on us. I mean, you saw how they were looking at us on our way over to this cafe."

"That's because all their women flocked to us," Aschner said. "They're jealous. They don't like their women mingling with us. How would you feel if a British soldier came over to America where you live and your woman gawked at him?"

"I would punch the poor bastard in the mouth," Andrew said.

We all laughed.

"Exactly," Aschner said.

Andrew shrugged his shoulders, now understanding Aschner's point and decided to remain silent.

Our soups came, and more useless conversations broke out as we ate. It felt nice to be in the company of my friends. This was a day we needed to get away from the strict military rules of our daily lives and just be ourselves. For the first time in many months, I felt normal again; an ordinary human being in the real world, mingling with the common folk. I forgot what it felt like. On this day, I was just me and not a soldier. The more time we spent in Salisbury, the less I thought about being away from home and the preparations for a war. But all of that would soon change—because I was not prepared for what was to come.

TWENTY-ONE

MY FOOT SLIPPED off the thick rope net as I climbed my way down into the Higgins boat from a large ship. I had practiced this exercise many times during my training, but slip-ups happen. We were off the coast of Normandy, France, about five kilometers. The weather is dreary, and the seas are rough. The early morning daylight is dim as overcast hid the sky from above. Harsh waves crashed on the side of the British transport ship, making the climb down into the Higgins boat difficult. Half of the troops from C Company crammed the inside of the boat. Our destination is section Dog Green of Omaha Beach. Regiments of the 1st Infantry Division and the Rangers had been assigned to fight along with us for the assault onto the beach. I learned in a briefing that Omaha would be the most challenging area to breach because it was the most important. It would be heavily defended with mines and enemy fire. Our objective: to clear the beach and the bluff of Germans to provide landings for the Navy and allow heavy artillery, such as tanks, safe access to the beach and ready for deployment across France. Operation Overlord was now underway.

But I feared I wouldn't make it to shore as I clambered down the net, struggling to hop aboard the Higgins boat. Due to the swells, I had to time my jump so the distance from the ship to the boat would be shorter. But I missed my mark as I performed my jump. A large swell pulled the Higgins boat away from me as I caught a hold of the edge of the boat after my plunge.

"Pull him in!" Hull shouted amongst the men.

Several men scrambled to my aid, pulling me over into safety into the boat before colliding with the ship and by chance, crushing my legs.

After the men hauled me up to my feet, I caught a glimpse of Roland smirking at me because of the incident.

Once onboard the Higgins boat, I felt sick. The boat bounced up and down with force, and to make matters worse—I couldn't sit down due to the boat being overcrowded. It amazed me it didn't sink due to all the weight of the men and the overabundance of necessities for the upcoming battle. After several minutes, I vomited along with other men, either by seasickness or anxiety, or perhaps both. The deck soon became slick with vomit. The foul smell of vomit and salt lingered onboard.

As I waited, the thought of going into the unknown filled me with many emotions. The emotion I remembered most of all: dread. I'm scared, and I'm willing to admit it. My body shook from tension. I was nearly killed climbing down a ship before my participation in the assault even began. After all the years of training, it's all coming down to this. I'm here now in a boat with twenty-nine other men—armed to the teeth with weapons, grenades, and ammunition for the upcoming assault. This is what I asked for when I left the comfort and the safety of the farm and by signing up for the army. And now there is no backing out. I'm here to engage the enemy and to do my civic duty, even if I were to be killed.

More daylight peaked through the clouds as we all stood in the boat, waiting with impatience for something to happen when a wave of planes passed overhead, and then thunderous blasts of artillery from the battleships launched. There were many boats ahead of us as they progressed towards land, but we remained in position. The noise from the artillery fire became deafening. I could feel every nearby blast that sent shivers through my body and I could see and hear the scream of large shells landing in the water all around us. Huge splashes erupted, swaying the boat. Cold water splashed my face. The taste of salt filled my mouth. I expected a shell striking the boat and blowing everyone on board to bits and pieces as the firing went on. We were defenseless. Men, including myself, covered our heads with our arms to hush the artillery blasts and shrieking shells flying from all around. At times, I would force myself to peek around to observe everything happening. Smoke from the firing of artillery filled the sky. The artillery blazing from the ships lit up the sky that reminded me of fireflies zipping through the air. I glanced around at the other men. Some vomited, and some prayed to themselves, terrified of what is taking place.

The artillery fire continued for half an hour as our craft prepared its course towards the beach. I became anxious as I clutched my M1-Garand rifle in anticipation. It wouldn't be long now before our boat would touch down on shore. I observed other Higgins boats making their encroachment towards land. As we moved closer and closer, I felt myself becoming hot. Sweat rained down my face. I realized the inevitable hour was drawing near. I took deep breaths to keep myself calm. But I vomited once more.

Karl made his way beside me as he squeezed through the troops from the front of the craft. "Are you going to be all right, Vince?"

"I think so," I uttered.

"Just remember your training. I will be with you when this thing lands on the beach. Andrew and the rest of the men on this boat too along with Captain Hull." Karl had recently been promoted to sergeant. A position he earned. He was favored among the men as he's well respected for his excellent attitude and willingness to always lend an extra hand with foxhole digging or lifting spirits when morale is low. There were talks among the men that if Hastings were to be killed in combat, Karl would be the possible candidate to take over 1st Platoon with Andrew at his side.

As our Higgins boat cruised on the choppy waters toward land, Captain Hull yelled out to us. Some of it I couldn't understand—not with all the mortar shells flying around and the blasts of artillery exploding not too far away from us. "Put your helmets on!" he yelled at the men who had failed to keep their helmets on during the boat ride. "Conserve your water! Do what you learned in training and you'll survive! Don't get too arrogant or you will be killed! Conserve your ammo! Only fire your weapon if needed. You're my Company so make me proud! Make your division proud! Make your president proud! Make America proud! Twenty-nine, let's go!"

I kept my eyes straight ahead—concentrating. Tension ran deep as I waited. My trigger finger repeatedly tapped my rifle as we drew closer and closer to land. The artillery fire from the ships died down as all the Higgins boats drew closer to the beach. It wouldn't be long now. I started my slow breathing exercises. I was counting on my fellow troops to help me get through what lied ahead. And I knew my platoon were counting on me to lead them through the assault. All the men in this boat with me were now my brothers. We all had to look out for one another. But some of these men I didn't know. I said few words to them here and there but nothing more. I didn't know what lives they had before entering this war. All I knew is these men were husbands, brothers, and sons. And now here they are, about to fight for their country and other countries. I'm proud to be among them. Proud to fight alongside them in this dark hour. I'm here now with them as we drew nearer to the beach.

———

"TWENTY-NINE, LET'S GO!" Captain Hull's voice roared out.

The boat halted as it approached the beach. The front ramp went down as a spray of bullets struck troops in front of me. The soldier's head in front of me snapped back. Blood sprayed my face. The deafening sound of machine-gun fire and mortar shells impacting nearby forced me to plunge overboard into the cold salt water to dodge enemy fire. My head just stuck out over the water as small waves came tumbling down on me as bullets sprayed the water from all around. I waded through the water with all my strength, in desperate need to get on land, but this proved difficult due to all the gear I hauled. My trudge out of the water was slow. Endless machine-gun fire burst through troops as I made my way to the golden sand of the beach. Along the way, I passed wounded and dead soldiers. I could hear a bullet's impact as it struck a soldier in front of me. He sank below the water's surface because of the weight he carried. I expected it would only be a matter of time before I would be next.

Men fell into the shallow water and crawled inland on the beach, in desperate tries to avoid gunfire. Some were injured as a haze of blood trailed after them in the water and the sand. I saw as troops pulled the wounded out of the water, but the endless and ruthless German machine-gun fire gunned down man after man.

My eyes burned from the salt water. My vision was cloudy, making it difficult for me to see far ahead, but I could see the faint light of machine-gun burst in the distance. By luck, I reached the sandy beach, and my training instinct kicked in. I crouched and fired my rifle towards the enormous pillbox ahead of me, but I recalled what Captain Hull had said about conserving ammunition. And the other issue was: what could a .30 caliber rifle do to a large concrete pillbox? I moved further inland away from water and spotted a hedgehog obstacle (a metal anti-tank obstacle with three metal beams crossed with one another). The barrier looked inviting; I needed to take cover from the oncoming machine-gun fire. Another soldier had reached it before I did and an eruption from a mine blew his legs off. A trap. His torso soared six feet into the air before crashing down on the sand. I stopped dead in my tracks.

I had to get somewhere safe, but that seemed impossible as I felt bullets breezing by my head. I moved closer inland—hoping to avoid mines. Mortal shells were landing on the shore—throwing any soldier near where they struck in to the air, blowing off limbs. Many soldiers who were wounded or dead were riddled with bullets as they lied on the beach. I made my way further in and dove behind some men who had cleared an obstacle of any mines. I looked at their faces to determine if I knew any of them, but it was no one I recognized. The blue diamond patch on their sleeves told me they were Rangers.

"Where's your captain?!" I shouted.

"Dead!" one man yelled. "Where's yours?!"

"I don't know! I guess I'm with you now!"

Bullets ricocheted off the obstacle as I curled up for protection. I surveyed the scene: men crouched behind hedgehog obstacles as bullets passed by and struck all around them, some men yelled out and wailed with fear, and troops struggling to make their way inland were going down like flies as machine-gun fire brought down everything in their path. Then someone I knew came storming behind me—Lieutenant Emmet Hastings.

"Sergeant Conroy! Are you all right?!" he shouted over the deafening noise of battle.

"I'm fine!" I hollered, satisfied to discover a familiar face. "Have you seen Captain Hull!?"

"No! You're the first familiar face I've seen!" He paused as he glanced around at the chaos happening before him. "Look, we need to get off this beach! We need to make our way to the sea-wall and get over it! There's a large pillbox about three-hundred yards from here! We need to get in there and stop this German fire!" Hastings looked around at the Rangers in our company, listening to everything he said. "I need all of you as well. We need to get off this beach now!"

More bullets impacted the tank obstacle and all around as more men were dropping dead on the sand and in the water as they attempted to run forward. More Higgins boats landed on the beach, but the troops trying to evacuate were immediately gunned down.

Hastings moved away from the obstacle and pointed in the direction of the sea-wall. "Let's move out!" But a bullet struck his hand. "Goddamnit!" he yelled. He was now missing a few fingers. He bent down and dug through his pockets in search of something to wrap up his bloodied hand with when a mortar shell hit near him, hurling him backwards a few feet. Yet, he's still alive with all of his limbs attached. He lied on the sand—dazed from the blast. I yelled at him to return, but he didn't seem to be aware of everything happening. The troops I were with were fixed in their positions, so it was up to me drag him back behind the meager protection of the tank obstacle. In a swift motion, I hopped to my feet and sprinted towards him, ignoring the bullets impacting the ground near my feet. I approached him and gripped him from underneath his arms and pulled him to his feet and I began to lead him to safety by his arm.

"We have to get back behind that obstacle!" I shouted. "We have to—" Several bullets flew through Hastings head and face. His body went limp and dropped to the sand as I released my grip on his arm. I dropped to my knees in shock. I peered at the remnants of what was left of Hastings face. There only remained a bloody mess. His lifeless eyes gazed upwards towards the sky. I stared into those eyes—not knowing what I was looking for. After a moment, I peeled my eyes away from Hastings and watched the scene in front of me. More soldiers were dropping to the ground. I turned to look towards the bluff as the land was exploding from all around. The ability to think straight was impossible. I couldn't move—not from fear, but from the horror I witnessed.

"Get back here!" I heard someone shout. I came to my senses and returned to the protection of the hedgehog obstacle.

"There wasn't anything you could do," the Ranger I spoke to moments ago said.

I glanced back and saw more Higgins boats with reinforcements arriving. Some troops were making it off the boats and out of the water and taking cover behind the hedgehog obstacles from the endless enemy fire. Mortars struck a few boats as the explosion threw troops into the air. More bullets whizzed by as I observed the giant pillbox and bluff that lay ahead. The daylight grew brighter as clouds drifted apart from above.

I turned to the soldier next to me, in need of his help. "What's your name?!" I asked.

"Private Jacob Holtzman!" he shouted.

"All right, Private Holtzman! We need to get off this beach! We can take cover at the sea-wall up ahead! And then we'll figure out what to do once we get there! Are you with me?!"

"I don't think I have much of choice! I'm not staying here! Especially if a mortar gets sent our way! And besides, some men are already making their run for the sea-wall!"

Jacob pointed, and I saw what he spoke of. Many troops had made their advancement to the sea-wall despite the machine-gun fire. "All right! We'll go on my signal, ok!"

Jacob and the other troops nodded.

"Get ready!" Bullets continued to pelt the obstacle as I waited for the opportune moment when the machine-guns moved away to another target. After a moment, the firing ceased. "Now!"

At once, we all hopped to our feet and ran as fast as our legs could take us towards the sea-wall. But being soaked in salt water and the gear we carried on our backs weighed us down, making our run sluggish. Bullets pelted the sand near my feet as I moved forward with my rifle in my hands. I could hear the other troops treading not far behind me. Time seemed to slow down as if this became the most difficult and longest run of my life.

And with a massive amount of luck, I dove behind the sizeable mounted sand for shelter. Other men came tumbling into the wall as well. Jacob being one. "Glad to see you made it!" I shouted.

"You're not the only one!" he yelled.

Machine-gun fire bellowed above us as more troops reached the sea-wall. I turned onto my belly to observe the scene. The barbed-wire fence ran along the top of the wall. There is no going over the top, for it would be suicide. I looked in both directions. Men were digging foxholes, seeking shelter. I studied the beach and spotted tanks and bulldozers reaching the beach, along with more soldiers making their advances. They hopped over the many dead soldiers lying at their feet as medics attended the wounded. Mortal shells dropped closer and closer to the sea-wall for the Germans knew where we were all hiding.

I had no Bangalore torpedo nor dynamite, so blasting my way through the wall would be impossible. And it would be too much effort to dig through. I needed to conserve all the strength I could. My only choice is to lie low and wait.

Jacob looked around. "What do we do?!"

"We wait!" I said.

"What do you mean we wait?!" he snapped. "We're sitting ducks out here! We will be killed if we just wait!"

"There's no way over this wall! We have to wait until troops blast trenches for us to go through! There's nothing much we can do right now!"

Jacob glanced around once again and patted my shoulder. "There!" He pointed at a dead soldier. A Bangalore torpedo lied next to him. "We have to get it!"

Before I could give the order, Jacob shoved of the sand and ran to the dead soldier to retrieve the Bangalore. Several bullets struck his torso. He hit the sand and screamed in agony from the pain as he tremored violently. The surrounding sand turned red from his blood. He shrieked out for help. I decided to run out to him and pull him back to the sea-wall. I had to leave the only shelter I had from enemy fire to save a fellow soldier. It took a moment before I moved. I held my breath as I lifted myself off the sand and ran to where Jacob lied. "Grab a hold!" I yelled. He nodded to let me know he understood I was here to help him. He wrapped an arm around my shoulder as I lifted him off the ground. I also reached for the Bangalore but several bullets nearly took off several of my fingers. Leaving the Bangalore behind, I helped Jacob back to the sea-wall. Our return was slow. Jacob hobbled on the sand as he clutched the fabric of my coat. He almost dropped a few times to his knees, but I refused to let go of him as we reached the sand-wall and back to safety. Jacob wrapped his arms around himself and curled up. "Stay with me, Private! A medic will be with you soon!" I wanted to keep his spirits up. But I knew if help didn't arrive soon, he would be as good as dead.

With Jacob back with me, I turned my attention to the task at hand. Officers were now at the wall, shouting out orders for men to blow trenches for passing through. I looked around for anyone in my company, but I was alone with strangers from the 1st Infantry and Ranger regiments.

Then to my surprise—Captain Hull, Aschner, and Roland rolled along the sea-wall by my side.

"Sergeant Conroy! I'm glad to see you made it this far!" Hull yelled out.

"I sure am glad to see you guys!" I said.

"Have you seen Lieutenant Hastings?!" Aschner asked.

"Dead!" I replied.

"A lot of us are being wiped out!" Hull growled. "Sergeant Lambert should arrive with a Bangalore at any moment." I was relieved to hear Karl had made it this far, but there was no sight or mention of Andrew. "Listen—once that Bangalore torpedo arrives—we will blow a trench in this sea-wall, and we are to get across immediately! We can't stay here, or we're all dead! Once we're through—we have to climb the bluff and fight the Germans head on!"

To my relief, Karl crawled to us with the Bangalore torpedo and nestled it under the barbed-wire at the top of the sea-wall. "When I light this—we have to move away from it!" he yelled.

"Light it up!" Hull shouted.

"Fire in the hole!" Karl shouted as he lit the torpedo and shoved it under the barb-wire. We all moved away and covered our heads.

The torpedo exploded—leaving just enough room in the sea-wall for one soldier at a time to pass through. Hull gave the order as one by one, troops made their way through the narrow trench in the sand. But before running over the wall, I patted Jacob's helmet. "You stay here, Private. You've done everything you could do. A medic will be with you shortly." He tried to speak, but no words came through his lips. He gave me a look of desperation. His faced turned pale. Blood seeped through his fingers as he clutched the bullet wounds on his body. The chance of his survival was slim if help didn't come soon. I gave him one last look of sympathy as I jumped to my feet.

I made way through after Karl and was glad to be off the beach, but there is danger still all around. During this time, more trenches were blown into the wall as other troops were making their way over. The next task at hand was climbing the bluff to attack the German position, but Hull gave the order to halt our posts. As I followed soldiers up the bluff, landmines were stepped on by unsuspecting troops.

But engineers were arriving and were needed to detect mines to avoid any more casualties. Working carefully to avoid fatal mistakes and yet fast, they scanned the area in hopes of not being blasted by mortars or stepping on any mines themselves. Along the way, the engineers marked a walking path with white tape as they searched.

Captain Hull gave orders for everyone to stay on the path and not step off after the engineers completed the sweep. When it came to my turn to move across, I took extra caution—treading carefully on the path and not running. But others were impatient and stepped off the safe path. Before long, bodies cluttered the minefield.

Once enough men were across the minefield, Hull rounded up a team to scale the bluff to engage the enemy and others to halt their position and attack the large pillbox on the bluff by hurling grenades into the portals where the machine-guns were shooting. But the Germans established defense with a nest at the top of the bluff. Machine-guns rattled with every movement in our direction, trying to ward off any progress as we took cover in front of the pillbox. Advancement past the nest proved slow. German troops were well sheltered behind a wall of sandbags. I glanced out from the pillbox and fired a few rounds with my rifle but only hit sandbags or nothing at all. Roland came to our aid after making it across the minefield. Many of us took shots in turns to give covering fire for troops to break toward the nest for an assault.

Captain Hull became impatient. "I want that nest taken care of now!"

A team of five men successfully reached below the enemy gunfire as covering fire continued. Grenades were tossed into the nest as the Germans fell back. Several explosions gave us the time we needed as Hull gave the order to maintain Allied advancement up the bluff and into the German trenches.

"Move your asses up that bluff!" Hull shouted.

Upon arriving at the trenches, we were matched with enemy fire as several men were killed unawares. But the ongoing assault of Allied troops quickly overpowered the Germans from every direction as more men mounted the bluffs, arriving at the top. Groups of soldiers now held outside the entrance of the pillbox crowded with German troops, pursuing their relentless machine-gun fire onto the oncoming waves of troops on the beach. Hull ordered Roland and me to toss grenades through the threshold behind the pillbox. A moment after the grenades exploded, Hull then assigned several men to storm inside and take out any remaining enemies. I paused outside the pillbox on my guard as several men, including Karl streamed in as the echoing sounds of gunshots broke out inside.

"All clear!" Karl called out.

"All right, men," Hull said. "Let's clean out these trenches!"

The Allied army now rushed throughout the trenches and from above, shooting and capturing Germans as the remaining pillboxes were cleared out of enemy troops. I witnessed Allied soldiers gunning down Germans after surrendering. But officers did little to intervene after witnessing this. Some prisoners claimed they were Polish. They pleaded with us that the Germans forced them to fight on their part against their will. Few of those men had been executed.

By this time, the beach and the bluff are now under our control as German units were spotted fleeing deeper into the land as more Allied troops advanced. We now had the upper hand.

In just the past hour, I became a man. And a horrible way to do so. A wonder I survived. No measure of training could have prepared me for the real thing. Throughout the morning, I watched grown men cower in fear and break down crying, wounded and helpless men cry out for help, and men saying their last prayers before taking their final breath. I watched a colleague die right before my eyes. Yes, this was war. And I am set on a course diving deeper into the uncharted.

———

THERE WAS NO TIME TO BREATHE. It wasn't long before officers rounded up the rest of C Company for action. I learned the 115th Regiment were making preparations to capture St. Laurent which is just over a kilometer away and now the 116th still had much work to do before the day ended. But the day was far from over, even though I wanted it to be. As soon as our section of the bluff was captured, the rest of C Company was required to provide help to the 2nd and 5th Ranger Battalions in taking Vierville—a village settled just below a kilometer from the beach on top of the bluff. As I had assumed, the fighting wasn't over. Instead of skirmishing on a beach or in trenches, we now proceeded through hedgerows. I became familiar with hedgerows during my stay in England, but the French hedgerows are different. They are mounds past six-feet tall and are made up of dirt with hedges on top. Going through or over a hedgerow is impossible. The only gaps discovered in the hedgerows were contained with MG-42s, fortified by the Germans.

The Germans waited for Allied forces to reach a hedgerow and then gun them down. They expected to massacre the Allies but what they hadn't expected was that infantry became accustomed to hedgerow fighting. An effective method adopted to drive the Germans out the hedgerows is to blow a hole with TNT away from a MG-42 nest from both sides and outflank the Germans by running infantry into the blown gaps.

Another issue the Germans did not understand is more Allied rein-forcements were landing on the beach and going into battle. Strength in numbers. The Allies were building up strength by each passing hour as the Germans were being forced back further inland.

The push towards Vierville had been slow. But eventually, C Company made its way into the commune with no enemy resistance. A and B Company moved south outside Vierville with the 2nd Rangers to hold a defensive position. And along with the 5th Rangers, C Company moved west to take defensive positions for the rest of the day. The reasons: German forces surrounded us, and with nighttime looming, it would be useless to go on until the next morning. Also, men were exhausted, and no longer had the spirit to continue without rest.

Karl and I helped round up German soldiers who surrendered on Hull's orders. We lined them all up side by side, about fifteen men, de-fenseless, as I rummaged through their uniforms in search of any weap-ons they failed to hand over or any propaganda. This was the first time I had gotten a real good look at the enemy face to face. Their uniforms were grey with black boots, and a steel helmet rested on their heads. And they all appeared as regular human beings, not looking much dif-ferent for Americans. I remember talks among the other men that the Germans were perceived as malicious in presence and conduct but when I set my eyes on the captives, I swiped that rubbish away. They were only human beings—a human being such as myself and nothing more.

Luckily, there were no other weapons to be found as they dropped and disarmed any weapons they had been carrying. I dug into their pockets and pulled out their wallets and searched through them in and out. I could not find any contents in their wallets pertaining to anything useful for the Allies. What I found were photographs of their wives and children and German currency. I hated to deprive them of their loved ones, so I placed everything back into their wallets and put the wallet back where I found it.

After ten minutes of searching, Captain Hull approached me. "Find anything useful, Sergeant?"

"No, sir," I replied.

Hull removed a pack of cigarettes from his coat pocket and handed cigarettes out to the prisoners who wanted them. He also lit them himself. "Well, keep looking. Some of these men are bound to have something useful on them."

I continued my search but found nothing: just photographs and German currency. After I searched the entire line, Captain Hull approached me again. "Sergeant—damn good work today."

"Thank you, sir," I said.

"You have my permission to rest for a few moments. Sergeant Lambert too. I want you both to be ready because we have a long day tomorrow."

"Yes, sir," Karl and I replied in unison.

"We've set up a solid defensive position here, but be on your guard. Those Germans could try to flank us at any moment, especially from the southwest. If they strike, we believe it will be from there. Once we get settled in more and reorganized—we'll be heading out to liberate St. Lo. It's gonna be one hell of a march. We're expected to be delayed by the Germans. So I need you to get some rest before we move out. I want men sleeping in foxholes in teams of two or three. Shifts will be taken during the night for watches. Is that understood?"

"Yes, sir," Karl and I replied in unison once more.

"Good. We plan to move out at 0700 tomorrow. Carry on."

I was grateful for the little time to rest, but I admit I could have used more than just a single nights' rest.

——

WITH THE NORTH OF VIERVILLE SECURED, I seized this opportunity to hike to the edge of the bluff alone to examine the beach, leaving Karl to mingle with fellow troops. The water and sand were stained red with blood—the beach, strewn with the dead. Bodies washed up on shore— torso's missing arms and legs. Medics walked about, inspecting the poor souls hoping to discover anyone alive. I knew the medics wouldn't find many. Thousands of Allied soldiers stormed the beaches of Normandy to fight the enemy, and many of those soldiers gave their lives. I had never seen the likes of it. And I hoped to see nothing like it again. The complete aftermath of the mayhem on that dreadful day spread out before me as I looked at it all from top of the bluff. The image of a bloody and battered beach is forever burned in my memory. A memory not forgotten.

There had been little sun the whole day, but now, the clouds had withdrawn, providing warm sunlight to shine down. But the air was cool as the wind whistled wildly, feeling it would push me off the bluff. My wet uniform made me feel colder. My feet were numb. I shivered from the chill. It's June here in Normandy and yet cold. I wondered if it was always cold in France. And if so, how could people stand to live here all year around.

Vessels now arrived at the beach. Obstacles were being removed from the beach to make space for the Allied forces. Ships and boats carrying other soldiers, heavy artillery, tanks, and many supplies. Soldiers hard at work finding and disabling any mines not yet discovered. The Allies were now invading France, and now it's time for this war to change momentum.

We soon had substantial control of the bluff and beach but had to be wary of any counterattack by the Germans. A counterattack never came, however. Speculation arose that the Germans didn't have the suitable forces available in the area for there were no reinforcements assigned— however, a German plane flew back and forth above the Allied fleet. The fleet opened fire but they never struck the plane. After several fly-bys, the plane flew away from the beach and never came back.

I continued to observe the vessels when a voice shouted out behind me. "You lucky son of a bitch!"

I turned around and saw Andrew standing just a few feet away with an enormous grin on his face. "You made it," I beamed.

Andrew rushed over and shook my hand. "I was worried to death over you. Is Karl ok?"

"Yeah, he's fine. He's around here somewhere."

As soon as I said that, Karl came running towards us. "What the hell happened to you, Andrew?"

"Nice to see you too, Karl," Andrew said as he shook his hand. "I got separated, just like a bunch of us did."

"Can you believe this mess?" Karl said as the three of us stared down onto the beach below us. "This is something I will never forget."

"You said it," I said. "This was pure hell. Too many men died today. Shit. . . it's just not right."

"Fucking Hitler," Andrew snapped. We all stood in silence, observing the beach for a few minutes. "Where's Hastings?" Andrew was unaware Hastings was dead.

I sighed. "He didn't make it. He got shot right in front of me as I tried to pull him to safety after getting thrown off his feet by a mortar."

"Shit. I'm sorry, Vince," Karl said. "I didn't know him as much as I wanted too. He seemed like a decent man though."

"Yeah, he was," I said. In some sense, I wanted to go out onto the beach again and search for his body. But I felt it would just be too difficult to look upon him once more. I lost a companion this day but I'm fortunate to have Karl and Andrew with me. It surprised me, however. Surprised that this battle had taken many lives, but both of my closest friends had made it out alive.

"I'm starving," Andrew said. "Where can we get some grub?"

———

THE THREE OF US LEFT the cold and windy bluff in pursuit of some hospitality and food. My belly grumbled from starvation. I advised that we should head back to Vierville.

Upon entering Vierville, the locals kept a close watch on the Americans as they traveled through. Andrew tried to speak to several young women, but they ran away in fear. They were all frightened. The Allies ward off the Germans, but they were unsure of who they could trust. Who can blame them?

We found an area where men were being served dry meat sandwiches, so we helped ourselves. After getting our sandwiches, we sat down against a brick building off the street and ate our sandwiches along with a few C rations (potato hash and beans). It had been a long day, and I had had nothing to eat since morning. I wanted my belly full of food before calling it a night, no matter how bad the food was.

We all ate in silence until Roland interrupted our meal. He walked towards us as if he had nowhere else to go. His eyes were heavy from exhaustion. For a moment, I thought he would collapse at our feet. He sat down next to Andrew and rested his head against the wall. "Any of you bozos have a cigarette?" he said in a slow and breathy tone.

"Sorry, pal," Karl said. "None of us smoke."

"Just my luck," Roland said. He removed his helmet and placed it next to him. "Well, do any you have any liquor? I've been dying for a swig."

"I'm afraid not," Andrew said. "But we do have plenty of terrible food."

Roland scoffed. "Well... I'm not hungry. If I don't find a damn cigarette or a shot of whiskey soon—I will go crazy." He then glanced at me and then at Karl and Andrew. "Why are you two hanging around this deadbeat," he said, gesturing at me with his thumb.

I felt my face burn hot with annoyance, but I knew Roland was trying to get at me, so I did my best to keep my cool.

Karl and Andrew glanced at one another. "Listen, pal," Andrew hissed. "We have nothing you're looking for. And we were doing just fine until you came along running your mouth. So I think it would be wise for you just to get up and walk away before I lose my temper."

Roland scoffed once more. "Take it easy there, buddy," He said in a bantering manner. "I'm only teasing. Just having a little fun is all. Can't a guy have a little fun?"

Andrew rolled his eyes. "Just watch yourself."

Roland took his helmet and stood up. "You guys are boring me, anyways. I'm outta here."

Before Roland could walk away, Captain Hull and Aschner marched in front of all of us. We bounced to our feet and saluted. "As you were," Hull said. "Sergeant Conroy, I have a proposition for you."

"Sir?" I said.

Hull stared at me for a few moments before speaking as if deep in thought. "It's unfortunate I lost Lieutenant Hastings in my unit. He was a good man and a damn good soldier. But positions need to be filled, however. And I need a staff sergeant. So let me applaud you on a damn fine job you did out there today again. You showed much courage and determination. You should be proud of that. Sergeant Aschner here from B Company has recommended you for staff sergeant. And he'll be promoted to sergeant first class and has requested a transfer to my company." Aschner smiled at me. "And I for one agree with that recommendation. So what do you say?"

At first, I was speechless. I could sense everyone's eyes on me, waiting for an answer. "Are you certain, sir? I'm sure there are men more suitable than myself for that position."

"You're damn right I'm certain, Conroy," Hull said. "So... what's it going to be?"

"Well, yes of course!" I realized this position would require much more responsibility, but I felt confident I was up to the task.

"Good!" Hull said. "I know you'll do just fine." We exchanged salutes. "Come along now, Sergeant Aschner. We have work to do. We'll meet up with you later, Conroy—to discuss formalities, but for now just get a little more rest. And remember, foxholes with two or three men taking shifts for watch outs."

"Congratulations, Conroy," Aschner said. We exchanged salutes as the two men walked away.

I turned to look at Karl and Andrew who now had huge smiles on their faces. I then looked at Roland who seemed perturbed. "Well what about that, Corporal Roland," I said, "This deadbeat just made staff sergeant." Roland's face turned red. He rolled his eyes at me and marched off, cursing under his breath.

"Well how about that," Karl said. "A goddamn staff sergeant." Both Karl and Andrew patted my back and playfully shoved my shoulders.

With the brief excitement over, we sat back down against the building wall and continued to eat and chat. I wanted to stay there against the wall until the war was over. But I knew D-Day was only the beginning.

———

KARL, ANDREW, AND I FINISHED DIGGING OUR FOXHOLE. Our muscles ached. We decided not to dig as deep as we should have. The ground was too much like a rock. Hedgerows enclosed us from all around so I felt somewhat protected. The hedgerows would give us at least some safety from German attacks if they were to come.

"Who'll take the first watch?" Andrew asked. We were all tired but speculated it would be best to sleep in shifts as Captain Hull ordered. If Hull caught all of us sleeping at the same time, there would be stiff penalties: a court-martial or even a death sentence. But I never knew this to be true or not. I suspected a death penalty is nothing more than a scare tactic superior officers used to frighten soldiers. But I never had intentions to discover the truth.

"I'll take the first watch," I said.

"The hell you will," Karl said. "I think the staff sergeant should get some sleep first. I'll take the first watch."

"Thanks," I replied. I said nothing further, relieved to get the first bit of shut-eye.

I wrapped my blanket around me and leaned back in the shallow hole, exhausted. But sleep would be challenging because of the chill, and I could hear the occasional thunderous sound of vessel artillery exploding in the distance. Every time I dozed off, events of the day kept flashing before me, jerking me awake—not nightmares but memories.

Eventually, I stopped trying to sleep and instead gazed upon the eternal night sky. Few clouds now hovered above, along with a few stars. I'm a long way from home. Nights on the farm back in Louisiana are remarkable. Many nights I would sneak out of the house and hike to the field and lie on top of a quilt outside the canopy of the great oak, watching the transparent night sky. When I was just a child, I used to think all the stars were fireflies that had flown so high in the sky to sur-round the moon. And that's where they stayed as they lit up their lights to illuminate the dark sky. I remember the night sounds of the cicadas, crickets, and owls. Some nights, I would just sleep there in the field and be awoken by the call of a loon in the distance as the sun rose in the early dawn. Those days now only seemed like a distant dream.

A steam of my breath disappeared into the night as I bundled up as best as I could with my wool blanket. I shivered from the cold.

"Are you freezing?" Karl asked as he threw his blanket over me.

"Thanks," I said. "What about you? You'll freeze."

"You need not worry about me."

I sat up moved closer next to Karl and wrapped us both up with the two blankets for warmth as best as possible. "I can't sleep. There's just too much going on in my head right now. After everything we went through today, I don't see how anyone can sleep."

"Looks like Andrew has no problems," Karl said.

I glanced at Andrew who was now deep in sleep, snoring. "He's lucky to have to go through hell and be able to doze off like that."

Karl yawned. "Well, I'm sure I will sleep like that tonight too. Try not to think too hard about anything, and you'll fall asleep, eventually. Or just try to think of something peaceful."

"I wish it was that easy." I sighed. "But there is one thing I know: I'm looking forward to sleeping in a real bed. Not a cot, not a foxhole, but a real bed with my woman."

Karl took a deep breath. "We will get out of here—the three of us. We will get home and return to our lives when all of this is over. I don't know how long it will take, but we'll make it there. All you need to do is not think of fighting and killing but think of home. Think about going home to your woman. Listen to the last songs from the birds before they settle down for the evening. Maybe one day, you'll have children. Your wife and your children are with you, snuggled up with you on a hammock at your home in your backyard, not caring about what's going on the world—just enjoying life, because everything is perfect for you. In the last few minutes of daylight, everything is quiet as it should be. It's getting close to the end of a great day, and you're looking forward to the next because it will be the start of yet another wonderful day with your family. That's how it will be. That's how it will be for you, for Andrew, and for me as well. We're all going to have families. We'll spend Thanksgivings and Christmas' together with our families. All of our kids will be good friends. We'll be like uncles to each other's children, and our wives will be like aunts. We're all going to grow old together. One day, a long time down the road—we'll be discussing our time together during this war with our children. They'll know what their fathers did for them, and their country and they'll be so proud of us. They'll be proud to say we are their fathers. It will happen, Vince. All of it."

"I want it to be true. . . I mean, I really do. It all sounds amazing." I rubbed my chest for a little warmth. "Do you think I'll be a good dad?" I didn't know why I blurted that question out.

"Of course you'll be a great dad." I was silent. "Something troubling you?"

"No, I'm just tired is all. . . I'm just tired. I think I will try to get sleep again."

"All right. I'll have Andrew wake you up when it's your turn. You can take last shift. And If you snore louder than Andrew—I will kick you in the gut."

"Not too hard though," I teased.

Karl wrapped me up with the blankets as I rested back down again. I closed my eyes and listened to the echoes of the night as I drifted off to sleep. I took Karl's proposal and thought of something peaceful. I imagined myself lying under the canopy of the great oak tree at the edge of the field, staring up into sky, watching the stars and fireflies above me. Before long, I was fast asleep.

———

I FELT MY LEFT FOOT BEING KICKED, which jerked me awake. Daylight peeked out through the clouds. I looked around confused, forgetting where I was, until I realized it had been Andrew that had woke me. The morning air was still crisp but not as harsh as the night before.

"It's time to get up, Sarge," Andrew said.

"Did I sleep through my shift?" I said half-asleep.

"Nope. Karl and I decided to let you sleep through the night." He crouched down in front of me. "You looked so peaceful, that we didn't have the heart to wake you."

"Well, that was very thoughtful, but you could have woke me." It felt as though I had slept very little. I still felt exhausted. My body ached, and my neck was stiff. I wanted a bed now, more than ever. But I then realized Karl wasn't among us. "Where's Karl?"

"Ah, he's talking to some Rangers," Andrew said. "I think he's trying to bribe coffee off of them."

"Let's hope he gets some," I said standing up, brushing off dirt on my uniform.

I spotted Karl in the distance speaking with fellow soldiers as Andrew had stated. I couldn't make out what was being said, but it seemed Karl was having no luck in getting coffee.

After a few minutes, he gave up as he shrugged his shoulders, walking away from the men, shaking his head. He stepped over towards us. "No luck on getting any coffee. We're supposed to be working as a team, but those guys are impossible to work with."

I grabbed my gear. "We should find out what's going on and try to find breakfast and not rations. I *really* could go for some coffee right about now."

Captain Hull then approached us. "Listen up, Sergeant Conroy: we're marching out soon towards St. Lo. It may seem quiet as of right now but those Germans are still hiding out in hedgerows somewhere, and it's our job to flush them out. So be prepared. You're a staff sergeant now, so I'm expecting you to take more initiative with these men. Is that understood?"

"Yes, sir," I said.

"Don't disappoint me," Hull demanded. He then stood back and called for everyone's attention as we were gradually surrounded by the troops. "Everyone grab your gear and get ready to move out. We have a long road ahead of us towards St. Lo. Now let's run these Germans out of France!"

TWENTY-TWO

AS IT TURNED OUT: D-Day had been an utter disaster but yet successful. Mistakes had been made in the beach landings, airborne drops, and
the Navy bombardments had been inaccurate. Most of the landing crafts
landed on the beach in the wrong areas on account of smoke, rough waters, and the stubbornness from officers driving the boats. Heavy mines
in the waters were also an issue. C Company arrived at Omaha Beach
minutes early than scheduled and landed left of the target on Dog White
instead of Dog Green. Casualties were high in the first hours of the assault, but despite all the errors of the day, the Allies were victorious.

　　With D-Day over, the Allies main objectives are to liberate the nearby
towns of Saint-Lô and Caen as the British Army were underway with
the liberation of Bayeux. The Canadian Army's target with the aid of
the British is to take Caen. Saint-Lô would be the American Army's
main destination. However, the US Armies needed supplies and reinforcements. Time was needed to gather more stability for the assault,
and it was vital for the Allies to liberate the town for it needed to be
captured at all costs due to its strategic location and advantage for the
war. I learned the Allies bombarded the town the night before D-Day

and finished the bombardment early the next morning.

But the objective to take Saint-Lô changed. First, we were to capture Cherbourg in the Cotentin Peninsula which would allow reinforcements to be brought directly from the United States. An advantage had been gained in the early hours on the previous day; paratroopers landed on the base of the Cotentin Peninsula and secured many routes for the US army to advance from Utah Beach. But until Cherbourg could be liberated, and until the 29th Infantry could be altogether reorganized, progress marches towards Saint-Lô were to be slow.

Before leaving Vierville, I went in pursuit to find Jacob Holtzman—the Private I saved on the beach. German machine-gun fire wounded him twice, and I feared he did not survive. I looked among the many anxious and exhausted faces, but I could not see Jacob. I spoke with Rangers, but they had not seen their fellow trooper. My only option left was to speak with the medics. Each one I found, I asked for Jacob's whereabouts, but each medic lead me to another. Eventually, I thought I had been lead on a wild goose chase until a medic gave me many blood smeared dog-tags to search through. It didn't take long to identify the one belonging to Jacob. I risked my life to save him, but I assumed he bled out on the beach-wall before a medic came to his aid. Jacob—along with many others I fought with became just another face. I wish I could have done more. By this time, I learned never to get to close to fellow troops.

Days passed. They were long which made the weeks feel longer.

On June 29th, the 29th Infantry received word the 4th, 9th, and 79th Divisions with the aid of Paratroopers liberated Cherbourg, but the battle for Caen was still going strong. It seemed the German Army grew reluctant to hand the town over to the Allies. But with Cherbourg liberated, our push towards Saint-Lô would soon be accessible for attack and our advancement march was renewed.

The time came to push our march deeper into Normandy towards Saint-Lô.

A positive note about marching through Normandy is the opportunity to observe the magnificent countryside. We marched through vast open green pastures past sparse wooded hills and alluring apple orchards. I would say it was all beautiful but bloated dead cows swarming with countless flies that had been caught in crossfire littered the lush ground we walked on. The carcasses foul stench drifted in the air causing men, including myself, to gag. I learned to breathe through my mouth and not my nose as we marched past the carcasses.

We marched little throughout the night, in fear of being ambushed. It was during this time, some men sang little songs to themselves. They sang for comfort. Perhaps for those few minutes of soft vocalizing, they could escape from the horrors taking place not far away. In the distance, the night sky would light up from explosions from a battle underway. And yet, the men still sang. The songs weren't depressing by any means but peaceful, elegant songs about love or a glorious hero winning a significant battle.

Often, after a night of rest, we'd be awakened by rain. The first two weeks of marching, I remember being wet most of the time. We marched in the rain just like any other day, stepping through thick mud that stalled our progress. By the end of a day marching through sludge, my legs felt heavy.

But mud wasn't the only problem we encountered; continuous resistance from the Germans came unexpectedly. We reached further inland mostly covered with hedgerows. German soldiers fired shots peering over the hedgerows, forcing us to take cover behind anything we could: trees, fences, and dead cows. If there is one positive thing to say about the opposing army: they are persistent. I can't help but to respect them for refusing to give up so quickly. In a way, the Germans mastered hedgerow fighting by using them for their advantage. But the Allies adapted to their strategy. We now had sufficient counter attacks for the Germans hiding behind hedgerows waiting to ambush. Our secret weapon was Sherman tanks. The tanks would blast a hole into a hedgerow, just big enough to send one through to counter the Germans attacks. German squads would retreat on account of being out manned, but hours or a day later, they would attack once more after being rein-forced by troops buried deeper into the shrubberies.

The Germans were persistent, but they were losing ground by each passing day. We pushed the German troops further and further back on our march towards Saint-Lô. And with each day, the troops I fought alongside with grew exhausted. Every morning we rose early, devour what rations we could and march further into the hedgerows—only to be expecting the enemy fire to rain down at any given moment. It was al-ways a satisfaction to escape the shrubberies and walk upon an open green meadow for a couple of hundred yards or so. That brief measure of time to walk upon open land felt like freedom. But the freedom is short lived as we marched into more hedgerows where German forces waited.

More days went by.

We had been marching for three weeks. Our spirits near broken be-cause of the endless marching and conflict, but some men had different attitudes for they believed we would escape the hedgerows for good within the next few days. How I hoped.

And after an intense day of fighting, our regiment had stopped for the evening. Only a small amount of sunlight remained. We nestled deep in the hedgerows, knowing the Germans are near—waiting. We would rest for the night and continue on early the next morning. It rained most of the day but for the moment, no drops of water fell from above.

I dug myself a small foxhole within a hedgerow next to Karl and An-drew, who had dug one together. It became difficult to separate those two men. Good as brothers they are. Always side by side. I couldn't help but to admire that. True friendship.

"Those bastards just keep coming out of nowhere," Andrew said. He stuffed his mouth with fresh vegetable stew from a tin can that had been cooked over a small fire. "Any more of this and I'll go crazy."

"At least we're making headway here," Karl said.

"If you say so," Andrews replied. "But it feels like we're not moving anywhere."

"Well, at least we made it through another day," I said as I stirred my can of stew with a spoon. The stew tasted bland and needed salt, but salt was scarce in our rations. "We can't say that for all those other guys we lost along the way."

"It's best to not talk about the dead," Karl said. "It's bad luck."

"Bullshit," Andrew said as he ruffled his thick red hair. "You're too superstitious. I bet you don't like to talk about the dead because you're scared you'll be next."

Karl laughed at Andrew's last remark. "Of course I'm scared, knucklehead. Any man out here would be a damn fool to say he's not. All I'm saying is that you can't let these worries of being killed in action get the best of you. We're here to do our jobs, and that is to win this goddamn war—even if we die in the process or not." Karl always had a way with words.

"I think I'm more scared of this food than anything out here right now," I said as I stared into my cup. My appetite was now gone. Karl and Andrew both broke out into laughs.

"Having a little friendly chat, gentleman?" Aschner said as he approached us.

"We're just having a little discussion about how great this food is," Andrew said.

"Yeah, I bet." Aschner crouched down beside us and looked around cautiously before exposing a small flask. "Care to join me?"

"What would the captain say if he caught you with that," Andrew asked.

"I know for sure that that hypocrite does the same thing," Aschner replied. "Where do you think this came from?"

"You *stole* that from Captain Hull?" I snickered.

"He *will* be pissed if he finds out," Karl said.

"He thinks he accidentally left it behind back at the bluff," Aschner replied.

"Well, it looks like Sergeant First-Class Daniel Aschner is a little prankster," Andrew said.

"There's no shame in having a little fun," Aschner said as he passed the flask to me. "You boys go easy on that now."

I took a small swig of whiskey and handed it to Andrew. This was a side of Aschner I never knew existed.

Aschner cleared his throat. "Anyway, I came to inform all of you that there has been a change in plans."

"What do you mean a change of plans?" I asked.

"The hedgerows will simply measure our advances from here on out. We will travel by four hedgerows tomorrow morning and then five the day after. Then back to four the day after and so on and so forth."

"Shit!" Andrew snapped. "It'll take us forever to get to Saint-Lô."

"From where we stand," Aschner continued, "we'll only be walking into the German's hands if we keep going the way we are now. These hedgerows are a serious issue. They can wait to ambush us at any time if we walk through them like we've been doing for the previous three weeks. Those Germans aren't foolish, guys. Eventually, they'll have counter attacks for our Shermans. It's a maze through these damn things, and I bet more than anything, the Germans know every nook and cranny out here. Offensive action from here on out will be problematic. So we have to be more careful. It'll be time-consuming—I know, but we have to strategize. So, we'll be marching little by little with each passing day. We're currently about twenty-eight kilometers from Saint-Lô. It shouldn't be too bad, gents. It's better to be safe than sorry."

The flask made it back into Aschner's hands. He took a hasty swig and placed it into his coat.

The looks on Karl's and Andrew's faces displayed disappointment. I for one was not delighted to hear about the new strategy as much as they were. Our march towards Saint-Lô would be longer now, and who knows exactly how long.

Aschner stood up and looked down on us. "You boy's should try to get some rest. We'll be moving out at sunrise." He walked away from us to talk with other men, leaving the three of us in a foul mood.

"Can you believe this?" Andrew hissed. "You know what this means do you? The longer this march will take—the longer it takes for us to get back home."

"There's nothing we can do," Karl said. "We have orders, and we have a mission. So we complete this mission no matter how long it takes. But I wish we could get it all done sooner."

"Well, that's that," I said, standing up and leaving my foxhole. "I need to take a piss."

"Don't go too far," Karl said as I walked away.

I found a place of seclusion not far from the other men to relieve my-self, but I felt a presence behind me as I was doing so. Eyes were on me—watching me. I buckled up my trousers and turned around to dis-cover Roland standing a few feet away.

"How are you not dead yet?" he asked. "I figured you'd be rotting in the ground somewhere by now."

Roland and I kept our respectable distances away from one another during our tenure here in Normandy. But I speculated I would be ap-proached by him sooner or later, despite my tries to avoid him. "Well, I hate to disappoint you, but I'm not that easy to kill." I wanted to be care-ful with my words and be civil as much as possible. My role as a staff sergeant was to be professional at all times.

"Well, I wouldn't get too comfortable in your position," Roland said. "Because as soon as you're dead—I'll be taking your spot."

I now grew annoyed. "Is that so? Let me ask you something, Cor-poral—if you don't mind."

"And what's that?"

"Do you enjoy being a pain in the ass?" Roland scoffed. "When are you going to get it through your thick head that you are not better than eve-ryone? Where has your attitude gotten you? You're still a corporal, and you've been in the army for well over five years. I'd figured you would have grown up by now, but you're still just a bully wantin' everything handed to you! Well, guess what? That's not how the world works, and I *highly* suggest you get with the program!" I became furious, not wanting to put up with Roland's obnoxious ego.

"You think you're better than me, Conroy?" he hissed. "Just because you're staff sergeant now—you think you're better than me? I'm so sick of you, you know that. You're just a fly continuously flying and buzzing around, annoying me. I swat and swat at you, but you can never go away until I finally get the chance to smack you with a rolled up news-paper. You just watch your back. There will be a time when I will be really sick of you, just like an annoying fly. And when the time comes—you *will* wish you never screwed with me!"

Listening to Roland's ranting reminded me of a young child throwing a tantrum. And the only way to calm the child down was to compromise. I thought it was best to try it. "I don't want to fight with you Roland—not anymore. Why can't we let the past remain in the past and start over? What's the harm in that?"

He said nothing—only glared. But the silence became awkward. I wanted to walk away, but now I believed our differences needed to be settled right here and now. I needed to stand my ground.

"You can't get rid of me that easily," he finally hissed.

"Is that all you have to say?" I said.

"Just watch yourself. You might just get sent home wounded or dead because of me."

"Is *that* a threat?!" I asked as I stepped up to him and stared him down with rage.

He laughed. "What are you going to do, Conroy? There's no way you can take me."

He was right. I couldn't fight him. And there were no intentions of striking him for I had no chance of winning a fight against him. But I had to make a stand for myself. No more am I to be harassed. "I will not fight you, Roland. I know better. But as your sergeant, I highly recom-mend you not to threaten your superiors, or there will be consequences. Is that understood?"

Roland was not laughing now. His face grew red. "What are you gon-na do, Conroy?"

"Return to your platoon, Corporal!" I ordered.

Roland turned from me, but by surprise, his fist knocked me to ground. I should have seen it coming. But I was quick to jump to my feet for retaliation but he grabbed a hold of me. One arm held me around my chest and the other arm wrapped around my head as if trying to snap my neck. The way I understood it, this would play out two different aspects: I would just take the beating or I could fight instead. I chose to fight, because I wanted this to be the last fight I would have with him. I'm a trained soldier, and now it's time to put all I learned to use. In this situation, I had to think fast or move on impulse. My legs were free— use my boots. I slammed my boot down on his right ankle and kicked his shins. When his grip on me loosened up, I elbowed him in his thick gut several times and kicked his shin once more as hard as I could. He let me go as he bellowed from the pain. This was the opportunity I needed. With all of my force, I kicked him in the chest. He stumbled back, hunched over as I plunged my elbow on the back of his head, which dropped him to the ground on all fours. I then planted an abrupt and ferocious kick to the middle of his face. He then rolled over. Blood spilled from his nose. I placed my right foot on his throat, applied pressure, and unholstered my pistol and stuck it into his face. Sweat beaded from my forehead as I took deep breaths from the adrenaline. My body trembled with anger. Roland's days of pushing me around were over.

Roland's face was bloodied. His eyes now revealed a fear I never seen before as I waved my pistol at him point blank in his face. My finger relaxed on the trigger. For a moment, I wanted to pull it. There was no doubt in my mind I would have. It all could be over with him right here and now. All I had to do is squeeze the trigger. I applied more pressure on his throat with my boot. A gurgling noise escaped his mouth as he choked for air. "No more!" I sneered. "No more!"

"What's going on here?!" a voice roared nearby. It was Karl. But he wasn't alone. Many men crowded around and witnessed the scene, looking concerned as they glanced back and forth at Roland and I. Karl stepped closer. He lifted his hand a little. "Easy, Vince. Just take it easy." He looked at Roland and then back at me. Roland continued to gurgle. "You need to take your foot off his throat, Vince. You're killing him." His voice was low and gentle, trying to calm me down. "Please, Vince. Take your foot off his throat and holster your pistol... please." He stepped within a few feet of me and stopped.

I looked down at Roland. His face began changing to a light shade of purple. "Vince," he gurgled. I did as Karl said and let my foot off his throat and holstered my pistol. Roland sucked in a vast amount of air and folded over on his side, coughing violently as several men scrambled to his side.

"Holy shit, Vince," Karl said, keeping an eye on Roland.

"The bastard had it coming," I said.

All the commotion caught Captain Hull's attention. I considered what would come of me: court-martialed? Maybe kicked out of the army and shipped back home to the United States? I almost killed a fellow soldier after being promoted to staff sergeant. Just my luck.

―――

I EXPLAINED TO CAPTAIN HULL every detail, exposing only the truth: Roland struck me first, and I was defending myself, but I also admitted I went too far. But luck was on my side. Several men confirmed this after witnessing the incident. They revealed to Hull it happened as I had explained it—that I acted out in self-defense. I expected this would help my case.

And so, I was not court-martialed or kicked out of the army or even stripped of rank, but only fined a month's pay for excessive use of force in self-defense. Hull fined Roland also for provoking me. A slap on the wrist for both of us. Nothing more. I expected this would be the last tangle Roland and I have. We were bitter enemies; no secret from anyone now. But now I believed our vendetta has at last came to an end. Or so I hoped.

"I won't allow my men to quarrel amongst one another," Hull scolded. "We are not here to fight ourselves. We are here to fight the Germans.

That's our mission. I understand that all of you are under loads of stress, but both of you are professionally skilled and trained soldiers. So goddamnit act like it! I want no more of this foolishness. So if there is an incident between the two you of you gentleman again—you both will be court-martialed. Is that clear?"

"Yes, sir," Roland and I said together.

"Good," Hull said. "Now get out of my sight."

Roland and I both saluted Hull but he ignored our salutes and went about his strategy for moving forward in the hedgerows with Aschner. I then returned to my foxhole.

Karl and Andrew kept a watchful eye on me as I settled in. They said nothing as they bundled up underneath their blankets and drifted off to sleep. I checked my gear and checked my pistol and rifle to ensure of being fully loaded. It was best to know I was prepared just in case of a midnight German assault.

As the night continued, I sat awake and watched the stars from above. The night air turned colder as I wrapped myself up tighter with my blanket. Several men began to sing songs with mellow voices. Roland was one of the men singing. His voice now raspy from my boot to his throat.

I closed my eyes and drifted off to sleep—listening to the songs of the night.

TWENTY-THREE

IT WAS THE FIFTEENTH OF JULY when the 29th arrived outside Saint-Lô. We were free from marching through miles of hedgerows for the time being. But days before reaching Saint-Lô, we marched through fields and small villages here and there, with ongoing conflicts with the Germans. They proved on the front line that the Allies would not overrun them without a struggle. The German forces constructed strong and difficult defensive battles, but the 29th Infantry, at last, prevailed in reaching the city. Casualties were high on both sides. Men I spoke with, had conversations with, ate with, laughed with, and fought side by side with left the battlefields wounded or dead.

And yet, Karl and Andrew remained—and Roland. Captain Hull, Aschner, Lester and even Robert Harris—the man I practiced hand-to-hand combat with at boot camp made it this far. But for how long? It's always best to not think about dying. Continue to fight. Be smart and survive. We are trained soldiers of the United States military.

Our marching halted upon arriving just three miles from Saint-Lô. The Germans were determined to keep the Allied forces from advancing any further as they fortified their strength almost two-hundred yards away from our patrols. The Allied officers ordered an attack; first: an artillery strike; second: charge the German Army head on. We took them by surprise and drove them back towards the city. But the raid had been nothing more but a temporary victory. Darkness became our enemy. The assault had been called off, and so we retreated.

Early the next morning, the Germans retaliated. Their forces blasted their 88s, mortars, and 105s for their attack. Further retreat was not an option, even after being taken by surprise. The 29th Infantry held their ground for over three long and miserable weeks. The casualties increased.

After days of fighting, tanks and howitzers reinforced from the rear. Now gaining the upper hand, officers ordered another strike that forced the Germans to retreat. The day after, the 175th Regiment came to our aid as the enemy counterattacked, but due to being unorganized, the attack was disbanded.

At last, the 29th Infantry continued its slow march towards Saint-Lô, enduring continuous battles with the Germans, but soon reached just outside the city.

We were to attack the northeast sector near the Madeleine River. But there came a serious complication: with little sleep, we were exhausted and low on ammunition after undergoing weeks of defense with the German forces that pounded us with artillery fire. So to conserve ammunition, we used only our bayonet's—fighting the enemy head-on. With little options available, we returned to the defense. Officers ordered to stay low at all times until prepared for an offensive movement. Wanting to survive, I followed orders and dug the best damn foxhole of my military career and stayed low in the ground.

What I remember the most about those days was not the enemy artillery fire or the bad food but the smell; the stench of dead rotting animals and soldiers. That smell is difficult to forget. But some men came up with a solution: they'd break apart their cigarettes in two pieces and shove the separate pieces into their nostrils. It was rather genius. I, however, had no cigarettes because I didn't smoke. But no one were willing to give up any of theirs, so I lived with the horrible smell.

Relief, at last, came on the twenty-ninth of June when an Allied bomber flew overhead and dropped loads of rifles, ammunition, and machine guns. It felt like Christmas; perhaps even better than Christmas. We were back in action and with our fresh supplies, we won new ground within a day of fighting.

The official attack on Saint-Lô had been scheduled for the eleventh of July. And after seven days of attacking and gaining ground west along the ridgeline against a tough German army, we advanced our forces in the city itself for battle. C Company are to march towards east of city to secure a bridge crossing over the La Vire River.

Upon entering the city, we marched through the ruined streets and architectures of Saint-Lô with caution. The Allies had taken the city, but German troops still prowled throughout the ruins, waiting to ambush. The Allied bombardment on the city that came weeks before had been crushing. I have never seen such destruction in all my life. Homes that gave shelter to generations of families gone in a blink of an eye. Sides of these homes and buildings were gone, revealing wrecked interior. Only a wall or two remained of many buildings. Rubble littered the streets along with battered vehicles, street lights, and bicycles. I only wished to have visited the city in its former glory and not witness it of what it had become: a city of ruin and disorder. I couldn't imagine all the innocent families forced out to avoid death and separation of loved ones. The debris and ruins that stood were once homes to these families.

"Keep low and conserve ammunition." Captain Hull ordered. "Only fire if need be!"

We continued our course through the city, keeping a watchful eye as artillery fire echoed in the distance when a single shot roared through the air and struck a soldier that was standing just a few feet from me.

"Take cover!" Aschner shouted.

Instinct took over as every man jumped behind anything for protection: a battered vehicle or sections of a demolished wall. I dove behind a door attached to a crumbled wall with Captain Hull. Near to me was

Roland, hunched down behind a fragment of a wall. His huge body just barely out of sight. He was an easy target for snipers, so his best choice is to stay hidden from enemy eyes searching for a target to the best of his ability.

Shots then rained down from the Germans, keeping us held down in our positions. After a moment, the gunfire stopped as they waited for someone to blow cover.

"It's a fucking sniper," Aschner said. "Who got hit?"

I peered out from behind the wall to glimpse the fallen soldier.

"Private Hunter Blake," he groaned. I knew little about him. Hull placed him in my platoon after D-Day reorganization. "I'm alive but hurt badly. I'm losing a lot of blood."

"Try to keep quiet and still, Private," Hull said. "We'll get you to cover as soon as we can."

I had to act out. "I can get him, Captain," I stated.

"I can get to him too," Robert Harris shouted out. "The both of us can pull him to safety."

"Now's not the time to act foolishly. The both of ya will get shot too. Just keep yourself down. We need to take out that damn sniper if we are to help him."

I saw Hunter pleading with his eyes at me for help. He would be dead if he didn't get aid from the medics. I wanted to rush to his side but disobeying a superior officer's orders is insubordination.

"Please... someone help me," Hunter groaned. He lifted his head, ignoring Hull's requests to stay still when another shot fired in the distance. The bullet pierced his forehead through his helmet. Blood sprayed the ground as his head dropped to the pavement.

"Goddamnit!" Hull shouted. "Did anyone see where the shot came from?"

Troops shook their heads not knowing until Karl's voice rang out from over them. "The shots came from a building just ahead of us—about thirty to forty yards north from our current position, sir!"

"Good, Sergeant Lambert," Hull said. He looked at me. "Conroy—I want you and Sergeant Lambert with three other men to get to that location as close as you can. I want a bazooka round fired into that building to allow the rest of the men to advance forward and take that sniper out, and whoever else is in there! But be careful. I don't want to lose any more men today. I need volunteers!"

"Second Platoon—I need volunteers!" I yelled.

"I'll go," said Andrew.

"Two more volunteers," I said.

"I'll do it!" Lester rang out.

"Ok, that's two," Hull said. "Who else? Who's carrying a bazooka?"

"That would be me, Captain," Arthur Bates said.

"I can go also," Robert squeaked.

"Too many men," I stated. "The captain only wants five men. You stay here with everyone else."

"Whatever you say, Sarge," he said, with a look of disappointment on his face. "Just be careful fellas."

Roland had not made a sound during volunteering. He only cowered behind the busted wall.

"Ok, that's five," Hull said. "You boys don't disappoint me. We'll provide covering fire. So find those sniping sons of bitches and give them hell! On my signal!"

I got to my feet in a crouched position, preparing to make a dash further up the road, unexpected of what may lie ahead of me. I checked and doubled checked my M1 rifle. A habit I grew into. "You men stay on me!" I yelled. I had an obligation to fulfill for my role as staff sergeant. Karl was my friend. And now Andrew volunteered as well; my duty now is to watch over them, along with Lester and Arthur.

"Covering fire!" Hull shouted as the troops in unison peered out from behind cover and fired at empty windows and doorways at the building Karl had pointed out.

I ran with Karl, and the volunteers while keeping low to avoid friendly fire and with hopes to evade enemy fire. Karl lead the way down the street to a partially destroyed building. There we took shelter inside the battered walls.

"If my assumptions are correct—" Karl said as he peered through an open window, "enemy fire is coming from just above us at that red brick building."

I moved closer to the edge of the wall and poked my head out just enough to get a glimpse. Shots fired and impacted the ground and wall close to my head. "Shit! Yep, they're there. They know we're here too. Ok. . . location is twenty feet north. Large red brick building as Sergeant Lambert pointed out."

"So what's the plan, Staff Sergeant?" Andrew asked.

I looked at Arthur. "If we provide covering fire—do you think you can get a shot with the bazooka at that building? We need to take them by surprise. One round will cause a distraction that should give the rest of the company time to progress forward."

They all agreed to my plan. "It won't be an accurate shot," Arthur stated.

"It doesn't need to be," I said. "It's a diversion." I checked my M1 Garand rifle to make sure I loaded it once more. "On the count of three. We'll provide covering fire as you fire a bazooka round. After you fire—we'll move closer to the enemy to engage and hopefully move the company further up from their current position for assistance."

I let out a deep breath and counted to three as we all leaned out from the wall and provided covering fire for Arthur to fire a bazooka round at the enemy. A rocket soared out the front as smoke poured out the end of the long green tube. The round struck the target building which blasted a huge hole in the wall. The remaining company that had been holding back rushed forward to my position—taking advantage of the little time to advance before the Germans retaliate as my team hurried to our next position, firing a round of bullets to provide more time to be where we needed to be.

"All right, men—give 'em hell!" Hull shouted. My team unleashed a firing brigade inside the building. Shooting into windows and tossing grenades into them above and below. I could hear the yells from German fighters from within.

After several minutes, I halted the attack.

"Let's make sure it's secure," I stated. "You guys stick to me."

Lester checked his rifle. "If I find one of them alive—I'm gonna blow his fucking brains out. And I hope it's the sniper."

Arthur strapped the bazooka on his back and unholstered his pistol as my squad peered inside the building. On the floor were six German soldiers riddled with bullets, lying in puddles of blood. I checked each one for traces of life, but they were all dead. Their eyes open and lifeless.

From above me on the second floor, there came a thud. "Someone's up there alive," Arthur said as we listened to the sounds of shuffling above us.

"It sounds like he's crawling. Probably wounded," I said. "Let's run up and get him."

With my last grenade, I stood at the foot of the stairs and tossed it up to the second floor. There came a shout from above before the grenade exploded. After detonation, Arthur and I were the first to rush up the stairs only to be met with a few rounds of enemy gunfire coming from a Luger pistol. I felt a bullet breeze pass by me as I fired a few rounds from my rifle at a German soldier sitting up against the wall. The rounds impacted the soldier in his chest, killing him. His head slumped forward as thick blood streamed out his mouth. I turned to look at Arthur who had fallen down the stairs. I rushed down the steps to his side. He lied at the foot of the stairs clinching his neck. Blood seeped through his fingers.

"Medic!" I called out. In just seconds, a medic and the other men from the company joined me.

What's the situation?" Aschner asked, looking down at Arthur.

"We removed the German threat," I said. "But Corporal Bates got shot in the neck when we tried to clear out the second floor."

The medic crouched down over Arthur and tried to remove his fingers from his neck. He was reluctant to let go, afraid of more blood gushing out. But the medic pried Arthur's hand away to get a better look. "It's the jugular," the medic said. Arthur gagged as blood squirted out his neck. His eyes were wide open, revealing fear. After a few moments, he lied still and not breathing. The medic sighed. "There wasn't anything I could do." Arthur lied dead. Those of us in that room stood around, looking down on him.

Aschner sighed. "Let's get him out of here."

"I'll help carry him," Robert said as he grabbed hold of Arthur's feet. The medic took hold of the shoulders, lifting him from the ground, carrying him outside.

Then Aschner, Lester, and I went up the steps to the second floor. A sniper rifle lied near to the fallen German soldier's body. Lester dug through the uniform for any keepsakes and found a wristwatch on his left arm and removed it. "You deserved it, you dead son of a bitch. I don't think you'll mind if I take this."

Aschner and I ignored Lester's looting and searched the rest of the second floor to find it clear of Germans. All that remained was antique furniture, rubble, and a wide hole in the wall left behind by Hunter's bazooka round.

"We lost another," Aschner said to Hull as we exited the building.

"That's a damn shame," Hull said, turning to me. "Is this building clear, Staff Sergeant?"

"Yes, sir," I said. "There was one man left alive upstairs—possibly the sharpshooter. He took a few shots at us once we reached the second floor. I fired back, killing him. But Corporal Bates got hit in the neck."

"Wasn't anything you could do, Sergeant," Hull said with frustration as he took his eyes off me. "Let's move out!"

———

DURING OUR MARCH EAST towards our destination, we came upon more German resistance. But troops from the 30th Infantry joined our company for support. Proper reinforcement would allow our liberation of Saint-Lô to come swifter. Two M4 Allied tanks accompanied the troops from the 30th to supply enough firepower to wipe out the lingering German troops hiding within buildings and homes.

Some German soldiers made it easier on themselves and us by surrendering. But some of them would remain to engage in a winless battle, only to be killed or wounded. The medics patched up the injured Germans. Perhaps the Germans would do the same. It's a decency among men to help those that need it, even if fighting on separate sides.

But The Germans killed several good men today. Arthur Bates being one. I didn't have the liberty of knowing him well. We spoke very little to one another during training and our time here in Europe, but in those few moments I spent with him clearing a building of Germans—he had demonstrated enough courage and determination that would count for over fifty men. The good soldiers don't live the longest. I know, because I witnessed it. I took the blame for Arthur's death. He perished under my supervision, and I let him down. I let Captain Hull down.

———

IT WOULDN'T BE LONG now until the Allies Liberated Saint-Lô.

By the end of the day, we arrived at our destination—a cobblestone covered bridge about twenty yards long and thirty feet wide. Underneath ran the La Vire River. We were to hold the bridge and wait for more reinforcements to arrive. With time to rest, we ate a quick cold ration meal (pork loaf, biscuits, and a chocolate bar).

The loud fire of gunshots and explosions I endured throughout the day rang in my ears. But perhaps they were real, proceeding from within the city but it became difficult for me to distinguish what's real and what's not.

I took a seat on the bridge with my back against the hard stone railing, I closed my eyes. I wanted everything to be over. We marched over twenty miles, and it took six weeks to arrive within the city itself. The entire time I had stepped foot into France, I had had little sleep, ate bad food, and drank bad coffee. I suffered aches and pains that made me feel like a fatigued old man. It tired me and I wanted nothing more than to go home, but I knew home, in time, was a long, long ways away.

I unholstered my pistol and aimed it at my foot. All it takes is one careful shot. I could just say it was an accidental discharge. They would believe me after I came this far—after everything I had endured. They would believe me. But I wouldn't shoot myself in the foot. It's childish and selfish. I holstered my pistol and leaned my head back and closed my eyes as the sun lowered.

"You showed a lot of guts out there today, Vince," Karl said as he sat down next to me. I opened my eyes.

"I'm just doing my job," I stated.

He scoffed. "Just doing your job? You make it sound like it's an everyday thing. Like a profession someone does without ever giving it much thought about the risks involved."

I chuckled. "Well, it's feeling like that. But the truth is Karl: I'm tired. I'm tired of being away from home and tired of this goddamn war." I looked at him. His eyes were diverted straight ahead, looking at nothing in particular it seemed. "It's only been six weeks, but I don't know how much longer I can keep going." I took a deep breath. "What did I get myself into?"

Karl let out a heavy sigh. "Shit, Vince—you think too much."

"Yeah, I know. It's a force of habit."

We sat in silence for a few minutes. I had nothing else to say. My mind wandered, daydreaming of my return home.

"Who was that woman you spoke of back home," Karl asked, breaking me out of my thoughts.

"You mean Catherine?" I replied.

"That's the one. Are you going to find a woman like her when you get back to the States?"

"What do you mean 'find'? She's waiting for me."

"Do you really believe so? You deserve to have a good woman to settle down with when you return. You're entitled to it. Hell, we all are. I just hope she's still waiting for you. But I if I were you—I wouldn't get my hopes up."

I shook my head. "Well, I hope so too. She's good to me."

"Well, who knows what'll happen when we get home. The stuff I told you that night back in Vierville—I meant every word. The two of us, along with Andrew—we will grow old together. Just you wait and see."

Karl smiled and slouched down as if preparing to catch a little sleep. But Hull and Aschner approached us and called out for the Company to attention. Karl and I jumped up at an instant.

"Listen up, troops," Hull said. "I just got word that C Company is to be relieved for two days." Nearly every man in the Company cheered. Hull waited a moment for the cheers to die down before speaking again. "We got the German army on the run. If we keep this up—this war will be over in no time. So all of your hard work has been regarded and appreciated. You all deserve a reward. So all of you are to head down to Agneaux at this very minute for showers, good grub, fresh uniforms, and rest in warm comfortable cots." The men cheered again. "So congratulations to all of you. You've earned it. So in two days, all of you are to report back here for your next assignment. Is that clear?!"

"Yes, sir!" we all shouted.

"Good," Hull said. "Dismissed!"

TWENTY-FOUR

AT LONG LAST, a few days' rest. The company earned it.

Agneaux, a small village just outside Saint-Lô had been untouched by any attacks. The civilians of the village regarded the Allied troops as heroes, greeting us with open arms as we arrived in the late hours of the evening. Few of us spoke French, but the language barrier was not necessary. Men, women, and children crowded the soldiers: men gave handshakes and hugs as children did the same. But the women: young, old, charming, unattractive, thin, or large—felt obliged to prove their gratitude to the men in different ways. Troops took pleasure in this for it was a temptation that no man could pass up, despite their commitments to significant others back home. The women's affectionate manner expressed that we did something right and valiant. We whooped and celebrated our triumph as we strolled through the village, swelling with pride—perhaps too much for our own good.

Arrogance. But most of us are young, so pride may be excused. After the company's successful part of the continuing liberation of Saint-Lô, we felt as if we walked on water. We were winning the war. Our constant push through France no doubt raised concerns for the German army. There was talk among the company that the war could be over sooner than expected. The Allies have momentum, and the Germans would predict there would be no signs of letting up.

Eagerness settled deep in the bones of C Company to finish the war as soon as possible to get back home. Even after being awarded a few days' rest, some men hoped to have the two days pass revoked to move out further into France and in due course into Germany. A day wasted is another day spent away from home and at last ending the war.

But after all my hard work, I'm grateful for a few days' rest. Captain Hull promised a soft cot to sleep in and I could not pass that offer up. It will be most a most welcoming break from sleeping in a filthy foxhole. But first, a shower, for I was in desperate need for one. It had been weeks and weeks before my last one. During the company's march to-wards Saint-Lô, if any ponds were come across, the men took it upon themselves to have a dip. The dips into the ponds were our baths. I questioned whether the water is sanitary and even raised concern but no one seemed to care. Our dips only lasted a few minutes, but despite our baths, we put on the same soiled uniform we wore at all times, so a bath didn't make much of a difference. But now, a shower turned into a luxury. So I hopped in line the first chance I got. Once finished with my shower, I put on only a clean t-shirt and a pair of P.T. shorts and got a much-needed haircut and shave, and walked to a small wash-house where young women were doing laundry, passing out clean uniforms, folded and wrapped, tied together with string in brown paper to troops.

I told one of the young ladies the size of my uniform and boots. "What is your rank, sir?" she asked in English but with a thick French accent.

"Staff Sergeant," I replied as I brushed my hand over my washed and trimmed hair. The young lady took a packaged uniform and a pair of boots and brought them to me. "Thank you," I said.

She smiled. It was an innocent smile, but she looked at me as if we were lovers. "You are most welcome, Sergeant. Thank you for everything you and your army has done for our village."

Her expression and eyes told me everything she wanted to say but not with words. Her appearance was attractive as her shoulder-length chestnut hair was skillfully styled, improving upon her angular face. She had thin brown eyes, a pointed nose, and a soft dimple in her chin. If I had to guess her age, I would suggest about twenty or a year or two younger.

"If you have time this evening, Sergeant. A few of my friends and I will be at the BRISTO for some wine. Perhaps you and a few of your companions could join us?"

I knew what she wanted, but I would have to disappoint her. "Thank you for the offer, ma'am, but I'm afraid I need much rest before my company has to move out again."

She frowned. "Of course—but if you were to perhaps change your mind. . ."

"I will know where to find you," I said as I reassured her with a smile.

She smiled once more and continued with her work, giving me the opportunity to leave the wash-house and the flirtatious French girl behind.

Afterwards, I went straight to the temporary barrack and untied the string holding together the brown paper and discovered my new clean uniform now came with the staff sergeant chevrons. It was official.

——

FEELING HUNGRY, I CAUGHT UP WITH KARL AND ANDREW so we could have a meal together. We were all starved, and a nice meal before sleep would be most promising. A mess tent had been erected and inside were several tables filled with food. Lines of men walked alongside the tables as servers planted food onto their trays: hot fresh bread, beef and vegetable soup, and proper black coffee. This stew was tastier than our stale rations we carried. From what I understood, the civilians of Agneaux helped with the preparing and cooking of meals. Nothing to complain about. The cooking, I discovered to be a delicacy.

Karl, Andrew, and I found a soft patch of grass to sit in away from other soldiers as we ate our meals.

But Andrew turned a distant shoulder at me. He had been all but quiet since our arrival at Agneaux. And when he spoke, it was only to Karl. His cold manner was different as he most often included an un-pleasant comment to any conversation we had. As his demeanor contin-ued through our meal, my curiosity got the better of me. "Are you ok, Andrew? You've been awful quiet this evening."

Andrew gave me a cold look, evident that something was on his mind.

Karl glanced back and forth at the two of us. "You must forgive An-drew tonight, Vince. He's in one of his little fussy moods."

I'm all too familiar with Andrew's absurd moods. I had witnessed an incident first hand one night back in Virginia; Andrew had a shooting competition with Karl: the first person to hit the bull's-eye five times would be the winner, and the loser would have to buy the winner rounds of beers for a full night at the BLUESTONE PUB. Karl won the competi-tion, putting Andrew in a most vicious mood. The whole night, Andrew cursed under his breath and mocked Karl. But Karl shrugged off any-thing said as if prepared for any ridicule to come his way. Andrew's ex-terior is timid and yet animated but there is more underneath; a side I've only seen a few occasions: blunt, serious, and indifferent. I always tried to avoid that side, but now I somehow crossed over into that terri-tory.

"I'm not fussy!" Andrew snapped, again putting on an angry face. "I'm just not too happy about how you called things out there today, Conroy. We lost a man today in that building we were clearing out which could have been avoided. *Why* didn't you call for backup?" His voice turned harsh, and his eyes burned with flames.

"Jeez, Andrew—calm down, all right," Karl said. "Casualties are una-voidable. There wasn't anything we could do to avoid what happened."

But Andrew didn't seem to listen. I had to speak up for myself and not allow Karl to continue fighting my battles. "I made a decision, Andrew. Maybe it was bad judgment, but we got the job done. I'm not perfect you know. And I make mistakes just like everyone else."

"Quite so," Karl said.

"Yeah, well don't expect any more favors from me," Andrew snapped. "You need to get your head on straight, or you will create a real shitshow for all of us. Because what happened earlier was a damn mess."

"You think it's *easy* being in my position?" I retaliated. "Maybe you should put on these stripes, and you'll understand how fun it is."

Andrew scoffed. "You're seriously fucked."

"Not as fucked up as you." I stood, realizing it's pointless to reason with Andrew. He needed to be left alone to cool off. Making myself absent would help his cause.

"Vince—come back and sit down," Karl said as I walked away.

"No," Andrew said. "Let the asshole leave. Screw him."

———

I LEFT KARL AND ANDREW and discovered a little pub nearby which turned out to be the BRISTO the laundry worker girl invited me to. I scanned through the windows. The laundry girl was absent from the scene. I watched soldiers mingling with the locals. Conversations scattered aloud among everyone as mugs of beers and short glasses filled with liquor were being consumed. Women sat in soldiers laps, as they flirted, and kissed them. A record player roared music as some patrons danced together joyfully. These are the times the men needed away from the misery of war. All work and no play is no way to live by.

"Why not?" I said to myself. "A drink or two won't hurt." I made my way in, and a few familiar faces turned and nodded. Robert being one. In his lap was a young French girl. Their behavior towards one another was not appropriate for the public. The kissing and touching was enough to force me to look away quickly in fear that I would blush. In the corner, sitting at a lonely table was Roland and Lester. Lester was speaking but Roland sat in silence over his mug of beer. Stepping up to the bar, I asked for a beer from a thin bartender. There were no stools, so standing was my only option. The bartender poured tapped beer into a large glass mug and set it in front of me as I tossed a few coins on the bar. The coins were French currency, so I tolerated the bartender to take the amount I owed for the drink. He perhaps robbed me, but it would be pointless to argue.

I sipped on my beer and discovered the lager to be tasty, smooth, and stimulating. There's not beer like this back in the States. I savored every sip, and after the mug was empty, I asked for a second round right away. I drank my beer and listened to the upbeat music coming from the record player when someone stood beside me at the bar. "A beer!" a voice sounded out. It was Andrew. Out the corner of my eye, I could see him glancing at me. He took a big gulp of beer as soon as he received it and turned to me. "Look. . . Vince, I'm sorry about what I said back there. I was out of line."

I stared at him for a moment with suspicion. "Did Karl tell you to say this?"

Andrew chuckled to lighten the foul mood between us. "Yeah."

"Well. . . you need not apologize if you don't mean it." I took a sip of beer. "It's difficult being in my position, you know. Sometimes orders have to be made for the sake of getting a job done, no matter the costs."

"Yeah. . . I suppose you're right. But I wanted to slug you though," We both laughed. "But a soldier should never strike his superior."

"I'm only a staff sergeant, and you're a sergeant, so I'm not much of a superior. And I wouldn't have reported it, anyway. So how about this— why don't you say we go out back, and I let you punch me square in the face." We both laughed again.

"No, I think I'll give you this one. Just this once," he winked. We clanked our mugs together and took a gulp of beer.

"Well, I'm glad to see we're all getting along again!" Karl's voice came from behind. He called for a beer after joining Andrew and I at the bar.

After taking a few sips, he put his mug down. "I've got to say. . . this is the best damn beer I've ever had in my life!"

"I was thinking the same thing," I said. "We need to enjoy this as much as we can. We have to head back into Saint-Lô in a couple of days."

"Where are we headed next?" Andrew inquired.

"My guess is Vire," I said. "We need to get to Paris. But I overhead Captain Hull saying that Vire is need of liberation. So that could be our very next stop."

"Vire, huh?" Andrew said. "I hope the US Military doesn't think the entire 29th Infantry can save all of France on its own."

"More reinforcements should come soon," Karl said.

"I certainly hope so," Andrew said. "This division is running thin."

We drank our beers as a small group of women approached us. There were three of them grinning at us. Among them was the French girl from the wash-room. They gestured to us with vague signals for a dance. "I reckon they want a dance," I said.

"Well I'll be happy to oblige one of them," Andrew said as downed his beer and set the mug down on the counter and took one of the women—a blonde with red cheeks and large breasts, by the arm and led her to a small space on the floor.

The other friend looked at Karl; a shorter woman with long black hair. "I can't leave a beautiful woman hanging, now can I?" he said as the two of them joined Andrew and his dancing partner on the floor.

I smiled, watching the four of them dance to upbeat jazz music. Karl and Andrew followed along as best as they could with their partners. But I thought the two of them looked a bit ridiculous.

The French girl I met earlier stood where she was, eyes fixated on me. She looked much the same as the first time I saw her but instead of wearing raggedy work clothes; she wore a neat blue dress. "You came after all. Care to dance?" she asked.

"I'm sorry, but I'm not much of a dancer," I replied.

I hoped this would get rid of her, but she stood her ground. "We don't have to dance—perhaps we could go somewhere more. . . private."

It was then I got a scent of her perfume over the smell of beer and lumber interior of the pub—a scent of fresh-cut flowers. I also discovered her French accent to be provocative—something I didn't realize before. And now the sight of her made me rethink my answer I was prepared to give her about her invite. But I didn't have the heart to turn her away although I wanted to. She was a sweet girl in need of company. But I'm determined not to give her everything she craved, needing to restrain myself from my sensuous needs. "How about a walk?"

———

"YOU'RE SWEET," the French girl said. "How does a sweet gentleman like you end up in the army?"

I sighed. "It's a long story."

We had been walking side by side throughout Agneaux for over an hour. Agneaux is small, so we wandered past the same spots several times, observing troops mingling with the civilians throughout the night. The Allies had taken over the town, but none of the civilians seemed not to mind for the Allies control will only be temporary. The night air is warmer than usual. And the explosion of artillery fire could not be heard in the distance. A welcoming change.

"Well, I have all night." Her tone became flirtatious, but I struggled to not fall for it. I needed to distract my attention to something else.

"You know—I never caught your name."

"It's Abella. And what is your name?" she replied as she hooked her arm underneath mine.

"Vincent," I responded. "But people just call me Vince."

"Vince. . . that's a nice name. But Vincent suits you better. So I'll just call you Vincent."

It's now I realized she had been speaking English this entire time, yet I never considered asking her where she learned it. "Where did you learn to speak English?"

"I taught myself. . . and I had a little help."

"Is that so? Well, you have my attention."

She let out a gentle laugh.

Travelers from many parts of the world come through here often, be-lieve it or not. Most of them speak English. There was one particular fellow who came here when I was just a small girl.

My parents own a Bed and Breakfast here in the village. Travelers come and go throughout the year. The busiest time of the year for guests is the summer and the slowest is the winter. During Christmas, there are rarely any travelers passing through the village. I always believed Christmas was a special time to embrace the fascinating and pure inno-cence of festivities with one's family. It's always been my favorite holi-day, for it's that one time of year, I can always be young and be filled with life. Every year, I never want it to end. I love the snow and the spirit it brings out of people, and overall—the uplifted feelings for loved ones. But every year, I always become disappointed—because Christmas ends and a new year has to begin.

So one night on a snowy Christmas Eve, after the night's festivities died down, I was sitting on the sofa in front of a warm fire in the sitting area of my parents Bed and Breakfast reading a book, when the front door suddenly opened. A gentle cold wind swept through the house that made me shiver. I wrapped myself up in a quilt around me for warmth as I peaked at the doorway to discover a large man carrying a suitcase enter the room.

"Keep that door closed!" my father shouted as he entered the room, unaware we had a guest. He stopped in his tracks as soon as he laid eyes on the stranger. "Oh, my apologies, sir. I was not aware we had a guest."

The traveler held up a big hand. "No need to apologize, my good man. I came in on the chance for an available room for the evening." The sound of his voice surprised me. It was light and mellow; not the sort of voice to come from a large man. I remember his hair was black and he had a long and wide face.

"Yes, of course," my father said. "It's just that we don't get many visitors during Christmas."

"Well, I'm not one for festivities and such. I always find the holidays to be the best time of year for me to travel, for the times are not busy." After the guest paid for a room and Father took his suitcase upstairs for safe keeping, the traveler stepped over to where I had been sitting. He sat next to me on the sofa and watched the warm glow of the fire for a moment before speaking. "I see you have your nose buried in a book. If you don't mind me asking, but what are you reading?"

I peeled my eyes away from the page I had been reading. "It's Voltaire's *Candide*," I replied.

"Ah, I've never had a taste for literature. For my passion is knowledge. There have been many, many books I read to understand everything about everything."

"What sort of books exactly?" I asked, now curious of our new guest.

His face brightened. "All sorts, my dear: history, the sciences, astronomy, and different languages."

I now became really intrigued. "Do you speak many languages?"

"I speak a fair few. But my specialty is English."

As soon as those words passed through his lips, I almost shot up from my seat on the sofa. "English! Oh, I've always wanted to learn to speak that language. But I'm afraid I own no books to learn by."

The traveler smiled. "Well then—it seems I have come to the right place. Perhaps I could teach you a little of what I know."

My face lit up like a Christmas tree. "Could you, sir?! Could you teach me?!" I never felt so excited in all my life. To this day, I don't know why I wanted to learn the language. Perhaps it had something to do with my craving for something new—something different.

He looked at me and smiled once more. "I can teach you. And I will."

The traveler was fluent in the English language. From that night on, the two of us sat on that same sofa in front of the warm fireplace every night for one whole month in each other's company, engaged in studies.

I always raced to the living area at night to discover the traveler waiting for me with his books, so we could begin our lessons. I learned so much. What started out as gibberish soon began to make sense as I learned the English alphabet and after the first week, I was saying words and saying complete sentences. It took time but I began to understand the language. It surprised me the traveler stayed with us as long as he did. Perhaps he had nowhere to go. Perhaps he liked our little village and wished to stay for as long as he could. But every night, I feared the time he would mention no more lessons would come because he had to leave but each night he paid for his room once more, and he made no mention of our lessons ever coming to an end. More and more I learned as days passed by. I made a friend. It was a friendship I didn't want to end.

Until one night I rushed down stairs to begin my lesson but the traveler was nowhere to be seen. I sat down in my usual spot on the sofa and waited for his arrival and yet he never made an appearance. I waited so long, I fell asleep and was woken by my father early the next morning. I asked the whereabouts of the traveler and my father told me he had left before I came down to greet him the night before. My heart sank. He left before we could finish our lessons. He left without saying goodbye. I think that hurt the most: I never got a goodbye from my friend.

"But he left behind a few books for me," she continued. "So I could continue to study my lessons on my own. And so I did. I read and studied those books for years until I perfected your language."

"Who exactly was the traveler?" I asked.

"It's funny—because I never asked him," she replied. "He never made any mention of his name. I just remember him being kind and gentle. But I often wonder what became of him."

"Perhaps he'll return some day."

Abella shook her head. "No. He left, and I believe he will never return here. And so I learned to never grow attached to strangers. For I never truly know anything about them or who they truly are. Strangers harbor secrets. They only reveal what they wish to reveal and nothing more. Because it's never wise to reveal too much. You have your secrets and you are just a traveler passing by, and I know I can't get too close to you because I'm afraid you'll leave me without saying goodbye."

I realized it was now getting late as I let out a yawn. I tried to hide it by covering my mouth with my hand but Abella took notice.

"You're tired, Vincent—I can see that."

We stopped back in front of the BRISTO. I glanced through the window to find Karl and Andrew and their dancing partners gone, but the party inside was still in full swing as it was crowded with troops and civilians. "Yes. . . I'm sorry, Abella but I must leave you. I'm in dire need of some sleep. And possibly tomorrow or the next day, I will have to leave you like that traveler did. Look. . . I enjoyed our walk together, but I'm afraid a walk and a conversation is all I can offer you. It's nothing personal. You're an attractive young woman, but the truth is: I have someone back home in America waiting for me. At least, I think I do. I write to her often, but I haven't received a single letter from her. Not in a long time. But I'm not giving up hope that she is waiting for me. So, it would be selfish of me to spend the night in bed with you."

She rested her eyes on me which were now full of tears, but her face told me she was neither disappointment nor offended. She placed her hand gently on my cheek and caressed it with her thumb. "You really are a sweet man, Vincent. The reason I am attracted to you is that you remind me so much of that traveler that passed through here. He was young and gentle just like you. I'm not angry. I'm just thankful that I got to spend time with you." She kissed me on the cheek and smiled. "Goodnight. Please get home safe back to your girl."

Abella left me there outside the BRISTO, fading into the dim lighted streets of Agneaux as she walked away. Part of me wanted to follow her back to her home. Follow her to wherever she would take me—perhaps out of Agneaux, out of France to somewhere exotic. Some place so far away that no one would ever find us. We could have a life together. All I had to do is to chase after her. But then what? Seduce her? Would she even have me now? Every man has his urges, and I was fighting mine. It had been several years since I had been with a woman. But instead, I stepped in the opposite direction than she had gone with only a memory. No picture. Just a memory for now. Perhaps when this war is over—I could return one day.

———

I RETURNED TO THE FOOD SERVING TABLE at the mess tent to see if the troops left any bread. Drinking those delicious beers and the walk with Abella made me hungry. Only a couple men stood under the tent as I searched for food, only finding a couple of thin slices of cold beef and I scarfed them down. But no bread.

Afterward, I jumped into a short, narrow ally to relieve myself. After I finished, I heard a faint giggling coming from the other end of the ally. Curious, I stepped towards the giggling, even though it should have been none of my concern. I reached the halfway point in the ally and flattened myself against the left wall in the shadows to get a better hearing of what was going on just outside. I heard a woman speaking French and then the sound of a young man's voice. American. A soldier perhaps. Then two figures rushed into the ally. The woman was heaved against the wall as the soldier pressing against her. She moaned as they kissed passionately. My cue to leave. Keeping myself flattened on the wall, I crept my way out of the ally to allow them to have their privacy.

As I had mentioned before: every man has his needs. But I felt envious. I had my chance with Abella but blew it.

I walked down the street towards the temporary barracks to sleep away the night, looking forward to sleeping on a cot. It was no bed, but a cot would do just fine. Each night, I only slept for a couple of hours, keeping watch, listening to artillery fire, and being uncomfortable in a foxhole. What I wouldn't give for a full night's rest.

I located the barracks and outside the flap, stood Aschner. "Staff Sergeant Conroy," he said as I approached. "Get your rest. We're heading back into Saint-Lô tomorrow."

"Tomorrow?" I groaned. "The captain granted everyone a couple of days rest."

"I'm well aware of *what* the captain said. But that has changed," he argued. "There's more work to do in the city, and it can't wait. We're short on men as our reinforcements have been arriving slowly and in little numbers."

"Yes, sir," I said, feeling disappointed. "I understand."

"Good. As you were."

Aschner left me and once inside the barracks, I found the cot with my belongings and lied down. Sleep is what I needed. I didn't bother to remove my trousers, leggings, and boots, only my coat. Many of the other cots were occupied with sleeping troops. Many of them snored, but snoring would not keep me awake tonight. The weariness from the weeks of marching and fighting crept over me. The cot felt comfortable. I closed my eyes and thought of Abella as sleep came.

———

I WOKE THE NEXT MORNING after the best night's sleep I had had in weeks. As I packed up my gear, a soldier stepped through the tent and gave me a letter. It was from Glenn:

Dear Vince,

How are you? Keeping yourself alive, I hope. I have been keeping up to date with the movements of the war on the radio and the newspaper. The news is depressing. It is difficult to listen to, but I listen because I worry over you. I'm glad I'm not involved in that mess over there, but I'm proud that my big brother is. You were never willing to stand down from a challenge. I learned that just from growing up with you. I bet that was why you were promoted to staff sergeant. You deserve that promotion.

Julia is living with me now. She asks about you almost every day. She misses you. And she wants you to come back home. It's difficult for me to explain to her the position you are in. She's just too young to know any better.

I thought it was best to remove her from Father's care after becoming concerned because I fear he may lash out violently at her. He's not himself. I believe he becomes increasingly perverse every day. I visit him when I can. He only works nonstop on the farm after firing a couple helping hands. So he does everything himself. He worries me. I'm not sure if he has gotten over Mother's death. The last time I visited him is when I took Julia with me. He was angry, and he shouted terrible words at Julia and at me. Julia ran to me, grabbing hold of my waist and cried. She never wanted to let me go.

But Julia has nothing to worry about now. I make a decent wage, and I have her in a good school here in New Orleans. She's making a few friends and getting used to living in a city now. It's a big adjustment from living on a farm. I remember I took a long time to get used to the city as well. I'm making quite a name for myself in New Orleans. Soon, I will move higher in my position at the law firm and work cases on my own, earning more money. You would be so proud of me.

Take care of yourself, Vince. Come back to us safe. Continue making Julia and I proud.

Sincerely,

Glenn

After I read the letter, I folded it and stuffed it into a pocket on my coat. It was the only letter I had received. I wrote to Glenn often and at last received a reply. But I longed for a word from Catherine. As each day passed without a single word from her, the more I accepted the fact she had moved on. I recalled the previous evening in the dark alley with the two unidentifiable figures fornicating. Now I imagined Catherine performing an act of such with another man back home. She admitted once being a prostitute but had she ever stopped such vile profession? The claim she had could have been a hoax. Had she played me for a fool?

Perhaps I fell in love with a woman who could never love me back the way I had done so? It would be too long before I could return home, this I knew. And yet, I somehow remained optimistic. A letter will come. I know it.

I put Catherine out of my mind along with my emotions and packed up everything I owned. After leaving the barrack, I searched for Karl and Andrew. I found them at the mess tent getting breakfast. I met up with them after I got a saucer of bread, sausage, and some black coffee.

"Can you believe this shit?" Andrew said. "The nerve they have to take away our rest from us."

"So you heard?" I said.

"Found out this morning," Andrew replied.

"I found out last night before I went to sleep," I said. "What a lying son of a bitch that captain of ours is."

"You got that right," Andrew said.

"Well think of it this way guys. . ." Karl said, "It won't be a few days wasted that will keep us from getting home. I say let's get in there, so we continue on our way and get this war over with."

"You always think too optimistically, as always," Andrew said. "But if you want to kiss the captain's ass—go right ahead if it makes you feel any better."

There was a silence for a moment, and then all three of us burst out laughing. It took a minute to find our composures. Afterward, we finished our breakfast and packed up to move back into Saint-Lô.

TWENTY-FIVE

"LISTEN UP!" ASCHNER SHOUTED OVER the gossiping troops.

The 116th Regiment all stood before Captain Hull and other officers under a large tarp canopy, waiting for a briefing. On a presentation board, hung a map, displaying our next plan of action.

The short break from the war came and went too quickly. Word was out that soon, the 29th Infantry would be on the move again as more reinforcements arrived within Saint-Lô, giving the 29th the spirit it needed to continue its march through France to liberate villages and towns and freeing innocent civilians from the hands of the Nazis.

Colonel Everett Greer took his place next to the map, standing tall with broad shoulders, wavy gray hair, and square face. His cold brown eyes scanned the room. "With Saint-Lô secured, the 29th is prepared to pull out with the 30th Infantry and 2nd Armored Divisions. Our target is the town of Vire," he pointed to the map with his finger, "just twenty miles southeast of our position. We, however, are not heading directly southeast. Instead, we will march south towards the town of Percy. Along the way, we will liberate the towns of Villebaudon, Tessy-sur-Vire and then finally Percy. Afterward, we will make our way southeast towards Vire. We have over twenty-eight kilometers ahead of us, gentle-man—so be prepared. The German forces are losing ground, but we are expecting fierce retaliation."

Captain Hull then took his place next to Colonel Greer. "We've come a long way since D-Day, gentleman. And yet still, we have more to do." Hull paused for a moment as if searching for the next words to say. "Now we lost many good men so far. . . but I'll be damned if I will let that slow us down—especially my men in C Company. But rough roads lay ahead, and there's much more fighting to do. And we will keep fighting until we run every single last damn Nazi out of France.

"So I want every one of you to be smart; be a fighter and survive. You're all soldiers, and I expect you to act like soldiers.

"We'll be moving out first thing tomorrow morning. So get your rest tonight. You'll need it. That is all."

Captain Hull spoke with a passion I never witnessed from him. His speech seemed to have lifted the energies of every man in the regiment. I swelled with a determination to win this war. And after Hull's speech, I did not want to let him down.

———

THE NEXT DAY, the 29th Infantry was on the move again past fields and scarce forests on winding dirt roads under the European sun, holding a watchful eye out for ambushes from the German army. Enemy troops could hide behind trees or within a ditch, lingering for the opportune moment to attack.

But with the 30th Infantry and 2nd Armored Division by our side, we now stood a better chance of fighting. Among them were replacements; men whom have just arrived in France with zero to very little battle experience. The veterans looked down at them. They were young and easily intimidated; pushed around and ridiculed. But they only forced a laugh from the constant teasing and vulgar name callings, wise to not start any fights. Just take the abuse. It's cruel, I admit. But even I took pleasure in giving the poor guys a difficult time—a feeling of apathy. Replacements are to get no respect until proving themselves in battle. It's a code veterans lived by. Stripes and respect had to be earned if they survived long enough.

The first morning on our march to Vire, a young replacement marched beside me, listening in on a conversation I was having with Karl and Andrew.

"The first thing I will do when I get back to the States," Andrew said, "is find me a nice woman. Hell, maybe two women—and have a real long night with them."

"Is that all you ever think about?" Karl asked.

"We've been in Europe for many months now, boys and I'm dying to have a good time with a lady."

"What happened to the lady at the pub a few nights ago?" I asked. "You know—the blonde with the large breasts."

"Oh her," Andrew said. "Well, she didn't speak a word of English. So she had no damn clue as to what I was saying. It's a shame though. She's a pretty gal. Let's just say the night didn't go according to plan. I tried to make a move on her, and I ended up with a hard smack across my cheek. But boys let me tell ya—if I get no action soon, I may need to cuddle up closer with one of you guys at nights."

"Just you try it," Karl chuckled. "It may be the last thing you do."

"What's the matter?" Andrew teased, pretending to kiss Karl's cheek. "Too afraid you might like it?"

"Ok, that's enough," Karl said, pushing him away.

Andrew fell back a few feet before catching back up. "Take it easy there. Can't take a joke?"

Karl said nothing but only glared up ahead, concentrating on the march.

"I thought it was funny," a young man's voice said from behind.

We snapped our heads back. The replacement looked no older than sixteen or seventeen: thin build, broad nose, and small grey eyes. His helmet looked too large for his head. It made me question how young he actually was. He walked in long strides, holding his rifle low as if too heavy for him.

"No one asked for your opinion, new guy," Andrew snapped. "Mind your own fucking business."

Realizing his mistake, the young replacement turned silent and low-ered his head. I felt pity. We are the men he looks up to—the veterans. But he had no place among us.

"Leave the guy alone, Andrew," Karl said, coming to the replacements defense. "He's not bothering anyone."

Andrew scoffed.

Deciding to take Karl's side, as I have always done, I spoke up. "What's your name, soldier?" I asked the young Private.

"Jeffery Barnes, sir," he muttered.

"Welcome to 2nd Platoon, C Company, Private Barnes. If you don't know already—I'm Staff Sergeant Vincent Conroy. And pay no mind to Sergeant Andrew Decker. He's just bitter because that lovely French girl turned him down once she got a good look at what he had to offer. And Let's just say—Sergeant Andrew was a bit too small for her liking."

"Fuck off, Vince!" Andrew snapped.

"What's the matter?" Karl laughed. "Can't handle the truth?"

"You guys can go fuck yourselves!" Andrew snapped again.

Karl and I laughed. Jeffery also laughed until Andrew twisted his head back and glared at him.

Jeffery's face turned lifeless. He looked away, covering his mouth with his hand. His face beamed red as he tried to hide his laughter.

"Just keep your mouth shut from here on out. Understand?" Andrew hissed.

"Yes, sir," Jeffery uttered, stifling a laugh.

"Goddamn replacements," Andrew said under his breath.

As soon as those words slipped from his mouth, enemy fire erupted further up the road. Our formations broke as the attack came without warning. Men dropped to the ground or fled into different directions, looking for cover. I did so in the dense forest alongside the road.

The sound of gunfire and mortars crashed through the trees, killing soldiers as men tried to shout over the gunfire to take cover. The 2nd Armored Division Sherman tanks fired at the German troops coming from a distance down the road but did little to reinforce the fight in our favor. I took protection behind a large tree. In the distance, the sound of fallen leaves crumbled underneath approaching feet. I peeked out from behind the tree and aimed my rifle to shoot, but the Germans were prepared, taking cover behind trees as well.

In the distance, the thundering sound of Panzer tanks were fast approaching as artillery fired at the Shermans but failed to make an impact. The Sherman tanks countered attack, blasting with fury in determination to push the Germans back.

Intense incoming machine-gun fire streamed down on the troops as the Germans advanced closer to the unorganized Allies. Once again, I peered out from behind my tree and took careful aim with my rifle, hoping to take down an enemy soldier. In the distance, I spotted several Germans lurching out from behind trees as I fired several rounds. The opposition was gaining ground as orders from Captain Hull and several other officers called out to push forward and engage with the Germans head-on.

"Fire into the trees!" Captain Hull's voice sounded out from a distance. "Push them back!"

Taking Hull's orders, troops peered out from behind trees and fired their rifles and tossed grenades at anything moving in the distance. Then in the act of determination, nearly everyman hiding jumped out from the trees and charged into the German's positions, firing their weapons.

I stepped closer and met Karl, Roland, and Robert. We aimed our rifles into the forest. Waiting for a shot to take.

"Glad to see you're all right," Karl said. "I lost Andrew. We got split up."

We moved forward step by step, firing our rifles at Germans who came into our view. Then enemy shots fired at us as we reached cover behind trees. I had to think up a strategy. I had to think hard and fast on how to proceed from our position. "Ok. Jump behind a tree after every ten feet. If you have a shot to take someone down—take it." I watched as Allied troops pushed forward at a slow pace to fight the Germans as a fierce gunfight between the two factions suddenly broke out. Many Allied troops fell dead as the German's relentless gunfire continued.

I fired my rifle like a madman at the Germans in hopes of at least getting one kill when my rifle's empty clip discharged with a ping. I took cover behind a tree as several bullets flew in my direction. After reloading my M1 Garand rifle, I shot a few more rounds before it jammed. Just my luck.

"Shit!" I grunted. "My rifle is jammed. I need to find another." My eyes searched the area at the fallen soldiers and spotted a rifle nearby ten yards away. But claiming the rifle would be risky. I had to leave the protection of the tree as enemy gunfire continued.

"You will get yourself killed, Sergeant," Robert screeched over the constant and deafening gunfire, mindful of my intentions.

"You worry about yourself, Corporal!" I said. I dashed out from behind the safety of the tree as bullets soared around me and struck the ground near my feet. I reached the fallen soldier and snatched his rifle. But I struggled to free it from his death grip. Bullets inched closer as I pried the stiff fingers loose. With the rifle now free from his grasp and in my hands, I jumped behind another tree. I looked back at my companions; their eyes glued to me, impressed with my fearlessness and stupidity.

"I have to give you credit, Conroy," Roland said. "You always had guts."

"That he does," Karl said.

Bullets pelted the trees as the four of us froze for protection. Robert unholstered his pistol and shot aimlessly behind him with his back pressed against the tree.

Captain Hull's voice rang out from not far away. "The Germans are retreating. I want every one of you sons of bitches to advance! Now!"

Enemy gunfire lightened as the four of us peaked out from behind the trees and advanced at a gradual pace. Behind us, Allied troops did the same.

I felt relieved. Sweat poured down my face from the excitement of a gunfight.

I returned to my companions as I reloaded my new rifle. "We should regroup with Captain Hull and everyone else," I said.

Karl glanced around. "Good idea. It looks safe."

But then, bullets soared through the trees, and heavy artillery fire crashed down nearby as we retreated behind trees once again.

"Goddamnit!" Karl shouted. "They must be reinforcements! They just don't know when to quit!"

The sound of battle grew strong. German machine-gun fire ripped through the trees, tearing down anything or anyone in its path. I waited for an order from Captain Hull or any other officer, but no order came. Troops yelled out in the distance to one another for orders, but still, no order came. I feared the officers might be dead. I listened to screams of wounded soldiers; listening to their cries for anyone I may know: Hull, Aschner, Lester, and Andrew but I could not hear their voices.

With the infantry unorganized, I had to think. As I looked around, I realized we were all alone. I could spot no other soldier within the forest, except for the fallen. "We need to flank 'em!" I blurted out. "We're just sitting ducks here. Let's move out west about fifty yards and close in on them. I'm sure we can take some of them out without them expecting us from the rear."

Karl and Roland looked at one another, uncertain of my decision.

"I think we should just stay put, Sergeant," Robert squeaked. "It's just the four of us. We don't know how many Germans we'd encounter if we flank."

I stared at Robert with annoyance. "It's my call. We're gonna flank them. I don't want to be here if they move in on us, or we'll all be dead."

"Harris is right on this one," Karl said. "It's just the four of us. We need support. I think we should just hang tight in our position. But like you said: it's your call, Sarge. However... if we are to move out, I think we should move further about seventy yards. We don't know how far the German line stretches. So I'd say seventy yards just to be positive."

Karl spoke sense about holding our position, but I was too impatient to execute my plan, not wanting to wait for reinforcements that may not come to us. But I agreed with his idea to move out seventy yards and not fifty. "Corporal Roland," I said, "Seventy yards sound good to you?"

Roland sighed and nodded his head. "I'd say so."

"Seventy yards it is," I said. "Let's move out then. You too, Corporal." I pointed a finger at Robert. He gave a reluctant nod. "Keep low and move fast." Enemy gunfire continued as we moved west further into the trees, stepping over fallen soldiers.

We jogged about thirty yards when a shout rang out nearby. A German soldier spotted us. He shouted with frenzy, giving away our position. We fired our rifles but failed to wound him. It wouldn't be long before more German troops arrived to reinforce. We would be out-manned. "Move out now!" I called out. "Move quickly!"

To evade the oncoming German charge, we moved deeper into the forest. I can't recall how far. But much further than we planned. Gunshots erupted not far away as we hustled through the trees. I kept my eyes glued straight ahead, not seeing a ditch and fell in along with my comrades. Dead leaves and tree roots filled the ditch, provided cushion from our fall. It was about five feet deep and six feet wide and stretched from what I believed to be a great distance.

After realizing where we were, we flattened ourselves along the dirt wall of the ditch, trying to keep out of sight from the Germans. It was several minutes before the sound of footsteps approached. We all stayed silent. The only noise was the continuing gunfight in the distance, footsteps on the ground, and our breathing.

Pressed against the dirt wall, Karl quietly unsheathed his bayonet from his boot and gripped it tightly, expecting to fight his way out of the ditch. Roland unsheathed his bayonet as well.

Karl looked up, waiting with confidence as a German soldier stepped to the drop off of the ditch. In his hands, he carried his rifle: a Karabiner 98 kurz. He spotted me as Karl and Roland latched onto the soldier's legs and pulled him into the ditch. Karl drove his bayonet deep into the German's chest as Roland covered his mouth with his hand to keep him quiet. The German struggled to free himself before coming still after repeated bayonet blows to the chest. After a moment, Roland released his grasp from the dead man's mouth. His dead eyes stared up into the sky. His face was lifeless. Karl then wiped off the blood from his bayonet on the German's coat.

I peeked my head out from the ditch and looked around. We had killed one, but there had to be others. And there were. I spotted several Germans, and they spotted me. They fired their MP 40s sub-machine guns as I ducked back inside the ditch. Karl and Roland unholstered their pistols and fired at the Germans fast approaching.

After taking several shots with my rifle, I ducked back down once again. A potato-masher grenade flew in, and without hesitation, I picked it up and tossed it out of the ditch.

I looked at Robert, crouched down and struggling to load his rifle. I gripped hold of his coat and pulled him toward me. "Get to shooting, Corporal! That's an order."

"I'm trying, damn it!" he shouted. He, at last, loaded his rifle and got to his feet, trembling from panic. I jumped up and fired at the Germans. Robert fired like a madman But suddenly, several bullets passed through his face. He slumped over—dead. His eyes glared wide open, surrounded with blood. A bullet left a gaping wound between his eyes. Another bullet charred through his upper lip, exposing flesh, broken teeth, and bone.

His sudden death caught me off guard. I couldn't help but stare at the bloody mess that was once Robert's face. "He's dead," Karl shouted, grabbing a firm hold of my coat. "Focus!"

I peeled my eyes away from Robert to focus on the Germans assault. I peered out from the ditch and fired a few rounds with my rifle and then took cover against the dirt wall.

Karl and Roland crouched down, with expressions of defeat on their faces. I had that impression of defeat as well. There was little we could do. The enemies were hiding behind trees and were waiting for us to run out of ammo so they can make their final charge on us to either capture or kill us. Winning this skirmish seemed impossible. I now regretted the decision to move out further in the forest, hoping to flank the Germans. My decision made me feel weak and irresponsible.

"We're in deep shit, boys," Roland said. "What were we thinking moving out?"

"It was stupid," I said. "... And I take full responsibility."

"Don't worry about that right now," Karl said. "We can still get out of this mess." He remained optimistic as he has always done so, but now I believed he was wrong.

"I don't see a way," I replied.

Roland looked at Karl and shook his head. "I don't either."

Roland shot up and fired into the woods with his pistol when a bullet flew through his upper chest. He dropped on his rear and pressed his back against the dirt wall. "Shit! I've been shot." Roland groaned with pain as he ran his hand underneath his coat and revealed several bloody fingers.

"We need to get the hell out of here!" I shouted.

But then came a distant sound roaring from the sky above. The sound of fighter and bomber planes. And fast approaching. The frightening echo of the jet engines and sirens pierced the sky; a warning for what was about to come.

Firing had ceased. As the moments passed, the sirens grew louder. I looked up into the blue sky and watched for the planes. Soon the bombs will drop as the sirens grew louder.

"Take cover!" Karl shouted.

With instinct, I crouched down and covered my head with my arms. I could hear the deafening sound of the planes almost on top of us. I drew deep breaths as I waited. My heart beat faster as I shivered with terror. It will be any moment now. The drops will come. Louder and louder the sirens grew.

I waited.

The bombs dropped. An explosion shook the ground near our position as it flung me back against the other side of the ditch. My head struck the dirt wall. My ears buzzed, my head ached, and my body became stiff and throbbing with pain as I moved in and out of consciousness. I struggled to speak—to cry out for help but no words came out my mouth. Over the ringing in my ears, I can still hear the sirens of the dive bombers. The drops were not finished. There were more to come as another explosion shook the ground and then another. And then another.

The ringing in my ears became louder. My head pounded.

Then everything went dark.

TWENTY-SIX

I COULD FEEL THE GROUND BENEATH ME as I scratched the soil and dead leaves. My back leaned against the ditch wall with my head hunched over. I opened my eyes, but my vision was blurry. A faint light is all I can see. My ears still rang from the blast, and my head pounded. But I was thankful for my helmet; it saved me from a more serious injury. I took a few deep breaths and smacked my lips. My throat was dry. I needed water as I reached for my canteen, but my limbs ached.

Everything is quiet. No gunfire. No shouting. Only silence.

My vision gradually returned after a few minutes. The faint light became brighter as the image of trees and earth crept into focus. How long have I been unconscious? The sun was set lower behind the trees. I estimated about several hours. I tried to move more than just my fingers and arms, but my body ached with immense pain. I had to take it slow.

After another minute or two, I examined the scene: Karl and Roland rested on the ground, face up and motionless. I feared they were dead. I groaned as my head pounded harder. But I needed water. Fighting through the pain, I took my canteen and drank. Now hydrated, I crawled to where Karl lied. His right cheek bloodied from where a bullet had grazed him. I saw no other wounds. I checked his pulse; alive, but unconscious.

"Karl?" I muttered as I shook him. "Can you hear me?" There was no answer. I could barely hear myself over the buzzing in my ears.

But the ringing in my ears eventually softened. I listened to the sound of the wind whistling through the trees and leaves. This is all I can hear. No songs from birds. No shouting from soldiers, gunfire, fighter jets, or the haunting shriek of dive bombers. Only silence.

Then came the sound of a faint moan. My eyes widened as I looked around. The moaning stopped and after a moment, came another, but this time louder. I traced them back to Roland. I built up all of my strength once more and crawled to where he lied. My legs felt insecure, making it difficult for me to stand; still suffering the effects of the blast.

"Roland. Are you ok?" I place my hands on his shoulders and shook him. Roland's eyes burst opened and looked at me. A wave of freight came over his face as he sat up, balled a fist with his right hand, wanting to take a swing at me. "Roland! It's me! It's Vince!" I trembled. His fist waved in the air as he looked me over. He sighed, remembering me and lowering his fist.

"It's just you," he said relieved. Blood from his wound had stained his coat. He groaned as he held a hand over it. I handed Roland my canteen. "Are we the only ones alive?" he asked after taking a few drinks of water.

"Karl's alive, but he's unconscious," I replied.

With my strength coming back, I picked myself up to my feet and stepped over to Robert's body to comb through his uniform for extra ammo. I also took his M1 rifle, M1911 pistol, grenades, and a canteen filled with water. He no longer needed all of this.

I looked back at Roland. "We need to get you to a medic."

"I don't know if that's a good idea to move out," Roland said. "For all we know, those German's are still around, waiting to ambush us."

"It's a risk we will need to take," I said, stepping over to Karl. "And I doubt those Germans we were fighting are still alive."

I bent down and lightly slapped Karl's face a few times to wake him. He didn't stir, so I unscrewed the lid of Robert's canteen and poured a small amount of water on his face.

Karl shook his head for a moment before his eyes came open. "What happened?" he moaned.

"We survived the bombing," I replied as I helped Karl sit up. "It was a miracle though."

"One hell of a miracle I say" Karl said.

"Roland is still with us, but he needs a medic."

Karl took a drink from his canteen. But his hand shook from the turmoil he just encountered. Most of the water spilled down his chin. "Are you sure it's us three?" he asked. "How about those Germans?"

"I see no one else, and it's quiet. If they are still alive, then we need to move out now and not wait for them to find us again. So we need to take this opportunity to get the hell out of here and get back to our regiment."

"Ok," Karl said. "You're the sarge."

At first, Karl had trouble standing up, but eventually, he made it to his feet without falling. The both of us then helped Roland stand, but he was weak from his wound and still felt the aftershock of the blast. His large size also made it difficult. But after a few tries, he stood on his feet.

I took my map from my pack and spread it flat on the ground to study it. "Ok, so we were headed to Villebaudon, just outside of Percy." I said pointing at the map and tracing my finger on the grid. "We had been marching for several hours before the Germans ambushed us. So that would put our position about here," my finger stopped, "about nine point five kilometers from Villebaudon. Now we moved off the road so I would say nine point six or seven kilometers away. I consider it's best to proceed onwards towards Villebaudon. We're close. But we should stay off the road and cut through the land. We could catch up with the rest of the regiment faster that way."

"What if they pulled out?" Roland asked. "We should head back to

Saint-Lô. We know the Allies are there and it'll be safe."

"He's got a point, Vince," Karl said. "Why should we go forward, not knowing what we're wandering into? It's too dangerous for just the three of us."

"We were gaining the upper hand during this ambush. The Germans were falling back. And it was stupid of us to flank them. I don't know what I was thinking." I became silent as Karl and Roland stared at me. "And It's my fault we lost Robert."

"It's not your fault," Karl said. "Things just happen. Nothing you can do about it sometimes." Roland didn't object. "But I don't like this idea about going to Villebaudon. Shouldn't we at least go back to the road to see what's going on? Maybe our troops are searching for us."

After a moment of understanding, I gave in to Karl's idea. "Ok. We'll go back to the road, but if we discover no one alive, we go on towards Villebaudon, and not back to Saint-Lô. I have a feeling Villebaudon is where we will meet up with our regiment."

Karl and Roland nodded their heads.

"Do you think you can walk?" I asked Roland.

"Yeah, I'll be fine," he replied. "I can take the pain."

"I don't doubt it," I said. "Ok, let's move out. Stick close together. I want none of us drifting away from one another."

The daylight grew dimmer, so it was best for the three of us to begin our hike back to the road, leaving this foreboding bit of hell behind us.

——

THE THREE OF US WALKED in the forest towards the road, taking every precaution. I led the way, taking a casual glance back at Roland. I worried he would drop dead at any moment. Karl kept close to him. Roland kept a hand over his wound, keeping an expression of pain on his face. He was losing blood and without medical help, he wouldn't live much longer.

Karl and I toted most of the gear, to relieve Roland of the stress. It's odd: Roland and I working together. We were two bitter enemies, but now we tried to keep one another alive. There is perhaps a time to set aside differences and work as a team under differing circumstances. After our fight in the hedgerows, everything felt unusual. Roland became different. The two of us set out on our mission as a team and not enemies. In the worst of times, even war can bring enemies together.

I realized this as I helped to keep Roland upright on our walk, relieving Karl. Over time, Roland grew weaker. His large frame and the extra gear I carried made it challenging to help him walk. My muscles ached with pain as I kept him from falling. Our pace slowed, but I was determined to keep the three of us moving.

After returning to the road, the evidence of an intense battle layout before us. All that remained were bodies of Allies and Germans and destroyed Sherman tanks. We found no man alive. I set Roland down on the ground to rest as Karl, and I searched dead soldiers for ammo and canteens. But everything had been picked clean. In the distance, came the sound of a vehicle approaching. Karl and I rushed back to Roland's side and stood him up and retreated into the forest to hide. We set Roland behind a tree as the two us laid low beside him with our sight on the road. The vehicle came into view: a black Admiral Cabriolet with the top pulled back, revealing a driver, two German soldiers, and an officer. The driver stopped the car and turned off the ignition as the three men stepped out and observed the carnage before them. In the soldiers' hands were Karabiner 98 kurz rifles.

With my rifle loaded, I took careful aim of the officer. I need one shot to bring him down and then the soldiers. My finger touched the trigger. Sweat beaded down my forehead as I prepared to shoot. But before I could fire, Karl's hand pushed my rifle down. I looked at him with fury, but he placed a finger over his mouth and pointed down the road. More vehicles were fast approaching—beige German VWs filled with soldiers, halted upon arriving behind the Admiral Cabriolet.

With more German troops arriving and in fear of being discovered, Karl and I hauled Roland up to his feet and quietly moved further into the forest. After half a mile, we stopped to rest. I took out my map to determine our specific location and moved on once more, heading toward Villebaudon. With many German troops in the area, the way back to Saint-Lô wasn't safe.

———

CUTTING THROUGH THE FOREST turned to our favor as we discovered a small farm as nighttime approached. The farm looked deserted. No lights shined through the windows of the house or the barn. We needed a place to rest. But unsure if the farm is abandoned, however, we decided to sleep in the barn, in the event the owners return to the house. We were all exhausted from our trials of the day and a nights' rest is what we needed.

I set Roland down against the outside of the barn's wall while Karl checked inside for safety. I took a glance inside at the door as Karl entered. Inside was pitch black and smelt of manure, hay, and dust—reminding me of home—reminding me of the many nights of sleeping in the loft. Karl took extra precaution as he searched. In the darkness, he found a kerosene lantern and lit it to allow a little light to chase away the darkness.

The barn was vacant of animals, soldiers, and civilians. I took Roland inside and laid him on a some hay on the floor and found a few old horse blankets, and covered the windows to hide the light from the lantern. The blankets hung over the windows by old nails protruding from the walls. It was shoddy work, but it had to be good enough.

After Karl and I made full inspections of the barn, I made Roland a bed out of hay and my blanket. He didn't protest about me giving up my blanket; I didn't expect him to. He needed it more than I did.

Our stomachs grumbled from hunger and exhaustion after our march, so we treated ourselves to some rations (chocolate bars and crackers). I watched Roland as he ate. I had to admit: he was tough. He marched for a lengthy distance after being wounded in the chest. He owned a deep sense of courage, despite him being nothing more a nuisance for me, and yet I couldn't help but to respect him. It was then I realized that Roland accounted for a great part of my success. I worked harder just to spite him, and it made me stronger. Without even realizing it, Roland became one of my greatest teachers. An unlikely ally.

When we finished our rations, Karl and I sat up against the wall while Roland sat in the bed I had made. We said nothing, only listening to the night, but the silence grew uncomfortable.

"How is your chest feelin'?" I asked Roland.

"Still hurts like a son of a bitch," Roland replied. "Do you think we got a chance to catch up with our regiment? Because who knows where they're at. For all we know, we could walk straight into the hands of the Germans. So, I hope you know what you're doing."

"We have to at least try to find them or any Allies. Divisions are spread out everywhere at the moment."

"I hope you're right," Karl said. "We're bound to run into our troops sooner or later. Perhaps we should have gone back to Saint-Lô? It would have been safe there."

"Not with the German army all around," I said. "I think we made the right decision. And we've been to Saint-Lô? If we go back with our tails between our legs, they will ship us out with another regiment to who knows where. I'd rather stick to what I know. We're C Company with the 116th Regiment of the 29th Infantry. That's where we belong. Those might be numbers and words to you but for me—that defines us. I'd soon die among my men than with strangers."

"I guess you're right," Karl said. "Believe it or not, Vince, but you will make a fine master sergeant someday."

I smiled. He always had a way to lift my spirits.

But before we could become too comfortable for the night, bright lights flashed outside the barn along with the sound of an automobile engine approaching.

"Shit," said Roland. "Kill the light."

Karl did so from the kerosene lantern and picked up his rifle and removed his bayonet. Roland and I did the same. We ducked behind a couple stacks of hay toward the rear of the barn, forgetting our helmets and packs.

The vehicle stopped outside the barn with the engine still running as the headlights beamed through the small cracks of the walls and windows. Just outside the barn doors, I could hear two voices. But It was difficult to distinguish what language was being spoken.

The sound of the engine had shut off but the lights, however, remained on. After a brief silence, the barn doors flew open. A voice speaking in German rang out. Then came the unmistakable loud click of a Gewehr 98 being loaded. The same voice spoke again and then came another voice.

If the men were here to search the barn, and with nowhere else to go, they will find us. The three of us remained dead silent and didn't budge from our positions behind the haystacks. This would be another display of surprise like hours before in the ditch. Karl readied his bayonet as did Roland and I. As far as we knew, there were only two of them and three of us. But we didn't want to risk firing our rifles for more German troops could be around. We had to fight these men in silence.

The only sound the German's made were their breathing and soft footsteps on the ground below. I listened closely. They stepped closer and as soon as they were about to step next to the haystack, I leaped up and lashed out with my bayonet—but he was ready for me as if expecting my attack. He stepped aside from my lunge and jabbed the back of his rifle into the back of my head, knocking me to the ground. Once more, my head ached with pain. I started to lose consciousness but fought to stay awake. I tried to move but couldn't.

(So the following is the best to my recollection, as I became dazed from the impact to the back of my head).

I witnessed a fight break out between the two German soldiers with Karl and Roland as I lied on my stomach on ground.

Karl grabbed hold of the rifle belonging to the German who knocked me down. A tug-of-war battle pursued.

Roland and the other German were on the ground at each other's throats. The German's rifle had been tossed across the barn during the fight. As the struggle continued, Roland gained the upper hand as he landed several blows to the man's face, but the tide turned when the soldier jabbed his thumb into Roland's eye. Now the soldier sat on top of Roland's chest, landing punches to his face.

The man Karl fought withheld him against the wall with the rifle still in their hands. Karl used all his strength and pushed the soldier away, and headbutt him. The German stepped back, giving Karl a chance to snatch his bayonet from the ground which had fallen from his hand moments before. He leapt at the German, lunging his bayonet, but the soldier remained cunning by dodging the attack for he expected it. The soldier then cracked the butt of his rifle into Karl's face. Blood drained from his nose as he fell on the floor, flat on his back, dazed. The German was then on top of him with a dagger he unsheathed from his belt and swung down at Karl's chest. Karl reached to grab the soldier's hand, but it was too late. The dagger penetrated his chest as he gasped out loud from the piercing wound. The soldier pulled the dagger out and lunged again over and over. Karl tried to fight back but was too weak to do so. His legs kicked as the dagger repeatedly went in and out of his chest. He gasped with each blow from the dagger. I could hear the gushing sound of the blade meeting flesh.

Then from nowhere, Roland swung down with his own bayonet into the German's back. He stopped his assault on Karl and was surprised by unexpected attack. Roland then threw the attacker off Karl to the ground and swiftly drove the bayonet into the German's throat. Roland pushed down with both heavy palms on the blade with all of his strength. The German gagged as large amounts of blood flowed from his mouth. Within a minute, he lied motionless.

Roland released his grip from the bayonet and stood up over the German. He looked down at him for a moment and then rushed to Karl's side. By this time, I gained full consciousness. I struggled to my feet and stepped to where Karl lied. He struggled to breathe as he gasped for air.

Blood gushed from his mouth. He looked at me with eyes filled with suffering. I dropped to my knees beside him and took a firm hold of his hand. He squeezed my hand hard. I tried to speak but couldn't. The realization of my friend dying before my eyes became too much. I could do nothing as he suffered. I wanted it to be over for him. He looked away from me and stared up at the ceiling as he let out his last gasp for air and then he lied still.

Roland dropped beside Karl and closed his open dead eyes with his hand. "I'm sorry I couldn't save him."

I still had a firm grip of Karl's hand, not wanting to let go. Everything Karl and I planned after the war faded away. We were meant to grow old together, but it all vanished in a blink of an eye.

I pried my teary eyes from Karl and glanced over at the other German soldier Roland fought with. He was dead, lying face down with his head surrounded by a puddle of blood. But there was something else too—an eyeball.

Roland took notice of what I was looking at. "That bastard tried to gouge my eyes out, so I did it to him instead. Don't worry. He won't be hurting anyone else."

"They both got what they deserved," I croaked. At last, I let go of Karl's hand and stepped over to the German with the bayonet still lodged in his throat. I inspected his uniform. By the looks of it, I'd say he was an officer: an olive field cap adorned his head, and he was cloaked with a black leather trench coat.

I then turned to Roland, who remained at Karl's side. "We have some work to do."

TWENTY-SEVEN

ROLAND READJUSTED HIS POSITION to get comfortable as he sat on the soiled ground of the barn with his back leaned against the wall. The finger jab from the German a few hours before changed his eye red and it was now swollen. He turned pale, and sweat rolled down his face as he lost more blood from his gunshot wound to the chest. He needed medical attention, or he wouldn't survive much longer.

The both of us sat across from one another over the faint light of the kerosene lantern, sitting in silence into the waning hours of the night. I volunteered myself to stay awake the entire night to keep a watch out for more German troops to allow Roland to sleep, but he stayed awake with me for the time being.

During the past hours, Roland and I buried the dead bodies under piles of hay and hid the German officer's automobile in the forest out of sight. We discussed a potential plan to drive the vehicle to Villebaudon or back to Saint-Lô, but I decided the idea was too risky on account of running into more Germans. We also considered wearing the dead officer's and soldier's uniforms for disguise, but our charade would be seen through if they had questioned us. They'll discover we couldn't speak the

German language. So our best option is to continue our walk towards Villebaudon in the forest, avoiding the road and out of view of look-outs. Early morning we will leave after Roland is well rested. He needed rest and much of it. We both did.

But my head still ached from the air raid explosion and the rifle stock. I learned any soldier can be trained with bayonets and hand-to-hand combat, but skill is also required. I lacked the necessary skills and patience and so, paid the price. My lack of know-how had cost the life of my dearest friend; for there are now two men dead under my supervision. The weight on my shoulders grew and grew with each passing minute by my guilt. But I now looked at the man sitting across from me— my enemy. And now I'm his protector.

"Can I ask you something?" Roland asked in a low and raspy voice.

This came unexpectedly. "Sure. What's on your mind."

"You know you could have shot me back there. It would of have been easier for you and Karl to put me out of my misery, than to haul my ass along with you guys... so why didn't you?"

"I'm not that kind of person, Roland," I said, confused by his question. "Why would you even ask me somethin' like that?"

Roland laughed but stopped in an instant. He groaned as he covered his bloody wound with his hand. "It's funny you say you are not that sort of person. It's funny because you are. I know you are. It's in you, Conroy. You're capable of killing someone."

"Of course, I am. I've shot at many Germans—"

"I'm not talking about Germans and I'm not talking about war. What I'm talking about is—you're capable of *killing*. I saw it that day when we fought in the hedgerows. You waved a gun around in my face but didn't pull the trigger—because you weren't quite... ready yet." He laughed again. "But it's there. You might not want to accept it, but it's there. You'll see."

I became agitated. "What the hell are you talking about, Roland? Are you implying I will be some kind of deranged murderer?"

"No. Not deranged and not a murderer, but an... executioner. A lyncher in other words."

I scoffed. "You couldn't be any more wrong, Roland. You really don't know me at all."

"I know enough. I know you are not a simple, innocent man who is always trying to do right and please everyone. No... that's just your shell, but inside you, there is something more. Something darker."

"You're wrong. The person who you are describing is yourself. You can't fool me. I don't see what you're playing at, but you're not gonna get into my head."

"Hey! Fuck you, Conroy! Let me tell you something—you don't know a damn thing about me." Now the Roland I knew emerged from his shell. Our peace seemed to have came to an end.

"I recognize a spoiled brat when I see one," I snapped. "Yeah, I know your kind. You perhaps came from a wealthy family: a mother and a father who pampered you every chance they got. They gave you whatever you wanted. You're the kind of person who thinks your shit don't smell. You believe the world owes you something, but the truth is, Roland—the world doesn't owe you a goddamn thing. So wake up and smell the roses!

"You can't fool me. And besides—you are the one always trying to do me harm. That day in the hedgerows, you started that mess, and you know it. You punched me, and I swear you were trying to snap my neck after you grabbed me!"

Roland became silent and shook his head. His face softened as if I struck a nerve. "Maybe I went a little too far," he muttered. "But I wasn't trying to really hurt you—only scare you."

"Well, I'd say you accomplished that."

"I wasn't *really* going to hurt you, Conroy. You need to believe me on that. But you don't understand—because you have it all wrong. My life is the exact opposite of what you described.

"I grew up dirt poor. I didn't have a father growing up—well, I mean I had one, sure, but I never saw much of him. He spent most of his time in Chicago, so he wasn't around much to teach me how to fight or how to take care of my mother. He wasn't there to teach me how to become a man. So I grew up learning how to fight for myself because I didn't have the luxuries of other kids. Other children always bullied and ridiculed me because of my size. Eventually, I had to stand up for myself. I was in constant fights. Some fights I won, and some I lost. But I never gave up after a loss. I fought, and I fought, until I wouldn't lose another fight.

"You see... my mother didn't earn enough money to feed the two of us. She barely made enough for rent in this little shit-hole of an apartment we lived in outside of Milwaukee. So I had to learn how to survive on the streets. I taught myself how to steal food and pickpocket people. I stole to survive. And my mother didn't know about it. Every time I brought home food, she questioned me about how I got it, and I would lie, of course. I told her I worked these small jobs during the day after school and then buy food with the money I earned. She bought it, at least I think she did. But somehow I had a feeling she knew where the food came from, but she didn't want to spoil a good thing, I guess.

"So one night in January, when I was sixteen, I just finished stealing several sacks of canned goods from a local market and was on my home through a shortcut in the woods when I heard this loud crying. It sounded like the cries of an infant. So I go in search of this baby through the trees, and then I find it. Someone had abandoned it in a basket in the middle of the woods. And did so during the middle of winter. You have to believe me when I say that winters in Wisconsin are brutal. I mean some of the coldest winters in the world. Well, I realized this infant would freeze to death, but there's a problem: I'm carrying these sacks of food. I didn't want to drop the food because my mother and I had to eat. So... I left the baby crying it's lungs out in that basket in the middle of the woods. And as I walked away, the baby just kept crying and crying and crying... and I did nothing. I just kept walking, neglecting the cries and the infant as if nothing was there at all.

"Later that night in bed, I woke up in the middle of the night hearing those cries but I was several miles away from the woods. I realized it was all in my head. But I kept hearing those cries throughout the night.

I couldn't block it out. I covered my ears with my palms, and yet, I still heard it. Needless to say, I didn't sleep much that night.

"So a few days later, I stole a newspaper as I passed by a newsstand, and an article caught my attention. It stated that an infant was found in the woods alone in a basket... frozen to death." Roland became silent. He stared at the light from the lantern between us. On his face, I saw a look of regret. "I could have saved that infant's life, but I was too selfish. I should have dropped the food and took that baby to safety but... I didn't. And there's a question I always ask myself after I read that article: is another human beings life any less valuable than your own? I live with that question and that decision I made every day since then. And I ask myself that same question every morning; because I can still hear those cries in the night. It haunts me. That crying infant in the basket is my suffering. I drink alcohol and liquor a lot to try to not think about it. I drink so much to block out the wailing just so I can sleep but no matter how much I drink—I can still hear the crying at night."

Roland's eyes swelled with tears. "And so, when I was twenty, I got caught for trying to pickpocket this wealthy bastard so I could eat, but instead, I was arrested. A judge reviewing my case gave me a choice: he said I could go to jail and endure hard labor or be a free man and go into the army. I chose the army. But I can't say I'm a free man. The army owns me now. And ever since I joined, I haven't spoken to my mother... or my father. I guess that's how I want it. Shit—I don't even know if they're still alive."

Roland became silent, still staring deep into the faint light of the kerosene lantern.

"I was seven," I blurted out, not knowing what came over me. Roland looked at me with his tearful eyes. "I'm sleeping in a room I shared with my brother—Glenn. That night, we didn't think to burn out a candle we had lit. At night, Glenn and I liked to make animal shapes with our hands and fingers on the walls and ceiling with a candlelight. It's fun with a candlelight and not a flashlight. Well, we talked mostly, and soon we talked ourselves to sleep. But we forgot about the burning candle on a little table right next to my brother's bed. I guess Glenn somehow knocked the candle off in his sleep. It fell to the floor and landed on some quilts. Well, the candle set the quilts on fire. And I woke up to discover flames covering the floor... and my bed. The fire had spread. Panicking, I looked around through the thick smoke and saw Glenn's bed empty. I'm alone in the room that's set ablaze. I realized if I want to survive, I needed to get myself out of that burning room. So I got myself out of that burning bed and ran through the flames and to the door before my father came rushing towards me with a pail of water. He saw me and threw me up against the wall as he went into the room to splash water on the flames.

"My mother found me and rushed me out of the house and outside, and sitting under the pecan tree was Glenn, eating pecans from the shells he had broken. I later discovered that my father got Glenn out of the room after he woke up smelling smoke. But he left me in the room while he grabbed a pail of water to put the fire out. My own father forgot me.

"What does that say? How can a father forget about his own son in a room that's on fire? I believe it was from that day on—I stopped respecting him. Maybe even hated him. How can you forgive something like that?"

There came a moment of silence. "What about your brother?" Roland said, catching my attention.

"What about him?"

"Do you hate your brother for not helping you out of that room?"

"No," I replied. "He didn't know any better. He was probably still half asleep when my father pulled him out of there." I let out a small laugh.

"What about your mother? Where was she?"

"Father didn't wake her until after getting Glenn out of the house." I shook my head. "She was in shock just as much as I was." Roland nodded his head. I decided not to speak about the subject we were on any longer. "It's getting late. You should try to get some rest. I will stay up and keep a watch out."

"Ok. You should try to get some rest too."

"Yeah, I'll try."

Roland dimmed the lantern as I sat up against the wall of the barn with my pistol in my hand. Now, my thoughts were all I had for company and conversation. "I'll be here in the morning," I whispered as he fell asleep.

I didn't think he would survive in the night.

———

I LOOKED OVER ROLAND as soon as day broke the next morning. He was alive but now had a fever as more sweat poured down his face and his shade of skin turned awfully pale. His condition worsened throughout the night. With so much blood loss, I gave up any hope of getting him to a medic. And now with the morning light spreading its way across the land, we needed to move out towards Villebaudon. But I didn't want to wake him. I let him sleep throughout the morning as I looked over how many rations and how much water we had left from Karl's pack and my own. We had plenty for a few days. I also cleaned our rifles and my pistol to keep myself busy.

Before I could go through our available ammo, Roland stirred in his sleep. A moment later he woke. He groaned from the pain and took deep breaths as he sat himself up.

"Take it slow," I said, giving him his canteen. "Can you eat anything?"

He took a large gulp of water. "I don't want to try," he replied with heavy breaths and slow speech.

"We need to move again," I said as I opened the barn door. A gush of wind hit me in the face, then it began to pour rain as thunder rumbled in the distance and dark clouds drifted from above. "You need to get to a medic, or I'm afraid you won't make it too much longer."

Roland nodded and stood. After taking a few slow steps, he groaned with pain as his legs buckled from underneath him as he dropped to the ground, too weak to move on. I rushed over to help him, but he shoved me away. He crawled to the wall and sat up against it, reached into his pack and took out a morphine syrette. "I will not make it any way you look at it," he said, injecting himself with morphine in his thigh. "Go without me. You can still get out of here and catch up with the regiment if they're even in Villebaudon. I'll only slow you down."

I could have left but didn't, afraid he would fall prey to the Germans. Standing at the door, I looked out into the rain and then back at Roland. "I can't leave you here by yourself."

"You need to leave, Vince. . . please. There's nothing you can do for me."

"No. . . I'm sorry, but I'm not leaving you."

Roland displayed an angry face as he unholstered his pistol. "Please, Vince. You can't stay here. More Germans can arrive any minute. Did you think about those two last night? They came from somewhere, and if they didn't return from where they've been, someone will come looking for them. And I suspect it will be more than just two this time."

I turned to look back to watch the heavy raindrops hit the ground, turning dirt into mud. A moment later, I looked back at Roland. His eyes were pleading with me to leave him behind.

Roland raised his pistol and aimed it at me. In his weak condition, he struggled to hold the pistol steady. "Go! Or I *swear* I will put a fucking bullet in you!"

I scoffed. "Is that supposed to scare me? You won't shoot me, Roland. You're better than that."

Roland kept his pistol aimed at me for a moment. His bottom lip trembled as a single tear rolled down his cheek. His arm then dropped to the ground, with the pistol still in his grip.

I called his bluff, knowing he wouldn't shoot me.

He drew a deep breath. Then a faint smile appeared across his lips. "Do you remember that time in boot camp—when you kicked Ramsey's legs out from underneath him, and then you beat him with that steel rod of his?"

"Of course, I do."

"That was something else, you know." His smile faded. "That was something else. . ."

"Roland?"

He looked at me again as he lifted his pistol. "No more cries in the dark." He put the muzzle of the pistol underneath his jaw and pulled the trigger. His head jerked back as blood splattered the wall and a red mist drifted in the air for a moment before disappearing.

I didn't know how long I stood there, staring at Roland's lifeless body: minutes; hours perhaps. I can't recall. After I broke out of the traumatic spell I was in, I stepped over to the Roland's lifeless body and knelt down. "I'm sorry. Another human being's life is equal to our own. What defines us are the choices we make. Whether they're right or wrong. We all need to make our own choices. Even over a matter of life and death. We do what we need to do to survive."

I stood up, leaving the pistol in his hand. Not wanting to look at him any longer, I picked up the blanket he slept on the previous night and threw it over him. Next, I rummaged through his pack and took out any extra ammo and rations along with his canteen as I did with Karl's pack. After stuffing it all into my own pack, I walked up to the open barn doors. I took one final quick look at Roland's large body hunched over on the wall hidden beneath the blanket before stepping out into the heavy rain to continue my walk to Villebaudon.

TWENTY-EIGHT

I HAVE NEVER BEEN A BIG BELIEVER IN COINCIDENCES, but sometimes, I have to admit that even I can't explain the most bizarre circumstance that would soon unfold after I left Roland and the barn behind.

I should mention I blame myself for Roland taking his own life. He sacrificed himself because I was too stubborn to leave him behind. But on the edge of death, he accepted his fate. The demons he fought with for so long, twisted his mind. It warped beyond repair as the agony became too much. I questioned his sanity soon after meeting him. And now I believe what little sanity he had left, guided his hand to put the pistol underneath his chin and pull the trigger. And yet, he possibly suffered from an infection from his wound that forced his hand. I considered his final moments to be the results of fatigue and delusions. But madness didn't force him to do it nor an infection. But desperation. Our mission was not over. No matter how great the odds are or how many men are lost, the mission must go on. Even if only one man is left alive. Roland saw himself as my burden to continue, for his part was finished.

During my walk to Villebaudon, I thought about Roland's comments from our conversation the previous night. It tormented me. I took offense of being labeled an executioner. Again, his words could have been foolish ramblings from the infection. But this time, I didn't believe it to be true. Roland saw something in me. . . buried deep inside.

Rain poured down—and the trees provided little shelter. I always admired the rain, but now it felt like a slap to the face. Like putting salt on an open wound. Exhausted, wet, and perhaps lost—my walk through the forest became delayed as I stepped through thick coats of mud. The mud made my feet heavier with every step. My back ached from the excessive weight of my combat pack. Fear escalated that I will collapse from physical and mental exhaustion. The fear crept through my brain like a disease. And yet, I continued on without stopping. For I'm a soldier. An infantryman. I'm trained to continue on no matter the circumstances. A soldier finishes the mission.

But my eyes became heavier as I struggled to keep them open. I wanted to drop face first into the soft mud and sleep, but I continued on. At times, I saw a German soldier watching me past the trees like a ferocious hawk waiting to swoop down for the kill when I least expect it. But in a blink of an eye, there was no one in my sight. Hallucinations perhaps? Were my weary eyes playing tricks on me? Fatigue can play tricks on the mind. Even drive a man insane. For my sake, I fought to control my sanity. But for how long could I endure it?

Despite the dilemmas, I continued my march alone with only my thoughts.

I wandered throughout the rainy day, only stopping to eat what little rations I had or to relieve myself. The day grew darker as the rain continued to pour down. I forced myself to take one step after another, but now I doubted if I could continue much further in these conditions. But then came new hope as I spotted a stone cottage nearby. A candle burned in a window next to the door and smoke rose from the chimney. Someone is in there. A local I hope. In dire need of shelter, a warm place to sleep, and hot food to eat, I went to the hardwood front door and pounded with my fist. But on account of my exhaustion, I couldn't think straight, forgetting my training to make sure it's safe.

After a moment, the door opened, to reveal a man in about his mid-thirties wearing dirty clothes and on his head, a brown wool flat cap. Behind him stood two small girls with long auburn hair dressed in white gowns. The two of them looked much alike and then I realized they were twins. The man locked eyes with mine as his face turned angry; a warning I should tread carefully. I held up my hands to show I meant no harm. "American," I said to communicate with him.

"American?" he repeated in a heavy French accent.

Keeping my palms up at my shoulders, I nodded. He nodded also letting me know he understood. The anger in his face vanished.

"Umm... food?" I said as I gestured towards my mouth with my fingers and rubbed my stomach to get through to him that I'm hungry. I no doubt looked like a fool.

He nodded again and opened the door wider, gesturing for me to come inside. Grateful for being allowed inside, I looked forward to getting a fresh meal and a night's rest to comfort my sore and weary bones.

———

THE FRONT OF THE COTTAGE is a moderate size room with a square table in the middle. On the left wall, a fireplace and on the right, chairs for sitting. My uniform and clothes hung on a rope stretched across the room beside the warm-lit fireplace to dry. Now naked, I wrapped myself in a thick quilt the Frenchman gave me to keep warm. The quilt smelled of pine trees. He also treated me with warm potato and vegetable stew along with a few slices of bread and a glass of delicious red wine. Nothing ever tasted so good. I ate with the gentleman and the young twins at the table. The twins watched as I ate, curious about their new house-guest. They may have been seven to ten years of age, with big doe eyes and curly hair. I devoured the meal within minutes, and the gentleman offered me more. I wanted to decline, but still, I was hungry and politely accepted a second serving. Not wanting to eat all his food and drink all his wine, I thanked him for the best I could after the second serving as I leaned back in the chair and rubbed my belly with two hands letting him know I was full.

After the meal was over, I slipped on my underwear and t-shirt as the Frenchman invited me to sleep in a small bed in the twins' room. The day had been long and tiring so I would not object to a small bed no matter how uncomfortable it would be. He had been most gracious with his hospitality, so I accepted the bed for the night.

I sat in the bed as his two children surrounded me, showing me little trinkets and toys. They tried speaking with me but I couldn't understand, so I only smiled at them and nodded my head. After half an hour, their father beckoned them to leave me be. Each of the two siblings gave me a peck on the cheek and crammed themselves into the other small bed. Before my kind host left me for his room, I shook his hand as he gave me a look of understanding and sympathy. What I wouldn't give to have a conversation with him. When we shook hands, I felt we did have a discussion. We both understood it without the use of words.

I lied back and positioned myself as best as I could on the small bed after my host left the room. I pulled a heavy and warm quilt over myself and closed my eyes and fell fast asleep with thoughts of Karl and Roland not far from my weary mind.

———

MY EYES SHOT OPEN as I sat straight up in bed. I groaned and rubbed the back of my head, still feeling the effects of my injuries I endured. After realizing where I am, I jumped out of bed and hustled to the front room. A faint glow of red embers came from underneath the fireplace. But the air was warm. Not as cold as I remembered. The Frenchman stood at the window next to the door, staring out into the calm night. But everything didn't feel calm. We both heard it.

The sound of a gunshot.

I joined him at the window and looked outside but discovered nothing unusual. The rain at last stopped. Outside, I can hear only the noises of insects. But I grew suspicious. I went back to the little bed I slept in and grabbed my pistol and rifle, careful not to wake the twins. Afterward, I slipped my uniform back on which was now dry thanks to the warm fire. I got to the front door and motioned to my host to keep quiet by placing my finger over my mouth. He nodded, letting me know he understood.

But before I could open the door, my host grabbed my arm and shook his head, as if he did not want me to leave. But I ignored his pleas as I opened the door and stepped outside the cottage. A thin fog covered the ground because of the warm night air and rainfall. I walked around to the edge toward the chimney, keeping low to find the source of the gunshot. But there was nothing to be found. Everything was calm. After coming around the rear of the cottage, I spotted a small cabin twenty yards away with a dim light coming from a small window near the door. Deciding to investigate, I stepped slowly to the cabin, keeping my eyes open and focused for anything unusual. Once I reached the side of the cabin, I ducked down in front of a window and took a quick peek through it. Inside, a lantern and several candles burned but I saw no one. But someone had to be around close by, I was sure of it. I rushed around the corner to the front but ran into something as I stumbled on my feet and fell hard on my rear on the wet ground. Looking up, a man stood over me with his face hidden in the shadows. He was dressed in boots, a dark uniform, and the unmistakable German steel helmet.

I lifted my rifle and prepared to jab the soldier with my bayonet when he threw his hands in the air. "Please, I will not harm you! No fighting! I swear! I don't want to fight!"

This surprised me on account he didn't wish to fight and that he spoke English.

He stood motionless as I sat on the ground with my rifle in my hands, still prepared to lunge with the bayonet. But I took a chance to trust him. The sound of his voice was sincere.

"All right," I said as I lifted myself off the ground, keeping my eyes on him. "Don't try anything. Understand?"

"Yes, of course," he replied. "Please come inside and sit with me and drink some beers. Let's talk. All I want to do is talk. . . ok?"

"Ok," I said. "Let's sit down and talk. And remember—don't try any-thing." I lowered my rifle but kept myself on guard as I followed him inside the cabin. The lantern and candle lit the modest room with deli-cate light revealing pieces of artwork and old photographs that decorat-ed the walls. At the left of the room was a small wooden table with two chairs.

"Please, sit," he said as he fumbled around in a small ice cabinet by the front door. He then presented a few glass mugs and a large bottle of beer. He sat down across from me at the table and poured a mug of beer for me and then for himself. After removing his helmet, I did the same. "This is the best damn beer in France. It's quite a delicacy here." He held his mug up. "Cheers."

I held my mug up as well. "Cheers." I took a sip of the cold beer as I kept my eyes on him. To my astonishment, he was right about the beer. I found the taste to be quite extraordinary: sweet, smooth, and flavorful. A sample of honey lingered on my tongue after the first sip.

We drank the beer in silence for a few minutes as I still held a watch-ful eye on him. But there was something about him. He seemed some-what familiar, but I didn't understand it. His eyes were deep blue and his hair sandy blond with a few thin grey strands.

"I can see you don't trust me," he said. He spoke in a low tone with not much of a German accent; it sounded American.

"It's difficult to trust the enemy," I replied.

He laughed. "I must assure you, that I mean you no harm whatsoever."

I cracked a smile. "You must excuse me if I'm cautious. I can't risk any chances. Surely you understand?" I knew by sitting down with him to have a chat is foolish enough. This man couldn't be trusted for he is the enemy. For all I knew, there were more Germans nearby, and at any moment, they could bust down the door and capture me. I could be tak-en prisoner or perhaps killed. What was I thinking coming in here and sitting down with him? I became reckless. I sat on the edge, expecting an attack from the German I was in the room with or from someone out-side.

"Of course. I understand quite plainly. You're a good soldier; I can see that. I've noticed you haven't taken your eyes off me since we sat down. That makes a good soldier. Never take your eyes off the enemy. Very cautious. But you have nothing to fear, my friend. All I wish is nothing more than a friendly conversation and a few drinks." The German gave me a friendly smile and a wink as he lifted his mug and took another drink of the delicious beer.

"I was investigating what I believed to be a gunshot," I said. "I heard it as I slept in the cottage out front. Do you know anything about that?"

"As a matter of fact, I do. It was me. I was shooting at a rabbit, but I missed. I can be such a lousy shot." He let out a laugh. "And yet I'm a soldier." He laughed again.

I grew suspicious. "You were shooting at a *rabbit* at *this* time of night and in *this* weather?"

"Yes. It sounds odd, but I grew up knowing how to hunt. The trick I learned from hunting at night is look for the animal's eyes. A glint of light in the darkness is a sign of an animal. Aim for the eyes... but as I had stated a moment ago—I'm lousy with a rifle. And I enjoy hunting in all types of weather. I love the fresh air, you see? Sunshine, rain, snow... it doesn't matter. I hunt."

"That's interesting. You seem to know about hunting. I can respect that."

"Well, please feel free to carry on that knowledge, my friend." He took a swig of beer and winked at me again. "Are you a hunter?"

"When I was little... yes," I replied. "But nowadays, I don't have the knack for hunting."

"That's a shame, my friend. Perhaps one day you will find the passion you once had for the sport and continue."

"Perhaps."

"As for myself—I enjoy the thrill of a hunt. I hunt all kinds of ani-mals. Deer, squirrel, rabbit, turkey. It's a passion I hope to teach my son someday."

Why does this man seem so familiar? It had been nagging since we sat down. "If you don't mind me asking," I said, "but what are you doing here all alone at this time of night?"

"Ah! I was accompanying several other men in a vehicle coming from Percy toward Villebaudon. Of the other men: a captain and a private. We arrived there to warn our troops that the Americans are on their way and that our attempts to hold Villebaudon would be suicide. But our armies have their orders. And so they stayed there, waiting to engage with the Americans. So bombings making way for the American assault further away sidetracked us. We stopped here after discovering that cottage just outside. The owner agreed for us to stay in here until the time came to move on." Now I understand why the Frenchman didn't want me to leave the cottage. He was trying to protect me from the German hiding in this cabin. "A night ago, my companions decided to drive to an abandoned farm near here to investigate. I was left here and told to wait for their return. But they have yet to return.

"So, I have been stuck here. I fear that something may have happened to my comrades. Perhaps they were caught by the Americans? Or killed? Who knows." He grew silent for a moment and took a big gulp of beer from his mug. "For these are dark days, my friend. Dark days indeed. There isn't much kindness in the world today. All this killing; I don't understand why we must fight one another. You see, this war is not our war. It's not mine. It's not yours. This war is an underlining fault that separates us all, and for what? What is this war truly for?"

"How about for peace?" I responded after a moment.

"Peace, my friend? No, It's not about peace. It's about understanding. Peace and understanding are two different trains of thought. There can only be peace when all is agreed upon. If there is agreement upon all men, upon all differences and creating all men, women, and children equal... the significance for war would become obsolete. What would be the point of war if all people agreed on the same issues?" He took a large swig of beer. "Now understanding, on the other hand, isn't about agree-

ing on all issues, nationalities, and religions among the people; but rather living together side by side and accepting people's differences.
There will be disagreements here and there, of course, but the need for
war would never have to arise if people lived together with understanding. So this war is about understanding. It's about acceptance.

"It's in the hearts of all men to live among other men with acceptance.
All men need not love one another. . . to like one another, but all men
should *respect* one another. Respect and understanding is what's missing from this world.

"You and I are enemy soldiers of different nations, and it's in our
hearts we should respect one another. Even in the most profound and
darkest of times. . . there should be respect." The German spoke with
such passion and vigor that I couldn't help but to admire him. "So what
about you?" he said. "Why are you here all alone? Are there any more of
your fellow troops close by?"

"No, not that I'm aware of," I replied. "I was on a march with my regiment after leaving Saint-Lô when we got ambushed. Myself and fellow
troops got separated when a counter-attack came. After the bombs fell,
we woke to discover the rest of the regiment were nowhere to be found.
We didn't know if they had moved forward or possibly retreated to
Saint-Lô." I decided not to mention the incident in the barn. "We
marched here when we were ambushed by a few stray Germans. I imagine they also got separated from their regiment during the ambush and
encountered us. There were maybe three or four of them." I lied. "I'm the
only man to walk away alive."

"That is unfortunate," the German said. "But these are indeed unusual circumstances, is it not? It's amazing that the two of us should
meet here tonight."

"Yeah, I guess so."

"So please tell me—where about in the US are you from?"

"Louisiana," I said as I took a sip of beer.

"Ahh, Louisiana," he chimed. "Believe it or not, but I once lived in
Louisiana."

I looked at him bewildered. "Really?"

"Yes," he said as he swallowed his beer. He stood up and brought back another bottle of beer from the ice cabinet and poured his mug full and poured the rest in my mug. I was eager to hear him return to what he had been saying. "I lived there with my wife—Katrina. We moved to the States from Germany in search of a better life."

Katrina! That's a name I knew all too well. Hearing that name sent a wave of emotion through me. But he couldn't be speaking about my Katrina. The same woman who spoke one of her poems to me, and who was always kind and gentle. I observed the German more closely. Everything came together now. I understood why he looked so familiar. Could it possibly be? Was this Aren I was chatting with? I wanted to tell myself 'yes', but I didn't believe it. The odds of me running into him here at this very point in time in this place across the globe was improbable; not impossible—but improbable.

I wasn't convinced this is Aren, but I had to make sure.

"We became farmers in Louisiana," the German continued. "Then one year, there came a great flood, and it forced us off our land to find refuge miles away. We went to this town called Natchitoches—I believe is the name of it. A family took us in. Sweet people. They let us stay there for as long as we needed."

As I listened to these words coming out of his mouth, I went into shock.

"There was a boy," he continued, "named Vincent. But he preferred to be called Vince. Katrina and I loved that boy. We thought of him as a son—a son we didn't have. He was exceptionally bright. Maybe a little rebellious and lazy but he was a good boy. Katrina and I truly missed him after we left.

"We returned to our farm and remained there for quite a few years until this war broke out. The community where we lived learned that we were German. Things were turning ugly for us, so we had no choice but to flee from our private land and return to Frankfurt. Our family helped us settle into a home there. But I miss my life back in Louisiana. To make things better for us, we took several trips to Quedlinburg. Katrina loves that little town. Quedlinburg is quite a magnificent place. It's beautiful. There's no place quite like it. She wanted to live there, so that's where we now reside. And so, a year after returning home, the Nazi Army called on me to serve." He took a gulp of his beer and studied me. "You know. . . you remind me of Vincent. It's strange, isn't it?"

"Indeed," I replied. He confirmed my suspicions. He appeared a little older from what I remembered. And I didn't want to believe it, but here he was—Aren. A man who I considered a friend but now is nothing more than an enemy. After everything my family did for him, he betrayed us. Hate began to grow deep from within.

Aren continued to drink his beer with large gulps as I only took sips, deciding that I should keep my head clear. "Where's your wife now?" I muttered. My manner changed as I spoke with a raw and somber tone.

"She is back home in Quedlinburg," he replied. "She is waiting for my arrival so we can return to our life together."

"I couldn't help notice that your English is superb. How did you learn to speak the language?"

"When I was a boy, my parents thought it would be of great interest if I were to learn a second language. So I learned English. I studied it for several hours every day in my youth before I became skillful in the language. Katrina didn't know much of the language after I had met her, so I took it upon myself to teach her. It took time, but eventually, she got the hang of it. She spoke little during our time in Louisiana when she was around anyone other than me. But the longer you speak the language—the accent attended with that language develop, if you haven't already noticed." He let out a laugh.

"Well, you could have fooled me," I replied.

Aren laughed again.

———

"WHAT WILL YOU DO WHEN YOU RETURN HOME TO THE STATES?" Aren

asked. His speech became slurred; a sign of inebriation. We had been chatting for an hour now. He was drinking his third mug of beer as I sipped my second.

"I'll try," I replied, "to pick up where I had left off when I left for England for training. But the problem is, there is nothing much there for me anymore. I didn't have much of a life when I left the States. No wife—perhaps a girlfriend. I wrote to her but never got a reply. It makes me worry if she stopped waiting for me. She promised she would wait, but now I'm not so sure."

Aren shook his head. "You mustn't think like that, my friend. Surely, she will wait for you."

"No. I don't believe she will. She must have moved on. But I have a brother and little sister waiting for me. But I fear if I ever get home... they won't even recognize me. They won't know who their brother is. This war has done a lot to me. To be honest... I don't even recognize who I am anymore. This war has done too much."

Aren smiled at me. He bowed his head and placed both of his palms flat on the table in front of him and leaned forward. "You worry too much, my friend. Things always have a way of working out. Sometimes for the worst but that will often lead to something good. Things get worse before they get better. Remember that." He sat back up once again and returned to drinking his beer. He became drowsy as he had difficulty holding his eyes open.

"Well, it seems you have everything figured out after this war. You have a wife and a home you are eager to return to. Do you have children?" I asked him.

"Indeed," he said, taking another drink of beer. "One son: Günter. Strong name."

I smiled. "But what if you don't make it out of this war? What will happen to your wife and son then? What would she do with herself?"

Aren stared at me. "I try not to think about those kinds of things. It would be best if you to try not to think about it as well."

"Forgive me for intruding," I said. "I sometimes think before I speak.

The truth of the matter is: I don't think I can survive this war. The possibility of me returning home grows dimmer and dimmer with each passing day. I've been through many close calls, but eventually, there won't be another close call—because it will be the real deal. My number will come. And I hope it comes soon. I've lost friends in this war. One of my closest friends. . . I lost a day ago.

"This war has torn my family apart. My father hates me, and I think I hate him as well. My mother is no longer alive because she suffered from the grief I had caused her because of my decisions. This war killed someone who was not a friend of mine, just the opposite, actually—but he impacted my life in more ways than any friend could ever do for me. I thought I would return to my future wife, but that illusion vanished into thin air. This war separated us. And I'm afraid this war has separated me from someone whom I thought was a dear friend of mine, but as it turned out—it was just a huge bullshit lie."

Aren lifted the perspiring glass to his lips and took a swig of the beer. When he set the mug down, he looked up at me and saw I had unholstered my pistol and had it aimed at him. I had been drinking with the enemy, and I couldn't allow him to fool me any longer. He swallowed that last gulp of beer hard. He looked at me with his blue eyes now sunken with despair. Tears swelled in my eyes. I don't know how long I sat there with the pistol in my hands. It felt like an eternity.

"My friend?" he trembled.

I pulled the trigger. The bullet pierced his chest as he flew black off his chair and hit the floor. I stood up and stepped around the table to look down on him. He was alive, gasping for air. I stood over him and pointed the pistol over his head and pulled the trigger again. His head jerked left and right on the floor as blood splattered all around. I shot again.

I stepped over him and pushed my back against the wall, dropping down on my rear next to him. The smell of blood lingered in the air. I leaned over him and dug through his uniform pockets: removing German currency, a luger, pistol ammo, several handwritten letters in envelopes, and a locket.

The ammo and luger, I put into my coat pockets and tossed the letters aside. They were written in German. So trying to read them would be pointless. I then fidgeted around with the locket. It was small and square-shaped with a tree engraved on top, and a thin silver chain ran through the top loop—just an ordinary locket. I opened it to discover a picture of a young woman; a black-and-white photo of a woman's face I could never forget—Katrina. I could never mistake her beautiful face as I gazed at the picture for a few minutes before shutting the locket. I clenched it in my hand and wept.

At last, I understood what Roland tried to tell me the previous night in the barn: I am an executioner.

I murdered an innocent man out of hate. These are the horrors inflicted upon soldiers during the harsh realities of war. Aren was a friend who in my eyes became my enemy. Yes, I hated him. I played the scene out in my head over a dozen of times: what if I had refused to pull the trigger? What if I had let Aren live and instead bring him to my regiment as a prisoner? Was there really a need for me to kill him?

My sobbing eventually stopped.

War.

That is why I killed him. Kill the enemy.

I took one last look at Aren's face in the hazy light of the cabin. His blue eyes remained open. His expression was soft as his lips were somewhat parted as if in a deep sleep.

Damn Aren. I didn't damn the war, but I damned him. "Better you than me," I said to his lifeless body.

After wiping all my tears away, I stuffed the locket into one of my pockets, leaned my head against the wall, and closed my eyes. And I dreamed the remaining night away in a deep and harmonious sleep.

TWENTY-NINE

"I KNOW A STORY," Aren said as he and Katrina tucked me into bed. "Would you like to hear it?" I nodded my head. He smiled as he pulled up a chair and sat down as Katrina sat at the edge of my bed. "This story happened not too long ago. It took place during a fierce and long battle in north-eastern France during the Great War." I listened to his words as the wind howled from outside and rain pelted the window. An angry rainstorm woke me up from my sleep. Being scared, I ran into the living area. But Aren and Katrina walked me back to my room and to my bed. Glenn was still fast asleep.

Two factions: The French and Germans have been fighting this battle for almost a year. But the end was near. Casualties were in the tens of thousands. Both sides were at the point of complete exhaustion of morale, and strength to continue. The German Army were ferocious in gaining land and momentum and yet as the days passed, the French Army retaliated, forcing the Germans to continue their fight.

In the final days, the German Army were losing territory they gained during the battle of Verdun. Their lines stretched thin. On a cold December day, Verdun was just one big haze of smoke. The occasional flash from a rifle dotted in the distance. But no artillery tore through the sky.

"Scheiße," Gerhard Oberleutnant swore under his breath. "Not even Hauptmann a week, and things are falling apart," he thought to himself.

His men had moved back off the front trench for the moment. The mud wasn't as bad back here as it was up by No Man's Land, but the air is still damn cold. Vogel ate half a loaf of dirty looking bread. He reached up and offered a bite to Gerhard, but Gerhard waved him down. Gerhard turned away and saw that Mayer was catching a few minutes of shuteye, sitting close to the small fire, his helmet tipped over his eyes to block out some of the sun. The sunlight came as a relief for it hadn't been sunny in months.

Gerhard looked away and rubbed his cold hands together. "Hey, Hauptmann Kühn," said a voice from behind Gerhard.

Gerhard turned to see who it was; it appeared Mayer had woken up from his nap. "Mayer, what is it?" asked Gerhard.

"Just wondering how long we stay here?" said Mayer.

"We head back up tomorrow," said Gerhard. "We've been back here since I took over for Hauptmann Klein. . . not too long after we lost Fort Vaux. I hear it's been quiet on the front. Snipers now and then, but no artillery hammering away at us like before."

"Makes me feel like a storm might be brewing," Vogel interjected.

"I don't feel great about it either," said Gerhard. "But we got our orders this morning. Let the men know, tomorrow at 0700, we head back to the front-line."

Vogel nodded, and Mayer shook his head. Both men turned from Gerhard and went around, letting everyone in the company know they'd be heading back to the front, and to report for debriefing at 2000 hours. Gerhard sighed, they must have been down to fifty men. He hated the front; it's wet and even colder than back in these trenches, and there was no clue as to when the French would start shelling again.

Gerhard sat down by the fire and pulled out a small notebook. He'd taken up sketching last fall, over a whole year ago. Mostly, he sketched birds, if he saw any. At times he sketched the men but found more solace in depicting nature. He started in on a sketch of one of his men, leaning up against a stack of wood, smoking a cigarette. He always started with the hands; he found them to be the most challenging to get right, so once he got the fingers in place, he felt more confident to put the time into the rest of the drawing.

Just as he had finished the left hand holding the extinguished match, Gerhard noticed a face he didn't recognize. It was caked with mud, and he looked out of breath. The man saw Gerhard and made his way over to him.

"Hauptmann Kühn," said the man with the dirty face, saluting to Gerhard as he spoke, gasping in between every breath.

"Yes, what is it, Gefreiter?" saluted Gerhard.

"I have orders Herr Kühn," said the man with the dirty face, extending his hand, holding out a parcel.

"Thank you," said Gerhard, as he accepted the orders. He scanned the page quickly, his eyes narrowing as he read the words. "This is a joke right?"

The dirty-faced man looked shocked. "No, Herr Kühn. I did not read the orders, but they came from General Erich Georg Sebastian Anton von Falkenhayn himself. I ran all the way here to deliver them."

"You've completed your task. Why are you still here? Run back," snapped Gerhard. There was more than a tinge of anger in his voice. The dirty-faced man appeared as if he was about to respond, but thought better of it, and instead turned and ran away.

"Vogel!" shouted Gerhard.

"Yeah?" shouted Vogel from about thirty yards away, down the trench. He gave the soldier he was talking to a pat on the shoulder and made his way over to Gerhard.

"New orders," said Gerhard, his face still etched with dismay, and his eyes narrowed. "Gather the men; we head out now."

Vogel looked shocked but knew better than to question Gerhard. He nodded and called out for the men to pack up now.

They were working their way back up through the trenches within thirty minutes. Vogel led, and Mayer took up the rear. The front was only about ten kilometers away, but trudging in the cold through the mud slowed them down. It took them three hours in the trenches to reach the front.

It was quiet.

Gerhard directed Vogel and Mayer to get the men set up in positions, replacing the men who had been here previously. They'd been ordered down the trench a way for unclear reasons. While Vogel and Mayer got all the men to work, Gerhard took the time to look around as best he could. From what he could see, this position was dead. He breathed a sigh of relief. After consulting with Vogel, Gerhard set his watch and dozed off in the mud, hoping to catch several hours of sleep.

Time passed. Gerhard woke to silence. "Another quiet morning," Gerhard thought. He noticed a bird sitting over at the edge of the trench. He hoped to get his notebook out in time to get a quick sketch down.

"Gerhard," said Vogel. "Guten morgen, feels like the cold is letting up, glad to see you got some rest."

"Guten morgen, Vogel," said Gerhard. "Thank you for taking command last night, I was apparently exhausted. Go get some rest now, I can take it from here."

Vogel nodded and walked away. Gerhard grabbed his sketchbook out of his pocket and sketched away at the bird on the other side of the trench, pleased it hadn't flown off. It must have been no more than three minutes later when there came a loud whining.

BOOM! Vogel disappeared in the explosion. Dirt and rocks rained down from where he had been walking. Then, more whining. Gerhard tried to shout over the sounds of explosions and the screams of his men. Dirt rained down from all over. The French began shelling again. Dreger, a soldier Gerhard served with for two years, was huddled up next to a support, clutching his legs to his chest. "Shell-shocked," Gerhard thought. He seemed not quite right back at camp. I should have said something.

The men all hunkered up against the wall of the trench closest to No Man's Land. Vogel was gone, so Mayer was second in command now, but Gerhard couldn't find him. So he grabbed the nearest man and screamed at him to find Mayer, and if he failed at that, then to run back to the general's camp and let him know the French resumed shelling.

Two days passed, and Gerhard hadn't seen the man again, nor Mayer for that matter. The French continued shelling, but he had seen no retaliation from German Artillery. Gerhard reckoned he had maybe thirty men left. The French had gotten some lucky shots in on the bunker, but Gerhard and his men held fast. He knew if they lost this position, it would mean breaking the front. That wasn't an option. In addition to shelling, the French advanced on the German position. Gerhard wasn't sure how close they had gotten, but the last time he ventured to look, a bullet grazed off the top of his helmet.

"Hand grenade!" was shouted over to Gerhard's left side. He saw a soldier leap forward, and then Gerhard saw the man's innards explode into a red mist as the grenade exploded.

"Shovels ready!" yelled Gerhard. He knew the French were close.

Men poured in over the edge of the trench. They were all hacking at each other, biting, clawing, stabbing to stay alive. Gerhard took a blow to the back of the head, and things got hazy. He managed to pull his pistol and shot the man in the gut. Not very clean, but a kill shot. He saw another man struggling and went to fire again, but when he had fallen, he'd gotten dirt on his pistol, and it had now jammed after firing once. "Scheiße!" he said, as he went to get out his shovel. As he raised his head, he was greeted with ten guns pointed in his face.

Gerhard's men were dead. The French broke through. Verdun was lost.

He dropped his shovel and raised his hands over his head. The men were spitting at him and poking at him with the barrels of their guns. He saw an older man with a very large mustache, probably in his late thirty's near the back of the group, looking as if he was thinking. He stepped forward and shouted something that Gerhard couldn't under-stand. The men stopped spitting and prodding, but then a scream came from the right. One of Gerhard's men survived and had just gashed a soldier in the back of the neck. Gerhard took the opportunity to lash out at one of the captors and was rewarded with a swift strike to the back of the head. The last thing Gerhard remembered was another scream fol-lowed by gunshots.

The light was bright, and it blinded Gerhard. It was unclear where he was at first. He tried to get up but noticed his hands and legs were bound, and he lied on something hard. It wasn't mud, but some kind of wagon, or back of a vehicle, maybe. He noted there was no movement. And he could hear voices around him, but they were speaking French, and he couldn't make out what was being said, having never learned much French himself. He felt something prod at his side, and Gerhard let out a yelp.

"Guten Morgen, I see you are a... a Hauptmann is it?" said the man who Gerhard believed was the mustached man from before. "I apologize for my bad Deutsche."

Gerhard said nothing as he sat up on the truck.

"You and your men put up quite a fight there at the end. There were so few of you. Is Germany running out of soldiers?" asked the man.

Gerhard said nothing.

"I admire your bravery most of all. Attacking my men, unarmed. Im-pressive. Especially from an officer, usually you throw your hands up at the first sign of trouble."

Again, Gerhard said nothing.

"You don't have to talk," said the man. "Verdun is won. The war will soon follow."

"You can't know that," said Gerhard.

"Ah, you can talk," said the man. "Ich Bisset."

"Your Deutsche is terrible," said Gerhard. "Ich bin Gerhard. Where am I?"

"Well met, Gerhard. Currently, we're heading to French command.

I'm afraid I must turn you over," said Bisset. "If you cooperate, I can put in a good word for you."

Both men chuckled. They knew it wouldn't matter.

Bisset reached into his pocket and pulled out a cigarette and lighter. He put the cigarette in his mouth and lit it. "Seriously, any information you could give me would be helpful."

Gerhard smiled but said nothing to Bisset.

"Tsk tsk. I'm sorry to hear that, Gerhard," Bisset patted Gerhard on the arm and took out a second cigarette. He put it up to Gerhard's lips and lit it. "And I'm sorry about your men."

"And I about yours," said Gerhard.

The men sat in silence as the truck began to move toward French command. Each smoking a cigarette, each thinking on the battle won and lost, and the friends lost in defeat, or in victory. The question of was it worth it was on both men's minds. What good are brave and coura-geous lads, who fight hard, and die young? The silence said it all.

My eyelids grew heavy. Aren stood from the chair and set it in the corner of the room as Katrina stood from my bed and kissed my fore-head. "Goodnight, Vince. Try to get some sleep now. The storm is letting up."

She turned off the lamp on my bedside table and walked with Aren to the door as he closed it behind them.

———

I FELT A HARD TAPPING ON MY BOOT as I opened my eyes, awakening me from a dream of a story Aren once told me when I was a boy. Andrew stood over me, staring at me with a grin.

"Shit, Vince!" he shouted. "What in the hell happened to you?!"

"It's a long story," I replied as I rubbed my eyes. "I'm glad to see you though. Who else is with you?"

"We're all here," he said. "The 29th, 30th, and the 2nd Armored. After that ambush after leaving Saint-Lô, the regiments became unorganized. We managed to fight them off further up the road, but more troops were on the way. We had to leave the dead and wounded behind. There was nothing we could do for them. Further up the road, we left the main road to take a detour toward Soulles to reorganize." Andrew looked at Aren's dead body lying next to me. "What took place here?"

My best advantage is to lie, not wanting to explain that I murdered an innocent man out of fear of the consequences. "I snuck in here and found him asleep at the table. When I approached him, he woke and looked at me and drew his pistol. But I was quicker as I drew my pistol and shot him."

"Must have been sleeping off a hangover," Andrew said as he walked over to the table and picked up the mug Aren was drinking out of. He then noticed the second mug of beer—the one I drank from. He picked it up and studied me with suspicion. "Did you see anyone else here?"

I played dumb. "No. Just him."

"It's odd that there would be two mugs."

I shrugged my shoulders. "Maybe there was someone else here but left to go on watch or something. I stayed here just in case he returned, but I fell asleep."

Andrew nodded his head. "Well, he couldn't have gone too far. In fact, he could be the prisoner we have outside right now. Where's Karl?"

I ignored his question regarding Karl. "You have a prisoner?"

"*We* have a prisoner. Sergeant Aschner and Captain Hull are outside, and I'm sure they will want to speak to you about what happened in here. And just where the hell you have been, by the way?

"I would ask the same thing," Hull's voice rang out. Hull and Aschner entered the cramped cabin.

I lied again. "I was with Sergeant Lambert, Corporal Archer and Corporal Harris, pushing forward on the Germans until we got overrun in our position. They pushed us further into the forest. Then Corporal Harris was killed during the assault. The rest of us fought them off until the airstrike came. The bombardment knocked us all unconscious, and we woke several hours later. We were disoriented, and so we became lost until we found a farm not far from here. We took shelter in the barn until several German soldiers discovered us. A fight broke out and... I was the only one to survive."

I looked at Andrew; his expression turned angry.

"Go on," Hull ordered with impatience.

"After I left the barn, I stumbled here on my way towards Villebaudon and caught a German off guard. I had no intentions of shooting him but once he laid eyes on me, he went for his pistol, and I had no choice but to pull my own and shoot him dead. And this morning, Sergeant Decker found me asleep from exhaustion while keeping a look-out for any other German soldiers."

I looked back over to Andrew. "I'm sorry, Andrew. But Karl didn't make it."

Andrew was silent. He stumbled backward a few steps, pulled off his helmet and rushed outside. I brushed past Hull and Aschner and followed him out into the damp morning. Lester and Jeffery Barnes watched over a lone German soldier with his hands tied behind his back. Andrew stepped up to the prisoner and struck him in the face with his right fist. The prisoner fell on his back as Andrew pounced on top of him, bashing him with his fist before Lester and a few others pulled him away.

"That's enough!" I shouted. "This isn't the man who killed Karl!"

Blood coated the German's face. His nose appeared broken, his right eye damaged, and blood spat from his mouth. But Andrew struck the captive once more when Lester released his grip.

"Remove Sergeant Decker from the captive!" Aschner shouted.

Lester and I pulled Andrew off the prisoner as he fell to the ground, but he kept his bloodied hand raised. He stared with rage at the prisoner, now gagging and spitting out blood. Several men helped the German to his knees when Andrew broke free from our grip, stood up and unholstered his pistol and shot the prisoner in the forehead. He fell on his right shoulder—dead.

Andrew dropped his pistol and fell back down to the ground again. He said nothing as he stared at the prisoner he had killed. His face turned pale and emotionless. Whatever feelings he had now vanished. He now looked empty of all life.

Jeffery appeared as if he was in a complete state of shock. His face was pale as if he would vomit from witnessing the scene that happened before him.

"What a big *fucking* mess we have here!" Captain Hull shouted.

"Sergeant Decker just snapped," said Lester. "He attacked him and then shot him in the head."

"I'm well aware of that, Corporal!" Hull spat.

Andrew kept his silence as he glared at the German with a blank expression on his face.

"Somebody get him out of here," Aschner hissed.

Jeffery gathered his composure as he and I reached down to grab Andrew by his arms but Hull stopped me. "Not you, Conroy. You come with me." He gestured at me with his index and middle finger to follow him back into the small cabin.

———

HULL, ASCHNER, AND I RETURNED to the cabin. A feeling of panic set in—unknowing if Hull had bought the misleading story I told him.

Hull noticed the letters I removed from Aren's pockets on the floor. He picked them up and flipped through the pages one by one after removing them from the envelopes. "I want to make sure I have all the information I need," he said as he tossed the pages on the table. He looked at me with a stern face. "Are you sure that everything you told me is to the best of your knowledge? Is there anything else you can recall?"

I had to confess about Roland. They will find him in the barn with a pistol in his hand and a bullet wound through his head and there will be no other explanation but the truth. I stammered, trying to find the words to say.

"Yes? What is it?" Aschner inquired.

"Well, it's about Corporal Archer," I said.

"What about him?" Hull asked.

"Corporal Archer had been wounded from our skirmish with the Germans after leaving Saint-Lô . He survived the night in the barn, but the next morning he was too weak to continue on. You'll find him there under a blanket with a self-inflicted gunshot wound to the head."

Hull and Aschner glanced at one another.

"Is that so?" Hull asked.

"Yes, sir," I said. "He wanted me to move on and leave him behind but I refused, and so he took his own life because I was too damn stubborn. I'm responsible for what happened. Have me court-martialed if you must." I knew my fate would be in Hull's hands.

Hull scratched his chin and paced around the room for a moment. "Let's not get ahead of ourselves, Sergeant. Well. . . I'll have a few men go to the barn and check it out to make sure everything you say is true. If it is, I see no reason for a court-martial. I know the two of you were not fond of one another but I can't imagine you putting a bullet through him. Damn shame about Sergeant Lambert and Corporal Harris, though. They were good men." Hull looked at me once more. "Anything else?"

"No, sir," I said. "That's everything."

Hull pulled the chair that I had been sitting in the night before out from the table and faced it towards me and sat down. "Ok, Sergeant— that's all in the info I need. Thank you." He picked up the letters off the table once again. "Sergeant Aschner—," he said, holding up the letters, "get our interpreter and see what he can make of these."

"Yes, sir," Aschner said as he took the letters and walked towards the door.

"Don't go just yet, Sergeant," Hull said.

Aschner stopped and spun around. "Anything else, sir?" he asked.

Hull scratched his neck. "I want you to check on Sergeant Decker and make sure he's ok. I'm sure he's just upset about his friend. I want him evaluated to know if he's mentally fit to continue on. Is that understood?"

"Yes, sir," Aschner said.

"Good. That'll be all, Sergeant." Aschner left the cabin with the letters in his hands and Hull looked back at me. "So what about you?"

"Sir?" I said.

"Do you find yourself mentally fit to continue? I mean that whole thing with Corporal Archer and losing those other men had to have been distressing. You've been through a number recently."

I felt as if Hull was testing me. I didn't feel as If I could continue with this war. Some part of me wanted to tell him 'no'. If I did, perhaps he will send me back home to America. Or at least, grant me a few days rest. I knew what I wanted to say but I couldn't bring myself to do so.

"Well?" Hull inquired.

"I'm perfectly fit to continue, sir," I said.

Hull stood up and clasped a heavy hand on my shoulder. "Good. That's what I wanted to hear. You're a damn good soldier, Sergeant. You make me proud, you know."

I smiled. "Thank you, sir."

"I have an offer for you if you are interested."

"Sir?"

"You've been doing a hell of a job for us so I presume it is appropriate for myself to promote you to Sergeant First Class. Once again—I believe you are the perfect man for the job."

"Yes, sir!" I chimed. "I'd be honored."

"Good. Then it's official. Gather up all of your gear and be outside pronto because we'll be moving to Villebaudon to run the German's out of there. We are expecting tough resistance, but now since we are reorganized, we should take the village by nightfall."

"Yes, sir," I said as I saluted him. "And thank you, sir, for this opportunity you granted me."

Hull didn't return my salute, however. "Get ready to move out," he said, walking towards the door. There he was met by Aschner with the letters in his hand. "Are the letters of any use?"

"I'm afraid not," Aschner replied. "The interpreter said they are only personal letters and nothing more."

Hull took the letters from Aschner and tossed them in a wastebasket by the door and left the cabin along with Aschner.

After picking up my rifle, I glanced back one last time at Aren's body. I removed the locket from my coat that I took from him and opened it to admire the picture of Katrina. It was one to cherish, for it reminded me of her beauty. I considered putting it back into his coat pocket but didn't, for I now had something to remember Katrina by. Aren didn't deserve it—alive or dead. He was a traitor—an enemy. And now will be nothing more than a memory.

I don't know why, but before I left the cabin, I picked up the letters from the wastebasket and shoved them into one of my coat pockets along with the locket.

——

I RETURNED TO THE FRENCHMAN'S COTTAGE to gather my gear. I thanked the owner for his hospitality with a hardy handshake and said goodbye to the children as they gave me kisses on my cheeks. Afterward I joined the troops on the road leading to Villebaudon.

Aschner began inspecting every soldier of the regiment as he walked past and halted once he reached me. "One of these days, Sergeant—I would like to know what really happened here last night," he hissed. His face turned somber. I said nothing as I tried to avoid eye contact. I had something to hide, and now Aschner could feel it. He leaned his head closer to mine and whispered into my ear, "Just remember one thing: you can bullshit the captain, but you can't bullshit me. I will be keeping a very close eye on you, Sergeant, so I highly recommend that you watch yourself." The change in his personality became evident—a man I once thought of as a friend had now become a superior, craving authority to impress Captain Hull.

Aschner stepped away from me and then continued his inspection of all the other men.

After he finished, Captain Hull arrived. "All right, listen up gentleman! We will continue our march to Villebaudon and then onwards to Percy!" He stood in silence for a minute, observing everyone as he paced back and forth with conviction. "Let's get our asses into gear!" he shouted.

My war was far from over. It's only the beginning. During those first several months, I escaped death on countless times. To perform such an act is not a skill but luck. I survive as others die. It's a burden I live with.

On I marched with my regiment into a vast countryside filled with trees, pastures, orchards, villages, and Germans. I marched on, not knowing what would be around the next corner. The vibrations of the regiments feet sent shivers through my legs as we marched. We took a glorious stride of relentless strength on our way to win this war. I know longer cared how long it would take. I was here now, and I would do my damndest to get home alive no matter the costs.

THIRTY

AREN'S LOCKET DANGLED from its silver chain at my fingertips in front of Dr. Gilliam. I had been speaking throughout the lingering hours of the day—verbalizing my story with feeling. Gilliam rested his chin on his hand, balled into a fist and focused on each word and every confession that slipped through my lips.

I glanced at my wristwatch: the time read three o'clock in the afternoon.

"Is all of that true?" Gilliam inquired.

I stood up and stretched, not ignoring Gilliam's question but only resting my raspy voice for a moment.

Dr. Gilliam adjusted himself on the chair and grew impatient. "Please, sit back down, Vince."

After my stretch, I sat down. "It's all true; every word. You don't believe me?"

"Is that the locket?", he asked, ignoring my question.

I had my suspicions that he doubted my confession—my secret. But I had to make him understand the truth. "It is," I replied to his question.

"May I see it?" I gave it to him. He opened it and looked at the photo of Katrina. "This is Katrina?"

"Yes."

"Very beautiful girl, I must say. It's nice to finally put a face with the name." He snapped the locket shut and gave it back to me. "So what's been troubling you is the incident with Aren that night in the cabin?"

"Yes. . . and this damn locket."

He nodded his head. "I see. But I have to admit—I'm still struggling to mull over the possibilities of you and Aren running into each other that night. I mean. . . the odds are unbelievable, to be frank. It astonishes me of the random chance of that meeting in that place and time is wondrous."

"I still can't believe it myself," I said. "But it's true, doctor. Every word I said is true."

He glared. "I don't doubt you, son. You must forgive me for my suspicions."

"It's ok. I understand." But he didn't understand. He doubted me. I knew it. The only proof I had is the locket, but that's hardly convincing. I could have purchased the locket in a second-hand store and stashed a photo of a random woman inside. But I believed it because it is the truth. There must be a way to convince him. I picked up the lockbox from the floor and set it in my lap, opened it, and removed a few brown pages aged with time. The scent of vanilla and musk flourished from the pages from being stored away for so long. "These are the letters I found in Aren's coat. The letters Katrina wrote. The writing is in German, and I can't speak, write, nor read the language. But names I understand. These were written in Katrina's hand because of her signature, and the greeting is to Aren. So perhaps these will convince you."

Gilliam took the pages from my hands and glanced through each page. "Ok, Mr. Conroy—I see your point. But how do I know these are just letters you found on a dead soldier and collaborated a story with these names?"

"Because you don't," I snapped. "You have to trust me when I say that you just need to take my word for it. I had no intentions of sitting in this room with you for all these hours and feed you a lot of bullshit."

He raised his palm. "Ok, son. There's no need to become offended." He cleared his throat and let out a heavy sigh. "So can you say the incident that happened between you and Aren has been haunting you after all these years? Is this the reason why you are having trouble sleeping along with panic attacks in the middle of the night. Do you feel guilty for shooting an innocent man. . . your friend? Is that what it is?"

"I do feel guilty. I've lived with this for so long and I know I just want it to go away so I can live peacefully."

"I'm sure anyone can overlook your misdeeds, my son. So do you believe killing Aren was immoral?"

I became overwhelmed. Gilliam's questions were all too much to answer at once. "I was wrong to do so, so yes. The only person I feel guilty about. . . is Aren. For taking him away from Katrina. That night I pulled the trigger was a selfish act of insanity. One thing I realize is that emotion can make you do terrible things. Emotion can control you as it controlled me that night. And I regret the decision I made. I was angry and tired of that damned war, and I thought one more dead German soldier is a step closer to getting home. I took Aren away from Katrina—away from his child—away from his family. If there were any possibility of taking it back, I would without hesitation. But the problem is, I can't. And I have to live with that decision every day."

Gilliam shook his head. "You are putting too much blame on yourself. It's not healthy for you, son. I have every confidence you will get past this."

"I wish I can believe that," I said.

Dr. Gilliam let out another heavy sigh, leaned back in his chair, and crossed his legs. "I want you to understand, Vince, that I am no psychiatrist—just a medical doctor. So, what I'm about to say is strictly between you and me only as friends. You can take it or leave it, for it will be up to you."

"I understand," I replied.

"Enemies can be friends," he continued. "Colleagues can be enemies.

If an enemy can lend out a helping hand during the conflicts of war, it is because of his nature as a respectable human being. Aren didn't see you as an enemy that night. He only saw you as another human being—as a friend even though he didn't know who you were. You on the other hand only saw him as an enemy—an enemy of war.

"Aren was your friend, Vince. Sure, the two of you were on opposing sides of the war but does that make him any more of an enemy than, let's say, a soldier on your side, like Roland, who was making your life a living hell?" I remained silent. "That night, you acted out in aggression. You looked across the table and saw the enemy and not a human being. And so—an innocent man died by your hand. And now, your past has caught up to you. Perhaps your past is catching up to you because it wants to tell you something? Have you thought about that, Vince?" I shook my head. "So what happened to your friend Andrew?" Gilliam asked, taking the conversation off of subject.

"Andrew was court-martialed for killing that prisoner. But medical personnel determined he was suffering from shock after finding out about Karl's death. It was too much for him. Eventually, he rejoined C Company at his request. He survived the remaining days of war—thank goodness. He lives on base with his family now. I still see him from time to time."

Gilliam nodded his head. "Well, your story *is* remarkable, *if* what you say is true. So I want you to listen closely to what I have to say, Vince. You must find a way to make peace with Aren. This is to become your task. How you go about doing that will be up to you. I can't tell you how to that. Only you can determine how. I can only give a suggestion or two to put you on the right foot, however, for you've been tormented with this for far too long. You must make peace with him."

I shook my head in agreement. "So what do you propose?"

"It's come to my understanding that Katrina only knows her husband is dead. She doesn't quite know how—that is, for she doesn't know the whole story. She only knows he's dead. I believe Katrina needs closure about Aren's death. Maybe that's what these sleepless nights are trying to tell you. She needs closure—and you're the only person who can give her that."

"That makes sense, I guess."

"There's another issue at hand too: your father."

"My father? What about him?"

"The two of you should make things right. Work your differences out."

"That stubborn fool wants nothing to do with me, nor I want anything to do with him. And this isn't about my father. I thought so earlier this morning but going back to everything I just told you, I feel as if trying to make amends with him would be pointless."

He sighed. "You've come here for my help, Vince, and I'm offering just that."

I gave in and decided to listen. "You're right. I apologize."

"Your father is an asset for your troubles," Gilliam continued. "You two may not see eye to eye on a few things or practically anything, but closing that gap you mentioned between you and your father is a step closer to recovery. Your relationship with him has been a burden for far too long. Not only do you need to make peace with Aren, but you need to make peace with your father as well."

"I don't know. But if you believe it will help—I'll try."

"No. Don't try. Do," Gilliam commanded. "Your relationship with your father has been the main source of your negativity. As you stated this morning—your father guided you into the man you are now. And the only way to erase this negativity from your life is to make amends with him. . . one way or another."

"I guess I could use some ideas on how to do that too. If I'm willing to reach out to him—what makes you so sure he will do the same?"

Dr. Gilliam leaned forward in his chair looking optimistic. "I don't. There is only hope. There is always hope. And for the issue at hand, I think I may have a solution. Have you considered writing to him?"

"No, I guess I haven't."

"You should write to him. If you never get a letter in return—keep trying. No matter what. Keep trying."

"Ok. . . I'll see what I can do."

There came a sudden knock on the door. "Enter!" Dr. Gilliam called out.

The door squeaked open, and Abella's head appeared through the narrow gap. Her eyes locked on mine. "It's getting late, hun. We need to get home soon."

Gilliam rose from his seat. "Ah, Mrs. Conroy, nice to see you again."

Abella greeted Gilliam with a smile. "Hello, Dr. Gilliam," she said with her alluring French accent. "I hope my husband hasn't been keeping you from your work?"

"Everything is fine, my dear. We'll be finishing up our talk in just a few minutes. We're just going over some. . . final details."

"I hope you don't keep him for too much longer," Abella chimed. "He's very much wanted at home."

"I'll be along shortly," I said. "Just a few more things to discuss."

Abella gave me a reassuring smile and closed the door behind her, leaving me alone once again with Dr. Gilliam.

"You're lucky to have such a beautiful woman, Vince," Dr. Gilliam said. "Do you know that?"

I smiled. "I am lucky," I replied. "Now you know how we met."

"But how did the two of you end up together?"

I smiled. "I'll leave that story for another day."

He returned a smile of his own. "Fair enough. As I was saying—" he sat back in his chair and gave me a stern look. "I've heard you say you despise your father and I refuse to believe that. You may say you do, but I know in your heart, it's simply not true." I open my mouth to speak, but Dr. Gilliam raised his hand to stop me. "Please, let me finish." I nodded as his hand dropped to his lap. "Now, every person has his or her own way of showing their love. Your father is no exception. I've concluded that your father was scared for you. Perhaps scared to lose you. You ignored his requests to stay on the farm by joining the army, and with each passing day, the thought of losing you became too much for him. He acted out irrationally because he didn't know how else to behave. He lost a brother in the Great War. And you are his son. Do you think he wanted to lose you? He only wanted what he believed was best for you. In his eyes, he didn't see you as a soldier, but as a son.

"Your mother accepted your decision even though she didn't approve. It wasn't your leaving that drove her to the grave; it was her lack of strength to fight over the heartache she suffered over you and your father's distant relationship.

"Could you have done more? Perhaps. But her fate was her own, much like Roland's. Not yours and not your father's." He glared at me with sympathetic eyes. "Do you understand what I am trying to tell you, son?"

I nodded my head. "Yeah. . . I think I do."

"Good. Write to him. You have an opportunity to make things right. There is never a guaranty of success but only hope. I know you'll do what's right."

Our discussion, at last, came to an end. We stood from our chairs and shook hands. Not another word was spoken. With an empty stomach and Abella waiting for my arrival outside, I left the cozy little office with a new direction.

And a new found sense of hope.

———

I LEFT FOR HOME with Abella after leaving Dr. Gilliam's office. My storytelling left me drained. It was difficult to relive those memories I uncovered. But I soon realized the closer I got home, the better I felt. I lifted a huge weight off my chest.

Abella sat in the passenger side of our vehicle—a green Ford Sedan, as I drove. We sat in silence. Out the corner of my eye, I caught her taking occasional glances at me. I'd only look at her and then smile to let her know everything was ok. She took her eyes off of me and stared out the passenger side window, watching the houses and trees pass by, appearing deep in thought.

I was also deep in thought, considering Dr. Gilliam's advice, fixating on every word he said. He was right—I needed to make things right with Katrina. She had to be told about what happened to Aren. And I'm the person to do it. But how? Is she even alive? But I had to try and find her. I then realized what must be done.

I took a quick look at Abella as she still gazed out the window. "I have to leave for Germany."

Her head turned away from the window as she looked at me with shock. "Germany?!"

THIRTY-ONE

"YOU'RE LEAVING ME AGAIN?" Abella asked as I finished packing my suitcase full of clothes in the early morning. Today is the day for my flight to Germany. I had to leave for Washington National Airport within the hour. This decision didn't come easy. I held this trip off for several weeks, but eventually, I gave in to Dr. Gilliam's advice to find Katrina so I can return the locket. I held off this trip because I was scared—scared to see my old friend once again. And scared to come face to face with the woman whose husband I murdered. And now the time has come to begin my search for this very woman.

I turned to Abella and held her by her thin shoulders. "Only for a little while this time."

"What about work?"

"I took leave from the recruitment office for a few weeks. I'm overdue for some time off anyhow."

She sighed. "I'm still not sure why you need to go."

"It's something I need to do. I need to make things right with a former friend of mine from my childhood. If I can do this, maybe—just maybe, I can feel better about everything that has been troubling me."

"I just hope you know what you're doing. Where you will start?"

"I have an address. I'll start in Quedlinburg."

"But you don't speak a word of German. Are you sure you know what you're doing?" It was obvious that Abella didn't want me to leave her. In my absence, she would be lonely.

"I honestly don't know what I'm doing," I chuckled to try to lighten the mood but she didn't crack a smile as she looked at me with bitterness. "But I need to fix this."

"For both of our sakes, Vince—do whatever you need to do then. But come back straight home when you are finished with whatever it is you need to do."

We both embraced and had a long passionate kiss. "I promise I'll return as soon as I can. I don't know how long it will take to find her, but I'll find her—one way or the other. I'll find her."

——

I CLUTCHED THE ARMREST as the airplane hurried down the runway and rose off the ground, departing from Washington National Airport. This was my very first time to fly, believe it or not. It was all new to me. I felt like a little giddy child experiencing something amazing for the first time. But that excitement faded after takeoff as the plane shuddered. I became nervous, even frightened as I took glances at the man sitting next to me in the aisle seat for reassurance. He appeared calm. A good sign I suppose. As the plane leveled out in the air, the shaking stopped. And as the minutes went by, I became more relaxed and began to enjoy the flight.

I leaned back in my seat and looked out the window as the airplane soared just above the clouds. I had seen nothing so majestic in all my life. It was almost like a dream. The sky was blue—as blue as I had ever witnessed it. The sun shimmered its elegant light throughout the morning sky. I watched the white, pillowy blanket of clouds spreading out for miles and miles from below in a trance, imagining myself walking on those clouds barefoot, feeling the softness under my feet and between my toes. I wanted to sit at that window and look down at the world for hours and hours, perhaps even days and I would still be fascinated by the beauty.

The plane was nearly full of passengers. I dressed myself in civilian clothes, not wanting to draw any attention, for my military uniform does just that. Men and women approach me in public, asking me many questions: Did you fight in the war? Were you wounded? Did many of your friends die? Questions I answered countless times before. But Abella told me I should smile and be polite and that the people are only curious. She stated it honors them to meet a soldier who fought in the war and they wish to hear stories. But the hardest part is acting polite when I only wish to be left alone. Privacy is difficult to come by nowadays. Most civilians do not understand privacy, especially privacy for veterans.

But on this flight, I didn't stand out among the other passengers; to them, I am another ordinary civilian. A civilian with no crazy stories to tell.

Some passengers lit up cigarettes in the cabin which reminded me of my fellow soldiers who smoked. I always thought smoking was a disgusting habit, but I could understand their decision for doing so. For it's believed smoking relieves tension—calms the nerves. I never tried it to know if it worked or not but I didn't care to try. Perhaps the passengers' smoke to relieve the stress of flying in an airplane.

Cigarette smoke filled the cabin air as the stewardess' made their trip down the aisle and asked the passengers for any refreshments. I only asked for water. They are polite and pretty. Beautiful women serving aboard a plane would make any flight enjoyable. But I wouldn't dare flirt with them. My heart belonged to one woman; and she was patiently waiting for my return home.

I never imagined Abella and me getting married. By mid-June, just one month after the war had officially ended, I received a long awaited letter from Catherine at Camp Grohn, just outside of Bremen, Germany. The 29th Infantry had set up a command post for organizing military government. After several years of never receiving word from her, my hands shook as I opened the envelope:

Dear Vince,

I'm sure you are possibly wondering as to why I haven't written you after during these passing months and lingering years. It's been a long time, I know. Before you left to fight in the war, I promised you I will wait for your return but I can't any longer. It's too difficult for me to do so. Because every day I worry. I worry you will forget about me. I worry you will return home a changed man and not the man I fell in love with. But most of all, I worry about receiving a telegram letting me know you've been killed in battle. And your body will be left behind and forgotten in a foreign land, far away from home.

This is no way for me to live. It's not fair to you and not fair for me to have to wait one more month or one more year for your delayed arrival. So I think it's best we move on with our lives without one another. There is no life I can give you that you deserve.

But I want you to know that in the briefest amount of time we were in one another's company—I was happy—the happiest I had ever been. And it's because of you—I decided to travel elsewhere. I think of myself as a gypsy. I can't be tied down to one place for too long because I need to be free. You taught me how to be free when you never judged me for the person I am. I told you who I really was but instead of condemning me—you loved me. You loved me like no man has ever done before. And for that, I am sincerely grateful.

Don't hate me. I won't blame you if you resent my decision but please—don't hate me. Maybe one day, years after the war when you are sitting on the front porch of your home with a wife you deserve along with your beautiful children—you can forgive me.

Goodbye, and I hope you know I will always remember you and always love you.

Catherine

I read the letter over and over again. I read it so much; I memorized every word—every detail to comprehend her message. Divided by heartache and relief, I came to accept the letter's true meaning. I loved her and always will. I remember our first kiss and her gentle touch as I held her in my arms. But Catherine was now a part of my past. A fragment. So I burned the letter, leaving behind that part of my life so I can move forward into the unknown. The unknown is a scary place and yet exciting. Good or bad, we all must move forward to the undiscovered parts of our story. More days are to come yet to be written.

I took leave from Camp Grohn, returning to the village of Agneaux in France. I made the trip there on the off chance of meeting Abella. My hopes were not high, however, for I assumed she would have found a man to be with it. But to my surprise, I found her in the same washhouse where we met months ago, and unmarried. I stepped through the door dressed with style in my military suit, decorated with my ribbons, medals, and badges with my Sergeant First Class insignia displayed on my sleeves, with a bouquet of purple irises in my hand. She stood behind a counter, alone, wearing a white dress patterned with small blue flowers smiling as tears rolled down her cheeks. She then came to me, embraced me, and kissed my cheek.

"You came back," she whispered in my ear with her arms folded around my shoulders.

"I did," I replied. "I came back for you."

"For me? Wanted to see me before you leave for America? And are those irises a goodbye gift?"

I smiled. "No. I came back because I missed you."

She gave me a peculiar look. "Missed me? Why would you miss a poor French girl when you have a woman back in your home of America waiting for you?"

"Because," I blurted out, "she's not waiting for me. Not anymore."

I gave her the bouquet of irises as she pressed the petals to her nose, breathing in the fragrance of the blue flowers. "They're lovely," she smiled. "Thank you."

It was the same day I asked Abella to marry me and emigrate to the United States to live with me in Virginia. Earning the rank of Sergeant First Class had its monetary perks. Perhaps now I can afford a home and at last, leave the base.

She agreed, and after receiving permission from her parents and the United States Army, she left France behind as my fiancé to be with me eleven months after my return home to America in December of '45. She sailed on a ship leaving Southampton, England and journeyed across the Atlantic to New York Harbor, along with many other brides and brides-to-be, awaiting to be reunited with their loved ones. The ship arrived in New York City on a cold December day in '46. I watched the passing faces of women. My heart pounded. One by one, they exited the ship to reunite with their husbands. It had been minutes when I had, at last, saw her, bundled up in a thick winter coat. She looked around the crowd of people, frantically searching for me when she finally spotted me as I approached. Tears rolled down her cheeks as she rushed into my open arms. After a long embrace, I held her face in my hands and wiped her tears away.

We stood in silence, staring into one another's eyes, with smiles gleaming. Eventually, I spoke. "Here we are."

"Here we are," she complied. "You came back to me in France. Now I come back to you here in America. This will be my home now. But all of this is new to me. It'll take time to get used to."

"I'll be here with you the whole way," I said.

As I waited for her arrival to America, I got a loan from the bank to put the down payment on a two-bedroom house in Richmond, Virginia. It would be a surprise.

The first time setting foot into our new home, Abella stepped throughout the house, excited about her dreams to come. She could see the house filled with people as we host supper parties and she could see our children running about the house, playing games and getting into trouble like children do. It was a fantasy I wanted to make a reality for her. I did this for her. Although we were not married as of yet, it felt like a marriage.

And we did marry. On a fair, humid day in August, we had a small wedding at the base chapel. I was dressed in my Army Service Uniform; Abella wore a delicate white wedding gown and a short veil over her chestnut hair. Glenn and Julia attended, along with Aschner, Lucy, and Andrew. Even Lester. But not Father. Nor Karl—though I know he would of have joined me on my big day if he was still alive.

Andrew was never the same after the war. The shock of Karl's death impacted him deeply. He was no longer the playful and yet offensive man I came to know. In some ways, Karl's unfortunate death had been a measure of maturity for Andrew. In time, we need to leave our youth behind for development. Perhaps a bond as strong as love can impact us many different ways. Even after death, a person's love can leave a profound impression on our character.

Abella and I stood together, hand in hand at the altar. I can smell the scent of her rich floral perfume. Father Davis stands before us, performing the wedding congregation. When it came time to speak our vows, I spoke carefully as to not slip up, but I did a few occasions. Remembering the wedding vows is not simple. But Father Davis was there, guiding me along. After I finished, Abella said hers. She looked more relaxed and confident and said them to perfection.

Father Davis then blessed our rings and then I slid Abella's gold diamond ring onto her finger. Her face lit up. She then slid my gold wedding band onto my finger as Father Davis gave his final blessing and then announced us as husband and wife and for me to kiss the bride. I lock lips with Abella. Now it became official—we were married. I was a husband. Abella was my wife.

—

HOURS PASSED AS THE FLIGHT CONTINUED. I listened to the loud noise of the jet engines. The engines droned over the pilot's voice on the intercom. I only made out a few words. But I didn't let it trouble me.

Soon, I would be off the plane.

The flight is to be almost nine hours, but I wanted the trip to be longer. The first stop is London and then to Frankfurt. There I will catch a train to Quedlinburg. The more I thought about my purpose for this trip, the more I felt uneasy. I told Abella the truth—I had no clue what I was doing. Did I have any chance of finding Katrina? The possibilities of her being dead or untraceable crossed my mind.

But I had to search. I had to try.

Many simulations ran through my head if I was to find her: How would she act? Would she believe me? Would she shoot me on the spot with a gun? I couldn't help but to laugh at the last thought. Then again, the scenario of her shooting me seemed logical. It would almost be a joke; after everything I had survived through, I die by a gunshot wound from a woman whose husband I murdered.

I laughed again at the thought.

I looked out the window and realized the plane is flying over the Atlantic ocean. The ocean below is beautiful, reminding me of my time aboard the *Queen Mary*. I could possibly look down on the direct course that the great ship took on the ocean on its way to Scotland. The first trip to Europe was by boat and my second trip back is by plane. It felt strange almost.

As the plane flew closer and closer to its destination, I began to sweat. My heart pounded. I unbuttoned my shirt at the top and drank a little water.

No, this can't happen now. I can't have an episode on the plane. Not

in the presence of all the passengers. I unbuckled the seatbelt and excused myself pass the gentleman sitting next to me, almost tripping
over his feet. Several passengers stared as I passed their seats on my
way to the lavatory. Once inside, I locked the door and splashed cool
water on my face. I dropped on the cramped floor, letting the episode
pass.

This was not fear of flying. But fear of meeting Katrina. Here I am,
years later, afraid to death of a woman I loved. Afraid of a woman who
will learn the truth. Now I regretted this decision to search for her. Fear
pursued me. And it will not let up until the task is done. So I hope. I'm
burdened with the choice I made that night in the small cabin with
Aren. I pulled the trigger. I took his life. And now, I've been granted the
undertaking of making matters right for both of them.

After several minutes, I got back to my feet and wiped my face off
with a napkin and then returned to my seat. The passenger's faces still
glued to me. I asked for more water from a stewardess. She returned a
moment later and gave me a small cup of water and took one look at me.
"Nervous about flying?" she asked.

"You could say that," I replied with a fake grin.

"Well, it won't be long now until we land." She gave me a warm smile
and returned to her duties.

I leaned back in my seat again and looked out the window, watching
the waves of the ocean far below me. I looked further out and spotted
land in the distance. Then the city of London. The sun vanished below
the horizon as the minutes passed. Darkness caught up with the plane
as it made its slow descent from the night sky. I clutched the arms of my
seat as we descended and I stiffened when the landing wheels contacted
the pavement. The plane jerked and rumbled on the ground as it sped
through the runway. It then started its gradual decline in speed as it
approached the tarmac before coming to a complete stop.

THIRTY-TWO

WHAT AN EERIE FEELING it was to be back in Germany. It was a short plane ride to Frankfurt after my transfer to London the next morning. I spent the evening in a hotel room in London for rest and returned to the airport early to not miss my next flight. At Frankfurt, I exchanged some of my American cash for German currency and picked up a map of the country, along with a little German language translation booklet containing simple phrases in English translated into German—just in case I needed it.

As I stepped outside the Frankfurt Airport, I bundled myself up in my coat to protect myself from the cold air and caught a cab to the train station. The cab driver held a watchful eye on me in his rearview mirror as he drove through the streets of Frankfurt. He didn't trust me—a foreigner, who should have stayed where he belonged. His watchful eyes made me uneasy, so I gazed out the window.

From the looks of it, Germany is a different life from America. It's difficult to believe just some years earlier—this country was being controlled by a dictator who inspired the Second Great War. Germany and much of Europe were still putting their lives back together. It would be a long and difficult trial. The Allies had bombed Frankfurt during the war and the scars left behind are still visible—in the streets, the architecture, and the community. During my time in the war, I never entered the city. After the battle of Vire, instead of proceeding south or east, the 29th Infantry moved west to take part with the assault on the city of Brest in northern France on August 25 of '44. Afterward, the 29th moved east through France and Belgium by train to stand firm in temporary defensive positions at the Teveren-Geilenkirchen line in Germany. Once on the attack, we reached the Roer River. And after taking defensive positions yet again, eventually crossing the Roer, we pressed on to Munchen-Gladbach and joined the Allied Expeditionary Force on March 31 of '45 and mopped up any remaining German resistance. The Elbe River would be the end of the 29th's fighting in the war. There we met up with the Soviet Army. Pleasantries were exchanged by the two armies for we were all in good spirits. We knew the war would be over soon enough. The German Army was breaking, and then on the seventh of May, Germany surrendered. And after spending nearly two years of endless and grueling training and fighting, the war in Europe was at last over.

The war took many lives—far too many. But somehow—I survived. I was awarded the purple heart after being struck in the leg by shrapnel after a German mortar struck a building near to where I stood during the Battle of Brest. My platoon was scrambling to reinforce Aschner's platoon as they were assaulting a German squad hiding behind a wrecked building. A mortar struck a building, not ten meters from where I had been standing. The blast threw me to the ground. My ears rang, reminding of the dive bombers outside of Saint-Lô. Then I felt the pain in my left leg. Shrapnel from the mortal stuck out of my thigh. I tried to move, but the blast left me dazed. The ground shuddered from beneath me as more mortal shells exploded from all around. Fearing that my time had come, I felt hands grab me from underneath my armpits. I looked up to realize that Lester had a strong hold of me as he pulled me across the pavement. Several times he yelled, trying to communicate but my ears still rang. But the mortars kept coming. The explosions from the mortars forced Lester to release his hold grip on me when striking nearby. But he never gave up. Eventually, he dragged me to safety. I owed Lester my life that day.

"You're lucky," Lester said as the medic pulled out the metal shrapnel in my thigh.

"That you are," the medic said.

The ringing in my ears had stopped, but a headache lingered. "Is this my ticket outta here?" I laughed.

"I'm afraid not," the medic snickered. "Looks like the shrapnel just barely missed an artery. I'll stitch you up, so just keep it clean, and you should be all right."

I didn't go home after that day. But after Brest had been liberated—I made a personal recommendation to Captain Hull to have Lester promoted to sergeant. Hull accepted my recommendation and Lester accepted the position with enthusiasm.

Like myself, Lester returned home. I had trained with nineteen other men in boot camp and out of that nineteen—only five, including myself, remained. Andrew came back to the front lines after his court-martial and evaluation. But the shock of Karl's left an everlasting effect on him. He was just another victim of the horrors of war—as we all were. Andrew may not have lost his life, but the war had taken something else. Wounds heal in time, but not all. Some wounds cannot heal. Those wounds remain with you throughout the years. They are unseen, but they are there—deep beneath the skin and the flesh. Buried deep into the heart. That's where those damages lie. I have wounds of my own, perhaps too many than I like to admit, as with all soldiers who took their place on the battlefield—soldiers I stood with and fought alongside with. In time, those wounds will try to break you, but I will not let that happen. I will allow them to make me stronger.

As the cab traveled through the roads, I became mesmerized by the charm of Frankfurt. Beautiful monuments and massive cathedrals brought meaningful life to a city that was still rebuilding. Many gabled houses along with bakeries, coffeehouses, and restaurants—old and new, filled every street, alley, and corner. Several long bridges crossed the Main River, connecting what seemed like two separate cities. I only saw Germany in the dark days of war. But seeing it for its true beauty for the first time is breathtaking.

After purchasing my train ticket at the station, the conductor told me the trip would be over five hours. The final stop will be in Goslar, and from there, I would catch a bus to Quedlinburg. Starting the trip in Frankfurt will allow me to see more of Germany's beautiful countryside. The train (a red and white VT 10.501 with a shape that reminded me of a bullet) roared to life as there came a slight shudder and squealing of wheels as it began to move on the track as I took a seat in an empty cabin. Looking out the window, the train station and the city of Frankfurt passed by. My hands trembled as I unfolded the map of Germany onto a small table in my passenger cabin. My fingers passed over the map starting in Frankfurt, then moving upwards to Hanau, Fulda, Kassel, Göttingen, Hanover, and Goslar.

Five hours.

I folded the map and tucked it into a pouch in my suitcase—the same pouch with the locket. I took out the locket and opened it, staring at the small black-and-white photo of Katrina. As I looked at her face, my heart pounded in my chest as it had done so on the front porch of my home and on the airplane. The locket fell from my trembling hand and onto the floor. Sweat beaded at my forehead. Remembering to stay calm, I leaned back in my seat and took deep breaths. Needing fresh air, I tried to open the cabin window, but to my discovery, it wasn't designed to open. I unbuttoned my dress shirt and fanned myself down with my train ticket. I'm grateful that I am alone; but how many of these attacks can I take?

Minutes pass. I stared out through the window as the bright sun lit up the moving green landscape. My nerves calm as I stare out into the scenery. I let out a sigh of relief. But I realize the locket is not in my hand. I panic as I looked around the small the cabin in search for it. I can't lose it now. But I spot it on the floor underneath the seat as I picked it up. I took one last look at the photo inside before snapping it shut and clenching it with a fist. It was not lost. Only misplaced is all. I clasped the locket in my fist as I pressed it against my chest. I didn't want to let it go again. Not until I find Katrina. I let out another sigh of relief as I sat down. I let it drop as I unclenched my fist, letting it dangle by the chain at my fingertip. Then I pull the chain over my head and let it drop around my neck. Now I can't let go. I can't lose it.

———

I STEPPED OFF THE BUS in Quedlinburg in the cold late afternoon. The sunny day had now vanished. The sky is gray, obscuring the low sun, and the wind is calm as many fat snowflakes gently fell to the ground from above. I pulled my collar up on my coat, strapped my scarf around my neck for more warmth, and removed Katrina's address I had written on a small sheet of paper. I politely asked an elderly woman with a wooden walking stick, bundled up with thick wool garments at the bus-stop for help in finding Katrina's home. My lack of understanding of the German language only caused confusion for the first several minutes, but eventually, she understood what I tried to ask her as I pointed to the address on the slip of paper with my finger. She nodded her head. "Ja. Ich nehme dich mit," she said, taking me by the arm and then leading me into the heart of Quedlinburg.

As I walked through the snow-powdered streets of Quedlinburg, I could see why Aren and Katrina admired the little town. Many colored half-timbered houses lined up and down cobblestone streets while old castles and churches towering from above gave it a charming medieval atmosphere. Walking through the town was much like a maze. At times, I thought we were lost, but I had no choice but to trust my guide. Slowly I walked side by side with her with arms interlocked from one corner to the next. Her walking stick thumped the pavement with each step, sending a distant echo throughout the streets.

The early spring air grew colder. I remembered how cold it would get during my time in the war. Hard to forget. Digging foxholes had been near impossible. The frozen ground was much like rock, digging through several feet of snow and then through several layers of ice. Staying warm was a challenge. Superior officers prohibited fires at night in fear of German snipers in the area. Soldiers would bundle up together with friends and fellow troops with as many blankets they could get for heat for the long winter and spring nights. Hot breath would steam out their mouths, creating a faint mist above their heads. The cold was always there. Some nights, the cold forced my mind to wander. Instead of staying on guard, I only thought of being warm around a cozy fire out of the harsh winds with a mug of hot coffee in my hands.

I also remember the snow covering the grounds. After battles with the Germans, the snow turned red with blood, reminding me of the red water on Normandy beach. I had seen much blood during my time in the war. Too much.

The daylight grew darker. I feared we were lost until I looked up at a street sign which read: Heidenfeldstraße. The very street I was in search of. Walking down the street, we passed many half-timbered houses until halting just outside a yellow house with a red roof. "Wir sind hier," my guide said, pointing at the yellow home.

I gave the elderly woman a warm smile. "Danke," I said.

She gave the back of my hand a few gentle taps with her palm before letting go of my arm and stepping away as her walking stick continued to thump the cobblestone.

At last, I reached Katrina's residence. I only hoped she still lived here after all these years. I faint light came from inside through a window. Someone is home. After reaching the front door, I hesitated to knock. My fist hung in the air. And after a few deep breaths, my fist tapped the wooden door: one knock, two knocks, three knocks. After a brief moment of silence, there came the sound of a latch being unfastened and the door creaked opened. Gazing back at me in the crack of a door was a tired and matured looking woman. "Ja? Kann ich Ihnen helfen?" she said.

She looked like Katrina but was it truly her? I took the chance to speak to her in English. "I'm sorry to bother you, ma'am—but I'm looking for Katrina Bauer."

"Are you American?" she asked. It relieved me when she spoke English.

"Yes, ma'am. I'm American."

"Well, I'm Katrina Bauer. What do you want?" It is her. She had aged. Her long hair, now ashy blonde, hung over a worried face. It was not the delicate blonde hair I remembered all those years ago back on the farm.

"I was hoping I could speak to you about something. It's important."

She looked at me with uncertainty. "I'm sorry, but I don't allow strangers into my home."

"It's about your husband, Aren!" I boasted as she began to shut the door in my face.

The door stopped in place and opened further once more. She looked at me with speculation. "Aren?"

"Yes."

"My husband Aren has been dead for years now. What is this all about?"

I could feel the chill in my bones as I bobbed up and down at the front door. I was getting cold. "There's something I have to tell you about him. Please, can I come inside, and then we can discuss it. It's kind of cold out here in the snow."

Katrina sighed and opened the door to allow me to come in. "All right," she muttered. "Come in." I was inside in a matter of seconds, a pleasant escape from the bitter cold. She closed the door behind me and locked it. "Please, sit by the fire. I'm making some hot tea, would you like some?"

Hot tea sounded splendid. "Yes, please," I replied as she disappeared into the kitchen. I set my suitcase down and sat in one of the comfy armchairs in front of the fireplace to warm up. I rubbed my hands together and held my palms up to the fire. My cold fingers grew warmer by the second. Inside, her home is cozy with a slight musty scent in the air. Looking around the room, it's decorated with knickknacks on small side tables, a large bookcase filled with various books, and on the walls are several portraits and paintings of landscapes. The only light in the room was coming from the glow of the fire.

A moment later, Katrina emerged from the kitchen and gave me a cup of steaming tea on a small saucer. She sat down on the armchair next to mine in front of the fire. "So what is this all about?" she inquired before taking a sip of tea.

Not knowing how to reveal to her what I had done to her husband, I stammered. "I‑err. . . well, I came a long way to see you. I suppose you don't remember me but you and your husband—Aren, came to live on my family's farm in Louisiana in America after the great flood when I was just a boy."

Katrina looked at me with suspicion. "I remember that. Aren and I migrated to the States many years ago for a short while." She leaned forward, staring closer at me. I can now see the brightness of her blue eyes. "Are you. . . Vincent?"

She remembered me. "Yes. But I always preferred to be called—"

"Vince," she blurted out.

It looked as if Katrina would drop her tea. Her hands shook as she set the cup and saucer down on a small table next to her chair. She leaned forward and gently laid a hand on my cold cheek, staring into my eyes and smiled. "It is you, Vince. It really is," she whispered with a hint of glee. "I can never forget those dark green eyes of yours. You've really grown to be a handsome man." She regained her composure, removed her hand and leaned back in her chair. "But why did you come here to find me? What do you have to tell me about Aren?"

I removed a brown envelope from my suitcase and set it in my lap. "I have a few items that belonged to him, and I wanted to return them to you." My hands shook. After opening the envelope, I removed the letters and gave them to her.

She looked them over. Her eyes swelled with tears as she read through them in the firelight. "These are letters we had written to one another during Aren's time away in the war. But this one... I never knew about," she said as she held up a single page. "Aren must have died before he could send it." She leafed through the pages of the letters once more.

"That's not all," I said. I loosened my scarf, unbuttoned my coat and pulled the locket chain over my head. "There's also this."

Katrina took the locket in her hand and opened it. She covered her mouth with her hand and gasped with emotion as she stared at the old photo of her for a minute. She then snapped it shut. "Thank you for returning these to me," she whispered. "But *how* did you get this? *How* did you get *any* of this?!" A few tears rolled down her cheeks as she looked at me. "How could you possibly have this locket and these letters? I don't understand. Why do *you* have them?!"

"Because I killed him," I blurted out, not knowing how else to say it. I just did. I had to tell her the truth.

Her eyes narrowed, and she shook her head. "What? What are you talking about?"

"I enlisted in the United States Army before their involvement in the war."

"You were in the war?"

"Yes. You see—my Company was making its way toward the village of Villebaudon in France when we got ambushed by German troops. I got separated from my troops. I made my way to a cottage in the forest, outside Villebaudon. It was there I met Aren. He didn't recognize me, or at least I don't think he did. Nor did I ever tell him who I was. He invited me to sit down with him and drink a few beers and chat in a small cabin behind the cottage. I didn't believe it to be him until he confirmed my suspicions by mentioning my family's farm in Louisiana—and he mentioned your name. After about an hour of talking, I didn't see Aren as my friend anymore. He became the enemy. So I shot him when his guard was down." Katrina said nothing and only stared. "That night, I just wasn't thinking straight," I continued. "I-I was a little drunk. And he meant me no harm, but I shot him with my pistol, anyway. So that's why I came to find you. I wanted to return his things to you and confess what I had done. I wish I came under better circumstances. But now I understand that it was wrong for what I did to Aren. . . and to you. I don't know how or why, we came to meet that night, but it just happened."

Katrina peered her eyes away from me and stared into the fire. Her lip quivered as tears rolled down her cheeks. I can see her face lit up by the orange light in the gloom. At this moment, I visualized her youthful self as I remembered on the farm. I remembered our nights in the field together—chasing fireflies, and lying in the thick grass, looking up at the infinite stars in the night sky.

Silence.

She closed her eyes and let a long and emotional sigh. The fire cracked as embers floated upwards into the chimney. Her head dropped, and she sobbed. I open my mouth to speak, but no words came out. I wanted to apologize but what good will it do? But as she cried, I wanted to take her in my arms and hold her. I wanted to hold my old friend and comfort her as she did me when I was just a boy. I wanted to lie her down in her bed and sit with her as she and Aren did on stormy nights and tell me stories, putting me to sleep. There was a moment I almost reached for her—to touch her—to caress her face and to wipe away all of her tears. But I thought better of myself and pulled my hand away.

With nothing else to say, I stood up from the armchair to leave.

"Wait," she sniffled as I approached the front door. She stood up slowly and stepped towards me, wiping away her tears. "Thank you for bringing me the locket and the letters. . . and thank you for telling me the truth. I know it wasn't easy. And there's something I want to show you. Please come with me."

———

KATRINA SLIPPED ON HER SHOES and grabbed a coat and a scarf off the coat hanger by the door and bundled up. I put on my coat and scarf also as we stepped outside into the cold. It was now near dark. Snowflakes continued to fall.

The snow beneath our feet crunched as we walked. I followed her through the streets of Quedlinburg as I did with my elderly guide not more than half-an-hour ago. I followed Katrina past every corner and alley, unsure of our destination. The streets were beautifully lit up with streetlamps that guided our way through the humble town. After twelve minutes, we stopped just outside of what appeared to be a castle.

"This is the Quedlinburg Abbey," Katrina said as she opened one of two large wooden doors. "In here." We stepped inside the huge interior room. Many long wooden pews lined up both sides of the room, filled with many people. The room was plain except for the many ancient columns that ran along just beside pews. At the back of the large room was an altar filled with a group of eight vocalists, harmonizing an enchanting chorus. Katrina lead me to the last pew, empty of individuals on the right of the room. There we sat down. She said nothing as she stared straight ahead listening to the vocalizing that filled the large room. I watched her, waiting for something to be said but after I moment I took my eyes off her and did as she did. We listened.

As minutes passed, I became entranced by the vocalists. I had heard nothing like it before. The variety of voices blended without flaw. The tone is serene and yet majestic. I didn't understand the words nor the message. But I didn't need to. All I needed to do was listen.

"Aren and I liked coming here," Katrina said at last. "He loved it here. We used to sit in the same spots we are sitting in now and listen to the beautiful music. After the war, we planned to live here permanently with our son—Günter. But after I had found out that Aren was killed—it devastated me. But I did what Aren would have wanted me to do—to live here on my own. I come here several times a week to remember him. I always believed he is still with me—sitting next to me when I'm here. Aren was a good man, Vince. He didn't deserve to be thrown into that ridiculous war. He didn't ask for it." Katrina became silent. She listened to the vocalizing at the altar once again as I had been. She then turned her head to look at me. "You see—Aren was drafted into the war. The Nazi Army forced him to fight on their side. He wanted no part of it. He wanted nothing to do with the Nazis. He hated them and everything they stood for." I listened to what Katrina was telling me. The inside of my stomach turned into knots. "There's no justification for you killing Aren. He was an innocent man." She removed the locket from her pocket and opened it.

"What's that tree on the locket?" I asked.

"It's the Yggdrasil," she replied. "It's a mythical tree of Germanic folklore. The sacred tree connects the nine realms of Norse cosmology. The tree creates existence. The branches extend to the heavens while its roots extend into other locations, such as divine springs. I think of it as my love and connection with Aren. This locket is very special to me. My grandmother gave it to me as a gift one year when I was very young. I gave it to Aren before he left for the war. It reminds me of that tree you took Aren and myself to in that field near the farm. I remember the picnics we had there. I remember the fireflies that came out at night, and we would catch them all and place them into jars. Sometimes I believed time would stand still after we released all the fireflies at once. They surrounded all of us so suddenly. When they paused for an instant in the air, I felt as if that was when time stopped. But for just a split second, I could touch one with the tip of my finger. It was a feeling—a feeling that nothing could ever take away my light—my light for love. It was my love for you and your family I gave for all the kindness that had been brought upon Aren and myself. Your family took us in when no one else would." Katrina stared at the locket in her hand and closed it. "You don't know how much this means. So thank you for returning this."

"Where is Günter?" I asked.

Katrina sighed. "He lives with my sister and her husband in Frankfurt. After Aren's passing, I didn't have the strength to watch over him. It was too difficult. But I see him a few times a month. His aunt and uncle will watch him until I am ready for him to be home."

The feeling of guilt and sorrow formed in the pit of my stomach. I felt ashamed for what I had put Katrina through. Unable to control my emotions any longer, I dropped my head, not wanting Katrina to see, and I covered my eyes with my hand and wept. "I'm sorry. I'm so, so, sorry."

I don't know how long I wept. But then came a touch of a hand on my shoulder—a touch that is gentle. My weeping soon stopped. I lifted my head and looked at Katrina. Her blue eyes stared into mine. Her face emitted a warm expression.

"I just want you to know I may never forgive you for what you did to Aren... but I also wanted to let you know I now have closure for his death. What I needed was closure. So now I believe I can move on. Thank you for the truth, Vince. As I said earlier this evening—I know this was not easy for you. So thank you."

My head nodded to show I understood. Katrina wiped away my tears with a handkerchief, and we said no more after that. We sat there listening to the vocalizing for over an hour. Somehow, I now felt at peace. It felt odd being in this place now with my old friend. We first met over thousands and thousands of miles away in a different land, in a different time, and now we sit here together, many years later in another country. The war divided us. It made us enemies, but now I understood that we were never enemies. It was an illusion—a trick played by the cruelty's of war. But now, I indeed discovered the real beauty Katrina owned; it was a gentle and loving nature. I only had a glimpse of it years ago in that kitchen as she voiced her poem to me. I felt light. As light as the breeze that flows through the sky. Time was irrelevant in that moment of harmony for the both of us. We had abandoned our suffering— our hardships for something more eternal—for something more wonderful.

It was for love and friendship.

THIRTY-THREE

IT WAS LATE AT NIGHT when I arrived home from Germany. With my trip over, I'm relieved to be back in my own bed as I slipped underneath the sheet and blanket next to Abella. My movements must have wakened her, as she rolled over and snuggled up next to me, draping her arm over my chest. I caressed her arm with my fingertips as she let out a slight moan.

I stared out the window as the full moon and stars lit up the night sky. Crickets performed their nightly lullabies. The pale light of the full moon seeped through the window and chased away the darkness of the night, exposing Abella's chestnut hair.

Abella opened her eyes and raised her head. She smiled. "Did you find her?" she asked with a weary French accent.

I took a moment to answer. "Yeah. . . I found her."

She kissed me on the lips. "I missed you," she whispered, her warm breath on my cheek.

Abella. It amazed me after all these years—she stuck by my side. I look forward to tomorrow morning, waking up next to her. And the morning after. A future lied ahead of us—a future with children perhaps. We discussed children in the past, and Abella wishes to be a mother. And she'll make a great one at that. With a good heart, she says I will make a great father. But It's difficult to imagine myself as one. The thought of becoming a parent is scary in a way. I was a soldier who fought in one of the bloodiest conflicts in history, and the image of raising a child is frightening. But the time will come eventually, but not until we were both ready. For Abella and I are both relatively young. And It's always better late than never. How many children? Will the first be a boy or a girl? Who knows? And I don't want to know. The future will bring whatever it so desires. For life is full of surprises and mysteries. There are more days to come in my lifetime. So I will wait for the undiscovered to find me.

But a question kept pestering me as if an insect was delving deep into my brain. "Am I a good person?" I asked aloud to myself.

Abella stirred. "Where did that come from?"

"I don't know," I replied. "Just talking to myself."

"It's best to talk to yourself so no one else can hear, you know." she giggled. "But if you want an answer... I think you are a good person. Maybe you don't know it, but you are. Because when I look at you, I see my husband. I see the soldier whom I struck up a conversation with all those years ago back in my home village in France. I see the man whom I want to spend the rest of my life with. If you're weren't a good person, I wouldn't be lying in this bed with you at this moment, speaking with you."

"I've done things I'm not too proud of," I said. "I've made mistakes. I've made choices that no man should ever want to make in their lifetime. Most nights, I'm back in Europe during the war—reliving certain moments over and over again: Normandy Beach, the air raid outside of Saint-Lô, the barn where I spent the last night with Karl and Roland, and most of all, that night in that small cabin outside of Villebaudon. That's the night I regret most of all. I hear gunshots throughout the night. They snap me out of sleep as if I was still there—in the heat of battle. It takes a moment to realize that I am here safe in bed with you.

The war took a lot from me. It took my closest friend from me. It took away men I was responsible for. It also took my sanity. It took pieces of me I can never get back. Too much. Too much had been taken.

"But I'm here. I made it out alive. Out of all of those poor souls that died during that war, I somehow made it out alive. But I didn't deserve to. All those young men, who were just boys, ran that beach me with me. I watched as they were gunned down by the enemy—their blood staining the sand and water red. I saw the aftermath of that day. All those young boys dead. Except they weren't boys. They became men that day—the dead and the survivors.

"I watched so many young men die right before me. But somehow, I survived. As to why I don't have the faintest clue. But I came to understand that after everything I had been through, the only thing left to do is to continue. I survived for a reason. Against all the unspeakable odds—I survived.

"There were nights I remember, bundled up in my foxhole, as snowflakes fell from above, and in the distance, I could hear a few men hacking up lungs from a sickness they caught from the cold. I was in no better position than those men were, but I never got sick. I would catch a cold or some sort, sure but not the sickness the other men got. Some of those men didn't make it. They died from exposure or caught some disease that couldn't be cured. It was during those nights I questioned if I was capable of pushin' forward. All those long days marching, fighting, and eating and drinking very little to preserve what small portions of rations I had took its toll. But I knew I couldn't quit. Many times I wanted to. But quitting was not an option, so I continued.

"But yet I wonder, why did I never catch any diseases like those other men? Why did I never freeze from exposure? I can't answer that question. Not now at least, or perhaps I never will. In some ways, I think it's a curse."

"There's no explanation as to why you survived," Abella yawned. "There doesn't need to be an explanation. Looking upon it as a curse is selfish. The only reason you're here is because you are. There's no defi-

nite answer to the course of our lives. There's no definite way of knowing what will come. It all happens because it happens. You survived
because you survived. Because nothing is written out beforehand. We
live each day one step at a time. What each step brings is a mystery.
But to discover what each step brings is courage. And you had the courage during the war to take those steps to come out alive. But you must
be willing to continue taking those steps tomorrow and the next day and
the day after that. Those steps lead to your future—to our future, because I am taking those steps with you. We'll do it together. And if
you're willing, we will see where our future takes us."

There is indeed a future that lies ahead of me. I don't know what it'll
bring, but I can only hope that it will be a good one. Perhaps I can still
have that life that Karl and I planned together. Maybe with Glenn and
Julia.

Glenn married some years back. He still resides in New Orleans and
has landed a permanent position at Baxter & Baxter Law Firm. We often write to one another and talk on the telephone. We also see one another when given a chance. Without knowing it, a strong bond had been
formed between the two of us. Bonds break as they always do, but the
one between Glenn and I seemed unbreakable. A bond as hard as a
stone. A brother's bond.

And Julia is growing into a fine young woman. I see Mother in her.
Not only in appearance, but in personality. It's sad that Julia is no longer the young little girl that loved to sit in my lap. How I wished she
could stay young forever. But in my eyes, she will always be that sweet
innocent little girl who would playfully jump into my lap and fall asleep
on me as I would hold her close or try to protect me from harm like that
day Father struck me in the face.

But most of all: I had Abella. My beloved and beautiful wife. And she
was right—I survived the war because of courage. And it is courage to
take every step forward. And the courage is in me to continue with our
lives together.

Beyond the innovation of what lied ahead, I looked forward to what may come. Now was the time—the best time to listen and not act. Listen to what needs to be said. Listen to the sounds around me. Listen to the quiet hours of the night. Listen to the crickets and cicadas. Listen to the chorus songs of the birds in the bright early mornings of the day. Listen to the rain as it pelts the ground, the windows, and ceiling. Listen to the boisterous roar of the thunder and the resounding strike of lightning in a rainstorm. It may only be my imagination to hear every detail of a day's events. Is it my imagination? Or is it my recollection of the tedious sounds of war echoed throughout time? To my time. But I am convinced of anything can lead me to a new beginning. A new beginning with Abella. A new life. A life without war. A life without regret. All I need to do is listen.

Just listen.

THIRTY-FOUR

KATRINA AND I KEPT IN TOUCH for several years after my visit to Germany. I gave her my address, and we exchanged letters every month. Looking forward to reading her letters, I waited with impatience each month for one to arrive. We wrote about anything and everything. Whatever positive went on in our lives, we discussed. After Lucille was born in the early month of May of '55, two years after I visited Katrina, I mailed a photo so she could see the new joy Abella and I now had in our lives.

Lucille had been named after Mother. I felt it had to be. In her infancy, she mirrored much of Abella as brown hair spread on top of her head.

With new life in our home now, I want to say things are perfect, but I must admit, everything is far from perfect, nor will it ever be. There are nights, I still wake from a deep sleep, confused about where I am. It's the dreams of war, or at times, I like to call them nightmares. True nightmares I lived through. It was what Dr. Gilliam believed: post-traumatic stress. And Gilliam assumes that the nightmares may never stop. It's a scar left behind on the mind. Through time, the scar will be less visible, but it will always be there.

But after each nightmare, after each night I woke drenched in a cold sweat, Abella was there to console me. We would hold each other in one another's arms, and then I knew I was ok. There were nights I never wanted to let go of her. Some nights I would discover her not to be in bed but sitting next to me in a rocking chair with Lucille in her arms, nursing her and keeping a watchful eye on me. "I'm here. Don't worry; you're safe," she would say to me. Her soft voice convinced me that everything was indeed ok as I lie my head back down to my pillow and drift off back to sleep with Abella watching me—keeping me safe.

Throughout the months, the nightmares became less frequent, but they were always there—always there to remind me of that time that took so much away from me.

As time passed, the letter exchanges between Katrina and I had become a sort of happening that needed no explanation. There was never a mention of Aren or the war. And that's how Katrina wanted it. With each letter I had received, curiosity would benefit my need to read what my old friend wanted me to know. Often, she wrote of times of her youth with her grandmother, for those were the happiest years of her life. It wasn't until a year that I noticed a pattern within the letters: Katrina had been writing to me her life story. Letter after letter had been set in a different place and different time of her life. But what is the purpose of her past? Is there something she wanted me to know? Something she wanted to tell me? It turned into a mystery, and I thought it would be best to go after it. I examined each letter again and again and could not come to any reliable conclusion. Why did she insist on telling me her whole life story?

Several times, I wanted to write to her and ask upfront, but if she wanted me to know, she would have told me what her true intentions were. But I believe I finally found the answer after several years of exchanging more letters, for there came a time when there were no more letters. I rushed home after every workday from the base in anticipation of finding a letter waiting for me, but there would be no such letter. I continued to write to her for several months, but still, there came no reply and eventually, I concluded that perhaps Katrina moved on. And if so, I would respect her wishes and no longer continue to send letters of my own. There were no hard feelings, of course. Perhaps it's for the best. Time to move on. But I knew I would miss my friend.

The letters stopped coming, or so I thought—until one day, an unexpected visitor came.

———

LITTLE LUCILLE SNUGGLED against Abella's chest, fast asleep, as we sat together in rocking chairs on the front porch of a lazy and mild Saturday afternoon in August. With my newspaper in hand, I read over the current events until I grew bored of reading and tossed the paper underneath my chair. Abella gently rocked in her chair, humming a sweet lullaby and looked down at Lucille and smiled. "She's just perfect, isn't she?"

"That she is," I replied.

I admired Abella's motherly instinct. It came without fault. She knew how to hold our daughter, feed her, bathe her, settle her, and protect her. My instincts as a father came as well. Much I learned on the farm after Julia's birth, but there is always more to learn. The first time, holding Lucille in my arms, I became amazed of the life Abella and I brought into this world. How can something so small and innocent be so beautiful? The first time Lucille opened her delicate hazel-green eyes and looked at me, something changed—and for the better. From her first cry in the early mornings and to her gentle breathing as she sleeps in her crib—I am there, to calm her and watch over her with Abella. I'm a father now. And that sort of feeling is indescribable.

"I wish they could stay this way forever," Abella said, still smiling down at the sleeping babe. "So she would never grow too old and leave us. But the coming months and years will pass by, and before you know it, Lucille will be a grown woman. And ready to leave her parents behind to begin a life of her own. I wish to myself that that day would never come." Then Lucille opened her small eyes, looked up at Abella, and yawned. She cooed as Abella kissed her forehead and rubbed their noses together. "You are too sweet, little one. And you are ours. Momma and dada love you to death." Down the road, the rumbling of an engine could be heard. It came closer as Abella took her eyes away from Lucille and looked ahead. "Someone is here to visit."

In the driveway, a black DeSoto Skyview came near the house and stopped. The rear door opened and a young man emerged, holding a brown envelope. I stood from my rocking chair and walked up to the steps of the porch as the young man came closer. "Good afternoon," I said. "Can I help you?"

"I'm sorry to disturb you," the man said in a German accent. "But I'm looking for a Mr. Vincent Conroy. I hope I am at the right address?" I now had a better look at him. As I stood there, staring at this young man, I couldn't help but feel as if I knew him. His facial features reminded me of Aren. He had sandy-blonde hair, and blue eyes, much like Aren's own appearance.

"Well, you found him. What can I help you with?"

"Mr. Conroy, I came all the way from Germany to speak with you. It's about my mother—Katrina."

"Katrina!" I belted.

"Yes. And it's very important I speak with you."

Abella rose from her chair, holding Lucille carefully in her arms as she stepped beside me. "If it's important, then please come in," she smiled. "I'll make us all a pot of tea."

"Tea sounds very nice, ma'am. Thank you." the young man replied.

———

"SO WHAT IS THIS ALL ABOUT?" I asked, as the young man and I sat in the living room. Abella was busy in the kitchen, preparing the tea after lying Lucille down in the crib in the nursery. The door was left wide open, just in case she started crying.

He tapped his knee with the envelope in his hand, looking nervous. "You knew my mother, yes?"

"Katrina?" I nodded my head. "I know her."

"And what is your relationship with her?"

I laughed. "You like to get straight to the point, don't you?"

His eyes darkened. "I came a long way to understand something, Mr. Conroy. You see—I've been pursuing a mystery that I wish to solve. And this mystery involves you and my mother."

My smile faded. "You're Günter, aren't you?" I asked without doubt. I had a feeling of who he really was.

"Yes," he said, confirming my suspicions. "You know of me?"

"I do. And I know your mother. . . and I knew your father."

"Aren?"

"Yes. We were. . . good friends. You look very much like him, you know."

"My aunt and uncle always tell me that. There's not much I remember about my father. He died when I was young."

"How old are you, if you don't mind me asking?"

"I'm nineteen."

"I'm impressed that you speak English so well."

He smiled. "Mother forced me to learn English at a young age. I'm quite fluent now."

Abella returned to the living area and set a large saucer with a pot of tea, and three teacups down on the small table next to the sofa. She filled each cup with tea and passed one each to Günter and I. "Well it's a pleasure to have a guest in our home," Abella said. Günter smiled. "I couldn't but overhear from the kitchen—but why exactly did you come from Germany to see my husband?"

Günter let out a sigh. "I came to tell you that my mother has passed away."

I was in shock. "She's passed?"

Günter frowned and bowed his head, unable to look me in the eyes.

"Yes."

"When did it happen?" I asked, startled by the unexpected news.

"No more than three months ago," he said with his head still down.

I let out a heavy sigh and shook my head. "I'm sorry. She was... an extraordinary woman. I'm sure you know—but your mother was uncommonly kind. She was gentle, and loving and loved me in ways I can't explain." Abella held my hand with her own, knowing how much Katrina meant to me. "So you came all the way from Germany to tell me your mother has passed?"

Günter raised his head. "I saved up currency throughout the years, and with help from my relatives, I am able to afford this trip. I've always wanted to visit America for a long time now. But before making the trip here, I've been going through my mother's materials, and I found letters you had sent her. And there is something else: just before she died, she wrote one final letter for you. And she asked me to mail it to you. But I wanted to meet you in person because I want to know what sort of relationship the two of you had and why you were so important to her."

He wanted the answer I should give him, but I knew I couldn't. I couldn't find it in my heart to tell him about his father. I walked that path with Katrina but to do it once more with their son would be far too complicated. "There are some things we can't return to; either because it's too difficult or too painful. Yes, I knew your mother. We had a story, but that story has ended. And I can't go back to that. I'm sorry. I understand your concerns and that you are curious—as you should be. But your mother and I were not lovers, if that is what you think. We were only friends. She and Aren came to America many years ago to live in Louisiana. One year, a great flood ran your parents off their farm, and so they came to live on my parents' farm. And that's how we met. We became close friends. And nothing more."

Günter nodded his head. "I understand. I have one more piece of business before I go." He handed me the envelope he had been carrying. "This is the letter she wanted delivered to you."

He stood from his seat and looked at Abella. "Thank you for the tea, ma'am. But I must ask—do you come from France? I have an ear for accents."

Abella smiled. "Yes. I come from the village of Agneaux. It's where I met and fell in love with my husband during the war."

Günter looked at me. "If you don't mind me saying, Mr. Conroy—but you are a very lucky man."

"Thank you, Günter," Abella and I replied in unison.

"I must go," Günter said, walking to the front door.

"Can't you stay?" Abella asked. "I'm sure my husband and I would love to have you a bit longer. Perhaps you could stay for dinner?"

"I would love to but I'm afraid I must leave," he interjected before I invited him to stay longer. "I only paid the cab driver for a half-an-hour wait outside."

I stood up. "If you are ever back in the States again—please come by and visit us. It'll be nice to have you around."

Günter and I shook hands. "I will certainly do that. Thank you for inviting me into your lovely home."

Günter went outside and disappeared into the taxi. Abella stood beside me as we stood on the porch. I waved to him as the cab backed out of the driveway and drove off down the road. The afternoon sun now settled low in the sky as a bright orange light spread across the land— my favorite time of the day. But this sunset I will cherish, for now, my story with Katrina is near over. Abella is there with me to witness such a magnificent event. It's amazing how a simple event such as a sunset can impress me. The beauty in the colors, the dropping of the sun in the horizon—disappearing below the earth, only to rise once more the next morning. It's an endless cycle of elegance. One day ends for another day to begin. And I will be here.

And then it all hit me: Katrina was telling me her whole story in her letters so her past would not be forgotten. She wanted me to know her life so that her story might proceed on and not be lost as many stories are. A person's story ends at their death, but Katrina wanted her story to continue. And so, I swore to continue both of our stories. One day will come when I will be buried beneath the earth, but before that time, I will pass down my life to another person so that Katrina's and my life will pass through the ages. A never-ending story that remains on from one person to the next. For some stories should never be allowed to come to an end; as sunrise and sunset should never stop a day's cycle.

———

ONCE INSIDE, AS ABELLA WAS CHECKING ON LITTLE LUCILLE in the nursery, I sat down on the sofa and opened the envelope Günter left with me. My hands shook as I ripped the top of the envelope open. Out fell the Yggdrasil locket. I held it in my hand—but felt somewhat confused. Katrina wanted me to have this? Perhaps something to remember her by? I opened it to discover two photos inside: the same photo of Katrina and one of Aren as a young man. I then discovered the envelope contained a letter. I unfolded the letter and read:

Dear Vince,

It has been a long time since I had written. I'm sorry, but I wanted to let you know that I had been receiving your letters and that I have not forgotten you. I have been spending most of my time in the hospital nowadays. I have grown ill, and I'm afraid the doctors are unable to treat me any longer. The only thing they can do is make me as comfortable as possible. My time is growing short. I have become weak. I can barely eat or drink. It is taking all my available strength just to write this one last letter to you.

But there's something I must tell you before I leave this existence. When you came to visit me in my home in Germany, I told you that I may never forgive you for what you did to Aren, but I am writing this letter out of love. For I wanted to let you know, I had made my peace with it. As I surely hope you had made your peace with Aren as well. You mustn't let the past haunt you. Choices are made, and among those choices, mistakes are made. None of us are perfect. But we all can learn from our mistakes. They make us stronger and for the better in the end.

I also want you to have the locket you returned to me. I now believe it is meant to be in your hands when I am gone. I have included a picture of Aren in the locket along with mine. So you now have photos of both of us to keep close to you. I hope that you cherish it. It means more to me than you may ever know so I believe that you should now keep it. It may be hard to believe, but I think that that locket had brought the two of us closer together—more than you could possibly imagine. It's strange how things work out in the end. For you gave me new life. To me, you will always be that little boy at that farm in Louisiana, listening to my stories about my grandmother and my poems. You were always there for me when I needed you.

There are only three more things I must ask of you—and that is first: to live. Live your life the way it was meant to. You mustn't be scared any longer. Let the past stay in the past, and now you must look forward to the future. For the past can no longer harm you. Second: take care of your wife and your beautiful daughter. You have a wonderful family now. So protect them as a husband and a father. I wish I could have met them. And finally: please don't forget me because you will not be forgotten. I will remember you in my endless dream to come. I hope one day, we can meet again at that great oak tree in the field near your family's farm along with Aren as fireflies dance around us. It will perhaps come in the afterlife. And if so, I will wait for you there with Aren.

Goodbye, my friend.

Love,
Katrina

I wear the locket every day to keep Aren and Katrina close to my heart.

THIRTY-FIVE

SO THERE YOU HAVE IT, Father—all in my own words. My story. My confession. I, at last, wrote all of this down with the help of Dr. Gilliam who had recommended I do so. And with the consisted urging from Abella and Glenn to finish my story and send it to you, I hope now we could at least try to set aside our differences for us to become father and son once again.

The truth is, Father—I think about you often, for I worry. You can be so stubborn to understand what I had been through. But I'm not writing this to criticize you. I only hope to help you understand. So all I ask is, please find it in your heart to realize my struggles as a son and as a sol dier of war. I made sacrifices for us all, including you.

But I have another confession to make: it was wrong of me to tell you I was ashamed of you. I now realize that. I was young and naïve. It was wrong of me to call you a coward when the time to fight for your country came during the Great War. And you should not call yourself a coward as well. I was a coward, however. I was afraid of that damn lockbox filled with secrets I kept hidden away. But Dr. Gilliam expressed to me that secrets shouldn't be kept hidden. Secrets can drive a man insane.

But I had to be brave to face my demons and make amends to those I hurt. So I'll say again that you were no coward. Separation doesn't come between those who are brave or not. We all have our own faults. You ran away from the war not because you were a coward. It was because you had other dreams—better dreams. That was why you ran.

I had different dreams than yours, Father. Dreams you couldn't grant me. But I was determined to find those dreams on my own. I may have found them, but I found something else too. Something deeper—more meaningful. I found an awakening, for I concluded that no one is perfect. There are times I once believed I was, but this was selfish thinking. It was my bitter enemy who woke me up one evening about who I truly was: an executioner. I became that person—and it frightened me. And I never want to become that person again. But something good came from that night; I believe Roland and I finally had our truce.

So now, I am offering a truce with you. It's your decision to accept it. Can there be peace? Peace between father and son? I don't know. But we can at least try.

For there were times I was at peace. I can recall watching the sunset on the Atlantic as I sailed on the *Queen Mary*, traveling to Europe. Beautiful orange sunlight of a setting sun spread out along the endless waters of the ocean. There were days I roamed through the snow-covered forests of the Ardennes in Belgium as large snowflakes fell, coating the ground and pine trees with glistening white. It was like walking into a snow-covered fantasy land you only read about in books. I remember the stars and the moon at night in the vast open sky as I sat in a foxhole, imagining the stars are fireflies floating high from above as I had done so since I was just a boy.

Do you remember those humid nights back home in Louisiana, me staring up at the stars in the night sky with you pointing out all the constellations? Those nights were the times I recall the most. I felt close to you. Those were the times that should be remembered and not forgotten. Although your granddaughter Lucille, is still too young to comprehend, but I take her outside and show her the stars and constellations as you once did. "Look up there! Fireflies!" I tell her.

I don't wish for your granddaughter to grow up not knowing who her grandfather is. Abella wishes to meet you as well. She has been one of the best things that has ever happened to me. She gave me a beautiful baby girl and has done more for me than your or her could ever know. So perhaps one day, we can all be a family again. I would like that.

So where we go from here will be up to you. And so, this will be the last time I will try to contact you. Throughout the past several years, the letters I had written to you have been sent back unopened and unwanted. I hope at the least—you can take this one chance and read everything I have written because I had done it all for you. But if you were to choose to never want to see me again, then I will respect your wishes.

But I must tell you one last thing, Father. Recently one night as I drifted off to sleep—I had a dream—perhaps it was a vision. I'm walking alone in a forest with no destination in mind. Everything is silent and dark. I feel afraid until I see a delicate light creeping through the trees. I step toward the light, stumbling upon a clearing and in the distance, there's a great tree. It was then I realize I am standing at the edge of the field. The very field near the farm. The very field with the huge oak tree I loved when I was a child. As I walk out among the trees, the sun is setting beyond the dense clouded horizon as the faint, but bright sunlight warms my face. It's evening—my favorite time of day. I look out across the field at the oak tree and standing just beneath the canopy of dangling limbs and Spanish moss are people waiving at me—beckoning me to join them. I step out from the trees and toward the middle of the field, feeling the tall grass at my fingertips as I glide my hand at the top of the reeds. When suddenly, I'm surrounded by a mist of glowing fireflies. And as I get closer to the oak tree as the fireflies dance all around me in the setting sun, I see Mother, Aren, and Katrina—waving at me to join them. They all appear youthful, not aged as I remembered. As I approach the tree, I am embraced and kissed on the cheek from Mother. She keeps a strong grip on me, never wanting to let go of her son again.

I am then embraced by Katrina and then Aren, for there are no ill feelings, only happiness. We are all at peace. We are all together underneath that oak tree in the field—my escape from the world. But there is someone else there waiting for me. And yet, I don't know who. There is only a glimpse of a human being, faded against the sunlight of the setting sun. I try to focus, but the image isn't quite clear.

I then wake in the middle of the night with Abella sleeping peacefully next to me. But the dream made me think: was this a vision of my death? Will this happen in my afterlife? I suppose everyone has their own personal paradise after death; your own realm no one else can control. And was that obscured image of another human being underneath the oak tree you, Father? I want to believe so. For the image to come into focus, you must decide to wait for me when that time comes. So will you be there to greet me along with Mother, Aren, and Katrina after I'm dead and gone? Will you be waiting for my arrival underneath that great oak tree that stands just on the edge of that field, among the fireflies?

Acknowledgements

I spent many countless hours collecting research for this project and without these sources, this would not have been possible: Stephen E. Ambrose's *D-Day: June 6, 1944: The Climactic Battle of WW II*; Joseph H. Ewing's *Twenty-Nine, Let's Go: A History of the 29th Infantry Division in World War II*; Waldo H. Heinrichs' *Threshold of War: Franklin D. Roosevelt and American Entry into World War II*; Ian Ousby's *The Road to Verdun: World War I's Most Momentous Battle and the Folly of Nationalism* and John M. Barry's *Rising Tide: The Great Mississippi Flood of 1927 and How It Changed America*

I want to thank Mick Spry for his inspiration and very humorous stories of boot camp.

I want to give a very special thanks to Ina Kinzel for her endless enthusiasm and support for this project.

And finally, I want to give thanks to all of my friends and family who supported me and waited patiently for me to finish this. I do hope it was worth the very long wait.

About the Author

Douglous D. Clampit was born and raised in Louisiana and now currently resides in the Milwaukee area of Wisconsin. *In the Hearts of Soldiers* is his first novel.

Facebook: DougAtCypressGate